THE OVERSEER

BY JONATHAN RABB

HALBAN
LONDON

FOR MOM AND DAD

First Published in Great Britain by
Halban Publishers Ltd
22 Golden Square
London W1F 9JW
2006

A catalogue record for this book is available from the British Library.

ISBN-10: 1 905559 00 3
ISBN-13: 978 1 905559 00 8

Printed in Great Britain
by MPG Books Ltd, Bodmin, Cornwall

Three executors and an overseer make four thieves.

—OLD ENGLISH PROVERB

The Owl of Minerva takes wing at twilight.

—G.W.F. HEGEL

In the summer of 1531, Medici soldiers, working for Pope Clement VII, tortured to death an obscure Swiss monk, Eusebius Eisenreich. What Eisenreich would not reveal was the location of a simple manuscript.

The Pope never found it.

Prologue

WOLF POINT, MONTANA, 1998 ✄ The wash of moonlight through the trees shadowed the underbrush and speckled the arms and legs of the three darting figures in an eerie glow. In and out of the slats of light they moved, swiftly, urgently, without a sound. The biting chill of the night air lashed against the few patches of revealed flesh on their faces, but they had no time to think of such things. *The road. Get to the road.* Taut young bodies, made fit through hours of training and drills, had learned to shut out the burning strain that now crept through their limbs. Two weeks of subzero temperatures had left the wooded floor a hardened mass of soil and roots, uneasy footing; even so, they were making excellent time. Another ten minutes and they would be through.

None of the three, however, had fully considered the options beyond that. They knew only that they would be alone, outside the compound, far removed from the near-idyllic world they had inhabited for the past eight years—a place where young boys and girls had learned to excel, to challenge themselves, all the while content to be a part of the whole. Insulated and surrounded by others of "equal promise," reared for a purpose, a destiny. It was what the old man had taught the children, what they themselves believed. Memories of lives before Montana—families, friends, places—had long ago faded. Everything and everyone they needed had always been here. There had been no reason to look elsewhere.

No reason until the three had begun to see beyond the rote commands, beyond the need to please. Perhaps they had simply come of age. Young girls grown to women. Whatever the reason, they had come to understand what the old man expected of them, what he expected of *everyone*. And it had confused and frightened them. No longer willing to accept without question, they had begun to talk among themselves. They had begun to raise questions.

"You are not meant to ask," he had said. "You are meant to do. Is that clear?"

"We don't understand," they had answered.

The punishment had been quick and severe. "A kind reminder," he had told them. But it had not been the days without food, the days shut away and beaten that had caused them to question the world they had known for so long, nor even the none-too-subtle hint that they might somehow be expendable should their concerns ever arise again. It had been his answer: *"You are not meant to ask. . . . You are meant to do."* Autonomy stripped away in a single phrase. And still they had wondered. Had that been the message all along? Had that been what he had trained them to believe? No. They knew there was no challenge in that, no inducement to excel—only the brutality of the threat.

And so they had decided to run.

They had left just after midnight. Silent jaunts from separate cabins had brought the three of them to the gate, the youngest, at fourteen, with a genius for things electronic; she had taken care of the trip wires, a simple matter of misdirection to give them just enough time to slip through the fence and into the cover of the trees. Nonetheless, there had been a moment of near panic, a guard appearing not more than twenty yards from them just as the two thin beams of light disengaged. Each girl had frozen, facedown in the brilloed grass; but he had moved on, unaware of the three figures lying within the shadows. Evidently, their jet black leggings, turtlenecks, and hoods kept them well hidden.

Now, the first minutes into the woods were passing with relative ease. A few sudden ruts in the soil ripped at their ankles, branches everywhere tore into the soft flesh of their cheeks, but they were moving—an undulating column of three bodies dipping and slashing its way through the onslaught. The intermittent streaks of light were making the ruts easier to see; they were making *everything* easier to see. One guard on the deep perimeter and they knew they would have little chance of making it through. They had hoped for pitch-black, or perhaps even a heavy cloud cover. No such luck. At least the downhill gradient was helping to propel them along.

Coming into a small clearing, the last of the trio was the first to hear it. Distant at first, then with greater urgency, the sound of pursuit. For a moment, she thought it might be an echo, but the cadence was uneven, the tempo accelerating with each step. There was no need to tell the others. They had heard it as well. As one, they quickened their pace, arms and legs less controlled, knees buckling under the strain. With a sudden burst, beams of light began to crisscross the trees around them, instinct telling them to bend low, lead with their heads as they pushed through the mad swat of limbs that clawed at their faces with even greater intensity.

"Split," whispered the girl at the front, loudly enough for the others to hear. They had talked about it weeks ago, had understood that one of them had to get through, explain what was going on inside. Their best chance for that would be alone, apart. One by one, they flared out, no time even to glance back at one another, no place for such thoughts. *The road. Get to the road.* A moment later, the first barrage of gunfire erupted overhead.

A stooped figure stared out into the night sky, hands clasped to his chest in an attempt to gain a bit of added warmth. The thin cardigan draped over his ancient shoulders had been the only piece of clothing at hand when the message had come through. For some reason, though, he was enjoying the cold, perhaps as penance for his failure. The young ladies had compromised the fence, just as he had predicted. The team was closing in; and yet, he felt only the loss. He had hoped they would have learned. He had never liked these moments, the few occasions when fate forced him to hunt down his own. The three boys in Arizona. The two in Pennsylvania. And now this. Especially at so crucial a moment. There was no time for such distractions. But then, what other choice was there? They had been foolish. They had failed to understand. Or perhaps *he* had failed to awaken them to the possibilities.

A voice crackled through the radio clutched in his hand.

"We're closing in on two of them. Do we shoot to kill?"

The old man slowly drew the radio to his mouth. "You are to stop them. You are to bring them back." The delivery precise, meticulous, without a trace of emotion. "The method is unimportant."

There must always be a place for sacrifice. The words he had read so long ago, whose truth he had accepted without question, once again flooded back. Somehow, though, their certainty could never explain why it was always the ones with the greatest gifts, the ones with the greatest promise, who ultimately disappointed. Fate seemed to be mocking him at every turn.

Several shots rang out, angry streaks through a silent sky. He waited, eyes fixed on the distant trees, the wide expanse shrouded in darkness. A moment later, silence. It was finished. He nodded and turned to the house, aware of the light flicking on inside the first-floor guest room. He had hoped not to awaken any of his visitors. He had hoped not to trouble them with tonight's little episode. No matter. They had always understood. They had never disappointed. They would understand again.

The first volley strafed across a tree not more than five feet from her, the bark ricocheting in all directions, a single piece glancing off her thigh as she dove to the ground. An instant later, a second burst rifled past her, the bullets seemingly inches from her head. Every instinct told her to scream, her throat too tight to offer little more than gasps of air, her chest heaving in abject terror. She wanted to move, but again a wave of bullets sliced into a nearby tree. *The road. Get to the road.* She tried to remind herself that she had been trained for such things, had spent nights in the freezing cold preparing herself for such moments, and yet now, with her own life hanging in the balance, she lay frozen, unable to move, unable to think. The road had become a hollow refuge amid the frenzy around her.

Another wave erupted, this time accompanied by a muted shriek off to her left; she turned, and a moment later watched as a figure staggered out from behind a tree. There, hands held out at her side, eyes wide, stood the youngest of the trio, a strange smile etched across her face. She looked dazed, almost peaceful, swaying ever so slightly with each step. It was impossible not to stare at her, the moonlight cutting across her torso, her entire body streaked with blood as she moved up the incline. She was reaching for a branch to steady herself when a final hail of bullets drove through her tiny frame, almost lifting her off the ground before collapsing her into a pile at the base of a tree. Only her arms, thin reeds draped around the trunk, lent the image a human quality.

Every flashlight seemed to zero in on the lifeless mass; instantly, figures appeared higher up on the incline, making their way down to the kill. For several seconds, the girl who had witnessed the macabre scene stared at her friend's corpse, unable to tear herself away. Finally, though, after what seemed an eternity, she sprang to her feet and clambered through the rapid descent of trees and underbrush, her fingers digging deep into the soil to grant herself an added leverage. She could give no thought to the lights that, almost at once, cascaded all around her, her only image the vague outline of a border, the road beyond drawing her closer and closer.

The first of the bullets pierced her upper arm, the momentary shock blocking out the surge of pain that, seconds later, drove up through her stomach and ignited her flesh in icy flame. The next tore into her thigh, jolting her legs out from underneath her, her torso and head dashed to the rock-hard ground, pummeling her body over roots and gnarls until her chest collided with the trunk of a tree.

And then silence.

She lay perfectly still, aware of the racing activity behind her, her eyes focused on the strip of road not more than fifteen feet beyond her. *The road.* A gleam of light appeared in front of her, her first thought the flashlights from above. With what little strength she had, she raised herself up and turned toward her pursuers, expecting to feel the probing glare of their high beams on her face. Instead, she saw only darkness. For a moment, she didn't understand; she then turned back. Lights on the *road.* Lights from a *car.* The pain in her leg now pulsed throughout her left side, but still she forced herself to crawl along the ground. The grassy embankment lay just beyond the tree line, only a few feet from her grasp. She looked to her right and saw the headlights bob up from the distance, the car now no more than a quarter of a mile from her. She tried to stand, but her leg would not respond.

The last wave of bullets drove into her back and pinned her to the embankment. Strangely enough, she did not feel them. Instead, they seemed to lift the pain from her body, the grass now warm, inviting, the lights bathing her in a soft caress. Everything weightless, still.

Numb, save for the sweet taste of blood on her lips.

"And there was nothing you could do?" asked the old man. "The driver pulled over before you could get there? You had no chance to retrieve the body?"

"None."

"I see." He shifted the pillow under his back and took a sip of water from the glass at his bedside table. "And the two others?"

"Secured."

He nodded. "You say she was dead?"

"Yes."

"But not when the driver arrived?"

"I said I couldn't confirm—"

"Yes, yes," he interrupted, the first signs of frustration in his tone. "You said you could not confirm that a sixteen-year-old girl whom you had just shot several times in the back was dead."

"If she wasn't dead when he arrived, she was dead within a minute. At most."

"Marvelous."

"It was an absolute fluke that the car—"

"Do not try to excuse your incompetence. You permitted her to get within five feet of that road. Fluke or not, the car was there. Which means that our young lady friend is now at some hospital, some morgue, or some police station, under the watchful eye of one of our local law-enforcement specialists. Not exactly what I had asked of you." Silence. "You will leave here at once. All of you. Weapons, clothing. You will see to it that the grounds are taken care of. No tracks. I want nothing that might lead them here. Is that understood?"

"Yes."

"You will then remove yourself until I call upon you. Is this also understood?"

"Yes."

"Good." The old man sat back against the pillow, the brief tirade at an end. "Your mistakes, of course, will not be impossible to correct. Difficult, yes, but not impossible." He nodded. "Still, you did well with the other two." The younger man nodded. "That is, perhaps, worth something."

A minute later, the old man lay alone in the dark, his eyes heavy, though as yet unable to rekindle sleep. *A fluke*, he thought. *Only a fluke*. How many times had he heard it? *Once again, fate has played her ace.*

Drifting off, he knew it would be her last.

PART ONE

1

Power clings to those who recognize its discord and who can turn that discord to dominance.

—On Supremacy, chapter **I**

"The failed putsch in Jordan. During Bush's little war." Arthur Pritchard looked up from his desk. "Who was onto that before any of us saw it coming?" His long face and bushy eyebrows invariably gave the impression of an angry stork ready to pounce.

"The putsch . . . ?" asked the man seated across from him, suddenly realizing who Pritchard was talking about. "*No,* Arthur. You know that's not possible."

Pritchard nodded, an air of New England refinement in the gesture. "True. Still . . ." He let the word settle; it was a favorite tactic. A product of the right schools, the appropriate clubs, Pritchard was anything but the dull-witted WASP his family and friends had tried to cultivate. When, at the age of forty, single and painfully aware that he had little to look forward to save another thirty years at the esteemed Boston firm of Digby & Combes, he'd pulled up roots and applied for a position at State. Washington. A city that had always held a certain fascination for him. The power? He often wondered. If so, his meteoric rise had brought more than he could have imagined.

Even through the mayhem of '74. Somehow he had managed to keep himself far enough from the fray; when everything fell back in place, he had been offered a most unusual position.

The Committee of Supervision. A nebulous title for a Truman brain-child instituted during, of all things, the desegregation of the military. A covert office within State to ensure that "*rules were being followed.*" Truman, of course, had given the Committee considerable leeway in defining those rules—and in safeguarding them, "*by whatever means necessary.*" Over the years, any number of *difficult* tasks had carried the mark of COS, and with each new enterprise, the Committee had consolidated every ounce of leverage thrown its way. Somehow during the power struggles of the seventies and eighties, when CIA and NSC had vied for favorite-son status, COS had quietly established itself as the most adept of the three— Nicaragua, Pnompenh, Iraq. In so doing, it had set itself apart. Above the competition. Autonomous. In fact, only a handful of people in Washington understood the Committee's capacity. Arthur Pritchard was one. It was why the Montana file lay on his desk.

"She's perfect," he continued, framed by a window reflecting Washington at dusk; ceiling-high bookshelves, oak paneling, and antique furniture added to the image Pritchard meant to convey. The beam from a single lamp shone down on the near-empty desk. "She's familiar with the dynamic, the motivation." He leaned back in his chair, swiveled so as to take in the last bits of the sun. "Why the hesitation?"

Bob Stein shifted in his chair, his thick cream white fingers squeezing into the green leather. His face, like his body, was pear-shaped, the entire effect accentuated by the small tuft of hair he kept close-cropped at the crown. Bob was most at home when staring at his computer or satellite printouts, painstaking hours fueled by diet Coke and cheese balls. Bringing his hands to his lap, he answered, "Look, I'm as anxious to follow this up as anybody, but she's not . . ."

"Yes?" asked Pritchard.

"I just don't think she's . . . capable anymore. That simple."

"'Capable'?" Pritchard turned and smiled. "To flip over a few rocks? Wasn't that what we were in Montana to do in the first place?"

"We were *there*," Stein explained, "to snap a few photos of the venerable Senator Schenten with a few men he's not suppose to be that chummy with. Ask the senator why he—champion of the New Right—has been meeting with Messrs. Votapek, Tieg, and Sedgewick, and then see where things lead."

"A general sweep," piped in the third of the trio, comfortably seated on the couch against the far wall, and busy unbending a paper clip. Infamous for his plaid shirts and short, fat, cream-colored ties, Gaelin O'Connell was one of the shrewder analysts at COS. He was a tank of a man, just over six feet tall, and easily 220 pounds, more and more of which was tending to jiggle with each passing year. A onetime operative with both the NSC and the Committee, he'd been with Pritchard since Watergate, brought in to deal with some of the stickier issues facing a government back from the precipice. It had been a short-term transfer that had lasted over twenty years, fifteen of which had seen him in the field. Together, the two men had molded a disciplined core of operatives, men and women with the cunning to survive in a highly explosive arena.

But survive alone. That had been the aim at the outset. Those in the field flew solo—a few words over a phone, a command from a computer—none permitted even to know the building from which their orders came. A single, unknown voice of authority. O'Connell had often thought it ironic that there was no room for group players in the Committee. Both he and Pritchard, though, had recognized early on that such an arrangement was vital to COS's integrity; and they had spent long hours creating an infrastructure that produced strict operative independence.

Not surprisingly, the two had grown on each other over the years. In fact, it had been Pritchard who had finally convinced O'Connell to get rid of the polyester pants. He was still working on the ties. "A minor operation to make sure that the money of politics remains ostensibly aboveboard." The Irish lilt was unmistakable.

"Exactly," answered Stein. "We track them, find them together, and start asking questions. Then, whammo, a dead girl turns up. This might sound a little weird, but I don't think we can ignore that given Anton Votapek's history. I told you we should have picked him up the moment we located him."

"'Picked him up'?" asked Pritchard somewhat incredulously. "For what? For something that happened nearly thirty years ago, and that no one's ever been able to prove? A few children go beserk in the woods of upstate New York during the Summer of Love, and you think it's linked to *this*?"

"The Tempsten Project was '69, not the Summer of Love," corrected Stein.

"Dating aside," O'Connell conceded, "he's right, Bob. A girl appears on a tiny strip of Montana highway, less than a mile from an area we've been watching for about a week—for reasons, lest we forget, that have *nothing* to do with teenage girls. *Nothing.* She's riddled with bullets; just then, some unknown character drives by, pulls over, clasps her in his arms, and has time to hear her blurt out one word before she dies. *One* word." O'Connell tossed the paper clip onto the coffee table. "Where's the connection?"

"All right," countered Stein, "but then, why no records? Less than seven hours after the incident, police and hospital reports, gone; the guy who picked her up, vanished. It's as if the girl never existed—no past, no family, not even dentals. If we hadn't been running the sweep, there'd be no trace at all. I'm telling you, it's a little weird given Votapek's history."

"*Votapek's history*," Pritchard repeated. "Wonderful. And because of that, you think our conservative senator and his cronies are killing young girls." He turned to Stein. "Whatever the history, Bob, I find that very hard to believe."

"Then why the missing records? Why the complete whitewash?"

"We could always ask Schenten," smiled O'Connell. "'Excuse me, Senator, but we seem to have found a dead girl in your vicinity. Any comments?'" He shook his head and again picked up the clip. "We weren't even supposed to be there in the *first* place. You'll have to do—"

"Granted," Stein admitted. "But we still have the dossiers on the folks who *were* there—Votapek, Tieg, and Sedgewick. If nothing else, we have to see if there's a connection between their arrivals and the girl."

"And, of course, the dying word." O'Connell shook his head. "Which was . . . what, Bob?"

Stein hesitated. "To be honest, sound and visual distortions were tough. Our guys were over a hundred yards from the point—"

"Technoexcuses aside, what did she say?"

"As best as we can make out—*Enreich*."

"*Enreich*," exhaled O'Connell. "Now that's *very* helpful. He—or she—could be anybody. Or maybe it's not even a person."

"Do we have anything on it?" asked Pritchard.

"A former East German dissident—Ulf Peter Enreich—disappeared in the spring of '63," replied Stein. "The body was confirmed in '74. We're still running the name; something might come up, but Gael's right. Beyond that, it's a dead end."

"As you know, gentlemen, I don't like dead ends. Not at all." Pritchard took the file in his hands and leaned back.

"We could pressure Tieg and Sedgewick," offered Stein. "See where—"

"Because of the *girl*?" chided O'Connell. "Where in the hell do you get that? We don't even have an idea how the three *men* tie into Schenten, let alone to one another. And Votapek—the linkup there is pure guesswork. It might surprise you, Bob, but being a conservative doesn't make you a conspiratorial loony."

"Just someone with a misguided perspective."

"Whatever young Mao here might think," O'Connell continued, "all we know is that they've been visiting the senator with some frequency. Once in August, twice in October, and, now, two nights ago. Let's not forget, this was a *minor* operation. Snap a few photos; ask a few questions." He turned to Stein. "Why the cover-up, Bob? Maybe the sheriff was having a little something on the side. It got out of hand and he didn't want anyone to know. It'll be a made-for-TV movie. That doesn't, however, make it a Committee priority. Sorry, boys, but right now, our recently deceased young friend—"

"Is a dead end," interrupted Pritchard. He tossed the file onto the desk. "Which would seem to bring us back to my earlier suggestion."

O'Connell said nothing for a moment. "I thought we'd agreed—"

"To leave her alone?" answered Pritchard. "She's had time to recover."

"*Recover?*" The Irishman seemed unable to find the words; then, as if explaining something very rudimentary, he spoke. "She's now part of research, Arthur. At State proper—"

"And, no doubt, bored out of her mind."

"Which is probably a very big step forward for her." O'Connell waited for a response; when none came, he reminded Pritchard, "State's *not* Committee jurisdiction. You couldn't touch her even if you wanted to."

"We both know that's not true." He stood and moved to the bar. "She'll turn over a few rocks. Test her wings. Probably the best thing for her."

"Have you been listening, Arthur?" O'Connell had become far more animated. "Putting her back in the field, no matter how simple the task—"

"She's perfect. Her work in Jordan remains textbook."

"*Was* perfect, Arthur. *Was.*" He watched as Pritchard took a sip of his drink. "Or are you forgetting what she was like *after* Amman?" He waited until their eyes met. "This is not an issue for discussion. We leave her alone, Arthur. We let her get on with her life."

"Actually . . . she already has some of the information."

"*What?*" It was Stein who spoke. "That's all very sensitive—"

"Don't worry, Bob," Pritchard continued, avoiding O'Connell's gaze. "She has the absolute minimum. Names of organizations, various players— oh, and that Enreich thing. If nothing else, she might be able to figure out how that fits in. All of it's through our contacts in research, so there's no way to link it to this office."

"It's not this office I'm concerned with," snapped O'Connell.

"The report reads like a routine fact finder on the New Right," Pritchard continued, "no mention of Schenten, our operation, the girl—"

"*What?*" O'Connell was doing everything he could to contain his rage. "Her mental state aside, you brought her in *blind?*"

"The report's been put together so that she'll think she's doing a general file update. Don't worry—nothing to set off any alarm bells."

O'Connell stared for a long moment at his old friend. "As much as I agree that Bob is blowing this thing *way* out of proportion, these are major players here, Arthur. Being chummy is one thing, but if the killing *is* connected—if these men are *capable* of that—we'd have to ask why. We'd be throwing her into something potentially far more dangerous than Amman."

"And that's *exactly* why she's perfect." Pritchard's tone became far more pointed. "If it turns out that this is all a wild-goose chase, then we've wasted a little of her time, and saved ourselves far more by not having to mount an entire operation. If not . . . she knows how to take care of herself."

"*That* remains open to debate."

The two men stared at each other; Pritchard then arched his back and turned to the window. Streaks of pink and red darted through the clouds, sending a single beam of light onto the dome of the Capitol. "You know, I love this view. Insisted on the office. Smartest thing I ever did." The ice in his drink popped and sent a rivulet of whiskey over the side. He turned. "You have to trust me, gentlemen. Know me a bit better than that." He took a long sip. "I'll be watching her the whole way—pull her out if things get tight. Chances are, they won't, but we all agree. The files on our illustrious quartet could always be a bit thicker." He put his glass down. "Given the nature of the thing so far, something's bound—"

"To turn up?" O'Connell had heard it too many times before.

Pritchard smiled. "Exactly. And when it does, we pull her out. Fair enough? Look, the ball's already in play. If there is anything here, all she has to do is raise a few eyebrows. How hard could that be?"

Saddled with overnight bag, purse, and briefcase, Sarah Trent looked the typical attorney making her weekly trek to New York. The heavy winter coat bounced playfully just above her knees, revealing a pair of rather exquisite legs. At five foot seven, trim and athletic, Sarah was used to the turned heads, the long stares. She smiled back, her deep chestnut eyes flashing in response, as she moved along the platform to a nonsmoking car, the Metroliner surprisingly empty for noon on a Thursday. She knew she would probably be able to find two seats for herself, stretch out, and enjoy the three-hour ride to New York.

She had opted for the train rather than the shuttle for the simple reason that she needed more time with the files—two days hadn't been enough to digest all the material that had landed on her desk. A research update. "Just some background information for the new system," the note had read. "We've got the space, we need to fill it." Typical bureaucratic reasoning.

Now, finding a pair of seats midway through the car, Sarah swung the two cases onto the window seat, then dropped herself into the one on the aisle. She turned to the briefcase as she unbuttoned her coat.

She had spent the last two days on the phone, trying to piece together the strands of information in the files. Very little had come up. Most of the people knew less about the three names than Sarah already knew herself. And whenever she tried to dig a bit deeper, awkward pauses followed by curt responses had made it clear that she was not meant to look further. Brush-offs notwithstanding, a few names had popped up to catch her attention—organizations that seemed to fit into a category with various right-wing fringe groups but which remained just this side of respectability.

In all the digging, one name had continued to crop up. One Alexander Jaspers, a prolific academic who had spent the last few years churning out article after article on the "new decency in conservatism." His phrase. Sarah had leafed through a number of his pieces and, realizing she had found her font of information, had made an appointment to see him. His office had been a welcome surprise of cordiality, given her recent track record, staffed by a sweet woman who spoke with a thick German accent, and who had no problem accommodating her by setting up the meeting on such short notice. Mrs. Huber had penned her in for 3:30 today.

As the train emerged from the station, Sarah opened the one file that had intrigued her most during her first perusal. Tieg. The infamous host of *Tieg Tonight*—one of the country's more popular evening television entertainments. She knew more than simple curiosity was prompting a second look. Jaspers would be well up on Tieg's history, having mentioned him in at least two of the articles. Never comfortable with academic types—always a bit intimidated—Sarah was determined to hold her own with *Herr Doktor Yaspers*. Even the name daunted her. Another few times through Tieg's file would give her the necessary confidence. She settled into her seat and let her shoes drop to the floor, ready now to peruse the file more carefully.

The first pages were standard form: born '33 to Hungarian émigrés, public schools, regional wrestling champion, scholarship to St. John's. Nothing unusual until '51, when, in a period of less than six weeks, Tieg's father died, he dropped out of school, and he set sail for Europe. No explanation.

> What might have occurred during these three years is left to the
> reader's imagination.

Nothing. Not even the city, or cities, where he had lived.

It picked up again in '54, charting Tieg's rise from low-level peon to programming executive with the then-burgeoning television division of NBC. By '63, he had become a central figure for various regional affiliates and stood as one of the bright boys in NBC's future.

> His sudden dismissal in early 1969, and his subsequent blacklist
> at the other major networks, is yet another gap in the story.

Sarah took a moment to jot down a few notes and then turned to the last few pages. The story beyond '69 was common knowledge. Buying up a number of radio stations—the source of the initial capital unclear—Tieg had parlayed them into a series of local television outfits, and by '73 had the largest media package in the Southwest. Then the shift to telecommunications in '75, when he started to drum up business in Washington. His involvement in the early stages of SDI remained unclear, but by the time Star Wars hit its prime, he had severed all Washington connections. His current linkups included Europe, Southeast Asia, and South America. By '92, he had an estimated five to seven pieces of high-tech machinery orbiting, all under the aegis of the recently formed Tieg Telecom, headquartered in San Francisco.

And then, just as quickly as he had gotten into the technology, he moved on, turning his attentions to *Tieg Tonight*, the homespun talk show that blossomed from a four share in '93 to a twenty-two share by '97, a legendary rise by any standards. The ratings established Tieg as the premier "*pontificating politico*" on the airwaves.

A final page had been added hastily. Sarah read:

> His central aim is to maintain a reputation as champion of working-class sensibilities. In the last five years, he has allowed that persona a much more public face through the Centrist Coalition. Originally a small enterprise, the Coalition has gained considerable momentum, and it now stands as a beacon of small-town concerns. During the flood disaster in the Midwest several years ago, Coalition volunteers shipped in food, supplies, and medical technicians to some of the more remote areas hit. Tieg himself was spotted in over twenty different locations, not as speechmaker, but as one more pair of helping hands. While most agree that at this time he has no political ambitions of his own, it seems clear that his reluctance will be short-lived. In a recent election for a midterm replacement to the Iowa legislature, Tieg received nearly fourteen thousand write-in votes. He is *not* a resident of Iowa.

That was where the file ended. Sarah placed it on her lap and closed her eyes. She had read the last few pages without the attention she knew they deserved, preoccupied by the three-year hiatus Tieg had enjoyed in Europe. The question remained: Who—or what—was allowing him to escape the keen eye of the world's most thorough intelligence agency forty years later? How had those three years remained hidden? Three years of anonymity. Of unaccountability.

Her mind suddenly raced to memories of her own past, images breaking through to conjure an existence she had known a lifetime ago, and which now resonated with an unkind immediacy. *Her* year of anonymity, unaccountability. *Her* gap to be filled. A reality of shadows. A life created by the Committee, a persona shaped by COS that let her slip into the madness of a Middle East ready to implode. And how quickly she had been able to lose herself, abandon Sarah Trent, assume an emptiness without ties. A vacancy that had granted violence a chilling ease, a comfort. Memories still so close, never dulled by the passage of time, ever more acute by their distance.

Amman.

"BWI." The shrill voice of the conductor bolted her from the violent images. "Arriving BWI Airport. Three minutes."

She was cold; her hands shook as she reached for her coat. Not bothering to slide her arms through the sleeves, she draped the heavy wool around her shoulders and chest, the swelling in her eyes prompting a quick finger to her cheek. With a deep breath, she leaned her head against the soft slope of the seat and concentrated on the gentle slowing of the train. The numbing throb in her temples began to ease. She was learning to hold the moments at bay.

WASHINGTON, FEBRUARY 26, 12:43 P.M. ✍ The disc popped from the slot: forty seconds to download the information, twenty to initiate the delay sequence. Everything like clockwork. The young man at the screen took the disc and placed it in his pocket. He was dressed in coveralls, the usual attire for maintenance staff at Hodge Wentworth, bankers to Washington's elite for over 150 years. He had found the clothes at the drop-off point four hours ago; the ID badge and disc had arrived in the mail yesterday.

He turned off the computer and stepped from behind the desk. Pulling a lightbulb from his pocket, he proceeded to screw it into the lamp's vacant socket. It was, after all, the reason he had been sent, the reason security had let him onto the eleventh floor in the first place. He tossed the old bulb into the trash and tested the lamp. Perfect.

At the same time, having made his way to the subbasement, another young man—similarly clad, similarly instructed—stood in front of what looked to be a large medicine cabinet filled with wires and computer chips, a tangle of the building's phone and modem lines. He had snipped one of them and was now threading the second of the two strands of copper through a small black box. After a few seconds, the light on the box flashed green, then turned yellow. Attaching a strip of adhesive to its back, he affixed the box to the side of the cabinet and closed the front panel.

Three minutes later, both men stepped from separate elevators to the lobby, coveralls now folded inside attaché cases, new ID badges hanging from necks on silver chains. One set from the World Bank, the other from the fed. The blue blazers and gray pants screamed intern. No one took any notice as they moved through the revolving door toward a car at the curb and the young woman who sat waiting for them.

It had taken them twenty-seven minutes, four fewer than they had planned on. That meant an additional four minutes for the excursion to Dulles.

Reaching the car, they tossed their attaché cases next to the driver and settled into the backseat. Both slipped off their jackets and began to undo their ties as the young woman handed each of them a plastic bag.

Another set of coveralls. Another set of ID tags. Another black box and disc. As she eased out into the traffic, she glanced in her mirror at the two half-naked men in the backseat.

"Enjoying the view, Janet?" The two men laughed.

She smiled. "Not half as much as you like me watching."

"What would your daddy say?"

She checked her watch. They would be on the flight to Montana by two.

The train arrived at 2:45, on time to the minute. Sarah had been deep within the files at the time and was therefore one of the very last to leave the car. She placed the papers in the briefcase, pulled it and her bag from the window seat, and strode out onto the eerily empty platform. The maze of stairs and corridors that crisscrossed the underbelly of Penn Station sent her in several wrong directions before she broke down and asked a passing redcap for the quickest way to the West Side trains. When he simply pointed to the sign ten feet in front of her, she was mildly embarrassed. She had been to New York too many times to act the tourist.

Twenty minutes later, the iron gates of Columbia University and the smell of roasting chestnuts greeted her as she took the last few steps to street level. Smoke cascaded from the vendor's cart and lifted gently into the sky, lending an added haze to the wintry gray. As she passed through the gates and into the sudden quiet of the campus—its pockets of brown grass amid a backdrop of overbearing buildings—she noted the stark contrast to the bustle of Broadway. To her right, a lone stone structure, perhaps a hundred yards long, glowered at her through the single eye of an equally long window that stretched the entirety of its second floor. A building to be taken seriously, if only for the names that rose from its facade in huge sculpted letters: Plato, Cicero, Herodotus. An avenue of steps to her left led to an even more grandiose building, whose dome seemed to vanish into the intensifying slate of the sky. Other equally stern buildings completed the quadrangle that sufficed as the Columbia campus.

Following Mrs. Huber's instructions, Sarah ventured left, toward a set of narrow stairs and the Amsterdam crossway—a concrete platform that covered the avenue from 116th to 118th Streets. Arriving atop yet another set of stairs, Sarah felt the sudden swirl of chilled air unleashed by the open expanse of the crossway. She walked to its railed edge, fighting a gust of wind, to see Amsterdam continue on for miles and disappear to a fine point in the distance. Cabs raced along, somehow less frantic from her raised perch. As she turned away from the hum of traffic, an extension to the crossway drew Sarah's eye. Moving toward the peninsula, she neared what she assumed to be the Institute of Cultural Research. A simple plaque to the right of the door confirmed the guess.

The three-floor New England house—white wood shingles and all—stood out as an incongruous transplant alongside the more modern buildings that lined the crosswalk. For Sarah, the quaint anomaly conjured images of her own college days, the creaky buildings of New Haven's Prospect Street, with their faint aroma of damp wood. Mounting the steps, she pushed through the oak door and found herself in a windowed vestibule, the customary umbrella rack to her left. The cold white tile of the small enclosure seemed to heighten the chill and prompted her to move quickly through the second door and into the dimly lit carpeted entry hall. A large wooden banister greeted her, its swirling line leading up to the second floor and the sound of several electric typewriters. In the sitting room to her left, Sarah spotted two ancient scholars in a pair of deep, embracing leather chairs, the men rapt in heated debate. The whining cackle of a fire rose through the conversation.

From around the staircase, a young man suddenly appeared carrying a tray of tea and cookies. He seemed overeager to dive into the fray by the fire—food and drink clearly his means of invitation. As he tried to dash by her, Sarah said, "I'm looking for the office of a Dr. Alexander Jaspers." Tea in one of the cups swayed dangerously close to the rim as the young man made his abrupt stop. "Jaspers?" he asked, a furrow creasing his brow. "Right," his eyes suddenly wide. "He's on the top. The attic thing." He jerked his ear toward the sitting room, not wanting to miss any of the discussion. A smile touched his lips. "He's got it all wrong, you know," he confided in Sarah, nodding toward one of the two by the fire. "All wrong. Anyway, you want Jaspers. This staircase"—he indicated with his head— "and then the corner one at the far end of the second floor. Clara's always up there. Or usually. You'll find her. Must run. It's getting cold." And with that, the man darted into the room to take his place in the chair nestled between the two older men. He—or rather, the tea—was received with considerable enthusiasm as Sarah began to climb the winding staircase.

Two sets of stairs later, she emerged on the third floor, a large open area, a few chairs placed at center, amid ceiling-high bookshelves on each of the four walls. No doubt this was the Institute's attempt at a library, she thought, one with a very select clientele. Several desks jutted up against the stacks of books wherever one of about eight windows appeared, each distracting with a lovely view of New York. Only one of the desks was occupied, its claimant deep in the pages of an enormous tome. Directly behind the chairs at center, a set of stairs rose on a leftward slant; a note card tacked to the banister read JASPERS, followed by an arrow pointing up. Sarah's nerves began to kick in. Images of a wizened old figure bent menacingly over a desk came to mind, his cold stare cutting through her as she reached the topmost step. She tightened her grip around the handle of her briefcase and mounted the stairs.

The attic office—or offices—were a good deal larger than Sarah had expected. Although constrained by the sharp angle of the ceiling, there was enough room for a sizable desk—a small wooden plaque with Mrs. Huber's name positioned on its front lip—two chairs for those with appointments, and a midsection wall that divided the entire top floor into two separate areas. At the far end of the wall, a door—with Jaspers's name on it—stood slightly ajar. At the opposite end, a small copy machine was in full hum, at the moment operated by a tall young man in jeans, tweed jacket, and running shoes who looked the typical graduate student, no doubt making some extra money—and some helpful connections. Sarah checked her watch, realized she was still a few minutes early, and took a seat in one of the chairs to await Mrs. Huber, whose desk was unoccupied. The view from the small porthole-like window caught her eye as she settled back into the leather—Morningside Park at the first hint of dusk. For a moment, it seemed rather inviting.

"Waiting for Jaspers?" asked the young man while he tried to stack the papers he had just finished copying.

"Yes," Sarah answered, and placed the briefcase on the floor by her side. "I have a three-thirty appointment. Do you know if he's in?"

"Most definitely." The young man smiled, setting the papers on Mrs. Huber's desk and scribbling some instructions on the top page. He dropped the pencil on the desk and extended his right hand. "Alexander Jaspers. You must be Ms. Trent."

Sarah's eyes opened wide, an embarrassed smile forming on her lips. "*You're* Dr. Jaspers?" she said as she quickly stood to take his hand. "I'm sorry. It's just that I expected someone . . . older."

"I know," he laughed, sitting on the edge of the desk and motioning for Sarah to retake her seat. "It's all that 'Herr Doktor Yaspers' stuff that Clara insists on. Everybody gets it wrong." Sarah couldn't help but smile. He folded his arms across his chest and asked, "Would you like something to drink? We have coffee, tea, water, smelling salts."

She laughed, shaking her head. "No thanks. Sorry if I'm a bit early."

"No problem." He rose from the desk just as Mrs. Huber popped her head up from the stairs.

The tight bun of black hair seemed to pull mercilessly at her forehead, accenting the look of surprise on her face. "Oh my dear!" Her thick legs tried vainly to take the last few steps. "Oh dear! You are here already." The German accent was even more pronounced in person, thought Sarah. "I was only in the kitchen with some cookies for you, but, you see, they have disappeared, and I was expecting you at half past three. I am so sorry. I was to be here at the time of your arrival to make introductions." She was back by the desk, straightening with a frenzied neatness. "This is so dreadful of me."

"Clara," Jaspers interrupted with a little laugh, "it's all right. We managed to work through the introductions without any major disasters. Ms. Trent, Clara Huber." Mrs. Huber stood silently, bowing somewhat sheepishly as Sarah said hello.

"It's Sarah. And I'd like to thank you for being so nice on the phone. It was a welcome surprise."

"Oh?" A wide smile replaced the hint of anguish on Mrs. Huber's face. "That is most kind of you. You see, Herr Doktor Yaspers is an expert—"

"Clara is invaluable," Jaspers interrupted, somewhat embarrassed, "and I know Ms. Trent—Sarah—would like to get started. But since we're out of cookies"—he winked at Mrs. Huber—"and because I happen to have an awful sweet tooth, I was hoping you wouldn't mind if we do this at a little pastry shop not too far from here. Every day at four—it's a . . . family thing. Can I convince you to—"

"Yes." Sarah smiled back. "I'd love to have tea."

"Great. Let me get my coat." Jaspers disappeared into his office and a moment later returned in an old gray wool coat that had clearly seen better days. He thrust his hands into the pockets and stopped. "Right. The Domberg stuff should be sent to Bill Shane in Chicago and, if you could, try to get hold of Lundsdorf and see if I can steal some of his time tomorrow. Before I have to take off. Anytime before three." Clara nodded as Jaspers turned back to Sarah. "Sorry."

"Not a problem."

"Good. Tea it is."

Jaspers pulled his hand from his coat and gestured for Sarah to lead the way. Mrs. Huber was already busy at the desk as Sarah said good-bye and trotted down the stairs, Jaspers behind her, grabbing a scarf that hung on the banister. The two walked in silence until they reached the first floor, where the debate by the fire was in full flame. "Anything from One-twelve?" Jaspers poked his head through the archway to the sitting room. "We're out of cookies." The three faces turned, the youngest answering, "Some of those little crunchy ones with the green bits. That would be nice. If you could." Jaspers nodded. "Don't put yourself out for us," one of the older men said. "Only if its no inconvenience. But yes, the crunchy ones. Good choice." Jaspers pushed off from the archway and smiled.

"No inconvenience." He pulled the door open and followed Sarah through the vestibule and out into the cold air. "That rather imposing tri-umvirate," he said as they walked across the overpass, "all happen to be brilliant. If you want to know anything about the Middle East, those are the boys to go to." Sarah nodded and pulled the collar of her coat tight around her neck as they took the steps down to the open quadrangle of the campus.

"And they're all cookie enthusiasts." She needed to shift the topic. "They were digging into a fresh batch when I arrived."

"Didn't you know that about academics?" Jaspers asked. "If Enten-mann's or Nabisco went out of business, the wheels of education in this country would come to a grinding halt." He was about to continue when he noticed a familiar figure moving slowly not too far off in the distance. "Professor Lundsdorf," he shouted, a slight quickening in his pace. He turned to Sarah as she tried to keep up. "I'm sorry. That's the man I need to see tomorrow, and I could save myself some time if I set it up now. If it's all right, this'll just take a minute." He continued to hurry them along.

"Why don't you run ahead," she said, slowing. "This pace is a little tough in heels." Jaspers looked down at her shoes, back to her, and smiled in apology. "Don't worry," she added, "I'll catch up."

He raced off, his coat billowing behind in the wind before he reached the side of the older man. Sarah watched the two in conversation as she passed a small fountain on her way down to the central walkway. Nearing them, she saw the older man place a hand on Jaspers's arm, the two a moment later lost in laughter. Sarah arrived to hear Jaspers say, "—without Parliament. Otherwise, there would have been legitimate claims of tyranny."

"I am sure that is right. Yes, quite sure. So you will see what comes of it." Sarah stood at Jaspers's side.

"Oh, I'm sorry," Jaspers said. "Professor Lundsdorf, this is Sarah Trent, from the State Department. For some reason, she thinks I'll be able to help her unpack the New Right." Here, at last, Sarah thought, was the old wizened character she had expected in Jaspers's office. But once again, all fears were quickly allayed when the five-foot-five Lundsdorf, slender and somewhat frail from age, and tucked deep within several layers of clothing, took her hand and offered a little bow.

"Enchanted." The twinkle in his light green eyes betrayed the spirit of a man who had once fancied himself something of a ladies' man. Even now, Sarah was unsure whether the venerable professor was flirting with her.

"The pleasure is mine," she said as he released her hand.

"How kind. *Herman* Lundsdorf," he corrected Jaspers. "I have known this young man for fifteen years, seven—no, eight—as a colleague, and still he insists on calling me 'Professor.'" He winked at Jaspers, who fidgeted under the scrutiny. "One day perhaps. One day, he will not see me as so frightening an old man, my dear. Be that as it may, you have certainly come to the right man, and I, unfortunately, must take my leave of your company and get out of this cold weather." He nodded again to her and looked at Jaspers. "Tomorrow at two will be fine." A short bow and Lundsdorf started to walk away, piping back over his shoulder, "And your coat—button it up if you want to live as long as I have." With that, he tossed his hand into the air and waved good-bye. Jaspers started to laugh to himself.

"There goes my mentor. And mother. The combination is sometimes a little unsettling." The two walked through the iron gates and crossed over to the west side of Broadway. "One minute he's explaining German parliamentary procedure; the next, he's telling me to button up." He shook his head. "I hope your shoes are okay on the ice."

"I'm fine. He seemed very sweet."

"Very sweet and very rigorous. He forced me to finish my degree in three years. I never worked so hard in my life."

"That's a little quick, isn't it?" asked Sarah.

"Lundsdorf wouldn't have it any other way." Jaspers dug his hands deeper into the pockets of his coat. "He's had it all planned out, ever since I got here. On average, it's eight years. So yes, it was quick."

"I'm impressed. That would make you—"

Jaspers smiled. "Thirty-three. And don't be. I wrote an incredibly mediocre dissertation, which the grand old man and I spent a year and a half reworking into a book. He kept on saying, 'Just get the degree, get the degree.' He was right. I got it, got a job, finished the book. . . ." He paused, his eyes distant for a moment. The smile returned. "Then I started doing stuff that was interesting." He stopped. "It's right here." Jaspers opened the door to a small café that smelled of thick black coffee; he waited for her to step through the doorway with her overnight bag and briefcase.

"You don't have to hold the door for me," she said.

"You're right. I don't," he replied without moving. "It's another bit of Lundsdorf. German propriety. I've been trained too well."

Sarah smiled. "In that case, all I can say is thank you." She walked into the dimly lit room and spotted a table against the back wall. She led the way through the legs and elbows at the packed little tables and began to disentangle herself from her coat as Jaspers slipped his off and draped it over the back of his chair. He waited until she was seated to take his chair.

"More Lundsdorf?" she asked.

"Of course." They sat. "I'd recommend a nice cup of tea and a piece of the raspberry chocolate cake, but not everybody's a chocolate nut."

"No, that sounds nice." Everything was nice, she thought—the idea of tea, the funny little café that wanted so desperately to evoke images of Paris or Berlin—and the company. There was something very relaxing about young Dr. Jaspers. Something that seemed so . . . unacademic. It was the only way she knew how to describe it. Jaspers lifted his hand, raised two fingers in the direction of the waiter, and turned back to her. "I . . . always get the same thing," he said almost apologetically. "They know me here."

"Must be nice."

"I guess it is." He smiled and shifted gears. "So, Clara mentioned the State Department and my articles. I can only guess we're here to talk about 'The New Right and the rise of conservativism.'" The self-mocking tone in his voice prompted another smile from Sarah. "The title of a very dull article I wrote."

"Not so dull."

Jaspers's eyes widened. "You've actually *read* it?"

"My job, Professor Jaspers—"

"Xander," he interrupted. "Everyone calls me Xander."

Again, she smiled. "One of the many I read . . . *Xander*. All very informative. And all quite different from the other articles on the subject. Your approach is . . . how shall I put this—"

"Unique? Probably the source."

"Lundsdorf?" A waiter arrived with water.

Jaspers grinned and pulled a thin well-worn book from his jacket pocket, several rubber bands holding it together. He placed it on the table. "Even older." The cover read *The Prince*. "Never leave home without it."

"Machiavelli?" she asked.

"Don't be so surprised. They were pretty bright in the sixteenth century. He was probably the brightest. Go ahead. Take a look."

Sarah picked up the book and gently unloosed its bands. The front cover came away in her hand, an inscription filling the page: "I'll always be with you, Fiona." She looked up to see Jaspers's eyes lost in the words. All traces of the smile were gone. She let the moment pass. "I'm . . . sure he was." She placed the book on the table, delicately slipping the cover on top. "The brightest, I mean."

He looked up, nodded. "Yes." He reached over and took the book. "He was."

"And now he's a man for all centuries," she said, watching as Jaspers stretched the rubber bands around the flaking pages, his smile returning.

"The nice thing about theory, Ms. Trent, is that it can apply to any number of situations." He put the book in his pocket. "It's the *way* you apply it that makes the difference."

"And your friend Machiavelli just happens to fit in with the New Right?"

"And the junk-bond market, and several LBOs, even a separatist group in Idaho—I'm not the only one whose seen a connection. I just keep it theoretical. It's everyone else who tries to put it into practice."

"Tell me, Professor—Xander—for those of us not quite so well versed, how exactly does someone use a book like that—"

"Oh ye of little faith," he cut in. "You'd be surprised. There's a group of young guns right now who are convinced that Machiavelli tells them how to play the market. One of them's just written a book—*The Machiavellian Manager*. Catchy, if a bit humorous."

"And you're not convinced?"

Jaspers shrugged. "Let's put it this way—it's not the Machiavelli I know. Theories are . . . susceptible to *broad* interpretation. That's what makes them so seductive. Look, I understand—probably better than most—what it is to ponder the practical implications. Sometimes, they're hard to dismiss. But at a certain point, you have to recognize their limitations. Wall Street hasn't seen that yet. They think it's about brute force, deception—"

"'Better to be feared than loved,'" she interrupted.

"Now I'm impressed. That's not, however, the whole picture."

"No, I didn't expect it would be," she added playfully. His gentle laugh and wide, if rather sheepish, grin, told her she had hit the mark.

"Rambling comes with the territory, Ms. Trent."

"I'll try to keep that in mind, Professor Jaspers. So," she continued, "it's all really just a matter of context—"

"Exactly," he replied. "Machiavelli wrote the *Prince* as a . . . how-to manual on wielding political power. What he really wanted was a job from the Medici—Florence's ruling family. The book was meant to catch everyone's attention by explaining things as they really were. Very bold for the times."

"But *specific* to the times."

"You *are* good at this."

"We try."

"Then you no doubt recall sixteenth-century Italy was politically very unstable—little more than a collection of city-states, all with their own agendas."

"Yes, I *no doubt* recall that," she teased.

Jaspers laughed. "In simple terms? Machiavelli wanted to protect Florence and inspire a bit of cohesion. His solution was a leader who could anticipate trouble and wield power with a bold hand, anything that might keep the people in line. For him, they were all a pretty bleak bunch—not to be trusted and not terribly bright. A little cruelty here, a little kindness there could keep things running smoothly."

"And that," Sarah asked, "applies to the market? It's a bit of a stretch, isn't it?"

Jaspers took a sip of his water. "Not if the market men think the book tells them what to do. It's their bible. Who am I to argue with the interpretation? And you have to admit, it is intriguing." He sat forward and rested his elbows on the table. "All Machiavelli did was to recognize the darker side of politics; along the way, he raised some pretty interesting questions about power, deception—tell people what they want to hear so as to maintain a power base. The modern implications aren't that tough to see."

"As long as it remains theoretical," she said. "In practice—"

"That's where the Wall Street boys make their mistake. Machiavelli was a genius, but he was a *sixteenth-century* genius, and we have twentieth-century questions. Where he talks about cruelty and military bravado—"

"We talk about corporations and grassroots politics."

"Exactly." The waiter arrived with two plates and two cups, a second waiter followed with the pots of tea.

"So you think he takes us only so far."

"Don't get me wrong," answered Jaspers. "I love the old guy, but he's a springboard, that's all. Those who see him as a definitive guide . . . I don't put much *stock* in that." He smiled as the waiters departed, then began to pour his tea. "A modern equivalent—at least for me—is what the New Right's been doing over the last few years. Except, instead of going directly to the people, they pander to any number of interest groups in order to maintain control. Theoretically, it's Machiavelli; practically, it's—"

"The 'new decency in conservatism.'"

"Bingo."

"The Centrist Coalition," she added.

"You've obviously been doing your homework."

"As I said, we try." She pulled a pad from her case; she was searching for a pen when Jaspers produced a rather gnawed ballpoint from his pocket.

"Sorry about the teeth marks," he said. "Hazard of the profession."

"Mine would have been no better." She uncapped the pen.

"To be honest, I've only just started looking into the Coalition, but it's an excellent place to begin."

Sarah flipped to an empty page and looked up. "Practically speaking."

WASHINGTON, FEBRUARY 26, 3:51 P.M. ⚔ The class moved through the museum room, a Veronese the highlight, each child busy with notebook and pen, jotting down the relevant information. The teacher, a woman in her late twenties, smiled affably at the guard as she led the small group to a far corner and a somewhat obscure offering by a young Tiepolo. All fifteen huddled around the painting, the teacher at its side, describing with great enthusiasm some of its more intricate details—the angle of Christ's head, the position of his hands. She kept her eyes on the guard, waiting for him to turn; the moment he did, she nodded once. On cue, one of the girls quietly sank to her knees, hidden by the other children as she removed the grating of the vent directly below the painting. With equal precision, she placed her pack inside the opening and slipped through. A boy followed, the grate immediately replaced. The sound of the teacher's voice drifted to the distance as they began to crawl.

They had no need of lights or maps; they had run the mock-up perhaps a hundred times in the last week. The schedule had called for three of them—*everything in threes*—but the old man had made a change. Lydia had remained in Wolf Point. They had not asked. It was not their place.

At the fourth duct, they turned. Forty feet along, they found a second grate; they dropped through, this time into a narrow tunnel, pipes and wiring running the length of the walls, enough room for the two of them to scamper deeper into the innards of the National Gallery. The girl checked her watch. Eight minutes. *Plant it, set the linkup, and return.* They had done it once in seven. The old man had been pleased.

Half a minute later, they heard the sound of cascading water directly above them—the promenade between the east and west wings. Cafeteria, museum shop—always popular among tourists. Both stopped and emptied their backpacks. To the guards at the entrance, the items had appeared to be books, pens, chewing gum, lipstick—the usual teenage fare. To the trained eye, they were far more. In less than a minute, they had fashioned the pieces into two large plastic bricks and a small black box, a copper coil connecting it to the wires along the wall. A yellow light on the box flashed once, then turned green. They retrieved their packs and moved on, scanning the duct above. Twenty feet from the box, they found the third grate, hoisted themselves up, and again began to crawl.

Several twists and turns later, they sat crouched behind another vent, another gallery room, another painting for the class to admire. They had done well. Six and a half minutes. He would be pleased.

⬧

"It's typical right-wing maneuvering," said Xander. "They don't want the government to tell people how to run their lives, but they're more than happy to be the country's moral conscience. The Coalition likes to do it through school curriculums. Abortion, sexual orientation—those are the big issues."

"Which doesn't make the Coalition any different from about a hundred other groups," Sarah pointed out.

"True, except they've got plans to develop private institutions of their own. Schools, funded by the Coalition, to compete with the public sector, giving them a blank check on what, and how, they teach."

She looked up. "Seems to me the Catholics have been doing that for years. Where's the problem?"

"Yes, but they don't have TV monitors in the halls and classrooms, all linked to some high-tech computers that function interactively with the kids. *Specialized* computers—if the stories are true—that sound quite extraordinary. I mean, imagine a kid being able to program an alternate plan of attack for, say, the Battle of Midway, and then watching it come to life on the screen; that would make learning exciting. Rumor has it, though, that the computers are going to be used to replace hands-on teaching. To make sure a clear, consistent message reaches all of the Coalition's devoted little followers. That's not education; that's indoctrination, and on a much wider scale than any parochial school ever dreamed of."

"Brainwashing?" she asked skeptically. "Computers have been around for a long time, Professor. Just because the Coalition's using them doesn't mean—"

"If they're the only things that tie Jonas Tieg and Laurence Sedgewick together—two men who haven't the slightest bit of interest in education—I'm not so sure." Jaspers stared across at her. "Have I struck a nerve?" Sarah said nothing. "Who else would you be here to talk about?"

"You might be surprised."

He drained the last bits of tea from his cup. "Want some more? I'm going to get another." Sarah nodded. She watched as he motioned to the waiter, the two fingers and the shake of the head. The waiter pointed to the plates of cake. Jaspers picked up the cup and mimed taking a drink; he then turned to her. "I've been known to have . . . two pieces at one sitting."

She smiled. "So, Tieg and Sedgewick."

"As I said, neither of them cares one whit about teaching. For Tieg, it's all politics. A way to rally his troops. More of the *Tieg Tonight* phenomenon. The school programs are simply a lure, the technology his bait. If the environment were more hip right now, he'd be focusing on that."

"And Sedgewick?"

"That's the interesting part." The waiter arrived with the tea, repositioning plates and cups to make room for the extra pots. Xander tried to help. "Didn't it strike you as odd that a man who had made his career as a financial whiz suddenly started developing computer systems for investment banks a few years ago?"

Sarah recalled the file. "Those were security networks. I thought they were designed to safeguard large investors—like himself?"

"Perhaps." The waiter moved off. "But who do you think helped him develop the prototype for the technology?" She shook her head. "A subsidiary of the Tieg Telecom Service. *That's* not in your notes. The trail's convoluted, but it's there. Trust me." He took a sip. "And now it's computers in the schools. No real connection, but . . . All I'm saying is, it makes me wonder."

Sarah nodded, jotted down a few words. With her eyes still on the pad, she asked, "And Anton Votapek?" She was about to repeat the question, when she looked up and noticed Jaspers's expression. He was staring at her, a look of sudden concern etched across his face.

WASHINGTON, FEBRUARY 26, 4:09 P.M. ✗ "*Repeat* that, please." National Airport's chief controller did little to mask his disbelief.

"*Every* screen in the tower just went *blank*," came the reply, the confusion in the background filling the speaker. "Auxiliaries are out, and we've lost radio contact."

"Is the beacon still operative?"

"No idea."

"What do you mean you have *no* . . ." He leaned in closer to the intercom as he stood. "Just take it easy. I'll be right there."

Two minutes later, he strode into the traffic tower, the slicing pattern of runways beyond already lit for the evening arrivals. "All right, people, let's see what we've got here. What do we have up in the air, and what's within closing range?"

"Four two-sevens, one noncommercial, and two jumbos, one from LAX, one from Madrid," answered a woman surrounded by a mountain of printouts.

"What about Dulles—"

"They've got the same thing. So does BWI. And College Park is completely unreachable. Everything went out about four minutes ago. My estimate—of the three majors—six planes in final patterns, another twelve that've been given clearance."

The man moved to the nearest console, its vacant face staring back at him. In twenty-five years, he'd never seen anything so terrifying. He turned back to the general mayhem. "All right, people"—he began to rub his hands together—"we reroute as many as we can through Atlanta; the rest can try—"

"That'd be great," the woman answered. "One problem—how, exactly, do we tell the pilots?"

✄

"Votapek?" repeated Jaspers. Sarah leaned forward to pour herself a second cup. "Are we talking about the same Anton Votapek? The Tempsten Project."

"It was actually called the Learning Center," she corrected. "The media dubbed it the Tempsten Project."

He shook his head. *"Votapek?"* He paused. "Why would—"

"It's about schools, isn't it, Professor?"

"Yes, but . . ." He was taking longer to recover than she had expected. "I mean, the man was a genius, the education guru of the sixties, but then . . . Tempsten." His eyes began to drift. "Some sort of high concept . . . *modular teaching*—"

"The *Modular Approach*—'education as a more aggressive means to creating less autonomous, more community-oriented children.' Very good, Professor."

"One more wild theory forced into practice." He continued to stare off, as if trying to remember something. "What was it, about ten children, all around eight or nine—"

"Actually, fourteen, some as old as eighteen. You seem . . . rather familiar with all of this."

He turned to her. "One of the darker moments in American education? If you care about teaching, Ms. Trent, you don't forget Tempsten." The reference had clearly disturbed him. He sat back, shook his head slowly. "Eight- and nine-year-olds, turned into . . ." He suddenly looked at her, his expression far more intense than only a moment ago. "You think he's linked to Tieg and Sedgewick?"

"I don't think anything," she answered. "I simply asked if his name had come up in your research."

Jaspers stared across at her. "I see." He paused. "It hasn't."

"Have I said something wrong?"

"Wrong? No. Of course not. It's just that throwing Votapek into the mix makes Tieg's connection to the Coalition somewhat more unnerving."

"Really?" She needed to see how far she could lead him.

"Well, now there'd be someone who really *does* have an interest in education, wouldn't there? A pretty frightening interest, and not just as a political stepping-stone."

"*If* there's a connection," she reminded.

"Right." His eyes remained on hers. "If." For a moment, neither said a word. "Now you've got me thinking."

"Sorry." She smiled.

"I'm sure you are." He began to fiddle with his spoon. "Trouble is, everything I've told you is speculation. I don't know about Votapek, but there's nothing in what the other two are doing that even hints at extremism. No neo-Nazis burning synagogues, no white supremacists making inane demands. That's why I label it 'decent.'" Again, he paused. "Votapek, however, would change that." He looked at Sarah as if expecting a response; she merely raised her eyebrows as the waiter arrived with the check. "Anyway," he said, tapping the spoon against the saucer, "that's the most detail I can give you. I think there's a link between Tieg and Sedgewick, but that's only what *I* think. And even if Votapek is involved, I still couldn't tell you what they hope to achieve. To be honest, as long as all three of them remain separate entities, there really isn't anything to worry about."

"But if they do somehow connect—"

"You'll have to ask why." He stopped playing with the spoon and looked directly at her. "What do they want? I'm not sure that's a question I'd like to answer."

"You make it sound so sinister." Sarah was finishing off the last piece of her cake.

"I hope Lundsdorf's right. He keeps telling me to concentrate on what I know and leave the conspiracy theories to the tabloids. Maybe I'm overreacting." Xander had finished his second cup and was trying to drain the last vestiges of tea. Finding none, he placed the cup on the saucer and said, "I'll leave the sinister side to you. Unfortunately, I do need to get back—"

"Of course."

"But I don't want to cut you off. Was there anything else?"

Sarah slipped the pad into her briefcase, snapped the locks, and reached for her purse. "I don't think so, but if we need to talk again—"

"Absolutely. After all, I wouldn't mind seeing *your* files."

She smiled and pulled out a ten-dollar bill before he had a chance to reach for his wallet. "I know Professor Lundsdorf wouldn't approve, but this is on the government." Xander conceded, more to the lovely smile than to protocol, and reached behind to grab his coat. As he stood, Sarah remembered something. "Oh, there was one other thing. This might sound strange—"

"I'm sure it isn't." He began to put on his coat.

"Enreich. Does that mean anything to you?"

Xander reached into his pocket and pulled out his scarf. He flung it around his neck as he repeated the name to himself. "Enreich?" He shook his head. "Doesn't ring a bell. I could look through some old stuff, but I think I would have remembered something like that. Sorry, not much help there."

She shrugged and stood, placing the briefcase on her chair and slipping into her coat. "If anything does come up"—she took a card from her purse and wrote the number of the hotel on the back—"give me a call."

"Will do."

She handed it to him along with his pen, picked up her briefcase and purse, and nodded to Xander to lead the way. Weaving their way back through the tables, they moved quickly to the counter, where he bought a box of the cookies he had promised the boys at the Institute. Sampling one, he pulled the door open and led Sarah out into the chill of Broadway.

WASHINGTON, FEBRUARY 26, 4:24 P.M. ⚔ The air erupted in a torrent of glass and water, metal driving up through the ground, a crater where the gallery's lower promenade had been. Screams filled the expanse, silenced eighteen seconds later by the detonation of the second bomb, which hurled its flame through the opening and encased body after body in a searing wave of gold. A sweet smoke followed, more deadly than the blaze, stifling breath and forcing its victims to what remained of the ground. Those who could ran haphazardly, men pushing women to the floor, parents grabbing for children, cradling them as they sucked in air they could no longer breathe.

It was over in less than six minutes. Some had been lucky. The initial blast had taken them unawares. Others had had to live through the gas, feel the flames lick at their flesh, endure their own incineration.

At 4:58, the first rescue teams made it through. It would take them fourteen hours to estimate the loss at 117, two more days to bring it to 130.

⚔

Sarah emerged from the subway on Fiftieth Street and continued toward Sixth Avenue. She had thought about a cab but knew she would save time with the train. Not that she was in a hurry. In fact, she had left tonight open so as to go over the information Jaspers had given her. Now, as she maneuvered along the snow-packed curb, the image of the young scholar hurrying them both along—so eager to get back to work—brought a smile to her face. He was so committed to what he was doing, so drawn into his little world where every moment seemed too precious to waste. *You're a lucky man, Xander Jaspers*, she thought. *Lucky to have that passion.* And yet, he had not overwhelmed her with it. Not once had he made her feel incapable. Somehow, he had allowed her to forget that fear. Instead, he had invited her in and had seemed so pleased when she had taken an interest. And how afraid he had been to bore her. She smiled to herself. There was a certain charm in that.

The large neon of Radio City loomed above her as she made the turn. The avenue was jammed with people all trying to wend their way through the chaos of rush hour. The fierce pace of the sidewalk seemed to sweep her up in its manic drive. All thoughts of the pleasant afternoon quickly drifted away. She began to lose herself to the crowd, to the gnawing hum of humanity.

And without warning, the buildings melted away in a rush of hands, feet, and arms. The rising pulse of movement swarmed in on her, echoing an Arabian madness that reverberated within her. *No! Not here! Not now!* A voice deep within pleaded with her, her head dancing in numb detachment above the noise and clamor, her mind slipping farther and farther away. *Fight it, Sarah!* Short of breath, her chest growing tight, she stopped on the sidewalk, staring about to find something, anything, to draw her back. People moved past with unkind stares, but she hardly noticed them as she struggled to retrieve her calm. *Let it go.* With great effort, she found her breath, the tremor receding, the buildings taking shape once more. *Look around you. It's New York. You don't have to hide here.* All was as it should be. As it had been.

As if a safe haven, the hotel came into view. She began to walk, reenter the flow of bodies. Even among them, Sarah moved in complete isolation.

Five minutes later, she stood at the front desk of the Hilton, the card to her room resting on the counter. Still shaken, she followed the bellboy down a wide concourse toward the banks of elevators and noticed a wide array of watches, rings, and necklaces in a row above windows built into the marble wall. A particularly radiant stone caught her eye, its color a deep, resonant blue, no less supple against the sterile white light of the open hall. She stopped and stared into the sapphire, its gaze somehow familiar.

"Would you like to see it, madam?" A man appeared at her side, dressed in a neatly tailored suit, his hair combed tightly across his scalp. Sarah gazed at him, for a moment uncertain. "Madam?"

"No. No thank you," she managed. "It's a beautiful stone."

"Yes, an exquisite cut."

"I seem to have lost my bellboy," she said, glancing toward the elevators.

"Of course." He stopped abruptly and offered a most disingenuous smile. "Perhaps later, then." He was already with another customer. Sarah peered once more into the sapphire—its invasive stare no less haunting— before turning to find the boy a good twenty yards ahead. He stood waiting by the elevators. She raised a hand and moved quickly down the concourse.

WASHINGTON, FEBRUARY 26, 5:27 P.M. ✗ His pace was slow, almost casual as he turned onto G, the lamps above already at full glow. Washington at twilight. Peter Eggart held his hands in his pockets, eyes peeled on the doorway perhaps two hundred feet down the street. As he had been told to expect, three Dutch diplomats emerged and began to walk toward him. They were lost in conversation, the woman at center apparently explaining something to her two companions. Eggart continued to walk, slowly pulling a gun from his pocket and clasping it tightly to his side as he drew closer to the trio. No one on the street seemed to take any notice until, almost on them, he raised the barrel and discharged two shots into the woman's chest, then one bullet apiece for the men at her sides. All three lurched backward, a sudden stillness, everything frozen, weightless.

Eggart turned to run, pushing past the few disbelieving onlookers, the night in slow motion as he reached the end of the block and crossed to Twelfth.

Only then did he stop.

Where was the car? He spun around, checked the sign to see if he had somehow made a mistake. No. Twelfth—where they had promised it would be. Screams began to echo from behind him, time once again accelerating to full tempo. He could feel the panic in his throat, the acrid taste of indecision. *Maintain focus. Understand the process.* He needed to remain calm, listen to the command in his head. There had been too many hours spent preparing to allow a last-minute hitch to get in the way. He started down the street, aware of the eyes staring at him from the buildings above, tracing his escape. Again, he began to run.

A car turned onto the street, oblivious to the mayhem it had just entered. Without thinking, Eggart darted out into its path, raised his gun, and aimed it at the windshield. The car screeched to a halt as the gunman moved to the door, pulled the driver from her seat, and threw her to the curb. Within seconds, the car was squealing in reverse toward the intersection. A sudden stop, the grinding of a gear; a moment later, it was gone.

Sarah followed the bellboy into the small but comfortable room, its view of Central Park. She placed the briefcase next to the mahogany chest of drawers, handed the young man a few dollars, and hoisted the overnight bag up onto the bed. Finally alone, she unzipped her dress and slipped off her shoes, the thick carpet a welcome relief from the confines of heels. Sliding her hands through the sleeves of her dress, she let it drop to the floor and then laid it gently across the bed. And she sat.

She was angry. A simple stone, and she had given in. It was always hardest during trips outside of Washington, trips away from the routine that helped to keep her in check. The unexpected conjuring memories of the all too familiar. Nothing more than a sapphire's hue, and she had been transported: the hotel on King Faisad Street, the noise of the al-Balad raging in the background, and the girl. Always the girl, staring at her, plaintive blue eyes, forcing Sarah to promise. *"You will come back." "Yes." "You will come for me." "Yes."*

No!

She forced her eyes open, only now aware that she had once again drifted back. For several minutes, she sat absolutely still as Amman receded to a distant pocket of her mind. With great effort, she stood and reacquainted herself with the room. The briefcase stared up at her. She knew she would be no good with the files now. She needed to walk. Out and unafraid.

She opted for jeans, a T-shirt, a pair of black boots. Transferring a few dollars from purse to pocket, she slid the briefcase under the bed, then grabbed her coat. The research update could wait.

Seven minutes later, the lights from the traffic on Sixth Avenue glared at her as she made her way downtown. She had little idea where she was heading, but she knew it was good to be surrounded by movement. Around Thirty-sixth Street, she realized she was hungry. She turned right and decided to try her luck on Broadway. Save for a few racing cabs, the Garment District was deserted, a few pockets of dark shadow spilling beyond the sidewalk.

The footsteps behind her only became audible halfway down the block. They were even and clipped, in close synchrony to her own, slowing and accelerating with each change in her tempo. She could feel herself begin to focus on the distinct pattern of the rubber-soled shoes, calculate the distance between herself and her would-be tracker, measure the road in front of her. *Stop it! Ignore them. They're nothing. It's someone on the street, anyone, damn it! Don't give into this—look back and see it's nothing!* But the signals were too well ingrained, too near to the surface now for her to shut them out with a simple plea. Twenty yards ahead, the sudden appearance of a second figure, an apparent drunk, confirmed her instincts. He seemed to weave along the street, but with each step, he drew closer and closer, tightening the net around her, forcing her deeper within the shadows. As she began to run, she could hear the quick sprint of the assailant behind, watch the drunk lunge up onto the sidewalk and block any means of escape. The trailer thrust his shoulder into Sarah's back and sent her reeling into the arms of the man in tatters towering above her.

With one swift move, he threw her into an alleyway shrouded in complete darkness save for the bare bulb that hung from an overhead fire escape. The cold brick scraped against her hands as she tried to cushion the impact, the wall's brittle edge slicing across her palms and forcing a momentary scream. "Not a word!" She fell to the ground, only to be grabbed by the shoulder and pinned against the wall. The pungent odor of the man's all-too-convincing costume caused Sarah to wince as he scanned her body, his eyes dancing with a lurid pleasure. The second man appeared over his shoulder and grabbed her by the hair. His eyes betrayed no such longing, no carnal desire for a prey well won. Drawing a small blade to the side of her cheek, he smiled, a sudden animation in the otherwise-vacant expression. "We've been sent to give you some advice," he whispered, dragging the flat of the blade across her lips and down to her chin. "Forget Eisenreich. Today was only the *first trial,* a promise of what's to come." He tightened his grip. "Walk away, or next time I won't be able to hold back my friend here. He seems to have taken a liking to you." The other man laughed and placed his free hand on Sarah's breast, pressing hard against her as he groped. The man behind continued to peer down at her, watch as his comrade enjoyed the moment, probe deep within her eyes for the fear, the revulsion that he craved.

No such terror stared back at him. Instead, her gaze revealed a strange emptiness, a cold indifference, a warning that he could not recognize. Trapped for a moment in the lifeless embrace of her eyes, he let his grip relax almost imperceptibly. And in that moment, the devastating precision of a killer schooled in the streets of Amman unleashed itself in an explosion of raw energy. No longer Sarah Trent, the assassin of Jordan drove her knee into the testicles of the man still preoccupied with her breast as her once-pinned arm lunged across the face of the second man, nails finding flesh in a blur of movement. Both men reeled from the onslaught, the knife clattering to the ground in the melee. As if programmed in her attack, she swung her foot into the midsection of the man now holding his bleeding cheek, the jagged snap of breaking ribs forcing an anguished cry as he dropped to his knees. The other man, somewhat recovered from the initial blow, tried to stand but was too slow to avoid the sudden jab of her elbow to his temple. His head smacked against the brick wall, a final burst of air shooting from his mouth before his unconscious body slumped to the hard cement of the alley floor. With equal force, she slammed her coupled fists into the prone neck of the man crouched two feet from her—clutching his chest—and watched as he, too, collapsed to the ground. Only the sound of her own panting breath cut through the silence of the alley. She stood frozen, her mind racing out of control, images of dark, sand-strewn streets forcing their way into her consciousness, tearing her from the cold embrace of the Manhattan night.

"You made the choice, Sarah. You accepted the responsibility." A solitary face shone through the dank haze, a girl no more than twelve, thin streaks of blood trickling from the bullet hole on her forehead. "Someone had to be sacrificed. Someone." With a frightened stare, her blue eyes faded to the shadowed recess as the bodies of eight young Jordanian soldiers appeared, each hung from a wire on the wall directly in front of her. The stench from their clothes filled her nostrils, forced her to move her hand to her nose. They dangled side by side,

twisting gently against the wall—faceless bodies of men who had squealed in death and who now taunted her with their silence. "Say something! Anything!" *she screamed.* "I had to take you, to stop you! You were the priority, not her! Someone had to be. . . ." *The bodies continued to sway in a single rhythm.* "Say something, damn you!" *Her voice became choked with a torrent of tears.* "Anything! Please, anything!"

The white light of the bulb cut through the shadows, extinguishing the horror before her, as a wave of nausea filled her throat. She lay back against the wall, at the mercy of trembling limbs and pumping adrenaline. A thousand voices reverberated within her skull, crackling against the deadly silence of the alley. Violence. Violence again, passionless and exact. She looked at the two men at her feet—still motionless. She had taken them without a thought, a swirl of activity that had come only too easily, spun from a part of her that longed for the anger, the destruction.

She had attacked. Provoked, yes, but she had been the one to unleash a blind fury, the rapid, staccato blows that might very well have killed them both. No thought, only pure animal instinct. Could she have killed? Would it have been that easy for her to slip so far back? She didn't know, couldn't make sense of the questions that hammered within her head. *Oh God! Oh God! I was out of control.*

Somewhere within, a single voice told her she had to move, distance herself from the bodies. Clinging to the wall and unable to tear her focus from the unconscious figures, she slowly edged her way along to the alley's entrance. A car raced by as she reached the sidewalk, forcing her to stare out into the empty street, to try to forget the men behind her. The cold calculation of the assassin was gone, replaced by a crippling fear, and Sarah stood alone, suddenly aware that her clothes were drenched in sweat. She began to tremble as she dug her hands into her pockets so as to fold the coat around her. *Somewhere safe. Find somewhere safe.* Again, the voice led and she followed in numb submission, back toward Sixth, back toward lights, people, and the security of others. She didn't run—somehow the voice would not allow it—but walked with a calm determination, unobtrusive and therefore unseen, unremarkable. As she turned toward the hotel, she felt the first tears of release wash over her cheeks.

Only when she had stumbled into her hotel room, a safe haven now from the attack twenty minutes earlier, was she able to concentrate on what the man had said. *"Today was only the first trial, a promise . . ."* What had they meant? *And Eisenreich?* She turned and caught her reflection in the mirror, her face a sea of black and red, her hair a tangled mess hanging precariously about her shoulders. But it was the eyes that stole her focus, the eyes not seen since Amman, the cold, unforgiving eyes that stared back and condemned in silence.

It was then that she began to think beyond the attack. *Why? What had provoked it?* A research update. That was all it was supposed to be. Nothing more. Nothing to prompt warnings—*first trial, Eisenreich . . .*

A cold sweat creased her neck as one name entered her thoughts: *the Committee.*

Sarah forced her gaze to the room around her, the box, holding her in, squeezing her, the safety of isolation. *Of course, the Committee.* It was all too familiar, too much of a life that had come so close to destroying her. *I won't be drawn in. Whatever this is, I won't.* She knew what she had to do. Give everything back. Files, notes—the job, if necessary. Let others take the responsibility. Let others carry the weight. Memories of the alley would pass. Memories of Amman. Of herself. She had to protect *herself.*

She reached for her briefcase and noticed the flashing red light on the telephone. For a panicked moment, she wondered whether the message in the alley had been sufficient. They had found her in the streets. No doubt they could find her here. *Ignore it. Let someone else play the game.* But for some reason, she couldn't. She had to hear it, hear them for herself, know she was running for the right reason. She slid across the bed, picked up the receiver, and dialed the operator. An electronic voice answered, informing her that a single call had been taken at 5:10. After a momentary purr, a second voice came on the line.

"Hi. Xander Jaspers at around six. Look, I don't know how I could have been so stupid, but when I got back to my office, it suddenly clicked. The Enreich thing. It's not *En*reich. It's *Eisen*reich. At least that's what my instincts tell me. If this does connect, it could be a lot more than either of us bargained for. Call me."

Jaspers. *Oh my God.* She wasn't alone; she wasn't isolated. He had made the connection. *Eisenreich . . .* And she had been the one to contact him, draw *him* in. *Whose responsibility, Sarah? Whose trust?*

She pressed down on the receiver, released, and started to dial.

2

Education . . . can turn aggression to fervor, obstinacy to commitment, and volatility to passion.

—*On Supremacy*, chapter IV

XANDER HAD RACED out in such a hurry that he'd left his scarf on the banister, and now, catching an updraft on Sixth Avenue, he reluctantly recalled Lundsdorf's warning: "*button it up if you want to live as long as I have.*" Sometimes he could be infuriatingly sensible. Xander walked up the taxi drive of the Hilton, then through the door and into the stream of warm air that embraced both neck and face. It was a welcome relief.

As he walked down the concourse, his mind returned to Eisenreich. The moment of revelation had come some two hours ago, standing over his desk, shuffling through various papers—astounding in its simplicity. And perhaps his own thickheadedness. *So obvious. So damn obvious.* At first, he had wondered whether it was just another crazy theory—one which Lundsdorf would dismiss with quick dispatch. Crazy, yes. But theory? No. It made too much sense to be fiction. Of course, he would have to run it by Sarah. After all, she was the expert, the one from Washington. *You're only the simple academic.* Even so, instinct told him he had uncovered something to make sense of his research, something that might shed light on whatever Votapek and Tieg had in mind. How Sarah and the government tied in, though, remained a mystery.

Inside the elevator, he glanced at the papers he had brought. Scanning one or two, he recalled the rush, the excitement he had known perhaps only twice in his life—the first, three years ago, when he had found an unknown manuscript by an obscure eighteenth-century theorist; the second, earlier tonight, when he had remembered Eisenreich. Of course, the eighteenth-century essay had turned out to be of little use—as Lundsdorf had predicted—but the thrill of the hunt, the chance to see something through, *that* was what had caused such stirrings. And what was now coursing through his chest. The elevator arrived, and he tucked the papers inside his satchel.

Before knocking, Xander paused to consider what he could expect from the woman who had called him just over an hour ago. Then, he had anticipated enthusiasm, even excitement at his discovery. Instead, a distant voice had told him to come by the hotel; bring whatever he thought might be important. And that had been it. *Not* the reaction he had hoped for. Even so, behind her apparent detachment, Xander had sensed urgency, a thinly veiled need for the two of them to meet tonight. Wrapped up in his own eagerness, he had put her surprising coldness from his mind. Now, he couldn't help but recall her tone on the phone, far from that of the friendly, delightful woman with whom he had shared tea that afternoon. And he had not been the only one to appreciate her appeal. On arriving back at the Institute, the fireside cabal had awarded him high praise for his radiant companion. Even Clara had lit up at the mention of the 3:30 appointment. Only then had Xander considered Sarah anything more than a Washington bureaucrat sent to tease his brain. A bureaucrat with a rather lovely smile, he had to admit. He had spent a good ten minutes in his office thinking of nothing else.

The sound of a double bolt releasing brought him back to the present. The door inched open and Sarah appeared through the shadows of a room lit only by a single lamp on the bureau. For a moment, the two stared at each other, until Xander smiled and asked, "All right if I come in?"

His own familiarity seemed to snap some life into her expression; with a gentle nod, she answered, "Sorry. Of course."

He stepped into the room; Sarah immediately bolted the door, then moved past him to the bed and her pillow propped against the wall. It was then that he noticed the television, her eyes riveted to the screen. She hadn't even asked for his coat. Without looking over, she said, "Take a drink if you want. It's a small bar, but it's well stocked." Xander saw the miniature JD on the table next to the bed, the hotel glass steeped high with ice and whiskey. Evidently, she had started without him.

"Thanks." He nodded stiffly, uncertain as to what he should do next. A drink. Right. He nodded again, placed his satchel on the rug, and pulled a bottle of water from the fridge. Her gaze remained on the set, her expression confirming the misgivings he had felt over the phone. He wanted to convince himself that the difference lay in the informality of a second meeting, her lack of makeup, her casual clothes. But it was clearly more than that. He stepped closer to the bed, his hand awkwardly in his coat pocket. "So," he said, "what exactly are we watching?"

Sarah turned to him, a momentary look of confusion in her eyes. "You haven't seen any of this?"

Xander shook his head, smiled. "I've been at the office. The . . . stuff with Eisenreich took some time to—"

"Then you should probably take a look." She picked up the remote and flicked from channel to channel. Xander stood watching as every station seemed to be covering the same set of stories—reporters amid the sounds of sirens, fire trucks, ambulances. Different scenes, all portraying the same confusion, the same controlled mayhem. National Guardsmen in evidence at every site. "You're looking at Washington, Dr. Jaspers." He slowly sat. "Not a pretty sight, is it?"

LURAY, VIRGINIA, FEBRUARY 26, 8:17 P.M.   ⚔   Searchlights cut across the thick wood of the barn, glaring white against a backdrop of open field, streaks of red and blue from police cars encircling the lone building. Intermittent pockets of steamed air floated into the black sky, men with rifles waiting for their prey, newsmen with cameras waiting for the latest installment from a night unlike any they had ever seen.

"I've just been told that all three of the Dutch diplomats are alive," blared a voice through the bullhorn. "Critical, but alive. Which means it's not murder. You still have a chance if you come out now." Silence. The FBI man turned to the agent next to him. "Are we set in the rear?" The man nodded. "We give him three minutes; then we go. And tell these reporters to move way the hell back."

From the darkness, a crow swooped down and settled on the frozen ground between barn and police. It stood quietly, head cocked to the left, drawn by the powerful beams. Half a minute passed before the sound of a hinge creaking broke the silence; the bird turned. A stooped figure appeared at the barn door, lost in shadow. The bird suddenly began to run at him, flapping its wings, the man at the door confused, his hands up to his face to shield the light as he tried to run.

A single shot rang out. Eggart's head snapped back; he dropped to the ground.

"Who the hell shot?" screamed the man with the bullhorn. He ran toward the body, two others in suits with him. "Jesus," he said under his breath, "I hate these local guys." The three men arrived at the body and flipped it over. The man shook his head and stood, then turned back to the lights. "No one's going anywhere. I want to know who fired that shot." One of the agents pulled a note from Eggart's pocket and handed it to the man standing. He unfolded it and read: "For the sins of all Sodomites and those who protect them. Our wrath shall be swift." He recognized the insignia at the bottom of the page. Another militia-inspired lunatic. "Seems he didn't like the fact that our Dutch friends came from a country that tolerates homosexuals." He placed the note in a plastic bag. "We'll see what the lab has to say. See if it connects to the rest of today's insanity."

Another pair of suits approached, these escorting a state trooper, a man in his late forties.

"Is this Trigger-happy?" asked the man. Both nodded.

"Grant, Thomas. Virginia—"

"All right, Mr. Grant, Thomas. What the hell happened?"

The trooper said nothing. *Sacrifice, my government friend. There must always be a place for sacrifice.*

⚔

Sarah had moved to the fridge and was refilling her glass. "At last count, eight distinct acts of terrorism. The city's been turned on its head—"

"Hold on a minute," Xander cut in, the last few minutes clearly having taken their toll. "In an *alley*? Did they . . . hurt you in any way?"

"No, they were professionals." She dropped the bottle into the trash.

"*Professionals?*" He shook his head slowly, his eyes fixed on her back. "I'm not sure I understand . . . *professionals*? How does that relate—"

"Exactly my question." She turned to him. "Why would they describe the chaos on that screen as a '*first trial*'?"

"They called it a first . . . " A sudden recognition crept across his face, his words following of their own will: "First trial of conjecture by experience."

"What?" she asked.

He looked up, his eyes still distant. "It's the way someone in the sixteenth century would have explained experimentation."

"In English, Professor."

He turned to her. "A dry run. Something to test the waters. That's what a first trial is. Why would they refer to Washington as a—"

"Because they wanted to convince me to forget about Eisenreich."

"*They* mentioned Eisenreich?" Xander could do little to mask his surprise. "How could they have known about Eisenreich? Even I didn't make the connection until . . ." Fear crossed his face. "Oh my *God.* Of course." He looked back at the screen. "They *are* Eisenreich."

Xander paced along the aisle created by bed and heater, a half-filled glass of scotch wedged firmly in his hands. Two steps, turn, two steps, turn. He seemed entranced, stopping every so often to lift his head and stare directly at Sarah, who was on the bed, trying to sort through some of the papers he had brought. After a rather uncomfortable five minutes, he slumped into the chair by the window and drained the alcohol in his glass. Aware that the strange routine had come to an end, she looked up.

"I can't make heads or tails of these. Half of them aren't in English."

"German and Italian," Xander answered, his tone distant.

"Right. Look, Professor—Xander," she said, trying to reassure, "I realize this isn't exactly the sort of thing you deal with every day—"

"That's putting it mildly." He placed his glass on the bureau. "If you recall, I do theory, Ms. Trent."

"Yes, I—"

"I sit in my nice little office, read lots of books and articles, and then I write about it. That's it. I don't do anything that might warrant an attack, *professional* or not. I suppose I expect someone else to see how the theories pan out." He stopped. "Which raises a very interesting question. Who exactly are you?"

"What?"

"I don't mean to be rude, but the little I know about State, especially its research branch, has nothing to do with dark alleys or professional assailants. You're like . . . academics. You don't get involved."

"I'm aware of that." She paused and looked over at him.

"Meaning . . ."

"I'm involved. So are you."

"That's not an answer."

"I might be able to figure out *why* if I knew what Eisenreich meant."

"I see." He waited for more; when none came, he continued. "Look, I'm happy to talk about Eisenreich. That's why I came. But I'd prefer to know if I'm dealing with the CIA or the FBI or whatever acronym is the most popular these days—"

"You're dealing with me," she said.

"That's cryptic."

"No, it's safer." She stared at him. "Eisenreich, Professor. How does it tie in to Washington?"

He returned the stare, trying to maintain his edge. After half a minute without success, he let out a long breath, then shook his head. "All right." He sat back. "Eisenreich. Not an it. A *he*. Swiss monk. Died about four hundred and fifty years ago under some rather unpleasant circumstances—"

"A *monk*? How does a monk—"

"Because of a treatise he wrote on political power."

Now Sarah shook her head. "A book is supposed to explain what happened today? Forgive me, Professor, but how dangerous—"

"Could a manuscript be?" He leaned toward her. "It's never the document itself, Ms. Trent. It's how people *use* it. Remember Machiavelli? As long as they trust its message, a piece of theory can create all sorts of trouble. If you need further proof, you can always flip to another station."

"You're telling me a manuscript did *that*?" she said, pointing to the screen. "That's sabotage on a very sophisticated level, Professor. We're talking about computer manipulation, high-tech explosives, acts of terrorism no sixteenth-century *theorist* could possibly have understood."

"He didn't have to understand—"

"A major U.S. city is on the verge of declaring a state of emergency. I find it hard to believe that a manuscript could be responsible."

"Don't. Peter the Great kept a copy of a book by a man named Pufendorf by his bedside. Wrote in his diary that it was the key to every political decision he made. Charles the Fifth had Marcus Aurelius. Cromwell, Hobbes. And Luther's ninety-five theses have kept Rome on edge for the last four hundred years. Remember, these people didn't have television or radio; Oprah didn't tell them which books to read. So they had to find their own guideposts. Those who couldn't read found theirs in the church; those who could found theirs in books; and those who sought power found theirs in a specific type of manuscript, a few of which have provoked some of the darker moments in history." He placed the remote on the set. "Can you tell me who invented television, Ms. Trent?" Sarah shook her head. "Exactly. But we all remember Guttenburg and his printing press."

"Then why this book?"

"Because it was supposed to make the Medici masters of Europe. Machiavelli had offered them only Florence." He seemed suddenly struck by something. Almost to himself, he said, "One city wasn't enough."

She watched as his eyes continued to wander. "Why 'supposed'?"

It took him a moment to regain focus. "What? Oh. Because . . . we're not sure it exists."

"What?" Her head snapped forward. "He never *wrote* it?"

"We don't know. There's a lot of . . . speculation."

"Then speculate."

WOLF POINT, MONTANA, FEBRUARY 26, 8:42 P.M. ⚔ Laurence Sedgewick stood on the veranda, his hands resting on the rail, the night hovering just below zero. He enjoyed the cold, his eyes tightening at the sudden gusts from across the open field. A shock of white hair—somewhat premature for a man only in his mid-fifties—lent an added distinction to a face that tended to draw stares for its extraordinary good looks: the high cheekbones, the supple lips, the gentle smile that seemed always to grace them.

Sedgewick checked his watch. The last car had been due ten minutes ago.

The sight of headlights bouncing through the woods allayed his concerns. Within a minute, the car appeared at the gate, its exhaust swirling in a gray cloud along the dirt path. As it pulled up, Sedgewick moved to the steps.

"Why the delay, Ms. Grant?" No greeting. No words to acknowledge a job well done.

"Turbulence" was her equally curt response. She waited for him to press further. When he merely nodded, she moved past him and into the house. The two young men followed. Inside, all three placed their bags and coats in a hall closet and stepped through the archway to the living room. A fire was at full blaze, the old man at its side, stoking in herky-jerky movements.

"I trust you had an easy trip." He thrust one last time at the wood, watched as the flame burst toward the flue, and then turned. "The car— what happened with Mr. Eggart's car? Why was it not in place?"

All three looked at one another, then at him. Janet Grant spoke. "It was on . . . Thirteenth. He never showed up."

"Yes, I understand that." He moved to the chair nearest the fire and sat. "I am simply asking a question."

"Did you know he'd been compromised?" Sedgewick appeared at the arch.

"Only . . . once we were in the air," she replied.

"But you were instructed to maintain radio silence." The old man spoke with little emotion. "How, then, could you have heard?" The woman did not answer. "I suspect that you failed to do as you were told because you were aware of your *earlier* mistake on *Twelfth* Street. Am I not correct, Ms. Grant?"

She kept her gaze straight ahead. "Yes."

"At last we have the truth." He stared into the fire. "Such a mistake can be costly. And, of course, there is always the matter of rectifying it."

"I understand—"

"You understand very little. Otherwise, this situation would never have arisen." The cold directness of the old man's response caught her off guard. He turned to her. "Your father has accepted the responsibility for your actions. He has always understood the process, the role he must play." He paused. "Do *you* understand that process, Ms. Grant?" Again he waited. "I trust that is something you will think about."

The young woman stood motionless, unable to answer.

"Fifteen thirty-one." The tale of the monk seemed to be calming Xander. "When the Medici resumed control of Florence, Eisenreich sent some excerpts of his manuscript as a gift to the returning conquerors. Much like Machiavelli twenty years earlier, he was looking for a job. In the pages he sent, so we're led to believe, he hinted at a method by which a few men— naturally, the Medici—could seize power not only in one city but on the entire continent. And not simply through military aggression. In that mess on the bed is a copy from the papal archives of a letter that Clement the Seventh sent to several of his cardinals at the time. Clement—who happened to be a Medici—describes the little he saw of the treatise as '*un lavoro d'una possibilita grande ma anche perigliso,*' 'a work of great but dangerous possibility.' More frightened than intrigued, Clement wanted the manuscript found and burned. Had he been a bit bolder, who knows what the map of Europe might look like today?"

"But why wouldn't the Pope have wanted to increase his own power?"

"To where? He was the head of the Catholic church, the largest source of social and political control in the known world, and he held the ultimate trump card. He was the Vicar of Christ. Excommunication was still a pretty potent weapon. He had all the power he could probably fathom. What he didn't need was one of his rivals—most likely Henry in England or Francis in France—to get hold of the document and threaten European stability."

"So Clement destroyed it?"

"That's the great irony. He found Eisenreich—or rather, his bastard son, Alessandro, Duke of Florence, found him—but tortured the old monk to death before he got any information about the whereabouts of the document. Clement probably spent some very uncomfortable weeks waiting for the manuscript to emerge in some other court, but nothing ever showed up."

"So it didn't cause any problems."

"For Clement, no. The manuscript never appeared. In fact, in a letter written to Alessandro about two months after Eisenreich's death, the Pope was already convinced that the whole thing had been a ruse—that no manuscript had actually existed, and that Eisenreich had created the threat just so that someone would give him a job."

"And so the whole episode was just forgotten?"

"If you think about it, in the early 1530s, Clement didn't have the time to dwell on the Eisenreich document. Henry the Eighth's split with the Catholic church was far more pressing than a hypothetical manuscript by a dead man."

"But it does reappear?" asked Sarah, picking out the copies of the Pope's correspondence from the pile. "Eisenreich *did* write the manuscript."

"Yes and no."

She stopped. "That's not the answer I was looking for."

"No proof, no manuscript. That's what most scholars believe."

"That's the *no*. What's the *yes?*"

"The *myth* of Eisenreich," he explained. Sarah shook her head. "Over the past few centuries, Eisenreich's name has turned up in letters, documents, even in notes on the side of a page, and always during periods of political upheaval. During the Thirty Years War, an entire treatise appeared: *Die Wissenschaft des Eisenreichs—The Science of Eisenreich.* Cute, but not all that coherent. Our monk pops up during the English Protectorate, the French Revolution, even into this century and the early stages of the Third Reich."

"So what, exactly, did they all think he had to tell them?"

"As far as we know, when and how to create chaos. Assassinations, the burning of grain reserves, destruction of ports. Sound familiar?"

"And you think the book could actually plot out—"

"It's not what I think that matters. You asked what the manuscript was supposed to tell them. Evidently, it's done a pretty good job. The problem is, no one has ever taken the references seriously."

"Why? Because the chaos never played out?"

"That, and because most academics believe that the very idea of the myth itself has been weapon enough."

Sarah looked up. "I don't follow."

"Think about it. If you want to consolidate your forces and make certain they have a common goal, what's the easiest way to bring them together?"

"A common enemy," she answered.

"Exactly. A threat that forces them to fight as one unit. Then, suppose you discover some old story about a manuscript that calls for, say, a severe restriction on individual liberty, a dismantling of the current market infrastructure, and so forth—and convince your compatriots that there's actually a group ready to impose those measures on the state. What do your followers do? They snap to attention so as to destroy the threat. And in the process, they destroy all opposition."

"And that's what Eisenreich has been?" asked Sarah. "A fictional device used by some savvy politicians to eliminate opposition?"

"That's what a number of historians believe. Even the name raises questions. In German, the word *Eisenreich* means *'iron state,'* or *'iron regime.'* The coincidence is . . . too good to be true."

"And you agree?"

"If I did, would I be here?" Xander got up and moved toward the bathroom, picking up his empty glass along the way.

"Wait a second," Sarah broke in as the sound of flowing water echoed through the room, "all those details about individual liberty and market restructures—how do you know that's in the manuscript?"

"We don't," Xander replied from the bathroom, a disembodied voice over the water. "Remember, this is a myth. It has a tendency to feed on itself. Over a four-hundred-year period, more *facts* are added; more little pamphlets appear expounding the wisdom of the great man. It all depends on what those savvy politicians require." He reappeared, glass and towel in hand.

"You're making a very strong case for the *nos.*"

"I realize that. So, this afternoon I did a little digging." He joined her on the bed. "Two articles appeared less than a month ago from a professor at the University of Florence—the one man who, over the last ten years, has defended the manuscript's existence. Carlo—"

"Pescatore," Sarah read from the top page in Xander's hands. "Eisenreich: La domanda risoluto."

" 'The question resolved,' " he translated.

"Does he?" she asked, trying to read over his shoulder.

"Not entirely, though he makes a pretty good case, from the little I read. It's all rather technical, but it's clear that he's seen what he believes to be authentic excerpts from one of the original manuscripts." He handed the pages to Sarah and started to rummage once again.

"What do you mean *one* of the original manuscripts?"

"Usually, there were two or three translations—versions if the master got lost or damaged before printing. As a precaution. For those of us who place stock in the Eisenreich saga, it's generally agreed that there were two versions. The one he sent to the Pope, and the one he kept for himself."

"And given today's events, you think Tieg, Sedgewick, and Votapek have one, Pescatore the other?"

"That would be remarkable, wouldn't it?"

"And you're telling me they could use it to construct—"

"I have no idea. Remember, it's what they *see* in it, how they *interpret* it. Take the Bible—think of how many different visions of the *Truth* people find in its pages. Spoon-fed in the same way, a book like Eisenreich's could create an equally dedicated following—one committed to a far more sinister truth." He went to the pile and pulled out the second article. "Plus, in this article, Pescatore seems to be saying that there's some sort of schedule linked to the manuscript. A step-by-step process, first for creating the chaos and then for building from it. That would make it a very powerful document."

"What if someone were to find the other version?" she asked, her expression more animated. "Would they be able to understand what our three friends have in mind, and not just as a . . . dry run?"

"I suppose . . . but—"

"But what?" she interrupted.

Xander had moved back to the chair. "Look, I could be way off base, here. It's a . . . theory. There's no proof to link—"

"The two men in the alley were very real, Professor. What happened today in Washington is no theory."

Xander stared at her. "I know." He shook his head. "It's just that when I came here tonight, I thought—"

"You thought it was part of some academic intrigue, something for your next article." He nodded slowly. "Well, it's obviously more than that," the words as much for herself as for him. "This is no theoretical exercise. If they know Pescatore has a copy, they'll want to get it back." She moved to the edge of the bed, her tone more deliberate. "And they won't want anyone else who might be able to decipher it to find it." She let the words sink in before moving to the other side of the bed and her briefcase.

"Look," he said, still recovering from the last few minutes, "I've kept up my end of the bargain. You know how Eisenreich's connected." He watched as she released the lock. "So, who exactly are you?"

Sarah paused, then looked at him. "To be honest, I'm not exactly sure."

"That's not very helpful."

"No, it isn't." She reached under the bed and a moment later was busy with her boots. "Put on your coat. Take everything with you." She could feel the operative returning. "We need to find a safe phone."

"A safe phone?" he asked. "Who the hell *are* you?"

VIRGINIA, FEBRUARY 26, 9:04 P.M. ✄ Thomas Grant, outfitted in a recently acquired Virginia state trooper's uniform, sat in the front seat, one FBI man behind him, the other driving. There were questions that needed answering. They had *suggested* he accompany them.

"You thought he was reaching for a gun."

"Yes," answered Grant.

"You actually thought—"

Grant suddenly reached over and grabbed the wheel, spinning the car into the railing. The man tried to regain control, but he had been caught totally unawares. A moment later, the car broke through, rocketing over the side.

"*Sacrifice!*" screamed Grant. "*Sacrifice!*"

The car crashed to the ravine below, exploding on impact.

✄

Sarah raked her nails along the brick face of the wall as she listened, the jagged texture helping to keep her mind focused. The booth was cramped, the seat offering a partial view of the bookshop at the end of the hall.

Benches and shelves were piled high with books; Tiffany lamps atop the three oak tables that lined one of the walls cast a warm glow on the small room. She had hoped the shop would distract Jaspers from the uncertainty at hand. The place had had an immediate effect, although he had been reluctant to stay by himself at first. A section on medieval tapestry had managed to ease his concerns.

"No," she said. "Completely unacceptable."

"All right." Pritchard's voice hadn't changed, the tone distant, even when trying to convince. "But it might be best for you to come in—"

"And take advantage of your *helping* hand?" She did little to mask her contempt. "I seem to recall an evening in Amman—"

"In which you made a choice. We've been through this. If you hadn't taken out Safad, the city—"

"A girl died because of that *choice*. That life—"

"Was expendable when compared to an entire city, perhaps an entire region. The repercussions with the Israelis—"

"Wouldn't have made any difference!" She stopped herself, heard the venom in her voice, a tightness in her chest, knuckles white as she gripped the phone. She shut her eyes and took in a strain of air. "So why the sudden concern?" She forced herself to stare at the wall. "As ever, you've been more than happy to set the pieces in motion."

"We weren't aware—"

Sarah laughed, enjoying the silence it provoked. "I'm sure of that. No," she continued. "I come in now, and you take me out to a nice little farm in the Maryland countryside, find out where the therapy went wrong—"

"As I said, we were all very impressed with your work in the alley. I can assure you, no one questions your—"

"I don't give a damn what you think."

Silence. "Then walk away, Sarah. Come in, turn everything over, and walk away." He waited. "I don't think there are any loose ends this time."

Loose ends. She could feel the rage rise in her throat, the need to lash out at the man on the other end of the line. Instead, she forced her eyes to the shop, to Jaspers, his stooped figure craning to read the spine of a book. The gentle academic, so clearly unaware, unprepared. *Loose ends.* The words battered at her, as they always had. *Whose responsibility, Sarah? Whose trust?* She had been taught to walk away, taught that it was the only way to survive. But she had never listened, never learned. "You have no idea what you're dealing with, do you?"

Again silence. "It would be best for you to come in. I trust—"

"Trust hasn't always been your strong suit. No, this time we play it my way. No last-minute surprises. No loose ends." Her eyes turned to Jaspers. "This time, nothing expendable."

⚔

Ten minutes later, she emerged to the shop's main room.

"Did your instincts pay off?" prodded Xander.

"They were expecting my call, if that's what you mean." Her tone was distant as she picked out a volume of Trollope from the shelf, more to keep her hands busy than for any other reason. "I need to see that manuscript."

"Wait a minute." His uneasiness had returned. "Who's the '*they*'?"

"Would it make any difference if you knew?" Xander remained silent as Sarah replaced the book and chose another. "Pescatore. Which department is he in at Florence?"

"Political Theory," he answered almost involuntarily. Trying to dismiss the question, he continued, no less agitated. "What do you mean it wouldn't make any difference? Remember, I've written about—"

"You haven't written about them." The intensity in her tone told him to press no further. "What I need from you is a letter of introduction to the Italian. Something that'll let me see what he's been working on. And I want you to take a few days off. There's a place in Delaware. I'll contact you when I get back—"

"Wait a second. . . . *You're* going to see—"

"He has the manuscript."

Her candor was a bit off-putting. "I see," he replied. "And what do you intend to do with it if, in fact, he lets you see it?"

"Let me worry about that."

Xander nodded, his unease turning to frustration. "I give you the letter, disappear, and you talk to Pescatore. Just like that." He continued to nod. "Unfortunately, I don't think it will work that way, if I know Carlo."

For the first time since her return from the phone, Sarah looked directly at him. "If *you* know him?" She could do little to mask her surprise.

"For the last ten years," he responded casually. "He's another of Lundsdorf's protégés. In fact, he was the one who got me interested in Eisenreich in the first place. I tried to tell you—"

"Did you? . . . It's perfect, then. Call him and tell him I'm coming."

Xander tried to control his impatience. "That simple?"

"Yes. I think I can handle it from there."

"Really?" He sat on the ledge of the shelf and crossed his arms. "And, again, what exactly are you going to do with the manuscript if and when you find it?" He waited. "It's either in Italian or Latin, so I trust you're fluent. And of course you know a great deal about sixteenth-century discourse, so you can wade through the endless pages of extraneous information, right? Oh, and by the way," he continued, gaining momentum, "Carlo won't be very accommodating. He might—and I emphasize *might*—let you take a quick look at a few pages while he peers over your shoulder, but that's it. He's easily the most protective academic I've ever met. Not to mention a little paranoid. He might even think I've sent you to steal his ideas. No. He'll be courteous, self-congratulatory, and more than a bit condescending. What he won't be is helpful. Moreover, he won't even be there." His directness had quickly turned to irritation, perhaps even a hint of comeuppance.

"And how do you know that?"

"Because, like two hundred other scholars in the field, he'll be at a conference in Milan for the next three days." Xander paused for effect. "I'm on the six-thirty flight tomorrow night. I'm *already* taking a few days off."

Sarah allowed herself a smile as she squeezed the book back in place. "I see." She sat down next to him on the ledge, clasping her hands on her lap in a show of mock surrender. "So what do you propose I do, given the fact that you're obviously three steps ahead of me?"

"Since you won't tell me who *you* are . . . let *me* talk to him."

"You were going to do that anyway."

"True." Xander smiled.

"What about the people who might not want you to find it? Their message tonight was pretty clear. On all fronts." She paused. "This isn't a game."

"It's a little late to be explaining the rules." Xander turned to her, greater confidence in his voice. "Look, you came to me. I understand you think I might be in some sort of danger now, but wouldn't it look odd to anyone interested in my recent activities if I *didn't* go to the conference? I've been planning it for months. So I decide to take a jaunt to Florence afterward—see an old friend. How uncommon is that?" He waited for a response. "You want to know how the manuscript ties in. Then you need someone who can decipher it, and who has access to Carlo. That would be me. I've done him some favors in the past; he'll put the paranoia aside for a few days. All I'm saying is that, on some fundamental level, you need me."

"What I need is someone who knows what he's doing." This time, it was Sarah's turn to think. There was little chance she could persuade him not to make the trip. And if he'd made the plans . . . maybe the sudden change *would* raise a few eyebrows, make him an even more acute target? *Acute target*—it was a phrase she hadn't let enter her mind in months, years. And now it returned with relative ease.

It also made it all the more apparent that Pritchard had known exactly what he was doing. Sending her out, letting her get tangled up with someone like Jaspers, her sense of responsibility. *"Then walk away."* He had never meant it, knew she would never take the bait. He had played her perfectly. *"No loose ends."* The question remained—why? Why force her back in?

She looked at the academic. His logic, much as she hated to admit it, was annoyingly on the mark. What exactly *did* she plan to do with the document once she had it? Once again, the voice—somehow fainter than before—broke through: *Whose life are you playing with, Sarah? Whose trust?* "Considering there's very little I can do to stop you—"

"Do you have a choice?"

"It doesn't seem that way, does it?" She stood and stared directly into his eyes. "You have to *promise* me that you won't do anything until after your conference, until he's back in Florence. Nothing more than casual contact."

"Why? Wouldn't it make sense—"

"No." The operative was now giving orders. "Remember, you're not the only one who knows he's been working on the manuscript. You have to lay low, at least until I get there."

Now it was Xander's turn to show surprise. "Until *you* . . . Isn't that the sort of thing that would cause our friends in the alley to take notice?"

His naïveté was losing its charm. "I've got some business to take care of in Switzerland. I'll be in the neighborhood anyway. And remember, I'm the one with the files on our three friends. If things do get rough"—again she held his gaze—"it would be nice to have someone there who knows what she's doing." She paused. "On some fundamental level, you might just need me."

⊀

Children scampered about, tossing quickly packed snowballs at one another, missiles whirling through the night air at targets almost unseen. The large expanse of open ground, nestled comfortably at the base of a long hill that tumbled down from the side of the redbrick building, served as the perfect battleground. Shrieks of laughter echoed, muffled by the sound of crunching boots racing through the near-frozen snow. The small wooded area that bordered the little arena lent the picture a calming quality.

A lone figure stood atop the hill, a cigarette between his fingers, his other hand clenched tightly inside a pocket for warmth.

Jonas Tieg watched as the smoke from his cigarette drew upward, colliding with the puffs of steamy air that poured from his nose. He knew it was a mistake; his doctor had told him to cut back, but Tieg had never been one to deny himself life's pleasures. At just under six feet, he had the stomach to prove it, although a barrel chest managed to hide a good deal of his most glaring indulgence. Two hundred and twenty-five pounds tucked judiciously within the confines of a double-breasted blazer.

The scene below allowed him a momentary respite—these children, so different from those in his own tightly woven world. He closed his eyes and let the last few months slip from his shoulders, the past day and a half fade from his thoughts. Memories of his own childhood—cackling laughter, sweat-soaked shirts and socks, panting breath, the cold wonder of a sudden explosion of snow on an unsuspecting back. So much easier. So much more tangible.

The cigarette began to taste sour in his mouth; he tossed it to the side of the hill and heard the momentary fizz as flame met snow. The sound of cars arriving, the sudden intrusion of headlights against the ethereal backdrop, drew him back to the evening's task. Turning to face the oncoming lights, Tieg heard the hurried steps of one of his aides as he approached. It was time to put on the determined face, the mask of authority that had come to characterize the most popular figure in the world of television rabble-rousing. Tieg smoothed back his jet black hair and walked toward the large brick building. As he made the turn toward the school entrance—his aide now at his side—the large letters above the two oak doors rose from the brick in majestic fashion: THE ELKINGTON CHARTER SCHOOL.

Tieg unbuttoned his coat as he made his way through the thick doors and into the small, tiled front hall of the school. An impressive glass case full of trophies stood directly in front of him; he removed the coat from his shoulders and handed it to the young man at his side.

"Keep it with you. I'll want to make a quick exit tonight." The aide nodded and moved off toward a set of doors at the end of the hall. A young woman appeared at the end of the hall, clipboard in hand, a harried look on her face. Amy Chandler—producer of *Tieg Tonight*—had been less than thrilled with the two-week-tour proposal that had landed on her desk three months ago. Fourteen shows in fourteen towns. Tieg had wanted to get to know his fans, hear their concerns. *Her* concerns had not been an issue.

"You've got about four minutes before we go to air," she said, moving toward him. "Your devoted fans—five hundred of them—are patiently awaiting the promised schmooze session. Give them a quick sweep and then head down. I'll spot you when we're at thirty."

Tieg started toward the double doors, adjusting his earphone before he answered. "I'll come down the center aisle," he said as they met at the door. She began to adjust his tie. "Pick me up with the forward camera just before I make my way up to the stage."

"Done." She pressed the tie against his chest, gave him a wink, and spoke into her microphone. "He's coming through. Cue them up."

Amy slipped quietly through the door; fifteen seconds later, a deep, resonant voice broke through the dull hum of voices just beyond the doors.

"Good evening, ladies and gentlemen, and welcome to *Tieg Tonight*." A smattering of applause accompanied the sudden hush of the room. "We'll be on the air in just a few minutes, so sit back and relax, and please give a warm welcome to the host of the show . . . Mr. Jonas Tieg." Tieg waited for the cue from Amy; a moment later, the doors opened in front of him, the applause considerably louder as he strode into the spotlight. The classic gym-cum-meeting hall, with ever-present stage and wooden floor agleam under untold layers of wax and varnish, served as the setting for this evening's off-the-beaten-path taping of the show. The studio equipment had been slotted into an area just below the far basketball hoop, cameras and booms at the ready for the on-air cue. Tieg raised his right hand in a fist of appreciation and then set off into the crowd. As he moved through the audience, he seemed a man with boundless energy; a man with vision, they would say.

"What a pleasure to come out here and listen to what you people have to say," boomed Tieg, shaking one man's hand and turning to another. He continued to wink and nod his way through the now-standing audience; two minutes into the ritual, he heard Amy's voice in his ear. "We're at thirty."

Tieg pulled himself away from one adoring young lady and started for the stairs at the far end of the stage. The set looked small, the bookshelves and desk pulled far down on the stage, but Tieg knew the cameramen would work their magic. He stopped just short of the steps and waited for the intro. "Smile, Jonas," came the voice in his ear as the familiar music swelled up.

He did as he was told, speaking under his breath, the tiny microphone on his tie keeping him in touch with his producer. "The plane's scheduled out of Rochester at eleven forty-five?"

"It'll wait if we run late."

"Not tonight, Amy. In and out. That's the plan."

"But what about your *adoring* fans?" He heard her laugh. "They'll want some time with you after the show, Jonas."

"In and out." He waved at a young man in the front row, smiled as he talked. "Not tonight."

The voice boomed over the music, the audience now at full pitch as Tieg took to the stage.

"Tonight, from the grand state of Vermont, the town of Elkington welcomes Jonas Tieg and . . . *Tieg Tonight.*" The applause sign flashed mercilessly, though without reason, the audience already in full lather. Tieg walked slowly toward the desk, applauding the audience and pointing to one or two unknown faces in the crowd. He got to his chair and sat just as the music reached crescendo. He then adjusted the microphone on the desk, moved a small stack of papers to the side, and looked up, a broad smile on his face. It was time to inspire, he told himself. Time to bring the vision to life.

"My, oh my, aren't we a spirited bunch tonight." The audience erupted one last time; Tieg waited for them to settle down—nodding, waving, stacking the pages—until, staring into the number-one camera, he continued. "Let me extend an Elkington welcome to everybody watching out there. As you can hear, we're a bit on the rowdy side tonight." Another wave of applause. "Folks, we've been in ten towns in ten days, and the amount of support we've been getting continues to astound me.

"Over the last week, we've tackled jobs, immigration, taxes"—a groan rose up from the audience as he turned to camera two—"and yesterday"—he paused, suddenly more serious—"well, we all know what was on everyone's minds yesterday." He let a silence settle on the hall. "To our friends in Washington, our prayers." Again he waited, then turned back to camera one. "Now, we're not going to rehash those stories tonight, but it seems pretty clear to me that they all carry the same message: What's happening to this country? Where are we supposed to place our faith when our jobs—our very lives—are at risk? Are we losing control?" A burst of applause forced him to pause.

"What it boils down to is that it's time for us to make our voices heard. That's what this two-week tour is all about. And tonight, we were thinking, What would be more appropriate—in this beautiful high school setting— than to talk about the state of education in this country. It's true—we might all need to tighten our buckles from time to time; we might even have to put a few extra locks on the door, but we've done that before. When it comes to our children and their future . . . that's when we really have to sit back and do some thinking." A number of voices rose in agreement from the back of the hall.

"As you know, I don't usually start out the show with a monologue, but tonight, well, I'm going to ask you to indulge me. I want to take a few minutes here and talk to you about something that's just too fragile to leave in the wrong hands. Our children's future." He took a sip of water and then placed both hands on the desk.

"There are some pretty strange ideas out there when it comes to educating children. Ideas that say morality isn't supposed to be taught in the school, that religious faith isn't to be encouraged. That strikes me as a little sad, especially when a school is meant to be a place where we shape young men and women into the sort of people who can make a difference. It's why we're here tonight, because we're sick and tired of a system that tells us—no, that *forces* us—to give up our own ideals, and claims that *our* vision is somehow unacceptable. Unacceptable?" Tieg allowed himself a quizzical laugh. "When we're the ones asking for a higher moral standard, a greater sense of community commitment, an investment in our children's future?" More voices from the audience. "I know. It makes no sense to me, either. The question is, Does that mean we're asking for a system that demands a bit more *control* over those young lives, that wants the same sort of freedom to choose what *not* to teach as others want in choosing what *to* teach? Perhaps. But what's so wrong with that?" The applause sign flashed as Tieg turned to camera two.

"Limitations, parameters—these are healthy things when they have a strong moral justification, when they help to define a character. As you've heard me say time and time again, too much time has been spent championing the fringe elements, the causes that only abuse the word *right*—in this case, a right to *teach* this, to *protect* that. Some things don't merit that kind of protection—at least not in the schools." Tieg picked up a newspaper from the desk and pointed to a headline. "I was reading this the other day, and it absolutely astounded me. 'COURT OPENS THE DOOR,'" he read, shaking his head while he stared at the page. "*New York Times*, tickled pink by a ruling that says sexuality *must* have a place in the classroom." The audience broke into laughter; Tieg looked up, a sheepish grin on his face. "Now come on, you know what I meant, folks." He laughed and turned to one of his cameramen. "We've got a frisky bunch tonight, Pete. Maybe I will have that glass of Vermont spring water." The audience applauded.

"But seriously," he continued. "Let me ask you—does my daughter *need* to know about birth control? Perhaps. But *not* in our schools. Does my son *need* to know about homosexuals and single-sex parenting? Perhaps. But *not* in our schools. Do my children *need* to come in contact with music that teaches pornography and hate? I would say never. But certainly *not* in our schools." Tieg took a sip from the glass. "That's why, by petitioning your school boards, we're asking to distance our children and ourselves from a system that, in the name of some constitutional freedom, claims the right to impose those standards—and I use the term *very* loosely—upon all of us. These aren't standards. They're an excuse. An excuse to give up responsibility for what goes on inside these walls." Another burst of applause.

"When I ask government officials—and I have—why my child needs to be indoctrinated by a bunch of liberal policy makers, they have no answer. At least none that makes any sense to me. It's become painfully apparent that they realize that schools are nothing more than holding pens, part-time jails for children who have no desire to learn about themselves, let alone anything else. They aren't *children*. They aren't *allowed* to be children, with all the mumbo jumbo that's thrown at them. Does a fourteen-year-old understand the questions abortion raises? Does a fifteen-year-old recognize the implications of a single-sex home? Can a sixteen-year-old distinguish between music and political brainwashing? I don't think so." The room erupted in applause.

"Standards." Again Tieg laughed in disbelief as he turned to camera one. "Standards imply caring—caring for those young minds, their spirits, their senses of themselves. And that's been lost." Again he paused. "Now, suppose I told you that the system, the chain that we're forced to wear around our necks, can't survive? And that when the time comes, we have to be ready with schools where children actually graduate with a sense of purpose, a mission. A *new* type of student, a *new* approach to learning and activism. How would you respond? How *do* you respond?" Waves of applause. "But the only way for that to happen, for those schools to pave the way and set those standards, is if we set ourselves apart *now.*

"Folks, that's what we're working toward. We have to be prepared to assert ourselves when the moment comes. We're on the brink of a powerful period of turbulence; too much is happening for us not to see it. I'm truly afraid that Washington yesterday was only the beginning. That's why this school, *these* schools, must be ready to take the reins, to stand as the very rocks on which our future is built. To pave the way to that future." He shifted his gaze to camera two.

"What does that future bring? And how do we prepare for it? That's what we'll be talking about tonight." He picked up the papers in front of him and placed them to the side. "You've been nice to let me have my say, but now it's your turn. When we get back, we'll see how far we can take this tonight. So start thinking, folks, and we'll be right back."

The bright light on his face dimmed and Tieg sat back. He pulled the earphone from his ear in anticipation of the makeup man, who approached from the wings for a few touch-ups. Amy was right behind him.

"Keeping them awake?" Tieg asked.

"Just keep it within reasonable limits," she answered, placing another stack of papers on the desk. "You were pretty close to the edge there at the end—'the brink of turbulence.' Let's stay this side of the apocalypse."

"Trust me, Amy. They were eating it up."

"They always do, Jonas. That's what's a little frightening."

"Are you complaining about the ratings?"

She smiled and picked up the earphone. "Stick it in your ear. We're back in thirty."

Tieg smiled. *Close to the edge,* he thought. Far closer than she could possibly imagine.

⚔

The whiskey glass was all but empty, resting gently in O'Connell's palm. He had turned off the overhead fluorescents and was allowing himself a few moments in the somber glow of lamplight. A reflection stared at him from the darkened window, his slouching body comfortably wedged into a leather couch. Somewhere through the glass, the icy waters of the Potomac ran silent and unaware, speckled by the light patter of a winter rain. The streaks of water slid along the window and cut through the still portrait.

The day had been filled with surprises, not the least of which had been the unexpected appearance of a dispatch from Bern. The operative fund. SARAH TRENT: ACCESS GRANTED. He had wasted no time in confronting Arthur.

"I thought we were pulling her in."

"She appears to be on to something," Pritchard answered, "and she's chosen to be a part of it. I wasn't going to leave her high and dry."

"'Chosen'?" snapped O'Connell. "*Jesus!* That's an interesting way of putting it. Did you at least fill her in on the rest of the file—Schenten, the girl in Montana?"

"Over the phone?"

O'Connell stared at Pritchard for a long moment. "You expected this, didn't you?"

"It was a contingency, yes."

"Why? Why would she come back in? What aren't you telling me, Arthur?"

Now he sat drawing the last drops of alcohol from his glass. His office was a bit smaller than Pritchard's, but it had all the amenities—desk, couch, and plenty of whiskey. No books. He knew he'd never read them, so why bother? And no Washington—just the river and Arlington beyond. It was the view he liked. Arthur had never understood. How could he? He'd never been in the field. He'd never needed a drink to soften the twinge of guilt. No. Arthur would never permit himself that sort of involvement. For twenty years, they had worked that way. It was, he supposed, why he had the ulcer and why Arthur had the bigger office.

He poured himself a second and picked up the phone. "Irene, my love, I need to see Bob as soon as possible. . . . Yes, I know it's all rather hectic, but he's going to have to start earning his money. . . . No, you get home safe. Have one of the boys drive you." He sipped from the glass. "I want the meeting off-line. . . . No, not even Arthur's log. Strictly off-line." He paused. "And erase this conversation. . . . Right. . . . Tell him I'll be waiting." O'Connell put down the receiver and brought his feet up to the couch. The rain had turned to snow, blanketing the window in a white veneer. He remained still, caught by the rapid descent of chalky crystal as it devoured the panes of glass.

She had found something, something to draw her back in. And this time, she was keeping the Committee at arm's length. Somehow, he wasn't surprised.

O'Connell gulped down his drink and waited for the phone to ring.

Xander downshifted the Fiat into second gear, its engine growling at the sudden change to accommodate a quick turn at the bottom of yet another winding hill. The sharp drop from the side of the road to the houses perhaps a hundred yards below gave the view the classic features of the landscape in any number of Italian Renaissance paintings. Even the somber colors of a winter sky, draped coolly over the rigid crags of the Apennines, couldn't diminish the luster of the earth and orchards below. Several times during the past hour, he had found himself dangerously close to plummeting over the side, caught for a moment too long in the splendor of the rolling Tuscan country. Now, with dusk creeping up ever more eagerly, he had no choice but to direct all his attention to the road that twisted mercilessly in front of him.

He had left Milan four hours ago, had made Bologna in good time— enough to stop and indulge a craving for afternoon coffee and sweet—and was now about half an hour from Florence. Somewhere over the next group of peaks he knew he would see the distant outline of the Duomo—the white ribbed crown of Santa Maria del Fiore—symbol of the Florentines' bravura, Brunelleschi's genius, and their faith in both God and artistry. Which they held in greater esteem was hard to know. Somehow, Xander thought, they had managed to sustain both commitments in a world that did its best to cultivate less impassioned interests, a coldness driven by the love of computers and mass communications and soulless art. Not that Florence had detached itself from the twentieth century completely, but its signal character had remained delightfully embedded in a consciousness, a fervor for the grandeur of its past.

He had chosen a rural route, forgoing the faster, if somewhat antiseptic, highways. There had really been no reason to monitor his time, since Sarah wasn't due until much later that evening. She had cabled from somewhere in Switzerland two days ago and had left instructions on which hotel he should check into once in Florence. And under which name he should register. That had seemed a bit odd, but the instructions had been very clear. *Instructions.* It was the kindest way he could describe the marching orders he had received. No questions about the conference, the weather—anything that might have lent the message some personality. So be it, he had thought. And, of course, she had told him to stay away from Pescatore. That, Xander now mused, had not been all that difficult, considering his old friend hadn't actually been there. No doubt he was digging ever deeper into the mysteries of Eisenreich, unwilling to tear himself away in order to take part in what had ultimately been a social gathering masquerading as an academic colloquium.

The sudden appearance of headlights in his rearview mirror brought Xander back to the road. Realizing he could barely see thirty feet in front of him, he flicked on his own high beams just in time to avoid a collection of rocks strewn across the pavement. With a quick jolt to the left, the car momentarily drove up onto the grassy slope of the hill with sufficient force to bounce Xander a good two inches above his seat. Another rapid swing to his right and the car was back on the road. He had to laugh. He had deserved the slight bump to his head, he thought. His overreaction to a few pebbles on the road had no doubt caused the driver behind him no small amount of anxiety. Checking his mirror again, Xander watched as the headlights—now creeping along—cautiously maneuvered the rocky spot. Within a few minutes, the car was once again only about forty yards behind him.

Forcing himself to concentrate for the last leg of the trip, Xander began to look in the mirror every ten to twenty seconds. He noticed that the car behind was drawing closer and closer, shooting along the road at near breakneck speed. It seemed rather odd, he thought, considering the care the driver had taken only moments ago. And yet, the car was looming ever larger in his mirror. Within a few seconds, the sound of its engine rose above the din of his own, the glare of its lights momentarily obscuring his vision. Luckily, the advent of a long, straight descent offered Xander the opportunity to slow down so as to let the car pass.

But the driver had no intention of passing. Instead, he closed within only a few inches of the Fiat and began to nudge the smaller car, jerking Xander forward with each tap. *What the . . .* Xander looked over his shoulder only to be met by the sudden shock of high beams cascading through his rear window. Trying to blink away the spots now dancing in his eyes, he hit the accelerator, shifting the car back down into third as the road began to climb. The churning of the fiery little engine, however, was no match for that of the car behind. The beams streamed in, reflecting off the windshield as Xander rocked from another jolt. He felt encased in light, almost unable to see the road in front of him, the small guardrail racing alongside his only guide. *Jesus Christ! What is this?* One word entered his mind.

Eisenreich.

Keeping his eyes firmly fixed on the thin sheet of metal, Xander eased the pedal closer to the floor, the small car screaming at the exertion. The car behind matched the Fiat's surge of power, careening again into the rear fender and thrusting Xander even more quickly up the incline. At the crest, the Fiat shot above the pavement, crashing down to the sound of crunching metal as it found the road again. Xander glanced at the mirror during a momentary respite from the blinding light, just long enough to see the car dart into the left-hand lane and disappear from sight as the road curved violently to the left. Crashing his palm into the gearshift, he thrust his foot onto the clutch and again listened as the engine nearly buckled at the strain. As the road straightened, the light from behind again invaded his car, making him wince and, for an instant, lose sight of the rail. Out of instinct, he pressed hard on the brake and began to feel the back of the car slide to the right and scrape against the metal protector that stood between him and a quick plunge to the orchards below. At that moment, the larger car raced past him on the left, unprepared for the Fiat's sudden change in speed. Xander immediately released the brake—his car readjusting itself to the road—and focused all of his attention on the taillights of the car now in front of him. It, too, began to slow, as if taunting him to pass so that the game of cat and mouse could continue.

As his own lights probed its rear window, he could make out the shadow of two figures, one—his head the egg shape of a fully bald man—clearly looking back from the front seat in order to keep an eye on the car they had inadvertently sped past. Xander wondered how long they would wait before making another move. He had no idea what to do.

Eisenreich had tracked him, had been with him in Milan, no doubt in Bologna, waiting. He had been foolish to think otherwise. But waiting for what? Whatever the answer, they seemed to be placing a great deal of stock in his ability to decipher the theoretical.

Theories, he thought. *Always theories*. The deceptively alluring panaceas that promised solution but that invariably disappointed. He had put his career in jeopardy too many times in the name of one of his pet projects, one of those theories that seemed so right at the time. And yet, he had made a name for himself in no small measure because of his imagination, a capacity to distill the crumbs worth saving when the theory began to fall apart. From those crumbs, he had managed to create some of the more insightful approaches to what ultimately proved to be unanswerable questions. It was always a game of knowing what had value, what was smoke screen. Lundsdorf had seen the talent, drawn it out of him, forced him to recognize his own passion for the bits and pieces that always lay at arm's length. Beyond the haze.

And he had run with it, all too often surprising even his mentor. The practical implications of a theory—the ways in which it could be implemented to good effect—remained somehow intoxicating. He had tried to convince Sarah otherwise with Machiavelli, but Xander knew himself too well. He was too good at lending the theories clarity to dismiss them as mere ideas. And now Eisenreich was stepping off the page. Frightening, given the reality of the men who had tracked him. Exhilarating, given his own passion.

The car in front of him broke left, turning into what looked to be a sea of black. Unable to react quickly enough, Xander found himself gliding by the red taillights of the car—the sound of its gears shifting into reverse forcing him to refocus his energy. He pressed down on the accelerator and down-shifted in an attempt to create as much distance as he could between the two cars. Once again, the lights bore down on him, sending his eyes to the rail for guidance, the rapid, sloping curves of the road coming with even greater frequency than before. Much to his relief, the change in terrain seemed to be preoccupying his assailants as well, allowing him to avoid more of the hammering from behind; even so, they were gaining with each new bend in the road. Any contact, he thought, and he wouldn't be able to keep the Fiat from careening out of control. The guardrail continued to whisk by, a token gesture against the imminent impact from the speeding car behind.

As if from nowhere, the distinct shape of the Duomo rose up on the horizon, an elongated orb floating atop a sea of lights—Florence. Houses began to fly by, less precarious on the hills, whose slopes now receded to a level plain. And the road accommodated the change, forgoing the snaking twists and turns for a straight and narrower path toward the lights. Xander shifted again, taking the car to the utmost limits its engine would allow. Through his mirror, he watched as the car behind responded equally well, cutting through the distance with voracious speed, and bearing down on him in anticipation of the kill. There was little Xander could do but will the yelping car to ignite a hidden burst of energy, a sudden swell of power to tear it from the oncoming assault. Clusters of houses shot by, forming a strangely amorphous wall through which the cars tunneled. Realizing that he was drawing closer and closer to the city, Xander became all too aware that the road would soon dissolve into the myriad streets and alleys of central Florence—a maze in which to get lost, or cornered. Or worse.

At the moment of certain impact, the road miraculously began to curve gently to the right, merging with what Xander guessed was the central highway from Bologna. Not slowing, he fired the little car onto the four-lane road, barely missing an ancient bus that swerved at the last moment so as to avoid the collision. The sound of its bellowing horn slipped quickly into the distance as Xander whipped through the light traffic heading into the city. Daring a glance in the mirror, he watched the large car try to make its way through, its bulk now a hindrance. With each passing car, Xander was drawing farther and farther away; within a minute, he had placed a hundred yards between them as the city began to appear all about him.

Its immediacy, the sudden rise of central Florence, had always struck him as overwhelming. Five minutes ago, he had been bulleting through the Tuscan countryside. Now he was doing his best to avoid the first hints of rush hour. Bringing the car down to a reasonable speed, he settled into the flow of traffic as he swung around the Piazza della Libertà and the old Porta San Gallo, a relic from the city's medieval past. The old stone figure glided by on his left, lit from below and bathed in a wafting glow. Xander had no time for its serenity. Turning into the wide avenue of the Viale S. Lavagnini, he again picked up the pace, darting through whatever gaps the cars around him would allow, slowing only at the Viale F. Strozzi and the circuitous approach to the railway station. It would be his best bet—a place to drop off the rented car and to lose himself in the crowds.

Directions to the rental returns began to appear as soon as he turned into the long drive of the Piazza della Stazione. Slowing, he noticed a gap in the parked cars and slipped the Fiat into an empty spot. He then pulled his overnight bag and attaché case from the backseat, opened the door, and made his way as quickly as possible toward the station's main entryway. Looking back at the small car, he was glad to find no apparent marks from the confrontation in the hills. More than that, though, he was relieved not to see a large car hurtling toward the station. He quickened his pace, striding through one of the entryway doors.

As the door swung closed behind him, the black Mercedes that had provided the recent entertainment turned into the station's drive.

3

Laws are no more trustworthy than the men who create them, and stability can never rest on human caprice.

—*ON SUPREMACY*, CHAPTER XVIII

XANDER MET A SEA of bodies as he pushed his way through the main station. The early-evening trains stood on distant tracks, waiting to whisk commuters from the city, conductors yelling out any number of obscure village names, muted by the sound of hissing locomotives. To his left, he spotted the Hertz counter, a woman dressed in the appropriate gold scarf manning a computer. Fighting his way through the throng, he reached the counter and handed her the bright yellow envelope that held all the rental information. She began to shuffle through the papers; Xander casually scanned the station, every so often turning his attention back to the woman in order to answer another question.

"Your Italian is excellent, Signore Jaspers," she said as she typed.

Xander had enough sense to smile. "You're very kind. Is there a phone somewhere?"

She handed him his receipt. "You may use the one here at the counter if it is a local call. Otherwise"—she pointed—"directly across the plaza."

Xander had no intention of staying by the counter. He wanted a good vantage point in case his friends were still following; a phone booth seemed the ideal choice. He nodded and pocketed the receipt, then made his way to the bank of phones, all the time keeping an eye on the entry doors. Slipping into an open booth, he fished out the hotel's number and dialed. Sarah had booked him under the name Fabrizzi. Waiting on the primitive pulses, Xander noticed a young man dart into the open atrium of the station, evidently searching for something. He wasn't difficult to miss, at least six-foot-five, a good 250 pounds, and completely bald. Xander stepped closer into the booth. *The man from the car.* He watched as the titan made his way to the Hertz counter and began to ask questions. Once again, Xander began to inch himself farther into the booth as he watched the exchange. The sound of a voice in the receiver startled him.

"*Pronto*—Hotel Donato." Xander gently replaced the receiver and continued to watch the man at the counter. The woman was of no help; he moved to a more central point in the station, where he stood for perhaps two minutes, slowly turning his body in full circle. Finding nothing, he moved off toward an exit, his hands tucked firmly into the pockets of his overcoat. For some unknown reason, Xander began to follow. As soon as the man pushed through the exit door, Xander hurried himself through the station, jostling one or two impatient commuters before cautiously making his way out into the cold.

Remaining within shadow, he scanned the parking area, headlights now darting all about. There, above the mayhem, he spotted a bald head making its way toward a large black car at the exit. Xander watched as the man opened the door and bent in, evidently to relate the futility of his search. A heavily bearded man sat in the driver's seat; his reaction, however, was not what Xander expected. He *nodded.* No burst of anger, no blame meted out on a subordinate. Only a nod. And then, even more inexplicably, he turned and peered through the rear window. For an instant, Xander thought the man was looking directly at him, a smile beneath the beard. It was enough to force him to take a step back as the car started down the drive.

"Taxi, signore?" Xander tried to focus his thoughts—*He was looking directly at me*—his eyes now drawn to the grizzled figure at his side. "Signore?" the man repeated.

Still dazed, Xander started toward the curb. "Donato," he said, more rote reaction than command. He stepped into the cab and sat as the small man placed his bags in the trunk. Half a minute later, the man squeezed in behind the wheel, smiled back at Xander and said, "Hotel Donato. *Sì.*"

A plastic chair served as Sarah's final waiting spot. Lodged within a gaggle of similarly uncomfortable seats, it held the perfect vantage point for anyone interested in a view of the long concourse back to the main airport terminal. Over the last six hours, she had done her best to minimize her audience—the train from Bern to Zurich, the plane from Zurich to Milan, and now the express train to Florence. She had decided to make the trip in small installments for two reasons: First, there would be only one flight manifest, thus limiting her name to as few records as possible; second, she had wanted to bring Eisenreich out into the open. The somewhat convoluted itinerary had managed both. A small, nervous man had been at the Bern station, on the Alitalia flight, and was no doubt at this very moment somewhere in the terminal, frantically looking for Sarah Trent—the woman in plaid shirt, jeans, and boots whom he had seen exit the plane.

Now, sitting alone, she was a different person entirely, hair pulled back, its reddish tint an attempt to convey the vanity of an Italian sophisticate with a yen for things northern European. Along with the dark glasses, her face had a far more angular quality. Her clothes were also less obvious, muted colors of skirt and blouse beneath a heavy black coat. Subtle differences, to be sure, yet each effected with a trained hand; she was having little trouble blending into the surroundings.

The change had occurred two hours earlier, five minutes after she had cleared customs. She had ventured into a ladies' room off the main concourse and had spent nearly forty minutes redesigning herself, a skill she recalled with easy familiarity. Memories from her early junkets into the field as a member of COS. Those first years when a simple change of clothing had been sufficient. Until O'Connell had seen something else, something that told him that her *gift* lay not in the costume but in the alteration of her very persona. An ability to adapt beyond herself, to become little more than a reflection of those she was sent to manipulate. Pritchard, too, had seen the possibilities—the perfect infiltrator.

Staring at herself in the oversized mirror, Sarah had come to realize that it was no longer expedient to question why that past—with its numbing, calculating voice—had returned with such clarity. It was simply enough to put the instincts to use. This time, though, she would have to maintain a connection with Sarah, redefine the operative as something more than a sober casing for easy brutality. Once again, someone so thoroughly at odds with the arena was forcing the duality, the sense of responsibility. After all, wasn't Jaspers the reason she had let herself be thrown back in?

She had emerged without the slightest glance from her would-be companion. So different from her first encounter with the men of Eisenreich. The horror of the alley now seemed utterly foreign. Even some semblance of sanity had returned to Washington—the country all too eager to dismiss the hours of mayhem as a singular event. But Sarah knew better. *Only the first trial.* And yet she had nothing tangible to give her a lead. Too much remained hazy, obscured in the shadow of a manuscript she had yet to see.

What she needed were facts, pieced together in a neat little lump to clear away any ambiguity, set the patterns in front of her, allow her to set a course for confrontation. *Know these men. Meet them as they are, not as you are. Show them only reflections of themselves.* Orders from a distant past.

It was why she had contacted Feric. The name so like the man himself, cautious, deliberate, ferretlike in demeanor, with a curious talent for things destructive. His skills, though, were far more than mere extensions of a will for violence. They were tools, coupled with a loyalty that had nothing to do with the money Sarah left at his disposal. Over the years, she had kept him from the Committee, a private resource, unknown and untouchable. A combination rare indeed.

She had placed the ad in one of the Bern papers. As always, they had met at a small café along the Aare.

"The notice came as something of a surprise." He kept his eyes on the avenue, his words direct, hushed. "I did not think you would be returning."

"Things change."

"Evidently. You are in Europe?"

"For now, yes."

He nodded, took a sip of his beer. "And the contact point."

"Next week. Same column."

"Good."

"The money's been deposited."

He allowed himself a smile, placing a few coins on the table as he stood. In a somewhat louder voice, he said, "And, of course, remember me to your dear mother." Tipping his hat, he moved off, his hands casual at his sides.

The announcement for the train brought her back; she stood and moved to the escalator.

CHICAGO, MARCH 2, 12:15 P.M. ⚹ "We have a problem, Marty." The voice came over the intercom.

"Problem." Martin Chapmann, a thirty-seven-year-old whiz kid who had avoided the worst of '87 and now sat as managing director of the Helpurn Investment Group, scanned the numbers on his private screen.

"We're overextending," answered the analyst. "Some of these options— I just took a look at the last two weeks of trades in grain. Have you seen this? I don't think we want to be going in this direction. At this rate—"

"What does the computer say?"

"The computer? The computer says . . . we're fine. But even a couple more hours like this, the market could be in serious trouble. The sell-offs on reserve grain stocks are climbing—"

"Then we must be fine." The words carried a finality.

There was a pause. "Let me take a closer look. Just to make sure."

Another pause. "All right, Tim. If you think that's best." He turned off the intercom and picked up the phone. A minute later, Chapmann had Laurence Sedgewick on the line. "Sorry to trouble you—"

"No trouble at all," the words delivered in a monotone. "What can I do for you, Mr. Chapmann?"

"The vulnerability. It's . . . beginning to show."

"It's a little early. . . . Still, all we need is a few more hours. I don't see the problem."

"I know, but I'm not the one controlling—"

"I understand that," said Sedgewick. "Is anyone aware that the trading positions are computer-generated?"

"No. We're up to about half a billion in bad bets. Someone, however, wants to check the numbers this end."

There was a pause. "That would be a mistake."

"Yes, I . . . I'm aware of that."

"Then you'll need to take care of it."

Several seconds passed before Chapmann responded. "And I keep buying those positions until—"

"It'll become clear when you've gone far enough."

"So we're actually going to take this thing over the edge?"

There was a pause on the line. "I thought we were clear on this?"

Silence. "I understand."

"Think of it as an experiment, Martin. A controlled environment to test the response. Let's just make sure the environment *stays* controlled."

A moment later, the line went dead.

Chapmann sat back, turned to take in the skyline from his fiftieth-floor perch. It was never more than that from Sedgewick—detachment with an edge. Chapmann had been with him since the last days of Warren Corp., part of the shake up that had left Sedgewick virtually isolated. Even then, the man had been cool to a fault, the loss of a $60 million venture tossed off with apparent indifference. He had been up and running again within three months. Chapmann had never asked how. Part of the aura. It was why Marty had remained so close to him. Sedgewick had earned his trust.

He inhaled deeply and flicked on the intercom. "How about a little lunch, Tim? Fill me in on what you've found."

"You buying?"

"Of course." He paused. "Isn't it always my treat?" Removing his finger from the intercom, he picked up the phone.

⚔

The Donato had been expecting Signore Fabrizzi and his wife up from Naples for a long weekend, Italians not required to leave passports with the concierge. Sarah had arranged everything, including the bottle of champagne in the room. Perhaps she had known Xander would need it. Given the absurdity of the last hour, he had come very close to taking a few swigs. He could almost forgive himself for his foolishness at the station—trailing after his pursuers. But the man's smile, that had unnerved him. He tried to push the thoughts from his mind as he settled into the sofa, his legs up on a small table.

A yellow glow streamed through the window and cast an uncomfortable glare across his eyes as he thought about giving into a nap. He knew he had the time; Sarah wasn't due for another two hours, but as he tried to maneuver himself from the streetlight's grasp, he could muster only enough energy to shift his shoulders. Evidently, it would take more than that.

Forced to wrestle himself up from the sofa, Xander opted for the cold wash of the Florentine night and ventured out onto the metalwork balcony that hung six floors above the Via dei Panzani. The burst of freezing air erased all thoughts of dozing from both mind and body. But it was the view to his left that truly made him forget his fatigue.

Don Quixote and his ever-faithful Sancho. The fat one on the left, the tall, thin one on the right. Xander's irreverence for perhaps the world's most striking architectural display brought a smile to his lips. Awash under a flood of lights, the Duomo and Campanile stared back at him, the central stained-glass eye of the cathedral penetrating the deep shadows cast by the powerful lamps from a hundred feet below. Clearly, their creators had been artists rather than builders. To Xander, the two seemed to be holding their ground, waiting for an unknown attack, comforted in each other's company. There was something very settling in their patience.

A chill began to rise on his back. He glanced wistfully at the glitter of the city street below and stepped back into the room, pulling shut the two French doors behind him. In an eerie unison with the click of the latch, the sound of a key at the front door drained the blood from his face. Images of the Florentine night immediately slipped away. In their place, an all-too-vivid picture of a bearded smile rose before Xander's eyes.

Xander's mind began to race, leaving his back frozen against the icy pane. He felt totally isolated, pinned against the glass, caught within the angry stare of the shaded bulb from the table. *Get out of the light, damn it! Get out of the light!* The words tore through him, an unknown source pulling him from his perch as the long seconds passed. He bolted toward the lamp, nearly striking his shin on the corner of the glass table before managing the switch. The room sunk into dim haze; only the soft stream of the streetlight cast odd silhouettes against the walls. Hearing the delicate turning of the knob and the creak of the door, he lunged to his right behind the childlike protection of a leather chair placed opportunely in the corner of the room. A broad wedge of light began to slice its way through the room as he groped for anything that might serve as a weapon. The bulbous outline of the champagne cork caught his eye; Xander clutched at the two-pound bottle, drawing it to his side, ready to flail about at even the hint of discovery. Focusing on his own breath, he tried to quell the rapid-fire pounding of his heart, certain that its echo could be heard throughout the room.

A shadow filled the expanse, rising across the ceiling and bearing down on his little enclosure. Daring no movement, he listened intently to the measured steps as they crept farther and farther into the room. Cautious footsteps, testing the waters. Again, the word *professional* taunted him, added to the strain in his fingers and lungs, and began to sap what little energy he had for the instant of confrontation. The figure inched nearer, a momentary flicker of light from the street catching a hand, a wrist. And in a sudden frenzy, Xander sprang from the corner, clawing desperately for the shards of arm that had revealed themselves in the cutting glare of the street-lamp. His other hand, still wrapped around the bottle, began to swing for-ward in the aimless direction of the figure as yet unseen.

The sensation he felt was wholly unexpected. A jabbing pincerlike object tore into the soft flesh of his wrist, forcing the improvised weapon from his hand. With a single twisting motion, a searing pain shot through his arm as his legs seemed to disappear, kicked out from beneath him. His backside and head crashed into the carpeted floor—his arm still captive—the harsh leather of a shoe's sole planting itself on his throat, the pressure sufficient to bar any movement save for the sporadic gulps of air he struggled to take in. More paralyzed by his own fear than anything else, Xander waited for the final blow.

It never came. The viselike grip around his wrist loosened; the next moment, the shoe lifted from his neck. Xander lay very still, free but dazed. Slowly, he pulled his arm back to his side and tried to regain his feet, but the pain in his arm would not allow him to push up. Crouching on the ground, clasping his wrist, Xander looked up through the streaks of light. There, staring down at him, was the vague outline of Sarah's face.

"Jesus Christ!" A swell of emotion rose up in his throat, unsure whether to burst out in relief, anger, or anguish. *"What* the hell were you *doing?"* Again he tried to get up, but to no avail, his mind still swimming from the throbbing in his shoulder. "I mean what the *hell* were you *doing?"* Sarah reached under his arm and tried to help him to his feet. Almost involuntar-ily, he pulled back. The indignity of lying supine on the floor, helplessly pinned, could not be forgiven with the simple extension of a hand. He began to feel a sticky warmth seep through his fingers, the slight trickle of blood that ran from wrist to palm. Waiting for the pounding in his head to subside, he slowly pulled himself up from the floor, all the while making sure to stay well clear of her outstretched arms. "I'm *fine."* He did little to mask his anger and frustration. "I just need to get something for my hand."

"You're not fine," she answered, waiting until he had straightened him-self up before moving to the small entryway foyer, flicking on the overhead light, and shutting the door. The sudden brightness only compounded Xander's discomfort. "And I should take a look at that wrist." The concern in her voice, though well intentioned, had little impact.

"Oh, so now you're the doctor."

"I know what I did. It's not deep, but it'll bleed." She paused, once again trying to help. "I'm sorry. I thought you—"

"I was *what*? What could you possibly have—"

"You did *leap* out at me from the shadows. It's not what I'm used to." She started toward the bedroom.

It was his turn to pause. "Well," the edge to his voice suddenly less brusque, "I thought you were . . ." He tried to find his anger. "I don't know." He made his way to the sofa and gently lowered himself. Speaking in the direction of the bedroom, he continued. "Why did you creep in the way you did? Why didn't you turn on the lights?"

"Because I heard someone switch off a lamp," she calmly explained, returning with a small, partially wet cloth. Sitting down next to him, she waited for him to extend his hand. "Why *did* you turn off that lamp?"

"I thought you . . . might have been two gentlemen I lost earlier this evening." He gave her his hand. "I also wasn't expecting you until *later.*" A short jolt of pain raced up his arm as she began to dab at the opening. "And why wasn't there a *bellboy* with you?"

"I didn't realize my nails were this effective."

"They are." Another short spasm forced a quick breath.

"Because my Italian isn't very good, remember? I didn't want to advertize the fact, *Signore Fabrizzi.*" She began to tie the cloth around his wrist, tightly so as to maintain the pressure. "What two men?"

"Just outside the city. We played bumper cars." Sarah continued to tie the cloth. "Don't worry, I lost them at the train station."

"Good." She got up and moved to her overnight bag, which stood at the end of the foyer. "I'm going to take a shower. And then you can fill me in."

Xander stared at her in complete disbelief. "That's *it*?"

"I think so." She was busy searching for something.

"I just told you that I was nearly *run down*, that I thought you were some kind of *assassin*, that I might be *bleeding* to death—"

"You're not."

"And you're going to take a *shower.* That's *it*?"

"Yes." She stared at him for only a moment—more relieved perhaps than she was willing to admit—and pulled a cosmetic case and a few pieces of clothes from her bag before heading back toward the bedroom. "Keep applying pressure for about five minutes. I'll be out in fifteen."

Xander watched as she walked into the bedroom, the sound of running water a moment later strangely calming, given his irritation. Her apparent indifference left him alone to ponder the last few minutes, her uncanny ability to render a six-foot-two, 180-pound man utterly defenseless within a few seconds. And if he tried to fool himself that he had been anything but easy prey, the still jarring pain in his shoulder and the equally dense throbbing in his wrist were proof enough that he had succumbed almost effortlessly. Xander recalled the two men she had mentioned in the alley in New York. It was not difficult now to understand how easily she must have dispensed with them.

Waiting *four* minutes to remove his fingers from the cloth, he decided to splash some water on his face and change his shirt. He lifted it gingerly over his shoulder and let it drop to the floor as he made his way to the sink in the entry hall. The water felt remarkably refreshing, especially the handful he rubbed into the back of his neck. Even his shoulder seemed to appreciate the few rivulets of water that managed to slide its way.

Grabbing a small hand towel to his left, he patted his skin dry, inadvertently knocking over Sarah's bag as he made his way toward the sofa. His clumsiness brought a short wave of self-recrimination before he dropped to a knee to restore the few items. Opening the flap to the main compartment, he noticed the five manilla folders wedged neatly into the side of the case. He knew he wouldn't get another chance to take a look at them. A quick glance at the bedroom door, the water still at full throttle. With childlike eagerness, he slowly pulled the well-worn files from the bag.

Staring up at him were the two names he had been researching for the past two years, plus the file on Votapek. The Tieg folder was by far the thickest, but it held the least interest. After all, Sarah had used his own articles to gather the information. Though considerably less impressive, Sedgewick's file seemed the best place to start. He laid it on the floor and lifted its cover.

> Laurence Caryll Sedgewick, age fifty-seven, born into New York's Park Avenue set. The bulk of the wealth from real estate and small interests in various publishing houses. Parents both died in air crash in 1961. Early years primarily under the eye of housekeepers and a series of tutors.

Five years ago, left his position as chairman of Warren Corp., a highly diversified venture capital concern. Reliable sources confirm it was not an amicable departure, despite press releases. Rumor is that he manipulated several trading venues, some of which made a number of very high-profile banking houses extremely vulnerable. The Warren board discovered the tampering in time to avert any major disasters, then quickly demanded his resignation.

Xander browsed through the rest of the page, facts that seemed either inconsequential or of public record. Schools—Deerfield, Princeton—two marriages ending in divorce, one daughter at a private academy somewhere in Switzerland. Nothing of great moment save for one piece of startling information: two years at Eton—involved in something called "independent study"—prior to his acceptance at Deerfield. The years, 1953 and 1954. Xander stared at the numbers. *Tieg,* he thought. Same time frame. Sarah had evidently noticed the connection, as well. A small red check stood alone in the margin. Flipping the page, Xander continued to read.

Since Warren, he's created something of a cabal around himself, a mixture of some of the more powerful figures within the world of finance. Some prominent names are Simon Maxwell at Lehman, Diana Cox at Morgan, and Martin Chapmann with the Helpurn Group. What he intends to do with them is left to the reader's imagination.

Xander wondered why there was no mention of the recent computer venture; it seemed the obvious answer to the question.

Here, the report seemed to jump inexplicably. Several paragraphs had quite obviously been removed, and a very sloppy job of reconstruction had been attempted. The flow of the report became jagged, cross-references back to the missing sections deleted so as to maintain the contrivance. Evidently, something had happened in the last few months that someone considered too delicate to include. The inconsistency was glaring. *It's the computers,* he thought. *Why had they removed those sections? It's the obvious link to Tieg.*

The cessation of running water caught Xander by surprise. He realized he had about three minutes to breeze through the Votapek file and make it back to the sofa before Sarah reappeared. Flipping quickly past the other files, he opened to the two sheets that served as the entire report on Votapek. Not much, but certainly more than Xander himself knew. He began to read.

Anton Votapek. Born 1934? Some question as to the authenticity of his early background—parents, date of birth, etc. Records available only after age seven. Unremarkable upbringing, followed by three years at the University of Chicago as an undergraduate, one year as master's candidate in education. Ph.D. from Columbia in sociology, followed by several years abroad on various grants and fellowships. Returned to the United States in 1963 to take a position with the Cahill Group, an avant-garde educational forum intent on revamping primary-school education. Some question as to Votapek's relationship with Arthur Cahill. Indications are that a struggle for control of the governing council left Votapek out in the cold. He resigned in 1965. Plans for the Learning Center (later known as the Tempsten Project) began in late 1966.

Xander glanced through the next few paragraphs, a few more details about the tragedy that had taken place in August of 1969, but little to make him stop. And yet, for some reason, he had the sense that, once again, there was a break in the narrative, a rushed job of cut and paste that left too much unsaid but that clearly hinted at more. No mention of any names associated with the Learning Center—children, faculty, sponsors. Nothing. In fact, the information, save for the very enigmatic first sentence about Votapek's background, was readily available to any practiced researcher. No, the report was evidently leading somewhere, but it had been cut off, as if it was meant only to whet the reader's appetite. *And no Tieg or Sedgewick. Nothing beyond 1969. No connections made, none implied.*

Wanting to scan the last paragraphs for answers, he reluctantly slipped the pages back into the folder and delicately slid the files into the bag. Struggling to his feet—his shoulder more maneuverable than only minutes before—he draped the towel around his neck and, realizing he had no time to make it to the sofa, planted himself in front of the sink, turning on the faucet just as Sarah reemerged from the bedroom.

"I'm glad to see you're up and about. Didn't bleed to death while I was in the shower?" She had dressed in a pair of slacks, a turtleneck rounding out the outfit. Her hair was pulled back in a bun, its red tint far more pronounced when wet. It was the first time Xander had noticed the change.

"That's different, isn't it?"

"What?"

"Your hair."

"You're not the only one who's had unwelcome guests today." Sarah left it at that as she made her way to the sofa and began to browse through one of the magazines on the coffee table. Without looking up, she added, "I hope you found them interesting."

Xander flinched for only an instant, then continued to dry the back of his neck. As nonchalantly as he could, he strolled toward her. "Found what interesting?"

"The files. In my bag." She looked up, no sign of accusation in her expression. "Did they fill in any holes?"

"Some." He realized it was useless to play dumb. "How did you—"

"I left the flap closed." Xander turned to the bag. Open. He really wasn't any good at this, he realized. "How's the arm?" she continued.

"Better. Thanks." He was by the bedroom door, ready to offer an explanation. Instead, he smiled, turned into the room, and started to unzip his case. Digging through layers of clothing, he found it hard not to think about the woman who sat calmly in the other room and who had shown no emotion when pointing out his indiscretion. Was she the same person he had met over tea only a few days ago? No. That much was clear. The hair, the candor in her tone, the eyes. There was a self-assurance, certainly not lacking before, but which now seemed to define her entirely. It was, perhaps, best not to ask. Still, he couldn't help but wonder.

Finding a reasonably unwrinkled shirt, he walked into the living room, at the same time trying to manage the sleeves without lifting his right arm.

"Want a hand with that?" she said, tossing the magazine onto the table.

"Thanks." This time round, he would accept the charity.

He handed her the shirt, turned his back to her, and placed his hands at his sides. Slowly, she positioned the sleeves by his outstretched fingers and gently pulled the collar to his neck, draping the shirt on his shoulders. As she let the material fall, she momentarily caressed the injured shoulder, as if to apologize. For someone who had tried to maim him only minutes earlier, her sudden tenderness was pleasantly unexpected. "You have a nice back, Dr. Jaspers."

Her comment caught him completely off guard. After a very long moment, he stammered, "I . . . I row."

"That would explain the shoulders."

He suddenly felt very warm. Without turning to her, and trying to handle the buttons as quickly as he could, he continued. "I have one of those machines . . . in my apartment. . . . A rowing machine." He tucked the shirt into his pants with surprising speed, given his discomfort, and made his way behind the sofa, heading to the sink. "I try to use it every day . . . the . . . rowing machine."

"I can see that." She was seated again, a smile on her face. Xander was finding it difficult to meet her gaze.

For no apparent reason, he turned on the faucet and began to wash his hands. "Yes, well . . . the shoulder is feeling much better." And with that, he rinsed off his hands, dabbed them lightly on the remaining towel at the basin, and turned to Sarah, trying his best at a smile. "Dinner?"

"Yes." She looked at him and then reached across to the menu in the middle of the glass table. "It looks as though they have a nice selection."

"Oh." Xander was unsure for a moment. "I thought we—"

"Given the way things have gone today—for both of us—I think it'd be smarter to eat in. Just to play it safe."

He nodded awkwardly. "Right. That seems . . . right."

"Plus, it'll give you a chance to tell me what you think about those files before we go and see Pescatore tomorrow." She remained focused on the menu, though her words seemed to jar Xander from his momentary stupor.

"Carlo," he uttered. "You know, he wasn't in Milan."

Sarah looked up, all signs of the smile gone. "Does that surprise you?"

"It didn't." Xander sat down next to her.

"But it does now."

"Yes"—he nodded, more to himself than to her—"I suppose it does."

CHICAGO, MARCH 2, 12:47 P.M. ⚔ The lunch-hour crowds filled the streets. Martin Chapmann was deep in conversation with his young associate, debating grain's solvency between bites of a chili dog. Tim Gillespie was wiping his chin with a napkin as they walked.

"Then the computers are fucked, Marty. I'm telling you, the surge over the last two weeks could be based on a lot of high-risk bets—farmers selling off reserve stock at inflated prices. . . . Look, I don't think I have to explain basic finance—if grain doesn't go that way—"

"You think we'll have a panic on our hands. Come on, Tim."

"Well then, humor me, Marty. Let me trace the numbers, see where the positions are coming from. Worst-case scenario, I waste an afternoon."

"You really think—"

"I've already got the computer doing an initial search. Two hours max—"

A woman momentarily brushed by the two men, inadvertently scraping the hand of the young analyst with her bracelet. Gillespie hardly felt the pinprick as the woman turned her head to apologize, an instant's recognition from Chapmann as she continued down the street.

"Then again," joked Gillespie, "I could always spend two hours with her." Laughing, he turned back to Chapmann and began to walk. They had moved no more than ten feet when the younger man stopped. Chapmann saw the smile vanish from his face, Gillespie's expression one of confusion, disorientation. For a moment, he tried to blink it away. He grabbed on to Chapmann, who continued to watch as the analyst's face suddenly contorted in a wild spasm. A few seconds later, his body collapsed to the ground. Chapmann screamed for a doctor as he knelt by his friend.

But he knew it would make little difference. An aneurysm to the brain was fatal—a sudden, inexplicable, though entirely plausible cause of death.

✠

The early-afternoon sun glistened on the rolling waves, giving a strangely warming sheen to the frigid air on the Cape Cod beach. The sand, powdered with morning snow, parted easily under the feet of Anton Votapek, his wiry five-foot-seven frame wrapped in a long leather coat. He held his hands at his back, his shoulders hunched slightly forward as he trod just out of reach of the tide. His gait was slow, not so much because of the sand or snow but for the figure at his side, who was doing his best to keep up on the precarious terrain. The older man was on a slight incline, making the two roughly the same size as they sauntered along—tightly bundled bodies, each in Russian hat and walking boots, thoroughly isolated on the long stretch of shoreline. Three other men stood around a car perhaps a half mile away, alone in a parking area long abandoned by the summer crowds. The engine was running.

"As usual, they were not told that I was meeting with you," rasped the older man, his breath short from the demands of the walk.

"Probably best," nodded Votapek as he spoke. "Jonas and Larry have their hands full with the first trial. The economic phase should begin—"

"Do not concern yourself with such things, Anton." There was a hint of reproach in the tone. "Men must see to their own tasks." A phrase he had heard all too often. "Yours are the *children*. Remember this. Not the first trial." He smiled, the lesson over. "Still, you are right. Washington was remarkable. It sets the stage perfectly."

The accent, though almost entirely Americanized, hung upon the words and reminded Votapek of his earliest days with the man. Days spent expunging any traces of his own accent so that he could assume his place in a new world, a new society, free from the stigma of his past. America. He had embraced it then and had lost none of his fervor in the intervening years.

The problem was that things had gone terribly wrong. Yes, the war had been won, the sense of expectation—of real promise—profound. "But *fear had infested activism, indulgence had replaced direction, and empathy had diluted everything*"—more words from a book he had seen only once. As a young man, Votapek had watched as Cold War fixations had drained America of its very spirit. The result, faddism. No agendas, no claims to a future, because no one had been willing to muddy his hands, run the risk of using power to ignite real passion and commitment. Everything had become worthy of pursuit and thus nothing had been achieved. That brave new world, the society that had offered him such promise, had become nothing more than a breeding ground for every eclectic whim a people could foist upon itself. That wasn't *use* of power. It was an *affront* to it. And Anton Votapek had been groomed to treat power with greater respect. People needed to be taught, guided. They needed a moral vision. That was what the man at his arm had taught him all those years ago.

"The word from Montana is that everything with the children has returned to normal," Votapek added.

"As we knew it would. Thirty years, and only six such episodes. We have been most fortunate. It is a testament to your leadership."

Votapek nodded, then spoke. "Still . . . I should have anticipated the problem." There was a certain nervous quality to his voice. "We've had similar rumblings at seven or eight of the other sites, but we've managed to find ways to avoid . . . such extreme measures."

"You question the method?" asked the old man.

"No. Of course not. It's just . . . I should have been better prepared—"

"You are afraid of repeating your errors."

The younger man nodded.

"How many times do I need to tell you, it was not yours alone." The old man looked at his onetime pupil, a warmth in his eyes. "It could not have been. Those children were ill-adjusted, our program ill-designed to cultivate the right sort of passion without fostering a certain element of violence. Hatred is a powerful tool, Anton. More powerful than any of us understood. We needed time to learn how to control it. You cannot blame yourself for a certain level of . . . naïveté all those years ago."

Votapek remained silent.

"Anton, this sense of inadequacy, is it a result of the recent episode," he paused before adding, "or is it because it reminds you of the girl?"

Votapek took a moment before answering. "You mean Alison."

The old man stopped. "Yes, Alison." The warmth had disappeared from his eyes. "We have been through this too many times, and I will not hear of it again. Things are too far along for her to play on your mind. It was *thirty* years ago. You have done all that you can for her." He patted Votapek on the arm. "We should turn back. It is getting a bit cold for me." The old man clutched at the outstretched arm as the two retraced their way through the sand and snow. "The children, Anton. Think only of the children."

⚔

Sarah drew back the drapes, momentarily stunned by the sunlight streaming off the balcony. Sleep still heavy in her eyes, she pressed her cheek against the icy pane of glass to jolt herself awake. She had been to Florence only once before—as a student—and had been more intrigued by the young Italian boys, who had made her feel so welcome, than by the splendor of the city. Now, staring to her left, she watched as the sun spread across the ribbed dome of the cathedral, the tourists already thick within the open court of its square.

Pulling herself away, she shuffled toward the bedroom and knocked on the door to see if Jaspers was up. Given his injuries, she had thought it only fair he get the bed. It had taken considerable effort to convince him—at nearly two in the morning—that she would be far more comfortable on the sofa. Lundsdorf's etiquette aside, Xander had finally conceded, due in part to fatigue, but more to Sarah's reference to possible unwanted guests in the middle of the night. Who better than she as the front line of defense? Of course, she had been kidding, but her suggestion had been just enough to break his resolve. The smile on her face now recalled his momentary look of panic.

She knocked again, surprised by the lack of response.

"Looking for me?" Sarah spun to her right to see him, tray in hand, walking through the front door. She pulled the blanket tighter around her waist. "I bring coffee and croissants."

"I didn't hear you get up."

"I'm amazed," a broad smile on his face as he moved to the table. "But there you were, fast asleep, when I emerged this morning. I thought it best to let you sleep."

"I guess I needed it." Sarah pulled the heavy chair closer to the table while Xander poured out two cups of coffee. As he did so, she noticed the thick piece of gauze lashed tightly to his wrist. "I'm sorry about that."

"Not to worry. The concierge had all this medical stuff downstairs and was only too happy to have a chance to use it. I think he went a bit overboard. It feels absolutely fine."

"I'm glad to hear that."

"As am I." Xander winced from the heat of his first sip. "Unfortunately, I tried to reach Carlo—from the lobby phone. No answer."

"Maybe he hasn't gotten to his office," she suggested, spreading a thick spoonful of jam onto one of the croissants.

"No. He's a workaholic. He's usually in by seven, seven-thirty at the latest. It's not like him."

Sarah stood, taking her cup with her—a large piece of croissant jutting from her mouth. She pulled a few items from the bag by the bedroom door and said, "We'll have to see. I'll straighten myself out, and we can get going."

✠

Twenty minutes later, Xander followed her out onto the Via dei Panzani, a broad avenue by Florentine standards. Thick rustic stones of brown and gray furnished a textured armor for some of the more overbearing buildings, crude second cousins to the smooth-polished stucco shops narrowly wedged in between. The most ancient of them seemed unable to hold themselves upright, resting ever so slightly on the buildings to either side. Their familiarity lent the tightly packed row a strange sort of camaraderie— wood, cement, and stone banding together against time and the elements. Xander drew up to her side, and she slid her arm through his; he did little to mask his surprise.

"Don't worry, Dr. Jaspers. It's only what the Fabrizzis would do."
Xander nodded, though she could sense a slight hesitation in his response
as they continued on in the direction of the cathedral. His discomfort with
her as a woman—evidently something he had only realized last night—
struck her, for some odd reason, as charming. Thinking about it now, she
couldn't help but recall with delight the episode with the shirt. She
squeezed his arm a bit tighter, only to feel a tension rise in his shoulder.
Knowing full well she wasn't, she asked, "Am I hurting you? Is that the one
from last night?"

"No. No, it's fine. It was the other shoulder," he replied. "Which . . .
seems to have recovered entirely." He swung the small case out in pendu-
lum style to illustrate the arm's mobility. "See."

"Good." She began to propel them along at a brisk pace. "So tell me
what we're looking at."

His immediate sense of relief was painfully apparent. It was only fair, she
thought, to consent to an impromptu lecture on Renaissance history and
architecture. After all, he had been through quite a lot in the last day or so,
and she knew a brief jaunt into his little world would relax him. It might
also make the burden of a rather attractive woman on his arm less taxing.
Listening with only one ear—on occasion nodding or offering an "I see"—
Sarah tried to extend her focus to the area around them, ever wary of any
sudden movements within the growing crowds. As they reached the Piazza
San Giovanni, the buildings dropped away and the tourists, until now only
a trickle, burst forth in a torrent.

The Duomo loomed with fitting grandeur over the open expanse, its
stained-glass and marbled facade reflecting a brilliant sun. Few seemed
deterred by the glare, cameras clicking in syncopated rhythm to the growing echo of footsteps. Perhaps out of instinct, Sarah asked if there were a
less-traveled route to the university. Xander stopped and nodded to his left
toward a small street just off the main square.

"It's the shortest way, but we'll miss the Medici Palace and a number of
other lovely—"

"I think we can pass on the sights for now." Sarah smiled up at the
young scholar, seeing her point register in his eyes.

"Right." He nodded. "The less-traveled route."

Unwilling to bypass the Baptistry entirely—the large nipplelike structure in front of the cathedral—he led them around several of its sides
before pausing at its easternmost door. Ghiberti's Gates of Paradise stared

down at them, scenes from the Bible rising from the bronze in rich undulating lines: the Expulsion from the Garden, the Sacrifice of Isaac, Moses on Sinai. Xander looked on entranced. Somehow, the sculptor had captured the anguish, the elation, the immediacy in these scenes. Sarah, too, found it difficult not to stare, to give in to the door's seductive lure. But an inner voice told her that they should keep moving. Too many people cluttered around them. She pulled at his arm and led Xander toward the smaller road and its comparative stillness. At once, she felt more in control within the confines of the nearly deserted street. Even the sun seemed less inclined to venture in with them, cut off by the high walls rising above the narrow lane.

Within a few minutes, they began to see the telltale signs of academia, students sauntering along, several clutching the uniform leather satchel prematurely aged through years of abuse. As the road opened to the Piazza San Marco—a large square serving as the foreground for a delightful church and its rather imposing monastery—Xander pointed to a placard on the side of a windowless archway indicating an entrance to the university. A few students brushed by them at a furious pace.

"It must be time for lecture," he smiled. "They never move that fast."

Venturing through a series of long arched redbrick passageways, they arrived in an open courtyard cluttered by a smattering of leafless trees and wooden benches, all surrounded by perhaps seven or eight fat little buildings, each an amalgam of late medieval austerity and seven centuries of alterations. Xander tried to remember which one of the buildings held Pescatore's office. "I think it's that one," he pointed. "Yes, definitely that one. With the funny slanted tree in front. He's on the first floor somewhere." Together, they followed one of the myriad crisscrossing paths that cut through the open court, stringlike pavements connecting each of the buildings.

Without breaking stride, Xander managed the uneven stone steps at the foot of Pescatore's building and pushed through a thickly grained oaken door, distractedly holding it for Sarah. She could tell he was now intent on the manuscript, with little time for Lundsdorfian pleasantries. Not waiting to see if she was through, he straddled another short set of stairs, and strode down an empty corridor to his left. Sarah remained a few paces behind, deeper in darkness as the door behind clicked shut, the few strips of sunlight slipping to shadow. To her eye, the long cavernous hall, streaked by several shoddy overhead lights, seemed to disappear in a wall of haze, swallowing

Xander in its ebbing glow. Only the sound of his eager footsteps filled the hall. Falling in with his rhythm, she lengthened her stride, drawing up to him just as his eyes lit up at the discovery of Pescatore's office.

Raising his eyebrows in anticipation, Xander knocked gently on the wooden frame and waited, leaning into the door as if expecting to hear the muffled footsteps beyond. After a few seconds without response, he knocked again, this time pressing his ear to the thick wood. Nothing. He turned to Sarah, a look of concern in his eyes.

"This isn't like him," he whispered. "This isn't like him at all." Just as he was about to pound firmly for a third try, Sarah pulled him away. She knew there was no reason to draw unnecessary attention, especially as they didn't know who might be inside the other offices. Removing two thin metal strips from her bag, she glanced down the hall and delicately slid them into the door's lock. Xander looked on, utterly bewildered. With a short snap, the bolt released, and Sarah gently pushed the door open. Placing her other hand in the small of his back, she directed the reluctant scholar into the office.

The room was in a state of complete disarray, books and papers everywhere. Drawers from filing cabinets rested precariously on the tips of metal railings, ready to pull the five-foot-high units crashing to the floor. A few inches from the ceiling, an entire length of wooden shelving had been dislodged from its brace and now swung dangerously out into the room. Directly in front of the door, several chairs had been shoved to the center of the room, conjoined in a bizarre sculpture with legs jutting out in all directions. What little light there was streamed in from the hastily drawn curtains, a few slits here and there to scatter the sun and add to the chaos. Moving slowly, Xander approached the desk, lifting his case up toward the one area free from clutter.

"Don't touch anything," whispered Sarah, her tone direct, enough to stop him in midmovement.

The case swung back to his side as he turned. "Look at this," he said. "What *happened* here?" He needed an answer, some way to explain away the mayhem they had discovered. Sarah could tell he was not, as yet, willing to admit the obvious.

"You were right to be concerned." She turned and closed the door, shutting out the paltry light from the corridor.

"Damn it!" Xander continued to look around the office. "This wouldn't have happened if—"

"If you hadn't come to Florence?" Sarah shook her head as she moved beyond him to the window, angling her head so as to peer through a thin strand of light. From the little she could make out, there looked to be a second courtyard behind the building. It was empty. Still, given the state of the office, she knew they would have to be careful. And quick. She turned to him. "It wouldn't have made any difference. They knew he had the manuscript and they wanted it. Most likely because it could explain what they have in mind after the dry run in Washington. As you said, that would make it a very powerful document." She began to look around the room. "The question is, Did they find it?"

"I don't know." He sounded somewhat dazed. "I . . . can't imagine it would have been that hard, if they knew what they were looking for." Xander watched as Sarah dropped to a crouching position behind the desk. He then glanced about the room, still trying to piece things together. "According to Carlo's article, it's about seven inches long," he added, "and about an inch wide, bound in old leather, with the Medici seal—six balls on a shield."

"It obviously wasn't that easy to find. Otherwise, why the mess?"

"I suppose." He shook his head in disbelief. "Carlo's stubborn, but he's not stupid. If someone wanted something that desperately—"

"He would have given it to them." Her voice rose from behind the desk.

"Exactly," he nodded. "What are you doing down there?"

A long silence passed before she answered. "He might not have had the chance." She stood and brushed the dust from her knees.

"And what exactly does that mean?"

"There are streaks of blood on the floor and on the leg of the desk. The carpet's ripped." She stared directly into his eyes. "There was a struggle."

"*Wait* a minute." He began to shake his head, his words uncertain. "What are you saying? That's impossible. Why would anyone—"

"Because they needed to get the manuscript."

They stared at each other for a moment. "That's *not* possible," he said, struggling to find something to convince her, *himself*, that the suggestion was ludicrous. "It would be like Eisenreich's story replaying itself four hundred years later. They *kill* him before he has a chance to explain?" The impact of the single word seemed to strike at Xander. For nearly half a minute, he said nothing. Then, in a near whisper, he said, "He's dead, isn't he?" The words seemed to roll out, almost of their own will. "Isn't he?"

"I don't know."

He looked at the books scattered about the floor. "Because of a few pages of *theory*." Standing quietly, Xander suddenly felt shaken. There was a fragile quality to his voice. "He wouldn't have done anything, said anything. At least I don't think . . ." A hollowness rose through his body. Choosing to ignore Sarah's warning, he sat on the lip of the desk and placed the small case by his feet, his arms folded about his chest as he began to sway back and forth. Sarah watched him drift farther and farther away, lulled by the gentle movement of his own body. Stepping through the papers, she drew up to him and placed her hands on his arms, tightening her grip until his eyes met hers.

"But you don't know *them*." She could see he was beginning to question his own motives, his own culpability. She'd seen it too many times not to recognize the expression on his face—an indulgence she could not permit. Him or herself.

"You know, I don't get you. I don't get you at all." No rebuke, merely a statement of fact. "You're able to look at all of this with . . . I don't know . . . such detachment." He shook his head. "I wish I could do that."

Sarah peered into his eyes. Another innocent. Another choice. "I don't think you mean that." She held his gaze for a moment, then added, "The manuscript. Is there anywhere Carlo would have put it?"

"Just like that."

"Like what?" she answered.

"Back to the hunt." She said nothing and released his arms. In an attempt to get his mind working again, he rubbed his hands down his face. "Right." He began to look around the room. The simple movement seemed to rouse him from the moments of self-recrimination. "The manuscript." He nodded. Brushing by her, he moved to the center of the room.

"Put on your gloves," she insisted.

Without stopping, he did as he was told, already focused on a large pile of books at the base of the shelving. "Now think," he began. "If he's as clever as you know he is, where's he going to put it?" Kneeling, Xander slid his fingers across a number of spines, the titles eliciting only shakes of his head, until, with a sudden burst of insight, he shot up. "Of course. In another book." Sarah watched as he looked up to the remaining bookshelves and then to the floor, all signs of panic and whatever else momentarily forgotten. "So where did you keep it, Carlo?" His eyes darted about. "And where would they have tossed it?" Sarah could do little but wait. The researcher had returned.

Impatient, she prodded. "Kept what?"

For the first time in the last minute, he seemed to remember she was in the room. "This might sound strange, but my guess is that somewhere in this mess is a rather old volume of Saint Augustine's *Confessions.*"

"*Saint Augustine?*"

"Book twelve, section twenty-four, I think." He was back, and at full throttle. "It's the chapter where he explains the vitality of interpretation. It's actually a very eloquent, and quite forward-thinking bit of writing on the freedom of thought." As he spoke, he continued to look about the room. "It's all about Moses, and how no one really knows the word of God, and how we're not allowed to insist on one reading because of our ignorance, and so forth." Sarah watched him pace the length of the wall, his head tilted to one side so as to read each binding. "Rather ironic for the man who set down all those strict rules of Catholic dogma." Xander might have been giving a lesson in theological history, but his eyes and fingers were now lost in the shelves by the door. "Basically, it's a diatribe against dogmatism. '*Don't* tell me what to believe'—that sort of thing. Carlo always thought it was one of the more important statements Augustine made. Talked about it all the time. It's *exactly* the sort of thing he felt he confronted every day of his life—the struggle against narrow-mindedness. Everyone dismissing what he was doing with Eisenreich." Looking up to Sarah, he added, "Well, evidently they were wrong." He turned his focus again to the books and added, "my guess is that he would have put the manuscript in his copy of *Confessions.* Where *his* interpretation would get the respect it deserved." Finishing with the books by the door, Xander moved out into the middle of the office. "Look for something big, and dense. A good fourteen or fifteen inches long, maybe two and a half inches thick, with the word *Confessiones* in Latin on the spine." He knelt down.

Joining him on the floor, Sarah began to sort through the stacks in her corner. Within a half minute, her eyes caught the faded gold inlay on the spine, the large *C* almost entirely lost. She picked up the book.

"Is this it?"

Xander looked over his shoulder and immediately sprang to his feet; he took the book from her as he moved back to the desk. "Bingo. Now, let's see if I know him as well as I think I do."

Clearing a wide-enough space on the desktop, Xander laid the tome down and slowly opened its cover. A long dedication by someone named

Teggermann was scrawled in almost unintelligible handwriting. Xander lifted the thick yellowed page, expecting to find the small manuscript staring back at him. All he saw was the table of contents.

"Dead end?" asked Sarah as she watched from the side of the desk.

Not bothering to acknowledge her, Xander flipped to about three-quarters the way through the book. Scanning the tops of each page, he flipped farther and farther back. About forty pages from the end, he stopped.

Sarah looked down and saw the small leather-bound volume placed neatly in the center of the page.

"Book twelve, section twenty-*five*. I was off by one." He did little to hide his pleasure. As he picked up the manuscript, however, his expression of triumph quickly turned to one of utter disbelief; the front and back covers came together in his fingers. There seemed to be nothing in between. Tearing open the small volume, he could do nothing but stare at the centimeter-wide edges still clinging to the spine, the only remnants of pages razored out. The discovery was too much. "*Jesus Christ!* It's not as if they haven't done enough. They have to *destroy* this as well?"

"I doubt they destroyed it," said Sarah, her own disappointment less apparent. "They probably didn't want some customs official asking questions about a book with that crest on it. That's why they left it here."

"Then why put the binding back in the Augustine?"

"So as not to draw attention. I don't know."

Xander tossed the leather casing onto the desk. "So now what do we do?" She saw the determination begin to fade from his eyes, the recollection of Pescatore's death slowly return.

"What about files? Anything that might give us something on the contents of the book." She was trying to draw him back in.

"Files . . . right." Another task. Another distraction. "Knowing Carlo, he would have been very careful. They wouldn't just be lying around." Again, Xander glanced around the room, lighting on a section of the floor directly behind the desk. "They'd be in *there*," he said, pointing to the large computer wedged into the corner of the room, a thick link chain locking it to a steel hasp extending from the wall. "The problem is," he added as he knelt by the keyboard, "how do we get inside it?" Sarah reached over his shoulder and flicked on a switch at the back of the console. The screen lit up, casting a pulsating glow about the room.

"How about that?"

Xander didn't bother to look around. "Yes, thank you. You know that's not what I meant. He's going to have some sort of code to get in." A small flashing key appeared in the top-left-hand corner of the screen.

"If it's like the ones at State, it's probably nothing more than a simple software block," suggested Sarah. "You get three shots at the password before the entire system shuts down."

"Or worse, before it sends out a signal to the main frame and calls in the local security. I have that feature on mine as well."

"And your friend Pescatore didn't happen to mention the password to you at any point, did he?"

"*Carlo?* You've got to be kidding. To be honest, I'm amazed that the Augustine panned out. That was blind luck. Not that it got us anywhere." The two of them stared at the screen for a minute.

"What's your password?" she asked.

"Niccolò. Why?"

"Why Niccolò?"

"Machiavelli. Are we going someplace with this?"

"Well, who was Pescatore's favorite? Augustine."

Xander peered at her over his shoulder, a skeptical look in his eyes. "Isn't that a little obvious?"

"Do you have any better ideas?"

He turned to the screen and typed the word *Augustine* into the keyboard. He pressed the enter button. A small *x* appeared on the next line, followed by another flashing key.

"One down. Two to go. Any other suggestions?"

Sarah thought for a moment. "What about his first name. What was Augustine's first name?"

"*Saint.*" Xander glared over his shoulder, an even more incredulous look in his eyes. "I don't think he *had* a first name."

"You're not being very helpful."

"Sorry. It's just—" His eyes suddenly froze, an expression Sarah had seen before, an instant of recognition struggling to find expression. She watched as a grin began to creep up his cheeks.

"What? What?"

"No. That would be crazy." He paused. "What the hell." Turning to the computer, he typed in a few letters, pressed enter, and watched as the system engaged, the software beginning to boot itself up on the screen. A guttural laugh emerged from his throat, the grin now a broad smile.

"Well, what was it?"

Continuing to watch the system come on-line, Xander grinned. "Monica. Augustine's mom. Freud would have had a heyday with that."

The screen transformed several times—meaningless instructions and patent warnings flying by in quick succession—before a small cursor appeared to initiate the word processing. Xander typed in a few more commands, and a long list of files began to race by. "The software's familiar enough. I just hope my technical Italian is up to snuff." Sarah looked on as her new partner typed furiously, every so often stopping to read the screen—list after list of files—before moving on. He tried to explain to her as he bolted along. "He's evidently placed the files deep within the system, and I would very much doubt that he's given them friendly names like Eisenreich One and Two. He might have been clever again." Xander shifted his weight, the strain on his knees beginning to take its toll.

Three minutes later, his eyes lit up as a new group of files slid by. A list of about twenty names stood in a neat line across the top of the screen, for some reason worthy of special attention. "The right size and the right time frame," he said, and pulled his hands away from the keyboard. "The question is, Which are the important ones? Knowing Carlo, any number of these, if not all of them, could be meaningless. Or worse, he might have set a few of them up as booby traps, triggered to shut the system down and bring in security if they get called up. Carlo is famous for these things."

"Wonderful." Sarah nodded, pondering the man who had gone to such lengths to safeguard a few files. Xander, hands resting in his lap, eyed the screen with caution; a moment later, his head tilted back and his eyes squinted closed. He began to clench his fingers in slow intervals. "What are you—"

"Shhh." The strange ritual continued for about half a minute before he slowly opened his eyes. Sarah had moved to the window, her gaze again on the courtyard; it remained empty. "My guess," continued Xander, "would be these two." His finger landed by the words *Ternistato A* and *Ternistato B*. Again, his mysterious thought process left Sarah at a complete loss. She knew that whatever raced through his mind at those crucial moments had to spring from some logical source. What that might be, though, was beyond her. Still, it was keeping him occupied. He in his element, she in hers. Each with its own rules of engagement. *Hostile arena—know the surroundings. Anticipate the contingencies.* "If you recall," he explained, "the name Eisenreich translates to 'iron state.' If I'm right, Carlo was very much aware of that." He pointed to the first part of one of the words on the screen, Sarah more interested in the figure emerging from the eastern archway to the courtyard. She nodded distractedly. "Terni is one of the few remaining centers of Italian iron production. And I think—now I could be wrong—that it was also one of the main targets of Allied bombing during World War Two for that very reason." She had heard the last bit and wondered if all academics had access to such trivial information. "You know . . . Laurence Olivier on PBS . . . *World at War*? 'The furnaces of Terni'?" He was off in his little own world. Again she nodded. "*Stato* simply means 'state.' *Ternistato*—'iron state.' Eisenreich."

She turned to him. "That's incredibly far-fetched."

"I know, but that's exactly the way Carlo's mind works. Plus, I can't for the life of me think what he would have been working on that would have had anything to do with the town of Terni. I mean, it really is obscure."

"And yet you seem to be familiar with it."

"True. But I happen to be as nutty as Carlo."

With that, Xander called up the first of the files. Sarah waited for the screen to go black, or for a siren to go off, or for some deadly gas to pour from the console. Instead, Italian filled the page, densely packed notes on what she assumed was the manuscript. The smile on Xander's face, his eyes racing through each line, told her that his logic—based on a television show—had maneuvered expertly through Pescatore's defenses. Evidently, this was the stuff of academic insight. Not terribly inspiring.

As he continued to read, she again peered through the cracks in the drapery so as to get a better view of the courtyard behind the building. Her lone figure was now seated on one of several benches perhaps twenty yards away. The man, in a heavy dark overcoat, seemed well protected from the cold, his gloved hands peeling back the pages of his newspaper, cigarette smoke cascading through the air from under his wide-brimmed fedora. Sarah maintained her gaze, making sure to keep far enough from the curtains so as not to draw unwanted attention. From this distance, she found it difficult to make out any distinct features. Save for the beard. She inched closer. Xander had mentioned a beard.

One minute later, a second man appeared. He was exceptionally tall, his broad shoulders and thick arms squeezed mercilessly into the sleeves of the straining coat. He wore no hat, the sun reflecting off of his shaven scalp, a pair of thick hands menacing at his sides as he strode toward the bench. Within half a minute, the first man was on his feet, making his way slowly, casually, toward one of the building's side entrances. The second remained at the bench, and, for the first time, Sarah realized that his gaze was fixed on Pescatore's office window. She stepped back.

"Have you gotten everything?" she asked. At first, Xander did not reply.

"This is absolutely incredible." He was transfixed by the screen. "I mean incredible."

"We should get going."

"Why? We—"

"We've been here long enough. No reason to press our luck."

He was too wrapped up in the notes to offer much of an argument. "All right, but I'm going to have to copy these. That might take a minute or two."

"Do it." Sarah now moved to the door as Xander reached for his case and pulled out a disc. She watched him slide it into Pescatore's computer and type in the appropriate commands; the computer began to hum and click while he sat back and waited. Leaning against the hard wood and listening for any noise in the hall, Sarah asked—more to keep him preoccupied than anything else—"so what's so incredible?"

"It's really mind-boggling." His eyes remained on the screen. "Remember I thought there were *two* original versions of the manuscript. One Eisenreich sent to Clement, and one for himself. Well, when we found the pages ripped out of the binding, I thought that was it." He stopped and looked at Sarah. "According to Carlo's notes, however, there are three versions. *Three.* One in Latin, one in Italian, and one in *German.* For various reasons—" He suddenly noticed her odd position at the door. "Is something the matter?"

Sarah's hand shot up in the air to silence him, the sound of footsteps in the hall prompting the reaction. Both waited the uncomfortable half minute until the pitter-pat moved beyond the office. Still holding his breath, Xander flinched at the sound of the computer clicking a final sequence of copying. Two seconds later, he retrieved the disc and placed it in his case.

"Erase the files." Another order from the operative.

"That would *definitely* bring in security," he said, getting to his feet.

"Which might not be such a bad idea." Again she moved to the curtains, motioning for him to join her. She pointed through a thin strand of light to the courtyard and asked, "Do you recognize him?" Xander's eyes widened. He started to lean closer, Sarah quick to pull him back. "I'll take that as a yes. That's why we might want to call in security."

"That's the man from the station."

"We can be out of here in less than a minute; no security works that fast. It might be enough, though, to get in the way of our two friends."

Five seconds later, Xander typed in the erase command and watched as a small red dot appeared at the top-right-hand corner of the screen. He switched off the console and grabbed his case. Sarah was already in the corridor.

CHICAGO, MARCH 3, 2:14 A.M. Chapmann watched as the area beyond his glassed-in office continued to swirl with frenzied activity, the lights on his phone flashing in an equally manic rhythm. It had been like this for the past eleven hours—since yesterday at 3:07 P.M., when the computers had reached 2.5 billion, the gambit having drawn in three other investment houses during the run. By 3:14, hints that something was wrong had elicited the first calls from the other houses. *"What the hell is going on! There's no indication the market . . ."* When Helpurn's computers had crashed two minutes later, revealing the betting strategy as nothing more than an enormous software glitch, all hell had broken loose. Helpurn naturally was beyond salvation; having to sell two weeks' worth of bad trading positions would finish them.

That, however, was nothing compared to the grain market itself. Over-inflated, it was now highly volatile. Prices would fluctuate, then dive. By tomorrow morning, farmers would begin to hoard the grain that they had held on to, the few reserves that had not fallen prey to their greed. And with hoarding would come the question of distribution. The supply lines out of the United States would be pulled back. Cargill and ConAgra would be sent reeling. The tremors would be felt at every level.

Just as Sedgewick had predicted. A week when the world would have to reconsider the stability of a major American market.

All in the cause of an experiment.

Chapmann continued to stare. And wonder. Had he really understood?

Sarah ushered Xander out into the hallway, pulled the door shut, and once again maneuvered the lock with the two strips of metal. As before, a dull glow hung about the empty expanse. The bolt engaged just as the echo of footsteps rose somewhere off to their left; the main entrance was no longer a possibility. Sarah led him down the corridor, Xander inclined to glance over his shoulder every few seconds, ready to find a large angry figure hurtling toward them. About fifty feet from Pescatore's office, the hallway took a sharp right-hand turn, sending them farther away from the central courtyard from which they had entered the building. Behind them, shouts cascaded throughout the corridor, voices confounded by the locked door Sarah had left. A hand pounded against the door's frame, its thumping in counterpoint to the rapid patter of their own feet racing silently along the stone floor. Another turn and they pushed through a thick swinging door, its metal hinges letting out an excruciatingly high-pitched shriek. For a long moment, all sound seemed to vanish. Then, with a sudden explosion of voices, the clatter of running feet erupted.

Xander, visibly shaken, looked to Sarah, who was now scanning the small alcove in which they found themselves. To their left, a broad stairwell lead up, its wide oaken steps flanked by an ornate banister with elaborate carvings for support. The voices grew in volume as Sarah moved toward a large curtain hung curiously underneath the rising steps. She yanked it back and found a second set of stairs leading down, stark by comparison, narrow stone slabs, smooth and uneven from centuries of use, with only a thick piece of rope extending along the wall for support. The clamor nearly upon them, Sarah motioned for Xander to follow; she grabbed at the railing and started down. The heavy draped material swung back behind him, shrouding the stairway in near darkness.

The last few steps were less hidden, leading to a series of underground tunnels. Together, they stood in an open area, eyes as yet unaccustomed to the series of bare bulbs, each one dangling on the end of a frayed cord.

And then, for a frightening moment, Xander watched as Sarah's eyes become transfixed by the glare of the light, her head twitch almost imperceptibly, her breath shorten. He thought she might pass out, her face suddenly ashen. He grabbed her. Their eyes locked, hers so distant.

"Jessica?"

The word was barely audible. He knew the bulbs had triggered something—something he wanted to understand, something he needed to tear her away from.

But there was no time. The swinging door screamed again, the sound of angry voices pouring into the alcove not fifteen feet above them. Xander froze. Everything seemed to stop. His forehead felt as if it would burst, the blood thundering through, pounding with abandon. Every breath, each word from above rang in his ears as if spoken directly to him. And still Sarah stood motionless.

With a sudden flurry, the voices began to fade, grow more distant. They had decided on the second floor. Not taking the time to consider their good fortune, Xander pulled Sarah toward one of the tunnels, its curved ceiling forcing him to slouch as they darted along. Dazed, she followed, but with each passing second, he saw her sense revive. After several snake-like turns, they arrived at another open area, another set of stairs, another thick piece of rope leading up.

Now it was Sarah who took control. She grabbed his arm and flattened him against the wall. Before he could respond, her hand was over his mouth, her eyes screaming at him to keep silent. She listened intently, all memory of the recent episode clearly forgotten. Faint at first, then louder, the sound of a lone pair of feet shuffling along the tunnel floor began to rise in the distance. Urgent and controlled, the monotonous beat of the approaching steps provided an eerie backdrop to the sound of Xander's sti-fled breath. They continued to stare at each other, fully aware of who was in pursuit. Whichever way he had managed it, the man with the beard had somehow slipped through the chaos on the floor above, discovered the cur-tained stairway, and chosen expertly which path to follow. With a quick jerk of her head, Sarah motioned for Xander to move up the stairs, bringing her finger to her lips to make certain he maintained absolute silence.

Half a minute later, both stood within an alcove identical to the one in Pescatore's building, the only difference a rectangular window that offered a welcome view of the front courtyard. Somehow, they had arrived only a few yards from the arched entryway that had originally brought them from the main street. Xander started for the swinging door, stopped in mid-movement by Sarah, who grabbed him by the coat. She would not tempt the squeal a second time. Instead, she held him motionless, both waiting to hear the sudden cessation of steps, the rapid ascent of the stairs.

But none came. Nothing but the sound of footsteps racing by, tracking past the staircase and deeper into the maze of tunnels. There had been no shift in pace, no silence to indicate a change of direction, not even a momentary pause to consider options. Their would-be pursuer had plod-ded on without a thought for the stairs. Sarah knew they had little time to make their escape. Two minutes at most before the man below would recognize his mistake and double back. They could only hope he was not in radio contact with his comrade at the bench.

With her hands still enmeshed in Xander's coat, Sarah waited until the sound of the steps receded entirely. Then, positioning herself by the window, she unlatched the lock and slowly pushed the window out, this time no screaming hinge to bring unwanted visitors. The courtyard was empty. No signs of inner turmoil from the building directly across from them. No security men perched by the main entryway to apprehend the suspected thieves. And no sign of the bearded man's companion. They had been lucky again. Hoisting herself up onto the ledge, she swung her legs out into the cold and let herself fall the five or six feet to the clump of frozen bushes nestled against the building's facade. Turning back to Jaspers, she reached up to take the case from him and watched as he deftly maneuvered the ledge and leapt to her side. His agility surprised her.

Adjusting clothes, brushing off dried leaves, they moved swiftly to the archway, back through the redbrick passageways. They said nothing. It had been ten minutes. Ten minutes of choked-back breath, of small pools of perspiration gathering under their heavy coats, of unspoken fear and exhilaration. Ten minutes running from shadows, allowing the game to play them, and all for the single disc that lay innocently within an unassuming leather attaché case. As they moved, the murmur of voices, the appearance of others no longer caused alarm. Still, Xander clutched at Sarah's arm, aware that she was in control again, he happy to acquiesce, follow along, vest her with all responsibility. He had found the files. She would find them a safe place.

Emerging to the street, they cut across the square and opted for the wide avenue of the Via Cavour, its crowds now a safe haven from the two men who they knew would not be far behind. Blending gracefully into the flow of bodies, the Fabrizzis walked arm in arm, his knuckles growing whiter by the second from the nervous strain of the case in his hand. His mind was focused anywhere but on the bustle all around them. Xander was shaken, but, for the first time, he felt neither confusion nor disbelief. Instead, he felt only outrage—outrage at the destruction, at the callous indifference to a colleague's life, at the abuse rained down upon him and his work. And, perhaps most telling, outrage at the men who could transform the woman at his side into someone—something—so petrified within the world they had created. He would not soon forget the hollow terror of her eyes in the tunnels. He would not let himself.

Still lost in his thoughts, Xander found himself standing in front of a small building, its central wall a single sheet of glass. It took a moment for him to recognize the building for what it was—a small café, packed with locals and tourists taking a morning cappuccino. A bell jangled as they pushed through the door, Sarah leading the way to a table nestled in an ideally cozy corner—far enough from others for discretion's sake, close enough to warrant no special attention.

"I seem to go in circles with you," she smiled, a casual lilt to her expression, which Xander found impossible to mirror. She seemed entirely at ease. He sat amazed.

"Really?" He nodded, then stopped. "I don't understand."

"Hotel rooms, cafés. It's become a pattern." She adjusted her coat and added, "And try to look a little more comfortable. We are in Italy."

He brought the case to his lap as a waiter approached. "Whatever that's supposed to mean." Countering with something that barely resembled a smile, Xander asked her, "Cappuccino?"

A grin accompanied her reply. "*Sì.*"

"*Due, prego.*" The waiter nodded and moved off to another table. "Your Italian is improving."

"*Grazie, bello.* Your mood isn't."

"Funny that, but I'm expecting two large men—"

"They won't come in here." She leaned across the table, as if explaining something rudimentary. "It's too obvious. They'll have expected us to keep running. That's why we didn't." A knowing smile creased her lips. "So enjoy the coffee when it comes."

Xander accepted the rebuke. Of course she knew what she was doing. It was foolish for him to think otherwise. It was simply a bit unnerving the way she managed every situation with such ease, such composure. Perhaps that was why the episode in the tunnel remained so vivid. "What happened back there?"

"We got away." She pulled the scarf from her neck and laid it across the back of her chair.

"No, I don't mean that. I mean in the tunnels. You seemed—"

An almost imperceptible tension rose in her shoulders to cut him off. "I seemed gone?" She turned back to him and stared into his eyes. "Is that what you were going to say?"

He waited before answering. "I . . . suppose. Yes."

"No need to suppose. It's a very good way to describe it."

Xander could tell it was not a point to press. "Yes. It is." His fingers began to play with the edge of his napkin. "I felt a little . . . *gone* there myself. I guess one never gets used to any of this. Whatever *this* is."

"For now, *this* is the manuscript and the files. And three men in the States who are just getting started." She saw her words register. "Isn't that what you said differentiates this from Machiavelli—one city wasn't enough?" The cappuccino arrived. Sarah waited until they were alone before continuing. "Whatever happened in those tunnels, whatever you might have felt in that office, you have to remember that those men and those files are the priority. The focus. I'm sorry if that frightens or upsets you, but there really isn't any other alternative."

He let the words sink in. "You're right—I . . . shouldn't have asked."

"It's not about right or wrong. I appreciate your concern—I do—but neither of us has the time for it." She waited, then smiled. "So, there are three versions. That's helpful."

"Yes . . . it is." It took Xander a moment to gather his thoughts; he sipped at the piping hot coffee. "According to the files, he found the German one about three months ago in a small archive in Belgrade. The whole thing was misfiled and mistitled; no one had ever . . ."

His words faded to the background as she continued to stare at him. His concern had been so genuine. So gentle.

What *had* happened in the tunnel? It was too easy to explain it away as a flash of memory—the bulbs, the swaying body, the life she had not been able to save. The sacrifice.

"I can take General Safad's men out now! End this here. If I don't, we risk losing the girl." Static filled the receiver as a message appeared on the computer screen.

DELAY. MAINTAIN POSITION.

Another delay! There was no reason. She could kill them all and end the threat. But delay . . . she'd never be able to get through. And she'd told her, promised Jessica she would be there, but now . . . What choice would she have? What choice could she make?

". . . the interesting part is that, in its preface, it mentions that it's the *final* version of the manuscript, and then makes reference to the *two* earlier copies. Ergo, *three* in total." Xander stopped, noticing Sarah's eyes on his. "Are . . . you okay?"

For a moment, she said nothing. "Yes." She offered a smile. "Three copies."

Still unsure, Xander returned the smile. "You know you said something back there . . . in the tunnel . . . a girl's name. Jessica."

The reference momentarily caught Sarah off guard. "Really?" She looked at Xander. "Jessica *Conlon*. The ambassador's daughter." Xander remained silent. "It was a long time ago." For several seconds, neither said a word.

Finally, he nodded awkwardly. He knew it had been a mistake to mention the episode again. Still, she had seemed so lost. "Right. . . . Anyway, Carlo's convinced that the Italian one is still somewhere out there. From the little I read, it sounds as if he'd recently started looking for it."

She took a sip of her cappuccino. "Any luck?"

"I haven't read enough to know. We have to assume that the Italian was the first because it would have been the one Eisenreich sent to Clement. And there would have been no way for it to have made a reference to any other versions because, at the time, there wouldn't have *been* any other versions. The Latin—the one I'm assuming our favorite threesome have had for quite some time—must have been the *second* version and would have made references only to the first. It follows, then, that whoever found that translation believed for *years* that there were only two versions—the Latin and the Italian."

"And now, because of the razored-out copy—the one in German—they'll know there are three."

"Right. The only difference is that I have Carlo's notes. They don't."

"And you think the notes will lead you to the Italian version." He nodded. "That raises the stakes considerably."

It took him a moment to answer. "I guess that's true."

"Don't guess."

"All right . . . so what am I supposed to do now?"

"Exactly what you would have done if none of this had happened." She pushed her cup to the side and leaned across the table, her hand cupping his as she spoke. "They won't do anything to you. In fact, they'll *want* you to find the manuscript."

"And when I do, they'll want to *kill* me. Even *I* can figure that out."

"I'm not going to let that happen."

Sarah stared at him, aware of how much she needed to believe her own words, how much more they meant than mere reassurance. In some strange way, Eisenreich was offering her a chance at redemption, a way to put Amman behind her. Perhaps more. *Nothing expendable. Nothing sacrificed.* But only by diving back in. She continued to stare at him. Was there really any other choice?

"For some reason," Xander said, "I actually believe you." Her hand felt very solid in his. "So I just get on a plane for London."

"If that's where Pescatore's notes tell you to go." *London.* That would complicate things. She needed to get back to the States, to the men of Eisenreich. Whatever Pritchard had set in motion, the game was now hers. Alone. COS had betrayed her once. Not again.

It was time for her to find out how unified Eisenreich really was, create a little chaos of her own. Do what she did best—rattle the foundation and make those men question their own commitment to one another.

But to let Xander go—even if she knew he *had* to go—she would have to find a way to keep him safe, to protect him. She squeezed his hand.

"Stay at the Lowndes. Knightsbridge." She saw the question in his eyes. "Trust me." She began to gather her scarf. "We should be going."

He nodded and stood. "What about you?"

"Me?" She slipped the scarf over her shoulder and looked up at him, a smile. "Don't worry about me."

Before she could turn for the door, he reached out and pulled her close to him. It seemed to catch them both by surprise. So sudden, his arms cradling her back, her hands and head gently pressed to his chest. Only a moment. When he stepped back, his arms fell awkwardly to his sides.

"I, uh . . . sorry." He tried to find his gloves in his pockets. "I guess it must be all the excitement. I . . . I just don't think I'm going to have much of a choice—not worrying about you, I mean."

Again their eyes locked. For a reason she could not explain, she wanted to reach out to him. *Don't do that, Xander Jaspers. Don't take that kind of risk.* But she knew it was too late. She could see it in his eyes. Sense it in her own.

What she couldn't see was how much he would be willing to sacrifice, how much of himself.

And that, above all else, frightened her.

PART TWO

4

**Hatred, if directed properly, is a powerful tool. . . .
[It] makes the people docile and unimaginative.**

—*ON SUPREMACY*, CHAPTER XV

SENATOR SCHENTEN WATCHED as the tea bag spun gently above his cup, drops of liquid splashing to the creamy brown surface below. He had never been one to tie the string around the helpless bag, strangling the leaves for what little tea remained. Nor was he terribly good with bare fingers on the boiling pouch, having always suffered from a certain sensitivity. No, he simply let it drip, his eyes caught in the endless twists, the rapid butterfly flutter that would reach near standstill before reversing on itself for the winding flight back. With each series, the bag seemed to gain added weight, the turning less and less animated, until, with a final release, the little sac swung limp and cold at the end of its string. Schenten tossed the lifeless bag into the wastebasket at the side of his desk and lifted the cup to his lips. The tea had already passed from unbearable to piping hot.

Outside, a near-perfect winter morning stung the Washington skyline, raw and fine. A brilliant sun cascaded in all directions, promising warmth but providing little more than hollow protection against the chill that rolled off the water. The open expanse seemed timeless, frozen in a postcardlike sterility under a thin blanket of distilled air. Schenten could almost feel the cold on his neck as he lifted the cup for another sip of the searing liquid. At that moment, he could concentrate only on its pulsating heat. For that single moment, his mind was free.

The freedom he enjoyed, though, was not the simple release from the grind of weekly demands. Over the last forty years, he had become inured to the patterns that defined his hours on the Hill. His affiliations, express or tacit, created a neat sort of web that demanded a highly structured approach to daily activity. And, if pressed to admit it, he enjoyed the regularity, the opportunities his breakfast meetings or midmorning conferences afforded him to preach more of the gospel, to confirm his place as the "iron-willed senator," a reporter's onetime reference to Bismarck that had caused not the least bit of resentment in the feisty politician.

Given his rather public persona, the German terrier (often misprinted *terror*) knew only too well what his constituents had come to expect. A bulldog approach to government that ensured a strict adherence to free-market economy and strong national security, all in the name of "progressive stability"—a phrase he himself had coined, unaware or unconcerned with its apparent inconsistency. An inconsistency that had brought Reagan to the fore and had launched a grassroots conservative thrust sustained for eight glorious years. Heady days indeed, when everything had come together with a sense of urgency, promise, only to be lost in the mismanagement of skeptics and incompetents. Those who did not understand, had never understood, who had faltered under the preposterous challenge for *change*. To be so close and to have it all dashed away infuriated the old man. Such fumbling had clearly called for new tactics, new approaches—strategies to bypass the usual channels. No, it was not the accustomed requirements of his official duties that transformed a simple cup of tea into so powerful an elixir. More was at stake.

"I have no appointments until eleven, is that right, Amanda?"

"A Mr. Davis from SEC at ten, lunch with Senator—"

"That's fine, dear, thank you. See that I'm not disturbed until then." He released the button, unconcerned with the reply from the outer office. He had given himself an hour to scan through the little book hidden within the safe behind his desk. It was all he could afford this morning.

He had shown little imagination when they had installed the safe nearly thirty years ago, directly behind his desk and covered by an oil painting of the Montana home that had become the focus of some rather intriguing meetings of late. Swinging his chair round, Schenten pulled the frame back and set to work on the lock. *That* he had replaced. *Several* times. No longer the spinning dial and click, click, click of a tumbler; now a digital input and voice command opened the safe. It was better that way, given what was inside.

He pushed aside various legal papers, some cash, and a small box before finding the little book. He paused for a moment, his eyes glued to the box, a happy but painful reminder of a time gone by. He often asked himself why he hadn't destroyed them—a few letters, a young passion. An affair. He had kept them all, never rereading them. Margaret had never known. Or if she had, she had never let on. He knew it had been foolish to keep them. But even iron-willed old terrors had their weaknesses. Jean had been his.

Safe and painting back in place, Schenten settled into the leather chair and began to read. As always, he took notes. He would burn them before ten.

⚔

The reception at the Lowndes had been anything but warm. So unlike the Italians, thought Xander. So like the English. He had spent the better part of two years in London for his postgraduate work, always the perfect American—not one to assume the idiosyncrasies of his hosts, embarrassing both them and himself in the process. He recalled with a smile an old friend from high school who had spent a semester at one of those snottier public schools and who had returned to the States with the air of a royal, an affectation only slightly less ridiculous than his accompanying accent. Xander had vowed never to fall prey to any of that. Even so, a little something had rubbed off. At least enough not to raise any questions from a typically decorous concierge, a man who had been more than happy to print out two copies of Carlo's files. Xander recalled the twenty minutes he had spent convincing Sarah that the first copy should be sent to Mrs. Huber in New York—a nod to academic superstition. Reluctantly, Sarah had agreed.

Now, after an early lunch, he found himself tightly packed within a thick clutch of bodies all bound for the Russell Square station. It was a familiar route, one he had taken almost every day during the years of unencumbered research. He had always referred to those months as such, that brief period free from the demands of a dissertation or the watchful eye of Lundsdorf. Free to choose his own course, to explore at will within the environs of a slightly crumbling academic setting. It was the only way he knew how to describe the Institute of Historical Research, a self-contained building tucked neatly into a large university complex at the edge of Russell Square, far enough from the British Library to keep the toughest rigors of academic life at arm's length. Even within the cramped air of the tube,

Xander couldn't help but smile at the images of that past: the little alcove he had made his own on the third floor, the desk wedged into the single window overlooking a few barren trees and a silent walkway, the smell of ancient tomes hovering about him, his solitude disturbed only now and then by the shuffle of an equally ancient academic in search of a long-forgotten book. He could recall nothing but pleasure from those days. Nothing but the sheer joy of every morning, every evening, and the true contentment they had engendered.

But it had been more than the work, more than the camaraderie, even more than the sense of purpose that now colored the memories with such fondness. As much as he tried, Xander couldn't convince himself that all those distant comforts had been anything more than mere reflections, echoes of a deeper sense of peace that he had found with Fiona. At first so dangerously assertive, so much more enticing than coy, so slender-framed and fine-boned, she had made everything lovely and real. Lulled by the familiar beat of wheel on track, Xander began to slip back. Memories impossible to keep at bay. Impossible to deny. *Why England? Why did the notes have to lead here?* A faint wisp of lilac filled his breath, his eyes closing to the clawing tightness of a longing caught between self-pity and delight.

They had met at one of those parties, where everyone seems to know one another except for the strange American—always a novelty—who gets dragged along by a recent acquaintance who insists that everyone will simply love hearing about whatever he's doing at the Institute, rapid-fire conversations with the young absentminded academic, cheese and wine, and men with ponytails, and on and on. And so he had gone, well aware that he wouldn't fit in—everyone a bit too trendy—with "smashing" drinks and "beautiful" food and "darling" hors d'oeuvres. And he had found a domestic beer instead of wine and had been happy enough to play the wide-eyed American for the record executives and literary agents who swarmed about the party, ever eager to foist their opinions of "the grand old US of A" upon him.

And she had saved him. Thoroughly out of his element, unable to fend off the cutting probes, he had turned to her, a moment's break from the jabs masquerading as questions. Against the backdrop of contrivance—the noise of young culture—she had appeared real, genuine, and somehow approachable.

"Is it always like this for you?" she asked. "I mean, at parties. Do they always pounce on you as the Yank?"

"I don't know. I haven't been here long enough."

"Fiona Isaacs." Her handshake was firm, a clasping of wirelike fingers.

"Xander Jaspers. Conspicuous American."

And with that, they had spent the entire evening talking, laughing, the obvious trappings of instant attraction. Both had given in without a thought, something so new for him, something she would help him to accept. The phone calls, the long walks, his total disbelief that things were actually working out well, his writing never better, and the hint of lilac that was always there even without her. Month slipping into month, and a growing need for her that somehow felt right, perfect for the simplicity of it all.

"I can't fall in love with you. You know that, don't you?"

"And why's that?"

"You're far too beautiful. Dad told me never to marry a beautiful woman."

"I see. Well, your loss, then."

The wedding had been simple, a small ceremony in a garden, suit and white dress, drinks and finger food, two weeks in Greece. No one had quite understood the speed of the whole affair. And yet, they had all understood.

When she began to feel ill, sudden headaches and overwhelming fatigue— early signs of the cancer that would take her within the year—his heart broke and he cried. And she held him, because she knew he would have to live beyond it.

The day she died, she was again cradling him, allowing him to bury himself in her, until her hands no longer had the strength to rest on his shoulders.

She had died in the afternoon, which was somehow even more unfair. Not even the cover of darkness to comfort.

The car pulled to a sudden stop, sending several people into Xander's back, and forcing him to steady himself with a hand to the ceiling. His eyes glanced around, a slow realization that the station had arrived, that he would have to push his way through the throng. Stepping to the sticky heat of the underground platform, he quickly rubbed away the wet patch clinging to the edge of his eye, allowed himself a deep breath and the welcome relief from the cramped, if pungent, subway car. The English were not famous for their rigor with a shower and soap.

Fiona had always recommended the bus. Too slow, he had always answered. Too slow.

⚔

The bag of cheese balls sufficed as breakfast. Bob Stein licked at the neon orange on his thumb, dabbing his moistened fingers into the plastic for what few pieces remained. He was looking for somewhere to toss the empty bag when he noticed O'Connell just the other side of the reflection pool. Bob opted for his coat pocket, then began to brush the grit from his hands as O'Connell neared the bench. A pair of National Guardsmen—ubiquitous since the recent turn of events—ambled along in front of the Lincoln Memorial, hardly taking notice of the Irishman. Their arrival had brought an uneasy serenity to the city, a furtiveness Stein found unnerving. Still, they were there to serve and protect. Normalcy at a price.

That is, if one could ignore the aftershocks. The news this morning had been filled with stories of the tremors, no saga quite so devastating as the deaths of the forty-three children from Spain, killed in a midair crash over Dulles. Cut adrift for nearly twenty minutes due to the tower shutdowns, the plane had circled into a thick cloud cover, colliding with a 727 out of Miami. The group of twelve- and thirteen-year-olds—a church choir—had been scheduled to perform at the White House, their names and pictures once again in the news because of a letter from King Juan Carlos to the *Post*. Overwhelmed by the tragedy, he was insisting that he accompany a special envoy to retrieve what remained of the bodies; the State Department, however, was *advising* otherwise. As yet, they could not guarantee his safety.

Bob recalled several of the names, faces on a screen. Heartbreaking as the news was, he had no time for it.

"The last contact was Milan," he said as O'Connell sat.

"She knew we were there?" asked the Irishman.

"As far as we can tell, yes."

"Wonderful. That means we won't find her again unless she wants us to."

"We still have people in Milan—"

"Trust me, Bob. We *won't* find her. She gets in very deep. It's her *special* talent." He paused. "It's why she was so damn perfect for Amman."

Stein removed a second bag from his pocket and pulled it open. "I've never actually been all that clear on what happened there."

"Join the crowd." O'Connell let out a long breath. "No one has. It was supposed to be a basic op—for her. Infiltrate Safad's inner group, get comfy, then pull the rug out from under them. It was all going according to script until Safad told her he wanted Ambassador Conlon's daughter eliminated—a show of *good faith*. Sarah'd done that sort of thing before, but never with a kid. We told her we'd get the girl out. Never happened. Something with the timing. Sarah showed up with two of Safad's men, expecting to find no one, but the girl was still there. Sarah had no choice but to kill Safad's boys; after that, things went a little crazy."

"And that's how we lost the girl?"

O'Connell nodded. "The pickup never happened. No one's ever been quite clear on that—whether it was Sarah's fuckup or something else. In the end, it came down to stopping the coup or saving the girl. Not much of a choice, really. The girl was dead before Sarah could get back." He stared off at the Lincoln Memorial. "I was the lucky son of a bitch sent in to retrieve our Miss Trent when it was all over." His eyes remained distant. "Not a pretty sight." He shook his head slowly, then turned to Bob. "We have no idea why she's in Italy, do we?"

"We have no idea why she's doing this *at all*," answered Stein. "Why didn't she just come in?"

"Why indeed." O'Connell reached over and grabbed a handful from the bag. "I just hope to Christ she can keep herself together. She crashes again, who knows how much of her would be left to come in?"

⚔

The entrance to the Institute hadn't changed a bit. He had stayed away for obvious reasons, but he had expected at least a little something different in four years. Nothing. Even the porter looked the same, the all-too-familiar tap of the cap as Xander walked past the gate. Reaching the long outdoor corridor that connected the University of London library to the Institute, Xander paused. The logical choice would be to the left and the larger building with its impressive stash of books. Where better to start the search than with the card catalog or computer, if they had finally put everything online? Instead, he turned right through a pair of swinging doors, again right, two more doors, until he nearly walked into a small table, a guard at his station, the final barrier between Xander and his old stamping grounds.

Digging into his coat pocket, he pulled out a rather ancient-looking identification card, the signature too faded to make out the name. Even so, the Institute's crest was clear enough, the dates evidently irrelevant; the guard asked him to sign in. Xander scribbled something illegible and proceeded through yet another set of doors, finding the old stairs and the slow mount to the third floor.

The smell of scholarship met him at once as he pushed through into the European history wing. Like wet cardboard sprinkled with dust, the air had a definable taste. Taking in a nice whiff of the familiar, he nearly ran into a young woman, her brisk stride the sure sign of academic administration. Only his ability to flatten himself against the wall saved him from the open field tackle. He smiled and pressed on. Few lights were on, the rooms surprisingly empty. There was no reason to question his good fortune. He was distinctly less inclined, since Florence, to presume any sort of security within the walls of academia. Carlo's office. The mad dash through the subterranean tunnels. Lessons well learned. He had even gone so far as to alter his appearance. Sarah had mentioned a few things—in New York, they had seemed silly—but he was now serving caution rather than his own naïveté. He had moved the part in his hair from left to right, shaped several days of growth into the semblance of a beard, and worn two extra T-shirts to give his slim frame some added bulk. Certainly nothing that would deceive a *professional,* but enough to make him seem unfamiliar to a colleague of a few years ago.

Moving down the hall, he arrived at the second door on the left. Placing a finger to the glass, he watched as the room opened up in front of him. Three neat columns of shelves, along with the ceiling-high wall brackets, housed several hundred books, some the recent beneficiaries of long-needed care, others crumbling toward a slow and painless death. A sense of home. Of place. As ever, the little sun that managed its way into the room bobbed atop his old desk, the light from outside caught in the trees as it cascaded through the window. Books everywhere, yet all he could see were the alcove, the desk, the chair. And for a moment, caught by the flickering light, he was back, sitting, her small hands gliding over his shoulders to his chest, her cheek sliding by his.

His head flinched, the room suddenly darker, airless. She was not there. No soft caress, no scent of lilac to dispel the longing. Xander stared into the open space and slowly moved toward the alcove. He began to trace his finger along the hard edge of the wooden chair. *Two years.* He had lost two years of his life after Fiona. Not in the usual sense. There had been no wandering off, no extended holiday lost in self-pity. Instead, he had given himself entirely to his work. Machiavelli had once again taken focus, only to become his springboard to the New Right. A sudden obsession. He hadn't bothered to ask why. It was enough to be distracted. Even Lundsdorf had approved. *Ironic,* he thought. Tieg and Sedgewick. They had brought him full circle, back to the Institute, back to the alcove.

The fluorescent lights flicked on and Xander spun around, his eyes momentarily at odds with the sudden change.

"Sorry. I did not mean to startle you." A small man nodded in Xander's direction, his eyes darting about the room before settling on a shelf along the far wall. Xander watched him sidle along, thumbing his way down the long row of books, every so often stopping, humming before moving on. The pattern continued for several minutes until, with a long "Aah," he pulled the sought-after volume from the shelf and rested it on a nearby table. Examining a few pages, the man seemed so typical of the place—the weathered jacket, the slight hunch in the shoulders, the utter disregard for anything and anyone within a hundred feet. Save for the slicked-back hair. That seemed an odd touch, a hint of vanity unusual within the hallowed halls. The man looked up and caught Xander's eyes. There was nothing kind in the stare, nothing of the cheerful nod hello. And then suddenly a smile. Thin lips curling through sunken cheeks.

"It is not what I am looking for," he said, his accent northern European. Dutch, Swiss, German—Xander couldn't tell.

"Pity."

"Yes." He shut the book and placed it on the shelf. He then ran a hand through his hair. "Wrong room, I suppose."

"Yes." Again, they stared at each other, the man's eyes empty of all response. "Sorry to have disturbed you." He moved to the door, turned for a final nod, and then stepped into the hallway. The door closed behind him.

Xander's hands were trembling as the sound of the footsteps receded, a reaction, he knew, driven less by the man's appearance than by the place itself. He had allowed himself an indulgence. It was something he knew Sarah would never have permitted.

On the steps down to the main floor, his mind was already turning over the pieces of information he had begun to decipher from Carlo's notes. A brisk wind greeted him as he picked up his pace through the colonnade, its rush providing a much needed shock to his system. *Lock it away; leave it up in that room.* The numbness returned, all too familiar, all too reminiscent of the same distance he had seen only yesterday—in Sarah, in her eyes.

CHICAGO, MARCH 4, 5:14 A.M. ⚔ Janet Grant clamped the man's lifeless fingers around the gun, positioning his hand on the pillow as she had been told. She had never taken a life on her own, the deaths in Washington rationalized as something beyond her control. This morning's activities, however, could not be so easily dismissed. The old man had called it "her penance." For Eggart.

She scanned the room, the computer still purring away, screen after screen of files melting away to oblivion. She had not been told why it was necessary to erase everything; it was not her place to know.

She sat in a chair and waited, staring at Chapmann's lifeless corpse on the bed. An apparent suicide. A man who had questioned the process.

It was a lesson Janet Grant would not soon forget.

Sarah had flown in late from London the night before, but by 6:45 A.M., she had already had a very productive morning. Finding her old friend Tommy Carlisle—head of the Criminal Division at Justice—at the Old Ebbitt Grill had been easy. The 6:00 breakfast of kippers and strong black coffee—made ready at so early an hour for the Grill's *special* clientele—was a part of his daily routine. As was his perfectly tailored suit and crisp bow tie, famous among certain Washington circles. He had been the obvious choice, given what she was after.

"I need to see some files," she began.

"And naturally, you've got clearance from State."

Sarah smiled. "Tommy . . . I said it was a favor, not business."

He paused, then nodded. "I see. And what kind of files would they be?"

"Old ones."

"How old?"

"The type they don't put on the computers." Now she waited. "The ones stored in D-five."

His eyes showed a moments reaction. "D-five," his own smile distinctly strained. "And how would you know about that?"

Sarah said nothing, her eyes on his.

After a few seconds, he began to shake his head. "Sorry, dear. That's slightly out of *favor* jurisdiction. Not to mention the mess this past week; security's been punched up everywhere around town. We're all being rather cautious."

"I won't take a thing, Tommy, I promise. All I need is a level-seven—"

"I don't think we're having this conversation."

"You've got the clearance, don't you?" She waited, studying his face. She then spoke very deliberately. "You've got it on you right now."

Their long hug good-bye had given her ample opportunity to lift his ID from his pocket and replace it with a well-crafted fake. With Tommy out of town for a few days—her source of information on Carlisle had been top-notch, worth at least another thousand—she'd known he'd have no reason to use it, no way to discover the forgery. That she was about to breach the State Secrets Act was another matter. The boys at Justice would no doubt want an explanation; she was banking on the aftermath of Eisenreich's *first trial* to keep them busy for a time. At some point, though, she knew they'd be sending out a few friends to . . . *convince* her to come in and chat. It would make things a bit more complicated, but it was a risk worth taking.

Now, she stood outside a nondescript door, one of only two along an isolated corridor tucked deep within subbasement four at Justice. The plaque on the glass read D-FIVE. Thus far, Carlisle's card had maneuvered her through three separate checkpoints, each manned by a marine in full uniform. Recent additions. She had not bothered to ask. None of the young men had said a word, relying on various scanners to confirm her clearance. She had known before coming just how lucky she was; Justice remained a little behind the times—no retina scans as yet. Then again, she couldn't imagine who else would want to see the files on Tempsten, or, more to the point, who would have taken the time to track them this far. Sensitive, but outdated. That's what Tommy had said. Evidently, the combination was making her visit possible.

She placed the card on the unmanned scanner; six seconds later, the door clicked open, and Sarah stepped through, nearly bumping into a shelf no more than two feet from the door. Fluorescent lights immediately came on overhead, revealing D-five as nothing more than a very long hallway, files piled deep in ceiling-high shelves along the entire length of the corridor. She closed the door and noticed a small chart affixed to the near wall, arrows and boxes designating different years for every shelf. Nineteen sixty-nine stood three from the end.

It took her less than five minutes to locate the two thin folders on Tempsten, each filled with no more than five or six sheets, some of them handwritten, others hastily typed, smudge marks in evidence throughout the files. It was clear that no one had taken a look at them in a very long time.

The explanation for their placement in D-five was summed up in a few short sentences at the bottom of the first page. Sarah read:

The tragedy known as the Tempsten Project remains problematic. Those affected by it are between the ages of eight and eighteen; to subject them to further scrutiny in a public forum would no doubt have serious repercussions. It is, therefore, the judgment of this commission that all records of names, dates, and any other personal data be sealed for a period of no less than fifty years.

It was the next few lines, however, that put the commission's apparent concern into proper perspective.

We also believe it vital to maintain a close eye on the progress made by those children. From time to time, these pages shall therefore be updated with information relevant to that purpose.

Monitoring in the guise of caring. A classic ploy. The rest of the file was a detailed rundown of the events that had taken place in 1969.

At approximately 3:00 A.M. on the eighteenth of August, two children (estimated at ten and twelve years of age) arrived at the Tempsten Sheriff's office, bloody and beaten. Neither spoke for several hours, no explanation for their appearance. In response, the sheriff sent three deputies to retrace the boys' tracks; they led to an isolated compound, consisting of four cabins and a small house, three miles inside the Highridge forest. Arriving at daybreak, the sheriff described the scene as "beyond imagination, children running rampant, knives, bats, anything they could find for weapons." This was confirmed by several others in the party. By 6:00 A.M., they had rounded up all of the children, two of whom were dead, victims of apparent head injuries sustained prior to the arrival of any of the sheriff's deputies.

On inspection, the men discovered the cabins to be empty. Only the single house held anything of interest. Inside, they found two adults who had been gouged to death. Several documents were also found, included herein.

Sarah flipped through to the next pages. Whatever they had meant to include had obviously not made it to the files—nothing that might explain why the children had been there in the first place, or what might have triggered the violence. Instead, the file simply detailed the events of the next few weeks, the subsequent hospitalization of the children, and the attempt to track down Anton Votapek, whose name had appeared on several of the documents they had recovered. Failure to find Votapek had left the commission no choice but to label its efforts "a continuing investigation." The last page was dated January 9, 1970, various signatures underneath.

Sarah quickly turned to the second folder. Opening it, she was greeted by a list of fourteen names, ages, and phone numbers. The children at Tempsten. She read the list. She was about to flip to the next page when her eyes froze on a name three from the bottom. For a moment, she stared at the letters, not quite sure what she was reading. *That's not possible,* she thought. At first, she wanted to explain it away as some bizarre coincidence—it was, after all, a common-enough name—but her instinct knew better. She had found the name *here,* locked underneath seven levels of clearance, a place she was never meant to see. That she had no idea *why* his name had appeared mattered very little. She had found it, and that, somehow, was confirmation enough. It *was* him. The name, the age.

Walter Pembroke, sixteen.

Pembroke, the golden boy, third youngest VP in history. Somehow, he was a part of Tempsten.

There had to be more. She turned to the next page, hoping for further confirmation, but found only the updates the commission had so diligently prepared. Paragraph after paragraph on each child—each new address and number carefully noted, but nothing on Pembroke. *Nothing.* She read more closely and discovered that the paragraphs described only those children who shared one disturbing trait: they were all dead—some from injuries sustained at the compound, but most from car accidents. Checking the dates, she realized that only four of the fourteen had survived beyond his or her nineteenth birthday.

Sarah quickly scanned the names of the survivors. It took her a moment to make the connection. There was something familiar, something recognizable in the last two names . . . Grant, Eggart.

And then it hit her.

The shooting of the Dutch diplomats during last week's mayhem. Eggart, the assassin—gunned down at a farm in Virginia; Grant, the state trooper who had killed him, and who had then lost his own life.

Eisenreich's *first trial* confirmed yet again.

The simple facts she had wanted, the facts that would tie everything together, were staring her in the face. And yet all she had were names. Disturbing names to be sure, but still . . .

Sarah looked at the last name on the list. Alison Krogh. Next to it, a ten-digit phone number. No update. No change. No apparent connection. A six-year-old girl now in her mid-thirties. Somewhere.

Sarah wrote down the number and placed the piece of paper in her pocket. She then returned the folders to the shelves and walked back to the door.

Alison Krogh—that was where she would start; that was where she would begin to put the pieces together.

⚔

Xander had opted for a once-familiar tea shop near the library. He needed to take some time with Carlo's notes, and perhaps, more honestly, to distance himself from the Institute. The memories had all been a little too real, too vivid. He needed a few minutes of release. To that end, he had bought a copy of the *Trib*. The puzzle. Certainty in a fifteen-by-fifteen grid.

But he never made it beyond the front page. Walking along Store Street, he glanced at the lead article, the grain debacle—the panic that had hit the streets of Chicago sometime in the early hours of the previous morning. Sources described farmers in Iowa already arming themselves to keep government assessors from determing levels of available stock. In response, Cargill Agricultural had issued a statement: All shipments of grain from the United States were to be halted for an undetermined period of time. Xander scanned the piece, not wanting to admit to its connection with Eisenreich; he had no choice when a single name forced him to stop in midstride. Martin Chapmann. Dead, suicide, the investor responsible for the fiasco.

Xander stared at the words, recalling the files he had read in Florence. Chapmann. Sedgewick's cabal: *"What he intends to do with them is left to the reader's imagination."* Not anymore. The only question remaining was how far the first trial would extend. More frightening, if Washington and Chicago were merely *experiments*, how devastating was the chaos Eisenreich meant to unleash? How many other markets would Sedgewick send his associates to destroy?

The answer, Xander knew, lay in the manuscript. First, though, he had to understand it as it was, not as three madmen were using it now. That meant understanding its context, its lineage. And that meant Carlo's notes. He tucked the paper under his arm and proceeded to the shop.

Within minutes, Xander was deep into the manuscript's history.

"Eisenreich titled his manuscript *On Supremacy*. But who was to know that this innocuous little title was the beginning of something so daring, so bold?" Evidently not one eighteenth-century cataloger who had placed it among a group of fourteenth-century diatribes on spiritual supremacy. Not exactly the most likely spot for a document bent on redefining the nature of power. "Had this Ludovico Buonamonte taken even a moment to read the letter of dedication, he would have seen the mistake, and the manuscript might not have been lost for another two hundred years." Reading his friend's comments, Xander sensed both the elation and the frustration. There were a good four paragraphs on the incompetence of Signore Buonamonte.

Not surprisingly, the path Carlo followed to the German version of the manuscript had been anything but simple. In fact, it had taken him almost eight years just to find the *name* of the original. The difficulty was that what few references there were to the manuscript had invariably been either to the *Science of Eisenreich* or, more disparagingly, to *The Swiss Delusion*. "The second," the notes fumed, "is of no help. And the first—any child knows this is useless." No mention of *On Supremacy*.

As fate would have it, Carlo had come upon the title by dumb luck. While checking a few citations from a student's thesis on church courts during the Inquisition, he had run across a correspondence between two Spanish bishops, one of whom, rather intrigued by an unknown short tract, had described it as "an uncanny theory that describes how best to place full temporal authority in the hands of the Church." At the time, it had meant nothing to Carlo, until he had read the second bishop's assessment, describing the manuscript as "nothing more than a piece of Swiss intrigue." Its name, *On Supremacy*. Its author, evidently Swiss. A bit more digging, a few more letters, and Carlo finally located the author's name. One Eusebius Iacobus Eisenreich. "Today," the entry concluded, "we drink champagne."

Finding the name, though, had provoked greater difficulties. Why would two Catholic bishops have had access to the manuscript? And how could they have possibly thought it had anything to do with church supremacy? It was about power and chaos, authority and manipulation. "The pieces do not fit together. The church and Eisenreich? This makes no sense to me. No sense at all." The notes charted two shattering days, Carlo sitting and drinking cup after cup of coffee, nearly convincing himself that he had run into an insurmountable dead end. Nonetheless, three days later, the entry in the notes began, "This cannot be coincidence. I will not let you beat me again." Xander wondered how many times his friend had written the same challenge to himself, how many times he had forced himself back into the fray. So, taking time away from the university, Carlo had spent over two months combing through the endless volumes of archival listings at the Vatican Library. "Naturally, the idiots who compile these roles of paper find it too much to offer a single author's name. Only titles! When will these clerics learn?" The omissions had caused Carlo no small amount of inconvenience; they were a relief to Xander. No names, no cross-references. No cross-references, no easy access to a manuscript tucked neatly within the pages of a medieval collection.

Carlo had ultimately found six manuscripts on church policy titled *On Supremacy*. One had been the German version he had discovered in Belgrade. That volume, however, had been damaged considerably, water stains and torn pages leaving only bits and pieces from which to decipher the theory. Carlo's enthusiasm at the discovery had naturally been tremendous, but the book's condition had left him far from satisfied. "It is as if you are testing me, seeing how far you may stretch my will. But have faith, my Eisenreich. I will find you." Unfortunately, none of the next four *On Supremacy* titles from the Vatican list had proved to be by the Swiss monk. Three were eighteenth-century treatises, the other a tract on divine intervention. Carlo had found the last in Milan four days before Xander's arrival in Florence. "There is only one left. It must be the one. Of this, I am certain."

The sixth waited in the Danzhoeffer Collection, buried somewhere in the dark recesses of the Institute of Historical Research.

That it was now a reasonably simple task to find those documents and extract the manuscript had at first excited and then alarmed Xander. By his third cup of tea, he had begun to wonder, If it was all so clear, wouldn't it be the same for Tieg and his cohorts? They had found Carlo's copy, why not this one? And they had the name. Had had it for years. A quick search at the Vatican . . . The answer had struck Xander in midswallow. Tieg had only learned of the *third* copy a few days ago. There would have been no reason for a quick search at the Vatican, because they wouldn't have *known* there was something to search for. Even aware of the third version now,

Tieg would never be able to draw the connection between Eisenreich and the church documents. That had been a fluke. Even Carlo had described his discovery of the bishops' letters as "a gift from God. I will thank Him in full when I have the manuscript in my hands."

Those playfully irreverent words were the last Carlo had written. The lightness of style, the little jabs, the digressions on the best cappuccino in Florence—all reminded Xander of the man he had known since his first days with Lundsdorf. "That emotional Mediterranean," he had often called him. "Wonderful mind, but it gets all cluttered with . . . too much enthusiasm." If there had ever been a phrase to define the difference between the Teutons and their neighbors to the south, Lundsdorf had found it. When Xander had told Carlo of Lundsdorf's remarks, the Italian had at first dismissed them with a wild hand to the air, as if sweeping away an annoying bee. Then with a shrug, he had smiled, "Of course, he is right. Then again, what marvelous clutter it is." A quick wink, the slightly nasal laugh. Vintage Carlo.

More telling, though, was the detail. For a man who had seen only small pockets of a damaged version of the manuscript (selections of which were scattered throughout the thirty-odd pages of notes), Carlo showed an uncanny sense for its totality. Even more so, he allowed Xander to see Eisenreich in a light that challenged the stereotype that too many scholars had accepted. Granted, the theory of power and supremacy (from Carlo's extrapolations) made Machiavelli's approach look tame, even inviting, but Xander couldn't help but marvel at the apparent genius. If Carlo was right, Eisenreich displayed an understanding of statecraft that was at least two centuries ahead of its time.

The notes offered so much. It was now time to see how well the manuscript lived up to that promise.

⚔

Sarah had expected to find a disconnected number, or, at best, a forwarding address. What she found, however, came as a complete surprise.

She called from a phone on the corner of Eighth and D.

"Hello." The voice on the other end was a woman's, quiet, hesitant.

Sarah waited, uncertain.

"Hello . . . Anton, is that you?"

The question was enough to force another silence. *"Alison?"* Sarah asked.

Again nothing. "Who's speaking?" The tone carried no mistrust, no hint of insecurity, only a kind of innocent curiosity. "Hello?"

"Yes, hello. This is . . . Sarah."

"Hello, Sarah."

"Am I speaking with Alison . . . Alison Krogh?"

Another pause. "Yes. . . . Yes, this is Alison. Sarah who?"

"Sarah . . . *Carter.* Were you expecting to hear from Anton?"

"He has the number." Silence. "Did Anton ask you to call?"

Again, Sarah waited before answering. "Yes. He asked me . . . he wanted me to come and talk with you. Would that be all right?"

"I see." Another silence. "Anton gave you the number?"

"Yes."

"He said he wanted you to come?"

"Yes," replied Sarah.

"Then . . . it must be all right." She remained, however, less than forthcoming with the address. "Didn't Anton explain everything?" she asked.

"No." Sarah waited, then continued. "He said you would tell me, but only if you wanted me to come."

Another few moments of silence. "All right."

That conversation had taken place an hour and a half ago. Since then, Sarah had caught the first flight to Rochester, New York, rented a car, and driven to Tempsten. As much as she recognized the necessity of the trip, she had grown more and more uneasy at the prospect of meeting one of the last of the survivors. Still there. Still so close. She wondered why they had allowed her to live.

The small cottage, no more than three or four rooms—a screened-in porch at the front—stood along a quiet lane. Sarah pulled up to the curb and stopped the car. She noticed a shuffling at the curtains as she moved up the path, someone anxious to meet guests. Even before she could reach for the bell, the door opened; there, in a simple print dress, hair tied at the back, stood Alison Krogh. For a woman in her mid-thirties, she looked surprisingly young. Thin, elegant, a long trail of thick red hair flowing down her back.

"You must be Ms. Carter," she said, stepping back and ushering Sarah down a short hall to the living room. The place was sparsely furnished—sofa, two chairs, bookshelves, and television. Two glasses and a pitcher waited on the coffee table. "I hope you like lemonade," she said, taking Sarah's coat and hanging it in the closet. "I made it myself."

Sarah nodded and moved to the sofa. "Yes, very much." She waited for Alison to sit and then took a seat by her. "Thank you for seeing me."

Alison nodded, keeping her eyes from Sarah's.

"Do you live here alone?"

"Yes," she answered. "Except when Anton comes. Then I don't." She smiled and took a sip of the lemonade. The frailty was even more apparent in person, thought Sarah.

"Does he come often?"

Alison shook her head and took another sip. Still, her eyes would not meet Sarah's. "Why did Anton tell you to come?"

"He said I should talk with you."

"Like the others?" For the first time, Sarah heard an edge in her tone.

"Others?" she asked.

"The doctors. Who want to talk about . . . the school." Alison stared, saying nothing more.

"And that bothers you."

"I don't like to talk about it." There was no reprimand in the answer, only a simple statement. "I don't remember very much. Isn't that funny?" She tried a smile and took another sip of the lemonade. "I have some fruit. I grow it myself, in the greenhouse. Would you like some?" Not waiting for Sarah to answer, Alison stood and disappeared through a swinging door.

Alone, Sarah studied the few pictures hidden among the trinkets on the shelves, wondering what lay behind the frightened eyes of the woman she had just met. Beach scenes, a younger Alison wading waist-high in the ocean, an older man at her side—Votapek no doubt—smiles from ear to ear. But the eyes remained the same, distant, uneasy. Even in a fading picture. Something so familiar.

The door swung open.

"You have some lovely things," Sarah smiled.

Alison placed a tray on the table and nodded. "Gifts. From Anton."

Sarah waited, then spoke. "Do you ever talk about the school with him?"

Alison kept her eyes from Sarah, her expression completely blank; she then sat, her eyes now focusing on the bowl. For a few moments, she seemed totally unaware of anything else in the room. Finally, she looked up. "Would you like some fruit?" she asked, the smile tighter than before.

Sarah shook her head. "I was hoping to talk about the school."

Again, no reaction until Alison's eyes darted to the corner of the room, her struggle to maintain control evident in the deep breath she took. She turned to Sarah, eyes damp, the smile trying to hold back the tears. "I don't like to talk about that." A single drop glanced down her cheek.

Gently, Sarah pressed. "Then why did you ask me to come?"

"I don't have many visitors." Alison brushed the tear away. "It's . . . nice when people come."

"Is that the reason?"

For the first time, Alison looked directly at her, Sarah seeing something behind the stare; Alison quickly pulled a leg to her chest, her head resting on one knee, eyes again on the bowl. "The school was a long time ago."

"I understand."

"No, you don't." Again, nothing combative in the tone, only a statement of fact. "No one does. Not Anton. Not Laurence. No one." She looked at Sarah, eyes swelling. "Everything was fine, you know, just the way it was supposed to be. It was . . . such a good place." Tears began to trickle through the smile. "We all belonged; we all learned—that's why we were there, you know. How to be strong, how to take what was ours." Her eyes darted back to the corner, the smile dropping, "and then, everyone so angry . . ." Her words trailed to a near whisper, tears caught in her throat. She looked as if she might give in, let the torrent come, when she suddenly stopped. One long breath, and she turned back to Sarah. "Would you like some fruit?"

Sarah stared at her for a moment, her own emotions rocked by the outpouring, ever more familiar and so desperately real. Alison, locked in a stare, her eyes betraying nothing of the last minutes—only a strange tension, distancing herself from the memories.

"Do you mean the boys?" asked Sarah quietly.

Another moment of recognition, then nothing. Frail, quiet, struggling for control, Alison shook her head. "The boys? I don't understand."

"The boys who died," answered Sarah. "At the school."

The tears flowed freely; still, there was nothing in her expression to hint at the slightest reaction. Only her hand clenching, releasing, clenching. She shook her head, even as the drops began to slide down her cheek. "I don't remember any boys," she answered.

But Sarah knew. She knew because of her own memories—weeks, months denying the lives she had taken. Hands clenching, releasing, clenching—unconscious mechanisms implanted through a doctor's hypnosis to allow her a release from the horror. Memories erased until she could learn to accept them. How long, Sarah wondered, had Alison hidden behind those same devices? How long had the men responsible for them forced her to remain a victim of her own self-loathing?

"It's all right," said Sarah, her voice quiet, caring. "I *do* understand. You don't have to remember."

"It was a good place." Alison nodded, her eyes still distant. "And then it went wrong."

"How?" she asked. "How did it go wrong?"

Alison shook her head. Without warning, she looked up, her eyes suddenly focused. "It was wrong to try again, wasn't it?"

The reaction surprised Sarah. "Try what?" she asked.

"They'll go wrong again, won't they?"

Again? Sarah sat motionless.

"Anton doesn't think I know," continued Alison, her eyes on some faraway spot, "but I know. Even though he promised. Even though he said it would be fine, that he could stop it from going wrong." She looked at Sarah. "It was bad to do it again. I know. I've seen it."

Sarah forced herself beyond the shock. "What have you seen, Alison?"

The tight smile. A shake of the head. "It was bad to do it again. That's why I told you to come. You have to tell him it was wrong."

"Do *what* again?" Sarah knew the answer, but she needed to hear it from Alison.

They stared at each other. Alison then stood, walked to the bookshelf, and pulled several volumes from the bottom shelf, uncovering a single videocassette. "I took this from Anton. I took this so I would know." Fifteen seconds later, she was at the television, sliding the tape into the VCR.

Before Sarah could ask, the screen flashed blue. In large black type, the words PREFECT RELEASE—NONDISCLOSURE PRIORITY appeared. A moment later, they were replaced by a thin strip at the bottom of the screen, a time counter spinning off the minutes and seconds. The date of the filming, April 7, 1978. The place, Winamet, Texas. Nineteen seventy-eight, Sarah thought. *My God, it had never ended.*

The picture came alive with a cluster of young children, no more than six or seven years old, seated around a woman in the middle of a room, an area called "the Learning Circle." A sign hung from the ceiling in a crescent arc, each letter a different shade of colored paper, the evident work of tiny hands. The woman was in her late forties, with a tenderness essential for those who mold the very young. She was reading to them. After a few seconds, she placed the book in a pile and looked out at the children.

"Poor Cinderella," she began, "so many people who were so unkind. In fact, I can't think of a nice thing to say about her sisters. Can you?"

"They weren't nice at all," piped in one tiny charge, so eager to please that her words flew out in a rapid burst of syllables and gasps. "When the prince came to see their feet, and Cinderella had the right shoe on her foot, but her sisters were mean and angry because they couldn't go." The slight roll of the head, the coy smile, each an indication that the exegesis had come to an end.

"I quite agree," smiled the teacher.

"I hated them," remarked a small boy lounging off to the left, his head resting on an elbowed hand, not even the slightest bit of menace in his voice. Simple. Straight. To the point.

"*Hate*'s a very strong word." The teacher seemed to be waiting for an answer. The boy shrugged as only little boys do, shoulder high to the cheek-bone in unintentioned exaggeration. "But I think you're right. I don't think the word is too strong." She scanned the others' eyes. Sarah sensed that the woman had been waiting, even hoping for the response. Clearly, the Learning Center taught a very specific type of lesson. "Let's try and think of all the nasty things those sisters did," she continued.

In quick succession, the children shouted out a long list of infractions, the most poignant from a shy boy who had waited until all the others had quieted down to speak.

"They made her feel very bad and said that nobody liked her."

A silence filled the room, several heads turning toward the boy as the teacher, in her most motherly tone, added, "And that's probably the worst thing, isn't it? To make special people, like Cinderella, feel that they don't belong, that they've done something wrong." The boy stared at the floor, nodding as he continued to play with a small tuft of carpet in his fingers. "And people who do that," she continued, "shouldn't be our friends, should they? And we don't have to like them, do we?" A chorus of nos. "In fact, sometimes it's all right *not* to like certain people. People who scare us, or hurt us, or make us feel bad about ourselves—"

"Like strangers," yelped one ponytailed girl.

"Like strangers." The teacher nodded. "But other people as well. People like Cinderella's stepsisters, who knew how special Cinderella was, but who did everything they could to hurt her. It's important to know that you have to watch out for those sorts of people. And you shouldn't feel bad if you begin to dislike them. Dislike them so much that you begin to hate them."

"I hated them, too." Several children, once given the official go-ahead, were happy to voice their ardent disapproval.

"They were bad people," said one little boy. "Some people are bad and you hate them. And that's it." The no-holds-barred tyke leader of the hate patrol. Our Gang in SS boots. Sarah continued to watch.

"Some people are bad," continued the teacher, "and they're not just in stories. Sometime, you might run into someone like Cinderella's stepsister, and you'll have to know what to do, how to behave, how to treat them."

"I wouldn't let them make me do all the work in the house," one voice piped in. "Or make me stay at home when they're at the palace," offered another. The teacher seemed to encourage the whirlwind of enthusiasm from the children, most pleased when one little girl, shouting above the rest and in full lather, screamed out, "I'd make them do all the bad things and be mean to them!" The final crescendo—the little girl springing to her feet, jumping nervously, arms pulled tightly to her little chest at the attention and prodding from her tiny peers—thrust the little band into shrieks of excitement. The room seemed to explode in a cackle of delight as several others hopped up, trembling wirelike fists boxing the air in full release of emotion inspired by the near-glowing teacher. Catching the wave at its crest, she slowly began to quiet the children in firm but gentle tones. "All right, all right, let's find a calm place. Let's find a calm place." Code words which, within a minute, had the children once again in obedient order.

The screen faded to black; a moment later, it filled with snow.

Sarah looked across at Alison. The young woman stared unimpassioned at the television, her eyes again distant.

"Where are those children now?" asked Sarah. Alison did not respond. Before Sarah could ask again, the screen slid to black; a moment later, another group of children materialized, these older, perhaps twelve, thirteen years of age. The strip at the bottom read "October 14, 1981, Brainbrook, Colorado."

No one spoke, a class in martial arts, each child showing extraordinary proficiency in any number of techniques. But it was their eyes that Sarah watched—focused but empty, personality absent from the cold precision of the movements. The scene quickly faded to black.

Twenty minutes later, Alison reached forward and pulled the tape from the machine. Throughout, Sarah had sat mesmerized as ten other segments had come and gone, each from a separate school, each from a different year, each with its own skewed vision of schooling. The common lesson, blind obedience; the underlying theme, a cultivated hatred. Fifteen-year-olds taught to hunt out the weak; eighteen-year-olds taught to demonize in the name of social cohesion. A constant dosage of venom to focus the children's aggression and turn it into a zealot's passion.

Most troubling, though, was how they had been groomed to express that passion. The sniper's gun, the demolitionist's explosives, the computer hacker's manipulations—all vividly documented.

The blueprint for Eisenreich's assault on Washington. The blueprint for the world beyond the *first trial*.

Alison remained silent. She looked at Sarah.

"Now you see the process," she said. "Now you see why I asked you to come. You have to tell Anton to stop it. He must stop the *process*."

Sarah waited before answering. She looked into the frightened eyes, aware for the first time that perhaps Alison understood far more than she had let on. "How did you get a hold of this?" she asked.

Alison stared at her, then spoke. "You have to *tell* him to stop it."

Sarah nodded. "I'll tell him to stop . . . the process." The mention of the last word seemed to calm Alison. "May I have the tape?"

Alison stared into Sarah's eyes for several seconds, a penetrating look, something Sarah had not expected. "What makes *you* so sad, Sarah?" Alison held her gaze for a moment longer, then leaned over and placed the tape on the table. "Maybe you do understand." She picked up the tray and stood. "I'll get some more lemonade."

It took Sarah a moment to recover. "Actually . . . I should be going."

Alison stopped at the swinging door. When she turned, a strained smile creased her lips. "You're welcome to stay. I have other—"

"No," smiled Sarah, now standing. "I should be going."

A momentary pause; Alison placed the tray on the sideboard. "You're not a doctor, are you." Again, no accusation, only statement. Sarah said nothing. The smile tightened on Alison's lips as she moved to the closet and retrieved Sarah's coat.

A minute later, they stood at the front door, Sarah no more easy with her newfound confidante than she had been half an hour ago. The look of tender helplessness in the eyes was too long ingrained to find release in the gentle squeeze of a hand. "Things will be all right," Sarah heard herself say.

"Will you come back for me?"

The words tore through her, a simple request, but it was all Sarah could do to find an answer. "Yes . . . I will come back for you."

Again, Alison stared into Sarah's eyes. A moment's recognition and then a nod. Sarah squeezed her hand and turned for the garden path.

Halfway down the block, a sedan slowly began to inch its way toward the house, Sarah immediately aware of its presence. Gradually, she quickened her pace. A man in his early twenties—a broad-shouldered boy stuffed into a plain gray suit—appeared from behind a tree. He remained still, hands crossed at his front, eyes lost behind a set of dark sunglasses. *Requisite Justice attire.* Sarah stopped. Tommy had evidently been more careful than she expected. And quicker. The sedan pulled up behind her car as the man in the glasses started toward her.

For an instant, she considered running. The thought of Alison alone, however, made the idea of escape impossible. Sarah knew the woman was too fragile for the scrutiny to which the men from Washington would subject her, too close to the men of Eisenreich not to be held accountable. Another life drawn in. Another life Sarah would not allow herself to dismiss so easily.

She slowly turned toward the house.

What she saw took her completely by surprise. Alison was standing next to a third man, the smile wide on her face, her hand resting in his. Sarah froze, the scene strangely serene.

"Look who's here," cried Alison. "It's Willy and John."

Before Sarah could react, the man from behind her slipped his hand tightly around her arm. In a whispered voice, he said, "Mr. Votapek doesn't want Alison upset in any way. Do you understand?" His grip tightened.

Votapek. Sarah could only nod.

⚓

After two and a half hours of misdirection and incompetence, Xander held the essential pages in his hand, ripping them from one of the library printers. The odyssey had begun at the desk of the assistant librarian, who, at first, had sent him halfway across town to an annex; there, he had been told that the books he was looking for were *never* permitted to leave the main library. *Wonderful.* He had returned to Russell Square, only to receive a somewhat embarrassed apology—"I thought you wanted the *Dillman* Collection"— and another hour's worth of ineptitude before he had insisted on seeing the head librarian. Mrs. Denton-Fiss, far more apologetic than her colleague for the "unfortunate mix-up," had then taken him to the back office and the private computer files. Now, ten minutes later, Xander scanned the few pages he had been looking for all along.

The Danzhoeffer family had been quite generous, according to the list, donating four filing cases of documents, each with perhaps forty listings— letters, pamphlets, manuscripts—in no specific order. That meant he would have to plow through each case individually in order to find Eisenreich. Any sense of annoyance from the further delay, however, quickly disappeared as Xander's eyes came to a stop about a third of the way down the page, where two small words stared back at him: *On Supremacy*. He passed his thumb over the print. Caught up in the chase, Xander felt the same sense of exhilaration he had sensed in Carlo's notes. A slight tingling licked at his throat.

It was only then that he noticed the asterisks on the page. Some ten to twelve entries, including the manuscript, sported little stars alongside their listings. He quickly flipped to the bottom of the second page. No note to explain. The asterisks simply sat there, causing a momentary tightening in his stomach. *What now?* There was only one way to find out. Xander picked up his briefcase and headed for the stacks.

Three minutes later, his eyes took a moment to accustom themselves to the dimly lit area of the fourth floor. Typical of so many research libraries, the books lay hidden within dark recesses, pale screens of light slanting this way and that from the few overhead lamps. Directly in front of him, a long, thin alley ran the length of the floor, its black-speckled tiles crisscrossed by shadows cast from the row upon row of shelves on either side. Each row stood within a wall of black, waiting for that one passerby to switch on its private light and break through the somber pall of the place.

Slowly moving down the corridor, Xander read each of the catalog numbers tacked hastily to the topmost shelf brackets. Once or twice, he checked the number he had written down just to make sure he hadn't missed it. Two rows from the back wall, the listing 175.6111 CR–175.6111 FL brought him to a stop. He shoved the piece of paper into his pocket, and with a quick click, ignited the narrow tunnel in light, his eyes racing by the numbers printed on the books' spines. Halfway to the wall, he nearly tripped over four large cases protruding from the edge of the bottom shelf. He looked down and read the inscription, the tingle once again in his throat. He then squatted to the floor and pulled the Danzhoeffer Collection from the shelf.

The state of the documents was far better than he had anticipated. Granted, no one had done a thing except catalog them and then place them back in their respective cases, but at least care, if not logic, was evident in the ordering of the small stacks. Xander began to read.

The fifteenth and sixteenth centuries commingled in the first case—some rather forthright letters from a Cardinal Vobonte to several Popes, demanding dispensations for various French aristocrats. Tax cuts for his constituents, mused Xander. *Some things never change.* Next, he found a collection of poems by an Italian court musician, homage to Boccaccio's *Decameron.* Flipping quickly past it, Xander lit upon a large assortment of pamphlets on religious practices—guides to proper observances for any number of saints' days.

At first glance, the second case seemed equally unpromising. More poems, more pamphlets on the saints. Two-thirds the way through, though, the titles took a dramatic turn away from saint-day rituals to the heated topic of papal authority—someone's idea of a natural progression from fifteenth-century primers to sixteenth-century treatises. Whatever the rationale, Xander knew he was close—*very* close. Sifting through seven or eight dreary tracts on church jurisdiction, each with endless counterarguments to Marsilius' *Defensor Pacis,* Xander finally uncovered a small leather volume, the Medici crest still discernible on the weathered leather binding. For a moment, he stared at the little book resting comfortably among the various other papers. Nothing to distinguish it. Nothing on its surface to explain the sudden rapid-fire pounding in his chest. Letting the other manuscripts drop into the case, he brought the book up to within two inches of his face. Its edges long ago frayed, a strange smell of apple vinegar rose from its pages. Gently, he pulled open the front cover and saw the simple Italian staring at him:

From Eusebius Iacobus Eisenreich to His Holiness, the Most Holy Father, Pope Clement VII

The dedicatory letter—written in thick sixteenth-century script—continued on to the next page. Xander ever so delicately turned the page, less taken with the text than with the tangible reality of the book in his hands. It was here, in front of him, the key to the riddles, the answer to the skeptics.

Almost of its own will, the manuscript moved on to the next page, the title straightforward, the name in large bold print, the year 1531 below it, and, for some strange reason, the letters *v.i.* in the lower-right-hand corner.

It took Xander a moment to tear himself from the joy of discovery and try to decode the odd inscription: *v.i.* Undaunted, he thumbed through to the next page and found the table of contents, an ordered outline in twenty chapters. Machiavelli had needed twenty-six. How like the Swiss, he thought, to pick a nice round number. But no explanation. *v.i.* It continued to nag at him as he fingered through the pages, more so as he neared the middle of the book and had reached only chapter five. A distinct sense of unease began to displace the rush of only moments ago. *v.i. Volume one?* Three pages from the end, his fears were confirmed. *Chapter IX—The Roads to Chaos.* Then nothing. Xander immediately looked back in the case. No luck. *Two volumes—why?* The answer dawned on him as he eyed the little book. *Clement.* The Italian version, the one for the Pope, had been the *first* version. Eisenreich had been clever to send only an excerpt, one that included only the first nine chapters. The other eleven, volume two. A safety precaution. So where were they?

Xander slumped back against the wall, his mind racing to find an answer. It made no sense. Why would the library have only the first volume? And why were the crucial chapters missing? Up through nine, the headings were daring but not earth-shattering. Xander glanced back at the contents page: *III. How to Achieve Stability; VI. Those Components Which Make Up a State; VIII. How a State May Be Made Ready for True Supremacy.* Eisenreich would have his own personal prescriptions, but the titles themselves were only slightly brazen. Ten through twenty, on the other hand, were extraordinary: *X. The Road to Political Chaos; XI. The Road to Economic Chaos; XII. The Road to Social Chaos;* and most extraordinary, *XV. Why It Is Important to Cultivate Hatred.* The shift at chapter ten was clear. Eisenreich had kept the best for last.

And yet nowhere in Carlo's notes had there been any mention of *two* separate volumes. Hope was telling Xander that the two had found each other at some point in the sixteenth century. *So why the separation now?* He closed his eyes and began to rock. *Think, damn it.* Two minutes into the strange ritual, his eyes suddenly bolted open. From his pocket, he fished out the now-crumpled listing he had ripped from the printer downstairs. *The asterisks.* Quickly, he began to rummage through the filing cases, glancing every so often at the list so as to find another name. Fifteen minutes later, he had his answer. None of the ten marked titles was in any of the cases. Which meant that someone at the information desk would know why those volumes were missing. And that *someone* would be able to tell him where to find volume two of the Eisenreich manuscript.

Only then did Xander notice the figure standing at the end of the row, face and body obscured in dim light. Xander froze, his hand tightening around the manuscript. For what seemed an eternity, the two men stared at each other, neither moving. His knees seemed to lock in their crouching position as he gazed up at the man with slicked-back hair. *Slicked-back hair?* Xander's memory flashed on an image of the small figure, the thin, sunken smile, the hard stare of lifeless eyes. The alcove. *My alcove.*

With a sense of raw panic, Xander grabbed his briefcase and thrust it full force into the shadows. The movement took but an instant, but, to Xander's eyes, the slow-motion heaving and thrashing lent the chaos a certain clarity, a precision he had never before experienced. He could see everything, feel it all as the case drove up into the man's midsection. Xander pushed his way out into the long alley, his feet slipping along the waxed tile. He careened against several of the shelves, desperate to find his footing. No sounds from behind, no scream of surprise, no patter of feet in quick pursuit as he propelled himself toward the bright light at the stairs.

Time began to accelerate again as he reached the stairwell, his body now in control, turning, eager to fly down the steps.

Instead, he lurched to a stop. There, stepping up to the landing, came another familiar profile. Completely bald, large shoulders—the man from Florence. A quick intake of breath was all Xander needed to draw the man's attention, the glance immediate, the reaction, however, completely unexpected. The man stared blankly—no recognition, no anticipated discovery. In that instant of stunned disbelief, Xander leapt to his right, racing up the steps toward the fifth floor.

A delayed clatter of feet behind him filled the air as he reached the next landing. Knowing he had only the sixth and seventh above him, Xander spun away from the stairs and began to move down another darkened corridor. *Away from the light! Get away from the light!* Ducking down the nearest alley, he stumbled his way deeper into the maze of shelves, trying to remember the layout of the floors; but his mind was a blank, straining to hear any sounds of his distant stalkers. A minute later, the shelves took a sharp turn to the right, forcing him to scrape along various books, one or two crashing to the floor as he whisked by. The first sounds of emphatic pursuit rang in his ears. Finding the central corridor again, he darted across and into another web of shelved alleys, the light growing fainter and fainter as he ran farther into the pitch-black of the labyrinth. With each step, his sense of direction grew more and more remote, until the stairs were but a distant memory, an unknown port lost within an uncharted sea of metal and books.

And then, with his heart racing, his breath searing to escape, he stopped. He had to take stock, regain control. He was deep within the morass of paths, somehow secure under the blanket of books above him. A fleeting sense of calm swept over him, enough to grant a moment's lucidity. He crouched and concentrated all of his energy on the faint sound of darting feet coming from his left. It was not a single, even beat, but the syncopated rhythm of two sets—*pat-a-pa-tat, pat-a-pa-tat*—jostling their way from shelf to shelf, drawing ever nearer to the tiny segment of floor Xander had staked as his own. Relentlessly, the pattern rose, its echo stronger as the seconds flew by. He snapped his head over his shoulder as if expecting to find eyes peering at him, through him. But only the staccato menace of feet, the deafening whisp of panting breath, nearer and nearer.

And suddenly silence. An eerie quiet descended all about him, soundless and cold, propelling a surge of nervous energy within, the books no longer a barrier against what he could not hear, could not see. Oppressive silence. He sat like a cornered animal, waiting for the thrust of claws deep within his flesh, the stealthy gouging he could almost feel, prostrate and alone on the icy floor. Again, he spun his head round, certain that eyes were upon him, only to discover the black outline of shelf, the near-distant fade to nothingness that seemed to isolate him all the more. The silence began to suffocate, its emptiness draining, leaving only hopeless terror in its wake. He wanted desperately to find himself, to break out of the torment his assailants had so masterfully contrived, but his will was giving in, his hands able only to clasp the pages to his chest. He began to rock back and forth, slipping more and more into a numbing stillness.

A momentary shift in the shadow above broke the trance. Xander peered up into the lifeless eyes.

"You have the manuscript, Dr. Jaspers?" the voice whispered.

Xander could only stare at the man.

5

The demands of each realm are so severe that, for those who lead, there is no time to attend to anything but their own tasks.

—*On Supremacy,* CHAPTER VI

AGAIN, THE MAN PROBED. "You have the manuscript, Dr. Jaspers?"

Xander's eyes fixed on the face above, a narrow oval atop a thin neck. Had he been standing, Xander would have towered over the slouching figure. But he was trapped, knees drawn tight to his chest, a child caught, certain of unspeakable punishment. There was, of course, the alley of shelves behind him, the long expanse of shadow with its promise of escape, but what was the use? No doubt, the bald giant stood somewhere in the dark recesses, happy to let his more diminutive counterpart take the first crack at interrogation. The man seemed content to let his prey make the first move. Xander could offer little more than a nod to the man's question.

"Good." Again, the cold precision of the northern European accent.

Xander slowly raised the small leather book toward his captor, the weight of the tiny volume somehow too much for him.

"Oh, no, you hold on to it, Doctor. I would not know what to do with it."

Xander's hand stopped in midair. *"What?"* he whispered, more reflex than response. The little calm he had managed now gave way under the impact of the words, his mind racing to find a rationale, anger replacing fear as one image began to crystallize. *Of course.* They were playing with him, biding their time so that the assassin could hand-deliver his prize to

Votapek, or Tieg, or whoever else had concocted this nightmare. And yet, there was something strangely serene, nonthreatening in the man's candor. *Keep it?* Where was the sense in that?

"There is no need for alarm, Dr. Jaspers."

"No *need* for—"

"Ms. Trent sent me."

"You've got—" The name ripped through him, his mind overwhelmed by words he could not comprehend. *"Ms. Trent?"* A momentary flash of coherence. *"Sarah?* Sarah *sent* you—"

"Yes. I am Feric. Ms. Trent asked me to . . . watch over you."

Xander locked eyes with the man, the calm, icy demeanor somehow unreal, impenetrable. "Watch *over* me?" he echoed. It took a minute for the words to sink in. And with the first hints of understanding, the shock gave way to a mounting sense of resentment, the realization that he was being coddled. "What the hell does *that* mean?" Xander hoisted himself up, Feric mindful not to interfere, no hand extended. He had been told such gestures would only exacerbate the young professor.

"It means—"

"And that was *you* back at the Institute." Pictures began to fall into place. "All that browsing through the books. 'Wrong room.' Why didn't you say something?" He had regained enough composure to keep his questions to a loud whisper, his hands busy brushing off his pants. Suddenly, his head snapped toward Feric. "The *other* man. The *bald*—"

"As I said, no need for alarm. He has been taken care of."

" '*Taken care*'—what is it with you people?"

"There was no reason—"

"Look, I'm grateful—I think. But . . . *Feric?* She never mentioned—"

"She would not have done that. I can explain all of this *later.*" Words chosen to pacify now gave way to orders. "You have everything you need?"

Another calm voice to penetrate his confusion. So much like Sarah's, and in that, Xander recognized he was once again caught up in their game, playing by their rules. Such questions were meaningless, answers an indulgence. *Concern . . . neither of us has the time for it.* Sarah's words from the café. It took him a moment to respond. "No. I need to speak with a librarian."

For the first time, doubt crossed Feric's face. "Fine. I will leave first. You will follow. There is a pub, the Wayward Lamb, no more than—"

"I know where it is. I'll need half an hour."

Twenty minutes later, they were well into their first pint of beer. "The library sent out a total of ten documents for restoration," said Xander, seated across from Feric two-thirds the way down a cushioned bench that stretched the length of the side wall. The Lamb had that homey feel rarely found in London pubs, one of the few to have escaped the onslaught of Anglified American bars and French bistros. Deeply grained oak walls, heavy under a dull shine, stood firm but easy on all sides, cluttered by endless drawings of horses with jockeys, each enclosed in its own slightly decrepit gilt frame. The world moved more slowly here, a hospitality extended to those willing to give in to the easy pace of the surroundings.

"To Germany?" asked Feric, the waitress arriving with cheese and a basket of bread. He reached out and pulled off a healthy chunk.

"Yes," Xander responded, his eyes on the man directly across from him. Up to this point, he had accepted his new *friend* at face value. Now . . .

"You are hesitant." Feric nodded.

Xander watched as the man's strong fingers ripped mercilessly into the bread, the hunched figure sniffing at his food before popping a small piece of fondled dough into his mouth. There was something animal-like about him, the sharp nose, high forehead only accentuating the cheekbones that gnawed away in rapid, tight bursts. Disconcerting as the appearance might be, Xander had to admit that this little man gave off an aura of self-control, a quiet confidence. Straightforward, with no hint of pretension. "What do you expect?" he answered. "I don't know who you are, and you don't seem that eager to fill me in. All you tell me is that Sarah sent—"

"Monica," Feric said, continuing to chew, his eyes on the bread.

"What?"

"Monica." Feric looked up and placed the bread on the table, picking at his back teeth as he continued. "Ms. Trent suggested I mention it."

Ms. Trent suggested . . . The word suddenly registered. *Of course*. Monica. Carlo's office. Only Sarah would have known. Only she would have picked so perfect a signal to put him at ease.

"I see she was right." Feric removed a large wad of chewed bread, examined it, replaced it, and swallowed. "This book—this *second* part—it is in Germany?" he repeated.

It took Xander a moment to respond. "Yes. We've just been unlucky." Somewhat more at ease, he continued. "The good news is that they're obviously unimpressed with the manuscript. Keeping one volume and sending out the other—they clearly have no idea what they've got. According to the woman at the desk, library policy is to split up multivolumes so that—"

"Only what I need to know, Doctor."

Xander stopped, nodded. "Problem is, they won't get the last eleven chapters back for another month."

"And that is too long to wait."

"If Washington and Chicago are any indication, yes. I'd say that would be too long to wait."

"And you know of this place in Germany?"

"It's a small town called Wolfenbüttel, about half an hour from the old East German line."

"Why there?"

"It's got one of the great libraries of Europe. It's also famous for an absolutely first-rate book collector and restorer, Emil Ganz. He's about a hundred and—" Xander cut himself off. Trivial details.

"You are familiar with this place, then?"

"I've spent some time there. A conference about six years ago. It's not the sort of place to have changed. My guess is that the book is already there."

"I see. We should fly tonight, then."

Xander paused, then nodded. "Right. I . . . could probably use a few hours to read through it . . . maybe find something helpful for Sarah."

Feric understood. It was all moving a bit too fast for the academic. "That is true." He nodded. "All right. A few hours."

"And you know how to reach her?"

"Yes."

"Good." Xander was hoping for a little more, even if he knew it was in his own best interest to be kept in the dark. "I've been answering all the questions, haven't I?"

"Yes."

"And I'll learn how *not* to do that."

"Perhaps."

Xander took a sip of his beer and began to gather his things. "Then I should probably get back to the library."

"For what purpose?" This time, the question was not for clarity's sake.

"The *manuscript*? Remember? I need to spend time—"

"You did not take it *with* you?"

"Of course not," answered Xander. "You can't simply walk out of a library with—"

"*You*—" Feric's tone remained controlled, only his eyes showing utter disbelief. "Dr. Jaspers, I do not think you quite understand what this is all about. That bald man would have been happy to do a great many things one is not *supposed* to do in a library in order to get that little book."

"I put it in a safe place."

"I am sure that is what your friend Pescatore thought, as well." The words had the desired effect. "Now, so there is no more confusion, you and I are going to return to the library and take the book with us. You will then have your few hours with it, after which time I will get in touch with Ms. Trent; we will then find our way to Wolfenbüttel, find the second part of the manuscript, and remove it to a safe place. Have I made everything clear?"

The first lesson. Xander nodded. "Perfectly."

Feric rose, leaving a few coins on the table. "Beer is always overpriced in this country." Xander had no choice but to follow.

✠

Pockets of grass and fence slipped by, the New York countryside blurring against the backdrop of a saffron sky. The limousine shot along, maneuvering the two-lane road with surprising ease, only once or twice encroaching the thin line in its quest for greater speed. The driver seemed unconcerned with his three silent passengers, each content to stare aimlessly at the vanishing horizon, to play their assigned roles with quiet resolve.

Sarah's was simply to wait. She knew there was little she could learn from the two men with her. They were nothing more than envoys, men sent to retrieve, unaware and uninterested in the deeper significance of their quarry. There was no reason to upset the stilted calm with unnecessary chatter. She would take the time to plan. A bit more information from Jaspers would have been nice, but she would have to make do with what she had.

The thought of him brought a smile to her face. It had been difficult to let him go to London by himself. *Choices. Always choices.* And even though she knew Feric would be there to protect him, she couldn't forget the concern in his eyes as they had left the café. And the embrace. A surprise to be sure, yet one more inviting than perhaps she was willing to admit.

The limo slowed and turned off the highway onto a road running parallel to the outlying fence of a private airstrip; fifty yards down, a solitary booth rose from the wire fencing, a separate entrance reserved for the airport's special clientele. Once again, the car slowed to turn, no exchange as the guard recognized the plates and waved the black Lincoln through, nodding at the smoked glass as the limo bumped its way up onto the tarmac. A hundred yards to the left, a private jet waited, two red lights flashing under each wing. Sarah's attention shifted to the man sitting directly across from her. He continued to peer out the window, aware of her gaze, happy to ignore it. She would find no answers there.

Five minutes later, she sat belted comfortably in one of six chairs in the plane's main cabin, her two companions at either side. She wondered if her exploits in New York were responsible for their caution. *Unknown and out of control. Capable of anything.* They would watch her, but from a distance. It was a long drop from six miles up.

The quick acceleration of takeoff helped to relieve some of the tension in her shoulders, g-force strapping her against the soft cushioning of the upright chair and allowing her back to realign itself from the sheer physical pull. Even as a child, Sarah had loved the moment of explosion, the engines revving beyond all measure, and then the slight uplift as the nose broke free, the soft climb that seemed to stretch an unseen rubber band, drain it of its elasticity, until, with a final surge, all thoughts of a ground below would disappear in the soft blanket of clouds and sunlight. Now, as the plane leveled off, Sarah turned her head to the left and peered out the small oval window. A yellowed mist dusted past them, a cold sun bathing the wing in a metallic glow. They were heading southeast. She had always had an uncanny sense of direction. She closed her eyes.

Votapek. A first line of attack.

⚔

Stein was managing on very little sleep. They had picked up Trent through Jaspers, then lost them both somewhere in Florence due to "unforeseen complications" near the San Marco monastery. The on-site analyst had been unclear as to the snafu, even less helpful as to why the two had visited a Professor Pescatore in the first place. Of course, there hadn't been time to set up full surveillance in Europe, which meant that Jaspers had slipped conveniently out of the picture. Luckily, they had reestablished Trent at Dulles sixteen hours later, solo and on her own passport. Her message clear: Follow me; leave him alone.

Bob had done just that, even though some rather alarming news had begun to float in from Italy several hours later. Pescatore was missing, thought dead, his office in shambles, bloodstains in evidence. Early Italian news reports made no mention of the two unlikely visitors, but the police were playing everything close to the chest. Even well-placed Committee sources had been unable to unearth specifics. Bob found it very difficult to believe that either Trent or Jaspers had had anything to do with the disappearance; then again, he was having trouble understanding why a virtually unknown Italian political theorist would be linked with Schenten and his associates. Too many variables were bouncing around to prompt any meaningful conclusions.

Those sorts of twists and turns, however, were par for the course. What was causing trouble was the way he had been *instructed* to handle the op: the breakfast meetings with O'Connell—all off-line—the hedging whenever Pritchard asked for an update, the sudden overuse of his office safe for materials he would have happily left on his desk only a week ago. He couldn't be sure if he was getting caught up in some high-level power play, or if there was reason to suspect an internal breach. And to add to it all, O'Connell had become tight-lipped, mulling over reports, never inviting the usual dialogue that brought meaning to the otherwise-lifeless words on the page.

For some reason, the Irishman was pulling back. Bob had lived through similar mood swings—the worst after Amman. Then, Stein had chalked it up to a strange sort of empathy. O'Connell had been too close, too much aware, the onetime operative seeing himself reflected in the lost expression of a woman fighting her way back from the edge. He had retreated into himself—a two-week *vacation*, far longer than the usual two-day binge. Bob hadn't asked; O'Connell hadn't discussed it. And now Stein had to wonder: Would the Irishman slip away again?

That was why Bob had shut himself in his office, staring at his computer terminal for hours on end, bags of cheese balls littering the area around his wastebasket. Not that concentrated periods of seclusion weren't the norm, but this time he felt completely isolated, all links to the two other offices on the sixth floor severed with a strange sort of finality. Rattled by the recent shake-up, Bob had allowed himself to get lazy, step away from the information, consider the personal side of it all. Now, he was trying to find his customary indifference to turn the real-world intrigues into an insulated and anonymous game. He was letting too many factors compromise his capacity to play.

The answer had begun to fall into place about forty minutes ago when he had decided to refocus the search. Instead of tying everything into Schenten, he began to trace even the most remote connections among each of the central players. The cross-referencing had provided one very bizarre possibility: Eisenreich, a hypothetical manuscript that Pescatore had spent half his life researching and which seemed to unravel the girl's dying word in Montana. Somehow, the connection among Tieg, Sedgewick, and Votapek was wrapped up in a little book that no one had ever proved to exist.

Uncharacteristically, Bob had decided to keep things to himself.

The price for such resolve, however, was the burden of responsibility—the onus to piece together information that somehow explained the probable death of one academic, the disappearance of another, and the reemergence of an operative so fragile that she might not come back this time round.

It was a role he was not accustomed to playing.

The gentle drop of descent woke her, the slight shift in her stomach enough to unsettle a light sleep. She hadn't dreamt—at least nothing to get in the way—but she knew her subconscious mind had continued to sift through the pieces that had begun to come together. Always sifting. Always alert. She maintained a curious faith in her subconscious, recognizing that she, like everyone else, used no more than 3 percent of her brain at any one time. She trusted the other 97 percent to get the job done if left to itself. That's why sleep had always been so important.

The trouble was that, most of the time, her subconscious kept the answers hidden, so much so that she would have to rely on instinct to reveal the necessary truths at the appropriate moments. That meant working on her feet, trusting herself to tap into the arsenal waiting just below the surface.

It was the way she had always worked. She recalled Berlin nine years ago, an arctic night when she had discovered one Oskar Teplic, a diminutive lieutenant in the East German Stasi, a man who had slipped through, evaded the Soviet net drawing in its faithful as the wall came tumbling down. Even then, Teplic had given the empire only two years. He had tracked her, told her he needed a way out, but not to the West—just out, to a life he could control on his own. And he would be grateful. Sarah had seen the possibilities at once. Three days later, Teplic had died at her hands, and Feric had been born. A plan of simplicity in the abstract, of pure instinct in practice. Invented intrigues, *official* papers—information revealed at crucial moments to confuse the easy dupes of a crumbling East German secret police. *Facts*— incomplete as they might be—with which to prod, surprise, weaken her opponent. They might be only distant reflections of a greater truth, but they were enough to convince an adversary that he stood at a disadvantage. Enough to create fear and self-doubt.

Enough from a miserly brain that liked to hoard the discoveries of the subconscious ninety-seven.

Xander rubbed the back of his neck, the touch of icy fingers to tender skin a jolt to his system. His hands had always been that way, reduced to frozen pincers when lost in the turning and scribbling of pages. The dim glow of the lounge's overhead lights was making the notes a bit difficult to read, more so given Xander's impatience to board Lufthansa 202, the 5:35 flight to Frankfurt. He was tired, but satisfied, having managed all but two of the twenty-four pages, the Italian quite readable.

The first volume of the manuscript had come together far more quickly than he had initially thought, Feric granting him an hour before shuttling them off to Heathrow. At first, he had simply given himself over to the novelty of discovery, the excitement of first view, but his enthusiasm had been short-lived. Had there been nothing to distract him from the easy fascination of scholarly analysis, he might have enjoyed the reading. But his thoughts returned again and again to Votapek, Tieg, Sedgewick—the men who meant to violate the theory by channeling it into practice. It was all too easy to see how Washington had been merely a dry run, a twentieth-century extrapolation of a sixteenth-century theory. No longer a missing link in the neat canon of political thought, *On Supremacy* stood apart as a manual of manipulation and dominance, its modern ambition coloring every page with a dark reality that corrupted Eisenreich's daring and savvy.

Once or twice, Xander had allowed himself to look beyond the theory to the man. And each time, he had been forced to admit that there was something compelling, a certainty in the way the monk had organized his ideas. As if he truly believed it was God's will that he set it to paper. Xander had to hope that no such divine inspiration was driving the most recent trio of disciples.

More troubling, though, was the reference to a fourth man, someone behind the others—someone who pulled the strings. What he read made Xander all the more wary, not just for himself, but for Sarah. He knew she had stepped into something more dangerous, more immediate than either of them had imagined. *"Don't worry about me."* He was finding it more and more difficult to do.

"They are opening the gate," piped in Feric. "Put the papers—"

"I know . . . put them away." Xander had heard the phrase perhaps half a dozen times in the last hour, Feric insistent that the manuscript remain out of sight. So be it.

"I hope they have something other than the peanuts," mumbled Feric as the two men joined the line for boarding. "Very messy. Pretzels are so much neater."

NEW YORK, MARCH 4, 12:18 P.M. The view from the Brooklyn Bridge was splendid, lower Manhattan rising in clipped angles from the concrete. Traffic was light, the single-lane detour causing only minor delays. Behind the cones, three men worked with purpose on a huge tear in the tarmac, an emergency repair before rush hour. Strangely enough, the men had anticipated the call. Perhaps it was because they had been the ones to create the gash two hours earlier—a small device dropped from a speeding car. Two of the men had been with road repair for over three months. Somehow, their schedules had made them the most logical choice for the bridge maintenance. The last of the trio had flown in this morning. Demolitions expert.

They had carved out a neat sliver of road—four feet wide, two feet long—with a two-inch gulley running from it to the center of the bridge. No more than six inches deep, the hole now held four briquettes and a tiny black box, a rubber antenna stretching from its side to the surface. The gulley oozed with a yellow liquid resin, already beginning to gel. Slowly, the men began to spread a thick mixture of tar and gravel over everything, careful to keep the antenna flat along the rising surface. Within ten minutes, they had completed the repairs, only a tiny nub of antenna—nestled just below the guardrail—evidence of their work.

The demolitions man picked up his bag and started for the car parked at the entrance to the bridge. He knew it would be a long day. After all, Manhattan had so many bridges and tunnels in need of such *repairs*.

≱

They had changed planes somewhere in the Carolinas for the hop to Votapek's island, a double-prop aircraft fitted with water skis that now bounced along the surf toward the waiting pier. The single house, flat and wide along the bluff, seemed to rise from the rocks as the plane coasted in. A gentle rap of metal on wood told all that they had come to the end of their journey; thick air invaded the cabin as the door opened, a peach swath of sun angling its way onto the curtain that separated passengers from pilot. Once outside, the rocking of the dock helped to propel the three arrivals along, the even roll of wood and water sending them from side to side. Above, a steep incline of jagged rock climbed toward a grass plain that spread like thick swirling carpet in front of the house. The only access, a funicular that waited to the left at the end of the dock.

It was close quarters on the ride up, sounds of cable straining under the weight. As the car jolted to a stop, the smaller of the two men slid back the glass-paneled door and directed Sarah toward a gravel path. The house, perhaps thirty feet back from the cliff, eyed her silently as she moved along the narrow strip that seemed unwilling to break either in or out, content in its mindless circularity. As the front of the house disappeared to her left, an open gazebo came into view, a man-made jetty extending beyond the cliff.

There, between two far columns, stood a lone figure, his narrow shoulders rigid as he peered out at a tranquil sea. He turned. His eyes seemed to convey a certain restraint, his body unnaturally stiff as he moved to greet her. He was a far cry from the Anton Votapek Sarah had expected.

"Good evening, Ms. Carter," he said, pointing a wiry hand toward the two floral-print chairs—thick plastic with overstuffed backs—that stood on either side of a small metalwork table. Sarah noticed a pitcher and two glasses at the ready. "Won't you have a seat?" he asked.

She nodded and moved to the chairs. *Carter,* she thought. *He must have tapped the phone when I called Alison.* A second man appeared and pulled the seat out for her; she sat as he retreated to a shadowed corner. Votapek remained standing, clearly uncomfortable with the preliminary introductions. His suit and tie, though out of place in the tropical surroundings, were perfect for his slight frame, a body ill-designed for polo shirts and

Bermuda shorts. She could tell he disliked the scrutiny. "I trust the trip wasn't too difficult?" he asked.

"Not at all."

"A bit unexpected, I would imagine."

"The location perhaps." Sarah settled into the chair. "We needed to meet. Where and how weren't all that important."

He stared at her; he had not anticipated her candor. "I see." He sat and poured himself a tall glass of the lemonade. "Can I offer you some?"

"I've had my fill for the day," she replied.

"Yes, of course." He placed the pitcher on the table and sat back, content to gaze out at the clouds. "Alison is very fond of lemonade. Mine is a bit sweeter."

"I'm sure you didn't bring me all this way—"

"True," he broke in, his tone haltingly casual. "I brought you here because . . . I'm somewhat concerned about your visit with Ms. Krogh."

"Somewhat?" Sarah replied. "You've gone to a great deal of trouble for something you're only *somewhat* concerned about."

"Perhaps," he answered, adjusting his jacket. "Perhaps more than that."

"As I recall, you were far more than only *somewhat* concerned during our first encounter in New York. Granted, it's more pleasant here, but I'm sure the message is the same."

Votapek turned to her, a creasing of his brow. "Excuse me?"

"Your *first* warning," she answered, "in the alley. I trust those men have recovered."

He continued to stare at her. "You have me at a loss, Ms. Carter."

Sarah returned the stare; Votapek looked genuinely perplexed. "And I suppose you're equally unaware of events in Florence."

His expression had not changed. "Florence? . . . Is this leading somewhere?"

Again, she waited. "You have no idea what I'm talking about, do you?"

He blinked several times. "None." He brought the glass to his lips.

Sarah watched his movements; they remained stiff, but no more so than before. She had learned long ago to detect even the smallest traces of deception—the subtle shift in the eyes, in the choice of words, even in the angle of the body. But Votapek displayed none of the telltale signs. It was as if he truly knew nothing of her two run-ins with Eisenreich. "I find that hard to believe," she said, suddenly far more wary.

"What you believe is not my concern. Nor is your private life."

"So you flew me down here—"

"I've told you why I brought you here," he continued, his gaze far more pointed as he turned to her, an impatience in his voice. "I'm interested in Ms. Krogh. I'll ask again—*how* did you find her?"

Sarah had to make sense of the last three minutes. Florence, Pescatore, New York—could they actually mean *nothing* to him? Could he possibly . . .

Out of the loop. The phrase broke through, a flash of the subconscious ninety-seven to lend order to the questions stumbling through her mind. *Out of the loop.* A lifetime ago, she had described herself in the same way in order to distance herself, remain a free spirit disentangled from structures and systems. *Amman.* An operative secure only when autonomous. For Votapek, though, it made no sense. He was a vital part of the Eisenreich structure. Separation would only blur his focus; lack of communication would only open him to attack. So how was it that he could remain unaware of the mad scramble that had been the last week of her life? *How?*

The man in the shadows shifted, a stretching of shoulders that drew her attention. He had a strong upper body, thick neck, though his head seemed too small for his large frame. Oddly serene, he stood off to the side, oblivious to the cat-and-mouse game playing out in front of him. The perfect disciple, she thought. The perfect tool.

Sarah glanced back at her host, his lips pursed at his glass. And in that look, instinct and fact joined together to offer one resounding answer: Votapek was no different from the man in the shadows. In that instant, Sarah saw the world of Eisenreich as it was, as it *had* to be: designed to keep each man insulated and thus protected. Tieg, Sedgewick, and Votapek. Men who were isolated; men unaware. Votapek didn't know about New York or Florence because he didn't *have* to know. Someone else had managed that.

It was a weakness she could exploit.

"You'll have to be a bit more specific than that," she said, far more casual than only moments before.

⚔

Feric was finishing off his third bag of pretzels, a cup of beer perched at the edge of his tray as his fingers dug angrily into the helpless little bag.

"The rest is a bit more complex," said Xander, nibbling at some cheese.

"Then simplify." Feric wet his fingers and dabbed at the crumbs on the tray. "Anyone can make something complex, Doctor. The mark of real genius is to make the complex simple." He swallowed.

"I suppose. But I'm no—"

"The *mark* of genius," Feric added, "not genius itself."

Xander smiled. Six minutes later, he summed up as best he could. "It's a clever theory. He's not describing a cabal of political conspirators; he's talking about mass manipulation of the three dominant spheres within the state—the political, the economic, and the social. Considering how well he understands state structure, it goes a good deal beyond simple deception."

"Spheres? I don't follow."

"He's rethinking the way states are put together," Xander explained. "In the sixteenth century, the state was discussed in terms of its *political* role. Eisenreich expands that definition and includes the other two spheres as equal partners. That idea doesn't really get developed for another three hundred years. Even then, the idea of *controlling* the spheres is beyond most people. The breakthrough with Eisenreich is that he recognizes that to control the state, the leadership has to control each sphere *independently*. One man to one sphere. And he takes the word *independently very* seriously. They stay virtually unconcerned with the goings-on in the other spheres. Theoretically, they remain blissfully unaware of one another."

"But that would only create confusion," said Feric.

"That's what makes it so clever," smiled Xander.

NEW ORLEANS, MARCH 4, 11:35 A.M. ✍ Pushing off from the underwater pilaster, the young disciple of Eisenreich—scuba equipment having replaced the coveralls from his jaunt to Dulles just over a week ago—swam to the far side of the pier and attached the explosives to a shallow girder. As he had done with the previous thirty-eight packages placed throughout the underbelly of the industrial wharf, he affixed a small black box to its side; a light flashed green, then yellow. A moment later, the detonator on his belt flashed red. The relay was secured, the frequency established. He then checked the gauge of his air tank—sixteen minutes. Plenty of time to place the remaining four devices and calibrate their frequencies. He flipped on his side and dove deep toward the next pier.

He did not, however, take into account the sudden roll of the current, the wake from a ship somewhere above that threw him against the pier's jagged ridge. His air tank was the first to hit, the immediate squeal of puncture echoing within the water. A moment later, a second wave slammed him into the cement and steel, again his tank taking the full force of impact.

The squeal now turned to a groan, the loss of air instantaneous. More troubling, though, was the release of pressure that sent a burst of water to the surface, a signal to draw the attention of anyone above.

He had no choice, though. He would have to surface.

Releasing the tank from his shoulders, he watched as it sank, a moment later the pack in his hands following, four sets of explosives drifting aimlessly to the deep. He then glanced up to the surface. The reflection of a lone figure undulated in the water above. His only choice was the pocket of air beneath the pier. Slipping through the girders, he made his way up, breaking the surface without a sound. He stifled his breath. And listened.

He would wait for the dark before venturing out.

✄

"No," Votapek answered, no less on edge. "I would like to know how you found Alison. I would also like to know why you made up all that rubbish about my sending you to talk with her. Naturally, Alison believed you."

"I mentioned your name," Sarah said as she reached for the lemonade, "because I knew it was the only way she'd see me."

"And how did you know that?"

Sarah stopped pouring. "It's what I'm paid to know, Mr. Votapek."

"I see," he answered. "And who pays you to know such things?" He placed his glass on the table. "The *government?*"

Sarah allowed herself a smile as she shook her head. "The government couldn't afford my services."

"'Couldn't afford . . .'" He began to press. "How did you get that number?"

"How?" she said softly, knowing it was time to offer a glimmer of the truth. "It comes from a list," she continued, her glass now finding the table, "a list that names fourteen children, ten of whom are dead." She paused. "Actually *twelve* of whom are dead. The last two are recently deceased." She looked directly at him. "But you knew that, Mr. Votapek, didn't you?"

Far more wary, he answered, "Again, you have me at a loss, Ms. Carter."

"I'm sure I don't, Mr. Votapek."

He waited before speaking. "Clearly, you *are* with the government, otherwise, how would you have that information?"

"Let's not be naïve. Do you think anyone in Washington has any idea who Grant and Eggart are? Or how the vice president is connected to all of this?" Again she paused, waiting to see the concern register in his eyes. "If they did, you and I wouldn't be having this conversation."

His jaw tensed. "Those files . . . were sealed."

"True," she answered, "but they aren't the only source of information, are they?" A mode of attack began to form in her mind. Before he could answer, she added, "The files never mentioned Brainbrook, Colorado, or Winamet, Texas, yet we both know that they're far more interesting locations than Tempsten, New York." She let the words settle before continuing. "How did I get the number, Mr. Votapek? I think that's something you already know."

He looked at her for a long moment. "No one would have given you that information."

"Then how do you explain my having it?"

Votapek began to speak, then stopped.

"Don't let that concern you," she said, eager to discover how isolated he was. "What *should* concern you," she added, reaching into her bag and pulling out Alison's videotape, "is this."

Again, Votapek said nothing.

"It's a tape that makes clear why Brainbrook, Winamet, and several other sites are so important. A tape, Mr. Votapek, that charts a rather interesting history. You're familiar with the tape, aren't you?" She waited for him to nod. "Certain people want to know why Alison Krogh had a copy of it."

Votapek's eyes grew wide, a look of disbelief etched across his face.

"This tape," Sarah continued, placing it in her bag, "shouldn't have been in Ms. Krogh's hands at all. She should never have had access to a *Prefect Release.*" She paused. "From a certain perspective, it looks very sloppy."

" 'From a . . .' " his eyes shot up to her. "That tape was secured. I don't know how—" He stopped. "Whose perspective are we talking about?"

"Another question for which I'm sure you have an answer." Sarah glanced over her shoulder in the direction of the second man. "I think it would be best to leave it at that."

Votapek stared at her. What had been apprehension at first now bordered on distraction. She had struck a nerve; the hint of self-doubt, his shoulders slow to settle on the soft cushion of the chair. Almost to himself, he asked, "Alison had a tape?" He then turned, his eyes on Sarah, his voice flat as he spoke. "That will be all, Thomas." Without hesitation, the second man started off along the gravel path; a moment later, Votapek stood and walked toward the lip of the gazebo. He stared at the water below, waiting for the man's footsteps to fade, then turned. "Who are you, Ms. Carter?"

✄

"Why?" asked Feric. "Such realms would inevitably come into conflict. You would have the worst of the old Soviet empire."

"*Theoretically*," said Xander. "Unless one man stands behind the three *prefects*—Eisenreich's term for the heads of each sphere—and monitors them. That figure is his *overseer*. The basic structure looks a little like this." Xander picked up three crackers and a roll and placed them on the edge of his tray. "Let's say the three crackers are the prefects. To you and me, they seem totally separate. The roll," which he held about six inches above the tray, "coordinates the crackers without letting on that all four are actually working together. In other words, all we see are the three crackers, and we believe they're autonomous. They themselves know that they're *not*, but they have little idea what's going on in the other spheres. That's where the roll comes in, hovering above to make sure everything else runs smoothly." He flipped to a page in the stack and read. " 'In this way, republican virtue will blanket the government because power will seem divided among the many. The neat appearance of checks and balances . . . will satisfy the whim of the people.' "

"How wonderful."

"That division," added Xander, "ties in perfectly with what Eisenreich sees as the state's need to alter its appearance from time to time."

"Explain."

"Well, depending on what the people want at a given time—democracy, aristocracy, or even tyranny—one of the spheres asserts itself to appease that whim. The structure never changes, just the surface. So, you have a core group—the prefects—who determine policy within their spheres. You have one figure outside their spheres—the *overseer*—who makes sure that the prefects don't step on one another's toes. Meanwhile, the people are convinced that they're *not* being manipulated, because the three spheres appear to be acting independently. The people become happy dupes, and the four boys at the top run the show, taking the state in whatever direction they want." A look of concern crept across his face.

"If the last few chapter titles are any indication, that direction is not terribly inviting."

"And these spheres are controlled by our three friends."

"Who else? Plus, the whole thing rests on the assumption that the people believe everything is fine. That means you have to manipulate them. And that's where a highly developed system of education comes in."

"Votapek." Feric finished off his beer.

"Exactly." Xander paused. "They're following this thing to the letter."

"There is, of course, an obvious weakness," Feric added. "Cut off the head—get rid of this overseer—and the whole thing falls apart."

"*Theoretically* . . . The problem is, they're not working theoretically. What they did in Washington and Chicago coordinates perfectly with the last few chapter titles. Those episodes last week were a perfect test run for creating political chaos. And what just happened with the grain market, the economic chaos." He paused. "Imagine when they try it on a larger scale."

"Actually, it's Trent," she replied.

"I see," said Votapek, his disquiet more apparent. "So many surprises."

"It was a precaution. My role, however, isn't important. The point is, I'm here because several people have a great deal at stake."

"Several people? . . . Now, *you'll* have to be more specific, Ms. *Trent.*"

"Jonas Tieg and Laurence Sedgewick," she answered.

He raised his eyebrows slightly and then nodded. "I see."

Sarah waited for more of a reaction; when none came, she said, "But those aren't the interesting names, are they?" She knew she had no choice but to play the final gambit. "*Eisenreich* is." She paused to give the word its full force. "Does that answer any questions?"

Votapek stood frozen, his small frame silhouetted against a backdrop of sea and sun. "Where did you get that name?"

"Assuming that there are only a select group of people who understand its relevance," she replied, "the *where* doesn't seem all that important."

"Humor me, Ms. Trent. *Where?*"

Sarah stared at Votapek and then reached for her glass. "I was approached," she answered.

"Approached? By whom?"

She slowly brought the glass to her lips and took a sip. "By someone who cares about the manuscript." And, recalling a word from her conversation with Alison—a word uttered as if a coded signal—she added, "By someone who cares about the *process.*"

Votapek's reaction was immediate. His head snapped toward her, eyes wide. "The *process?*" he whispered, clasping his hands together and moving slowly back to the table. "You say he approached you?"

The question carried none of the authority of only moments ago. Instead, Votapek seemed to be asking more for himself than for her. *He approached you?* she thought. Not Tieg, not Sedgewick—their names had prompted only a raise of the eyebrow. No, something else was responsible for his reaction. Something . . . or *someone* else. It suddenly struck her. A *fourth* man?

"That's unimportant," she added, "unless you have doubts about Sedgewick or Tieg?"

"Doubts?" he answered, still recovering from the onslaught. "That's what you were doing in Tempsten—the extent of *my* loyalty, the depth of my *faith.*"

"Alison raises some very difficult questions, especially given how much she knows." Sarah's tone remained even.

"How much she knows?" The words again were half-whispered. "Alison is a child. I don't know how she got the tape—" He cut himself off and looked at Sarah. "The man who approached you, Ms. Trent—would he have a name?"

Sarah stared directly into Votapek's eyes, no sign of hesitation. "As I said—Eisenreich. That was the name I was given."

"The name you were given?" An impatience colored his tone.

"Clearly, it's not the man's real name." She knew it would be dangerous to press the advantage. Confirmation was enough. "And I would prefer to keep it that way. I'm not being paid enough to take that sort of risk."

"I see. And why would this *Eisenreich* want to hire your services?"

"Because I'm very good at what I do, Mr. Votapek."

"And that would be?"

Sarah sipped at her glass. "Given your access to State Department records, I thought you would know exactly who I am."

"Clearly not, Ms. *Carter.* And since we're alone, there's no harm in you bringing me up-to-date."

A single white gull appeared and perched on the low wall. Sarah kept her gaze on the bird as she spoke. "Five months ago, I was contacted by a researcher at the State Department—"

"Ah, then you *are* with the government," Votapek broke in.

"If you dig deep enough, you'll find that, until seven years ago, my status was quite different." Another glimmer of the truth.

"Meaning?"

"I was in the field."

Votapek paused. "*In the field.* So you were some kind of—"

"The term is irrelevant," she interrupted without raising her voice. "Until 1990, I split my time between Europe and South America; during the Gulf War, I was in Syria and Jordan. I'm surprised you were unaware."

"Don't be." Votapek's patience was growing thin. "Syria and Jordan—in what capacity?"

"My expertise was infiltration—political and military cliques whose aim was to subvert American policy. My job was to create internal chaos so as to destroy them. My last assignment was General Safad in Jordan."

"Safad?" Votapek had stopped, his eyes riveted on Sarah. "You mean—"

"The coup attempt." Her face showed no emotion. "Yes."

"You don't strike me as the James Bond type."

"I'll take that as a compliment."

"You can take it any way you like." Votapek was doing little to hide his anxiety. "And then what happened? A breach of trust, the *rogue* spy waiting to return to the field? The story's a little dated, don't you think?"

"It is, and it's not mine," her words precise, spoken without feeling. "My career ended when I lost my hold on reality." A strange emptiness washed over her eyes as she looked up at him, "I went over the edge, Mr. Votapek. In my department, it's called 'dropping.' Sorry to disappoint you, but judging from my visit with Alison, I suspect you're familiar with what I'm talking about."

Votapek let a long moment pass before speaking. "I see," his tone a mixture of uncertainty and self-reproach.

"There's no need for concern. I've recovered."

"Yes." Votapek was clearly uncomfortable. "Evidently."

TEMPE, MARCH 4, 9:40 A.M. ✍ The smell of freshly brewed coffee lingered in the air, the telltale sign of a change in shift at the operations center. Thirty computer terminals, subdivided into rows of five, defined the various sections of the cavernous room. Samantha Doyle, an employee of six weeks, sat in front of one of the screens, waiting for the call she had been told to expect at *9:50:45*. The light on her screen flashed green.

"I'll take this one, Karen," she said, adjusting her headset. "Good morning. Southwestern Bell. This is Samantha. How may I help you?"

"Yes, good morning," came the reply, "I've been having trouble with my phone. I keep receiving calls for a Mr. Eisen."

On time to the second. "All right, sir. I do need to ask if you want this call to be recorded by my supervisor?"

"No" was the answer. "I'm sure we can handle this ourselves."

Samantha moved her laser pen to the red recording icon on the screen; a moment later, the icon vanished. It was to be a private call. Immediately, she double-clicked her mouse and watched as a grid of the region's phone lines appeared, each of the central relay points flashing its routing code beneath. Without waiting for confirmation, a series of input commands streamed from the voice on the other end of the line, Samantha quick to enter them, uncertain what any of it meant. Every so often, she glanced up at the supervisor's booth to her right. No one was paying any attention. Within a minute, a small box opened in the lower-left-hand corner of the screen, zeros and ones racing by at breakneck speed. She continued to type as she was instructed until, in a sudden shift, every routing code for every relay point on the grid changed. The voice now asked her to confirm the new sets of numbers. Half a minute later, she had checked each one. A final string of commands followed.

"Now enter."

Samantha watched as the original codes appeared again on the screen; it was as if nothing had been changed. "The routing is back," she replied.

"Excellent," said the voice. And with that, the line disengaged.

⚜

It was time to lend the story greater reality. "There isn't a great deal to expect after endless months of recovery. You don't simply ask to be reassigned. Not that I wanted a new station. To be honest, I didn't know what I wanted." Sarah let her eyes drift to Votapek, a hint of a smile on her lips. "There's the cliché you've been looking for. Another? I was angry, confused—not, I'm told, unusual for someone in my situation. After everything we'd done, Hussein was as powerful as ever, and Jordan was a nightmare ready to explode. You can imagine how that might have made me feel. Everyone said it was natural to be angry, that I'd *work* through it. Their idea of work was rather vague. The man who approached me gave that work direction. How he knew to approach me, I don't know—or why, for that matter. I'm no zealot, Mr. Votapek—and I don't care to know who is—but things in that manuscript made sense."

"You've *seen* the manuscript?" He could do little to hide his surprise.

"Bits and pieces. Enough to spark an interest. Remember, chaos is my expertise." The reaction, though slight, was there, in his eyes, and Sarah saw it. "Not to mention that he knew a great deal about me."

Votapek nodded, placed his glass on the table, and moved back to the wall.

"The first meetings were casual, harmless—"

"All right," he said, turning to her, "let's assume that you are who you say you are. You still haven't told me what you were sent to do."

"Confirmation."

"Whatever that might mean." He did little to mask his resentment. "So you *did* expect this meeting. You were planning on it."

"In so many words, yes."

He nodded, his eyes scanning the horizon. After nearly half a minute, he asked, "What exactly happened in New York and Florence?"

"The first, as I said, was some kind of warning. The second . . . is a bit more complicated."

"Explain."

She knew he would find out eventually. "Have you ever heard of a Professor Alexander Jaspers?" Votapek shook his head. "He was in Florence looking for the manuscript."

"The manuscript was in *Florence?*"

"Not the original. The German translation. It's been recovered."

"The German?"

"I assumed you had that information."

Ignoring the barb, he asked, "What happened to this . . . Jaspers?"

Facts coupled with instincts. Sarah spoke. "Two men arrived to make it very clear they didn't want Jaspers to get near the manuscript."

"I don't see the problem."

"*I* had been sent to monitor Jaspers, and I had no idea who they were."

Votapek looked confused. "You're telling me that these two—"

"Appeared out of nowhere. We have no idea who sent them."

Votapek took a moment. "You're sure this had to do with the manuscript?"

"No question. A day and a half later, a man named Bruno Feric contacted Jaspers, and the two of them disappeared."

"And you say you have no idea who these two men were."

"None whatsoever."

Another pause. "This Feric—why is he of any concern?"

"Bruno Feric was a lieutenant in the East German Stasi—a highly skilled assassin with links to several political groups in Europe and the Middle East. After the Soviet collapse, he began to hire out his services."

"You're certain it was this Feric who contacted Jaspers?"

"I know the man." Now she paused. "I was the one who got him out of East Germany in 1989."

Votapek's jaw again tightened. "The question remains—why should any of this concern *me?*"

"Clearly, someone is very eager to keep me from doing my job."

"Your *job*, Ms. Trent, remains somewhat unclear."

"Does it really, Mr. Votapek?"

The momentary look of puzzlement on his face quickly gave way to an icy stare. "You thought that someone was *me?*"

"It still might be."

"*Please*, Ms. Trent. Are you implying that someone within—"

"I'm not implying anything." She now paused for effect. "But it would seem that someone, or some group, is making up their own rules."

"Explain."

Sarah spoke deliberately, measuring each word. "The *first trial*. Maybe someone's getting a little overanxious. Maybe someone wants to accelerate the *process*." She let the words settle before adding, "Or maybe that's been the idea from the start. It's one of the things I was sent to find out."

"*One* moment," said Votapek, his eyes fixed, controlled. "You're saying that someone, someone like Jonas or Laurence—"

"Your names, not mine."

"Is attempting to move ahead of schedule?" He shook his head, the idea gaining clarity. "That's impossible, given the need for coordination. *Ludicrous*. I know these men, Ms. Trent."

"Twice, Mr. Votapek. *Twice* someone has tried to stop me. In New York and in Florence. So I must be getting in someone's way. The fact that I'm here tells you that I'm not the only one concerned." She waited. "Eisenreich wants to make sure we're all on the same page." Again, she paused. "That's what I'm here to confirm."

Votapek remained silent as he sat on the low wall. He stared out at the lapping water below. He then turned to her. "I *know* these men, Ms. Trent."

Sarah could see him losing focus; she knew the conversation had run its course, the seeds planted, Votapek having taken the bait. "I hope you do." She stood. "Which, as I see it, leaves very little else for us to discuss. I will, of course, pass on the information."

He did not bother to answer. The gull flapped its wings in a flurry of motion, disappearing below the cliff almost instantaneously. "You will, of course, keep me apprised of your . . . analysis."

His request caught her off guard. It was nothing less than an admission of concern, a hint of suspicion of his fellow players. "I don't know if we'll be in touch again." Sarah smoothed out her skirt and reached for her bag. "This meeting is to be kept strictly private. No external confirmation." She smiled. "That's what I was told. He said you would understand."

"Of course," nodded Votapek. He stood. "My pilot will fly you back." Sarah started toward the gravel path. "Ms. Trent," Votapek interrupted; she stopped and turned. "You still remain something of a mystery."

Sarah looked directly into his eyes. "As it should be, Mr. Votapek. As it should be."

⚜

"My friend and I are taking a few days to visit some family, and then on to the south and the Zugspitze. Maybe some climbing." Feric's German showed no traces of the usual accent and instead lilted along with the thicker sing-song quality of Austrian Hochdeutch.

The official continued to examine their passports. "And you were in England for . . ."

"Business." Feric continued to crane over the high desk in the assumed pose of a harmless, if anxious, traveler.

"Yes," answered the guard, flipping through the weathered books, only once looking up to match pictures with faces, "and you return to Austria in . . ."

"A week. Ten days at the most."

A few moments of well-practiced silence, a quick burst of mechanical stamping, and the two holidaymakers were on their way. Xander had been to Frankfurt only twice and had forgotten the impressive layout of the self-contained monolith. He continued to stare up at the vaulted dome as they headed down the central escalator. Car-rental booths lined the walls below, each staffed by a garishly togged attendant, the glaring yellows, blues, and reds of the international competitors vying for attention. Feric moved to one of the indistinguishable carrels and placed his case on the counter.

"A car, please." Feric's German had now become stained with a northern Italian accent. Xander couldn't help but stare at him, the stance, the head cocked to one side, even the easy posture of the hands a far cry from the nervous Austrian of only minutes before. He watched as Feric dug through his pockets for a half-crushed pack of cigarettes—from Milan. Xander had to smile at the precision, no less so at the simple gesture with which the little man brought the cigarette to his mouth, only to be reprimanded by the rental agent, a finger pointing to the large NO SMOKING sign on a nearby wall.

"Ah, sì." A casual shrug, the cigarette remaining unlit between his fingers as he smiled up at Xander, pouring forth in impeccable Italian, "What can you do?" A knowing smile. "At least the Spanish let you have a good smoke while you wait for them to bang away at their computers." He turned back to the agent, and again in labored German added, "We have now just been within Spain, and in there they have smoking allowed."

The German continued to scan the screen. "This is not Spain, sir." Feric nodded affably. "Your passports, please."

Without a blink, Feric looked up at Xander and nodded for him to give the man the documents. Xander stood frozen until Feric, in a sign of apology, placed the cigarette in his mouth and fumbled in his jacket. A moment later, with a short laugh, he pulled two new passports from a pocket, handed them to the agent, and said, "No, me, I am having them."

Xander continued to watch the performance; the agent, cool against the backdrop of Italian noise, typed away. Within a minute, he placed an envelope and a set of keys on the counter, Feric nodding and shrugging, penning indecipherable initials at all the appropriate marks.

"*Sind wir fertig?*" Feric's extended roll of the *r* and the aspiration on the final *g* forced a pained smile from the agent.

"Yes, all is complete."

Pulling his case to his side, Feric placed the documents in his pocket, nodded again to the agent, and said, "First, some food." Then, hooking his arm under Xander's, he led them off into the underground maze. Five minutes later, they were in front of an Italian restaurant, the sign above in deep red curves, the name lost to letters in the shape of the seven hills of Rome.

"I always make it a point to eat here if I have the time. Excellent manicotti. You will not find another like it outside Rome." The old Feric had returned, the precision of the English the telltale sign, but somehow softened by a surprising remnant of the buoyant Italian alter ego. With jaunty step, he moved through the glass door and into the empty dining room. Forgoing three perfectly acceptable tables, he settled on a fourth along the near wall, dropping his bag to the floor as he sat. Xander joined him as the maître d' placed the menus on the table before ambling back to his perch by the door. Ceiling-high mirrors lent the thin strip a well-contrived girth, the clever placement of lamps and candles adding to the illusion. Feric watched himself tear off a thousand pieces of bread.

"That was quite a performance." Xander placed his elbows on the table, his back uncomfortable against the straight edge of the chair.

"You are too kind." There was a hint of self-satisfaction in the way Feric gnawed away, betraying an unexpected delight in his own bravura. "A boisterous Italian. He sees far too many every week to remember us."

"You enjoyed it nonetheless."

"Naturally. That is why I can be so convincing." A waiter arrived, took the order for two manicottis and a bottle of the house red, and vanished as quickly as he had appeared. "That expression on your face, Doctor, when I asked for the passports—now *that* I truly enjoyed."

The waiter returned with a carafe, Feric maintaining his uncharacteristic playfulness, eyebrows raised in anticipation of an Italian wine served by a German restaurateur. Both he and Xander were pleasantly surprised by the rich flavor that washed down the stray pieces of bread.

"I'm impressed," nodded Xander. "An excellent choice."

"Yes. It is at that."

"'In the midst of the hunt,'" piped in the academic, "'find a place to refuel—a good meal, some wine.' Lesson—what are we up to?"

"If that is the way you want to see it, yes. All of that can be very useful." Feric took a long sip of the wine. "However, at this particular time, it is much simpler than that. We have twenty-six minutes before we must leave, and I am hungry. They prepare the food here in record time."

The precision in the answer was a bit much, even by Feric's standards. "Twenty-six?" asked Xander. "What difference does it make?"

"The train to Göttingen leaves at seven twenty-seven, twenty-two minutes." Good to its billing, the food arrived, Feric quick to sprinkle heaps of cheese on the already-hidden tubes of pasta; he stopped when he noticed Xander's expression. "You did not think we were actually going to *use* the car, did you? It is the easiest thing to trace." When Xander did not answer, Feric continued. "If they are not that clever, then we have merely wasted fifteen minutes. On the other hand, if they are better at this than you think, they will eventually discover who rented the little Fiat. They found you at the library in London; why should they not be as successful here?" Feric dared a large forkfull of the manicotti. He continued, teeth splattered with marinara sauce. "Which brings up a question that has been troubling me since this afternoon." He wiped the sauce from his chin. "How did they know where you were going?"

The question caught Xander off guard. *How* Eisenreich had found him in London seemed slightly less important than the fact that they *had* found him. And the manuscript. "I have no idea. I assumed—"

"There are only two possibilities. Either Eisenreich has vast resources with which to trace a man—highly unlikely, given their obvious inability to keep track of you—or"—he reached for his glass—"you have not been as careful as you might think." He looked up to measure Xander's reaction.

The young scholar sat motionless, pasta frozen between plate and mouth. Not sure whether he had just been accused of stupidity or something worse, Xander momentarily was at a loss for words.

Feric saw no reason to press the point. "I do not think you have been *aware* of how it might have happened, but you might do well to consider the days since Florence. Perhaps Milan."

"Milan?" Images from the last week raced through his mind. "I didn't *know* about London until I'd read Carlo's notes. And I didn't get those until Florence. Nothing about the Danzhoeffer Collection—"

"Fine," Feric interrupted, seeing the mounting concern on his companion's face, "then you can dismiss Milan."

"And until I met you, I was flying under my *own* passport. It's not that difficult to trace someone."

"Granted. But why did they appear at the library? Certainly *that* was not in your passport. Why not the British Museum, or Cambridge, or any number of other places? Why *London*, and why *that* library?"

"Well . . . it wouldn't be that difficult to find out that I'd done most of my work at the Institute four years ago."

"Where is the logic in that?" Feric shook his head and again embarked on a slab of pasta. "Pure coincidence. Working at the library *four years ago* has no relation to the manuscript being there *now.*"

"Couldn't they have had someone waiting at the Institute?"

"For what purpose? And even so, you yourself said the bald man looked utterly surprised to run into you. Am I mistaken?"

Xander had to think. "He did seem . . . shocked. Then again, I could be wrong. I was running from you; I'd just found the manuscript—"

"All of that is true. Does it change your impression of the man?"

Xander slowly shook his head. "No. He was genuinely surprised."

"Exactly. And from the description Ms. Trent gave me, I spotted him before your encounter. It seems quite clear that he was there for the manuscript, not for you." Feric nodded and ripped off a piece of bread. "No. There must be something else—or *someone* else who knew where the manuscript would be. Someone who had access to Pescatore's notes and who could send our bald friend to London, regardless of your presence there—past or present."

"Someone *else?*" The words made no sense. "There were only two people who knew what those notes said—myself and Sarah."

"And"—Feric paused, his eyes fixed on Xander's—"the person to whom you sent the copy in New York."

A sudden tightness crept up through his neck. "That's different," he answered, recalling how long it had taken him to convince Sarah to let him send the notes to Mrs. Huber. "The copy went to New York the day I left for London. There's no way it could have reached there the *next* day. Even if it had, I can assure you that the person on the other end is *completely* trustworthy."

"Are you certain?"

"Yes," an edge to his tone. "No question."

"Let me determine whether—"

"I said no."

A set of eyes Feric had not seen before peered at him from across the table, no warmth, no self-doubt, none of the trappings he had come to expect from the scholar. Only conviction, perhaps a tinge of anger. He had to admit his new companion was showing real promise.

"I ask only because it is a possibility."

"I answer because I know it isn't."

Feric nodded, pleased with the response. "Good." He took a sip of wine. "That leaves only one possibility. Pescatore."

"*What?*" The suggestion was ludicrous. "*Carlo?*"

Feric removed an envelope from his pocket and placed it on the table. "There are *four* people who have had access to the notes. Your friend in New York, who, as you say, would not have received them in time to orchestrate the run-in at the Institute. You and Ms. Trent, who are clearly not at issue. Which leaves only Pescatore."

"That's impossible. Carlo's . . ."

Feric slid the envelope across to Xander. "I found that on our bald friend at the Institute. Evidently, the professor was not as reticent as you think. It's a note that details the location of the Danzhoeffer Collection. No doubt you recognize the writing, the signature."

Xander stared at the scrawl. *Pescatore.* He couldn't take his eyes from the page; it was clearly Carlo's hand.

"One wonders," added Feric, "if Signore Pescatore is as familiar with the whereabouts of your friend Ganz?"

NEW ORLEANS, MARCH 4, 3:31 P.M. ⚓ His legs burned; his arms tore at his shoulders. Several times in the past four hours, he had let himself sink, his body drift into the current for as long as his lungs would allow—moments of release—before propelling himself up to the pier. Only once had he let himself go too far, the sudden realization of consciousness ebbing, the frantic struggle to find the surface again. In all the jostling, he had nearly knocked the radio detonator from his belt. Failing to plant four of the explosives had been bad enough. Losing the detonator would have been unthinkable.

He had been ready to go half an hour ago. The arrival of a small tanker and its subsequent unloading, however, had made escape impossible. Now, as the sound of the last trucks faded to a distant part of the wharf, the soldier of Eisenreich slowly drifted out from his lair. He clung to the edge of the pier and made his way out into the Mississippi. Reaching the end of the cement wall, he dove deep, using his flippers to send him farther and farther from the light overhead. A minute later, he emerged to the surface, a good hundred yards from the pier.

The swell was overwhelming. He floated for perhaps half a minute, trying to find the strength to dive again, when he heard the sound of an engine no more than twenty yards from his head. A routine Coast Guard patrol. Fate was not being kind.

He dove, his legs and arms thrashing through the current, the pier his only chance once again. But his strength had left him, limbs cramping at the sudden exertion. He felt himself drift to the surface, the sunlight slicing across his face seconds later.

He knew what they would expect to pull from the water—a frightened, grateful survivor. The scuba suit and detonator, however, would quickly alter that picture. And raise questions—questions he could not afford to answer.

There must always be a place for sacrifice.

The words ran through his head as he slowly let himself sink. Pulling the detonator from his belt, he entered the code.

He felt nothing as the water around him erupted in flame.

A smattering of stars winked through the cloud cover, intermittent flashes of light speckling the rutted lane of German countryside. Sounds of late-night drinking spilled onto the street as Xander and Feric plodded on. Just ahead of them, the Schlossplatz, Wolfenbüttel's onetime home to Saxon nobility, edged its way through the mist, dwarfing the no less impressive Zeughaus, a three-story block of stone and wood that cast an ominous shadow and seemed ill-suited as home to one of the great libraries of Europe. Its counterpart, the more elegant Herzog-August-Bibliothek, stood across a short cobbled lane and offered a far more majestic profile. But it was in the Zeughaus, Xander recalled, that the real books were to be found and where he had spent much of that summer six years ago.

It was there, in the Lesungzimmer—the rare-books room on the third floor—that he had first met Ganz, a tall, scaly man with barely enough skin to cover his endless arms and legs. Xander had never forgotten that first glance, a pair of ice blue eyes peering over his shoulder as he had flipped through a manuscript, the smile that had crept across the older man's face as he had lured Xander to the small cantina on the lower floor, all the while describing his colleague—long dead—who had been the last to restore the book now again in need of repair. Xander had listened for hours, several cups of strong coffee in hand, as Ganz had relived in painstaking detail some of the more extraordinary finds of his long career.

The exhilaration that had reverberated in the man's voice had reminded Xander of someone he knew only too well. It had been a perfect match from the start.

After that, the two had continued to meet, mostly in the evenings, for no other reason than to add a necessary splash to their rather patterned lives, beer or pastry, and once, on a whim, for a long weekend in Berlin— Ganz's first since the war. Like many, he had stayed away, unwilling to tarnish his childhood image. A week of incessant prodding from Xander, and a reminder that the city was once again whole, had finally broken Ganz's resolve. Three glorious days in Berlin. The gift of an early German edition of Machiavelli's *Prince* had been his way of saying thanks.

Back in Wolfenbüttel, the two had continued their friendship, only once, Xander recalled, ever straying from the topic of books. On occasion, Xander would invite Ganz to his room at Pension Heinrich Tübing, where the proprietor would manage to provide a king's feast for his esteemed guests. "Two such men of learning," Tübing would say. "It is an honor to be of service."

And now, years later, Herr Tübing was proving himself the consummate hotelier again. His recognition of Xander's voice—even given the dreadful phone connection from Göttingen—placed the innkeeper in a class by himself. *No, there would be no trouble at all setting up Herr Doktor Professor's room. And his guest, as well? No difficulty at all.* The man's enthusiasm had been hard to miss. *Would he be staying for an extended period?* A few shouts back and forth to Frau Tübing (a woman Xander had never actually seen during that initial three-month stay), and all was put in order.

Now, bags in hand, they made their way alongside a lovely covered bridge, past a darkened row of shops. Turning right, they entered Jürgenstrasse, home to the Pension Heinrich Tübing—two floors, with perhaps ten rooms for guests upstairs, breakfast area and sitting room downstairs—all shrouded in darkness. Xander checked his watch. Ten to eleven, late by Wolfenbüttel standards, but Herr Tübing had insisted that he would be up to welcome his guests. And, good to his word, a light from above flicked on before Xander could knock, the front door pulled back a moment later, revealing the upright figure of Herr Tübing. He was in bathrobe and slippers, his eyes trying to adjust to the light.

"We've kept you up," apologized Xander. "We had no idea the train would take so long."

The older man shook his head once rapidly. "Pah, these trains are always the same. *Viertel vor elf. Prompt.* I keep the lights off for the electricity. Please." He indicated for his guests to enter the foyer. "I have given you your previous room. There was a young woman from Bremen staying. She has been kind enough to move."

"There was no need—"

"For the Doktor Professor, there is *always* need. She is merely a Privatdozent." He flicked on the hall lamp.

Xander smiled and followed his host up the narrow staircase, Feric directly behind. He had forgotten how strictly the Germans regarded the distinctions within the academic hierarchy. Doktor Professor, the grandest of the grand, and she *merely* a Privatdozent. For all Xander knew, the woman was fifty, far more distinguished than he, and had probably insisted on the move herself. It was a culture he would never fully understand. Turning left at the top of the stairs, the three moved along to the corner room; Herr Tübing unlocked the door and handed Xander the key. He then reached into his pocket for the spare for Feric, pausing before transferring the key.

"Ah," Xander quickly said, "this is—"

"Signor Caprini." Feric smiled the smile from the car-rental counter, his head in a gentle nod, cocked slightly to the right as he extended his hand. Again, the strained German stunted from his mouth. "I am assisting Doktor Jaspers in investigations for your magnificent libraries. I hope it is no convenience." He paused. "Ah, *Entschuldigung. In*convenience."

The German bowed his head and placed the key in Feric's hand. "There is never inconvenience where the Doktor Professor is concerned. I trust the room will be satisfactory."

"*Belissima,*" answered Feric, and moved through the door. He returned a moment later to carry Xander's bag through. Tübing bowed again, announced breakfast—"*Halb-sieben prompt*"—and turned toward his own bedroom, his back straight as an arrow as he disappeared around the corner. Xander smiled and stepped through, closing the door behind him.

The room was exactly as he remembered it. The same blue towels, the same thick white comforter and pillows on each bed, even the same brand of soap in the tiny dish at the basin. Xander recalled having placed the small desk by the window all those years ago—he preferred natural light—returning it to its original location before vacating the room. To his surprise, the desk was again by the window, another nod to Tübing's precision. Meanwhile, Feric had perched himself by the sill and was peering through a gap in the curtain at a small yard, a few shrubs, the beginning of a wood. The orb of a streetlamp glared down on the graveled dead-end street, where two cars sat quietly for the night. Feric let the curtain fall back, its thin material no match for the light outside.

"If I remember," said Xander, "the light goes out just after three."

Feric nodded and placed his bag on one of the two beds. Save for the short exchange with Tübing, he had been virtually silent since the changeover in Göttingen, his look far more concentrated than Xander could recall. He had felt compelled to make a few comments about German railway inefficiency, but had offered little more in the way of explanation for some of his directives: that Xander make the reservation at the pension, that he offer up the exact time of their arrival, that he mention the "colleague" who would be accompanying him, and that he *not* ask Herr Tübing if there had been any recent inquiries concerning the young Doktor Professor. If the men of Eisenreich had found their way to Wolfenbüttel—a possibility that seemed less and less remote—their first stop would no doubt have been his old haunt, number twelve Jürgenstrasse. Or perhaps their second stop. Ganz lived a five-minute walk from the central market. They could easily have rummaged through Ganz's material, found the manuscript, and simply been waiting at the station to dispense with a few more "loose ends." The fact that Feric and he had arrived without incident had eased Xander's mind only slightly.

Settling onto his bed, Xander watched the operative remove a pair of dark trousers, a sweater, and a black cap from his bag. Xander adjusted his pillow. "I have to admit, I'm somewhat relieved, given the way we rolled into town."

"Do not be," Feric answered. "Eisenreich would not have done anything to this point for the very reason that we *did* make our arrival clear to anyone who might be interested." He placed his shoes neatly by the bedpost. "*They* are the unknown quantity here, not you. *They* must be cautious." He pulled a second pair of pants, a turtleneck, and another cap from his bag and tossed them across to Xander. "Put those on." Feric stood and placed the wallet and passports in his pockets. Then, sitting down at the desk, he pulled a piece of stationery from the wooden drawer and began to write.

"What are you doing?" Xander was following orders, his shirt off, his fingers busy with his shoelaces.

"A note for Herr Tübing. Your apologies at being unable to stay. Sudden emergency. We will rest for a few hours, then go. Should something happen later tonight, the word *emergency* will have the proper effect, more so if the note is in my handwriting as your assistant. I will leave a hundred marks."

"That's twice what the room costs."

"You are a generous man, Herr Doktor Professor."

Sarah had the pilot fly her to Tempsten, Alison now too valuable to leave in the open; after all, she could tie the men of Eisenreich together, whether she realized it or not. And, of course, Votapek would want answers about the tape. Sarah knew she had to move quickly. To that end, she found Alison a place to stay and stocked it with food for a week. She also gave her a gun—a precaution. Alison took it without a word.

Staring at the weapon in Alison's hand, Sarah felt strangely detached, aware that she had lived the very same moment before, once again no choice but to follow through. *"You will come back."* *"Yes."* *"You will come for me."* *"Yes."* Alison *had* to be kept from Tieg and Sedgewick; Sarah *had* to confront them, undermine their resolve as she had undermined Votapek's. Find a way to the heart of Eisenreich and destroy it. She knew it was the only way to keep Alison safe.

The only way to save Xander.

Now, six hours later, Sarah was in San Francisco's Ghirardelli Square, her thoughts, though, six thousand miles away. She phoned into the relay point for Feric's message. They were in Germany, with only part of the manuscript. He did not elaborate. More encouraging, though, was his synopsis of the part they had found. It confirmed everything she had put together on her own—the isolation, the taboo on contact. And the fourth man. But it was his final words that brought the smile to her face.

"The Doctor is doing well. I am actually growing quite fond of him."

An uncharacteristic admission, but one she understood only too well.

As she replaced the receiver and stepped out into the flow of bodies, Sarah became acutely aware of the man following her. Her first thought was Justice, but he didn't fit the profile.

Needing an answer, she began to drift into the crowds, slowing so as to pull in her prey. The sound of his steps drew closer, almost on her, until, with a lunge, Sarah bent over, an instant later her torso colliding with his, legs and arms lost in a wild jumble. Before he could respond, her hand was buried in the small of his back, her grip viselike around the base of his spine. He winced as she prodded him to keep walking.

"You seem to have taken an interest in me," she said quietly. "Not a very subtle one, I might add."

"It wasn't meant to be subtle," he answered, his gait more clipped as she dug her fingers deeper into his flesh. "I'm with the Committee."

∗

Five minutes later, they sat in a coffee bar, two cups of caffè latte on the table.

"Would the Committee man have a name?" she asked.

"Stein. Bob Stein." He smiled uncomfortably, his thick fingers around the tiny spoon. "I wasn't quite sure how to approach you."

"Well, here we are."

"Yes." He removed the spoon from the cup, licked at the foam, and cleared his throat. "I'm with the Committee—"

"You've said that."

"Yes. Well, it has to do with your . . . *investigation*."

"Take your time, Bob."

"I've brought some files with me."

Sarah stared at him as he sipped his coffee. "That isn't Committee policy." Stein didn't answer. "Then why did Pritchard send you? A sudden pang of conscience?"

"No one at COS knows I'm here."

Sarah watched as he stared into his cup. "That's rather bold, isn't it, Bob? A bit outside the parameters of acceptable behavior."

He looked up, his unease momentarily forgotten. "It's a bit outside the parameters of *acceptable* behavior to send out retired operatives. But we've moved way beyond that, haven't we?"

Sarah smiled. "Yes, we have."

"Look," Stein continued, his voice now a whisper, "we lost both of you in Florence. I won't ask you where the good doctor is, because that's not why I'm here. You appear a day later on your own passport, which I took to be an invitation: Here I am; come find me. If it wasn't, tell me and I'll be happy to fly back to my desk, forget about all of this, and hope I haven't made some sort of horrible mistake. Otherwise, I think I'm here to offer help."

Sarah had not lost her smile. "Well then, I guess I should be willing to take it, shouldn't I, Bob?"

∗

A deep black sky had turned to slate when the two emerged onto Jürgenstrasse. They had been careful on the stairs, more so with the front door, and were now maintaining the same posture on the lane leading toward the center of town. A stoic traffic light guarded the only large intersection, its amber beam flashing at a road that drove on for countless empty miles. The stillness of the night, ideal for their purposes, only compounded Xander's concern. They were alone, scampering through a town locked deep in sleep. Xander held his shoulder bag tightly against his side, the premium on quiet in strict contrast to the easy gait of their first hike to Pension Heinrich Tübing. Beads of sweat began to form under Xander's turtleneck as Feric quickened the pace.

Passing the palace and libraries, the two arrived at the market center—as in most German towns, a pedestrian area walled in by shops and stores, too many of them overwrought boxes of cement and glass staring menacingly down at the roofs of the older timber buildings. Xander led the way along the wide cobblestone court, a few arteries crisscrossing the main thorough-fare in an endless maze of small-town life. Only the sound of rubber-soled shoes landing in contrapuntal *pit-a-pat* broke through the heavy silence. At the end of the promenade, the sustained green of a traffic light cast a wel-come glow on the street. Ganz's house, another twenty yards beyond, lay in deep shadow.

Xander stopped and nodded toward the small two-story home. From where they stood, the two men could make out the vague outlines of bushes dotting the lawn. As they drew closer, more of the house came into detail, including the sudden appearance of a car—from the profile, an ancient Saab—a monster with a hunched back, standing guard at the lip of the curb. They cut across the lawn, the grass brittle underfoot, each step prompting a hushed crunch, impossible to muffle against the sterility of the open yard. Within a minute, both stood on the second step of the front porch, the drip under Xander's turtleneck having grown to a mild trickle, his breath short and choppy, less from exertion than nerves. Xander gently rapped his fingers against the thick wood of the door, quickly pulling his hand back to listen for movement inside. Nothing. He tried again, more conviction this time, his heart jumping with each touch of wood. Feric was already by one of the windows, his gloved hand feeling its way round the wooden frame, his eyes lost in concentration. After a minute, he looked over at Xander and mouthed the word *alarm*. Then, pulling a small metal strip from his coat, he swept it along the gap between the window and frame, found the catch, and returned the strip to his pocket. He pushed the window up and listened; satisfied, he lifted the window higher and nodded for Xander to join him. The episode had taken less than two minutes.

Once inside, both men removed flashlights from coat pockets and began to examine the room. Ganz's kitchen, seen only through narrow beams of light, proved in far worse condition than any book he might have been asked to repair—cigarette burns dotted the tabletop, paint chips hung from the cabinets, and the smell of cheese filled the place. Xander recalled Ganz had been a widower for some twenty years, evidently never having mastered the finer points of housekeeping. Feric quietly led them across the room to the swinging door, whose ancient hinges threatened a squeak but mercifully remained silent as the two men moved out into the narrow hall. Keeping the light on the floor, they slipped down the corridor toward the staircase; Xander tapped Feric and pointed to the second floor. The study. That much he had remembered. If Ganz had the book, it would be there, next to the bedroom.

Taking the steps two at a time, they arrived on the upper landing, the sound of a radiator hissing the only accompaniment to their near-silent strides. Several doors stood ajar; Xander could make out stacks of papers and books in the rooms, storage areas for a man who had always prided himself on an unwillingness to throw anything away. The two doors at the end of the corridor, however, remained shut, the hiss growing louder as they crept along. Feric pressed his ear close to the first door, raising a hand for Xander to step back. A moment later, he pushed the door open, no sound from knob or hinge. Surprising even himself, Xander stood quite calmly as the entrance widened, Feric's head disappearing round the door before a streak of light momentarily caught the edge of a mirror. Even then, Xander remained composed.

Feric immediately retreated from the room. "He is not here."

The voice was only half-whispered, but the sudden intrusion of sound was enough to jump-start Xander's heart, his self-confidence evidently premature. Feric explained. "It is his bedroom. The bed is made, unused. We have been lucky. He is elsewhere tonight."

Xander drew in a deep breath and stepped back as Feric turned to the last door on the hall. With no less precision, he managed the handle and pushed the door open, this time not quickly enough to avert a squeak rising from the hinge. Xander's grip tightened on the flashlight. Following Feric through, he saw a lamp with fringed shade, the only image to have remained from his last visit. Somehow, it had a soothing effect. As Feric moved toward the desk, Xander turned to close the door.

Staring back at him, the metallic curve of a revolver barrel flickered in the thin beam of light, a pair of ice blue eyes above.

6

Education and aggression work hand in hand to assure stability.

—*On Supremacy*, chapter XV

SARAH SAT IN THE hotel room, scanning various pages, so caught up in the text that she flipped past the final sheet, expecting another. All she found was the back cover, the all-too-familiar government seal staring up at her. She turned again to the last page. "This is still very sketchy."

"Nice to see you remembered I'm here." Stein sat down next to her. "I didn't say it was perfect. I said it would help." He had spent the last hour watching her, every so often trying to offer an explanation over her shoulder, only to be rebuffed with a quick hand to the air. Her concentration had been unwavering, the intensity in her gaze almost hypnotic. It was a lesson in analysis, in the art of scrutiny from the woman he had known only as the assassin of Jordan.

"These sections were omitted from the copies I was given. Why?" The question was tinged with accusation.

"Pritchard thought they were too sensitive."

"That was *very* kind of him."

"His reasoning," replied Bob, "was that if we gave you the complete dossiers, you'd have no reason to look beyond them. You'd be in the same position we were in. He wanted to leave the loose ends so that you'd have to start from the beginning—something, obviously, we couldn't do anymore."

"I don't buy that. I can't imagine O'Connell would have—"

"He didn't," Stein cut in, knowing full well what Sarah was going to say. "And neither did I. Why do you think I'm here?" Sarah said nothing. "Look, I know you have no reason to trust—"

"Any theory on why Mr. Pritchard wanted to play it this way?"

"No."

"And you're absolutely certain he's shown you everything?"

"*Absolutely* certain?" Stein shrugged. "A week ago, I would have said yes. Now I don't know. Absolutely certain is . . . pretty absolute."

She turned to him, slightly less edge to her tone. "To be honest, I *was* expecting Gael. My invitation."

"I understand—"

"No, you don't." She paused. "You're right, I don't trust you . . . for the simple reason you don't understand this."

"And O'Connell does?"

"Not specifically, no." She stood and moved toward the French windows and the balcony. "But enough."

"Look, I didn't choose to send you—"

"Of course you didn't." She turned to him. "Let me paint the real picture. None of you had a clue as to what was going on or how any of this tied together, so you threw the unknown into the works. The unknown, Bob, doesn't have to have *perfect* credentials. In fact, she doesn't have to have *any* credentials. She just has to stir things up so that the big boys can see how the field is playing." She stared directly at him. "Well, it's playing a little rough, a little rougher than any of us expected." She opened the doors and enjoyed the breeze on her face. "So you're right—I wasn't the best choice for the job, if *choice* was ever applicable."

Bob was quiet for a moment. "No, I don't suppose it's Committee policy to give people choices."

She turned to him. "Is that why you're here, Bob? Is that what this is all about? They let you get in a little too deep, and now you're feeling responsible? If that's the reason you're here, you won't be very useful."

"I'm here, *Ms. Trent,* because I thought I had something you needed and because I thought you asked for my help." The words flew out, a stream fueled by pent-up tension. "Could be I'm wrong, but I don't think it matters a rat's ass whether I feel responsible or not. You don't want me to join in in your game, play on your *rough* field? Hey, then I'm happy to hop the next plane to Washington. But I don't think that's the case. I think the information I gave you, coupled with whatever Jaspers has turned up, may just be the only way to derail whatever these people have in mind."

The outburst caught her by surprise, genuine emotion from a man she had pegged as little more than an anxious analyst suddenly in water over his head. "It's nice to see that blood can boil under a bureaucrat's skin."

"Bureaucrat? You'd be so lucky."

"Don't worry, no one's got the time to blame you or anyone else."

"I'm not worrying." He lifted the pitcher of coffee, swirled around what was left, and poured out a stream of coal black liquid. The smell was enough to dissuade tasting. "So exactly how important is Schenten?"

"I'll let you know."

"That's the problem," answered Stein. "I've given you what *I* have. So I think we've come to the part where *you* reciprocate and bring me up-to-date on what you and Jaspers have found."

Sarah turned and looked at Stein on the sofa, his paunch at even length with the armrest. "I thought you were playing the Good Samaritan? I didn't realize you expected anything in return."

"Two heads are better than one, something like that."

"Perhaps." She sat next to him and produced a lovely, ingenuous smile. "I need a favor first. I assume you have access to my files."

"Yes," he replied, the answer more question than response.

"Good. Then you're going to need to destroy a few pages of them."

"*What!*" Stein nearly dropped the cup of rancid coffee in his lap. "You want me to *destroy* highly classified information that no one can get his hands on anyway? What the hell for?"

"Confirmation, Bob. Confirmation."

⚔

"Put the gun down, or I shall be forced to shoot Dr. Jaspers directly in the chest." Ganz's tone was hushed, no signs of his seventy-plus years in either voice or movement as he rose and remained by the door. Xander stood silently listening to the sound of Feric's gun landing on carpet, the movement slow and deliberate. Ganz stepped to his right—eyes fixed on the two men—and reached across his body to turn on a standing lamp. Each man squinted momentarily, Ganz measuring Xander, the blue stare somehow gentle, even warm, though out of place given the circumstances.

"Who is he?" asked Ganz.

It took Xander a moment to realize that the question had been directed at himself, his natural instinct to turn and look at Feric so as to describe the operative. At the first sign of movement, Ganz interrupted.

"Do not move, please. I ask again, who is he, Doctor?"

Xander exhaled, barely able to swallow with the pounding that had reached his neck. His words were muffled, half-asperated bursts, as a stream of wet nausea rose from his stomach, the revolver fixed in his stare.

"I am Bruno Feric," came the reply from behind. "We are here for the manuscript."

"I have many manuscripts," answered Ganz, his voice a monotone, his hand equally still around the gun. "Your name is not familiar to me, Herr Feric. How do you come in contact with Dr. Jaspers?"

"We are recently acquainted."

"I was not aware that he *acquaints* himself with men who wield guns."

"Then you might have to question your *own* familiarity with him."

"Do not be clever." Ganz showed no sign of emotion. "This revolver is purely defensive."

The sound of two native German speakers conversing in English finally shook Xander from his stupor. "He's helping me," he broke in. "I wasn't aware he'd pulled the gun."

"Move away from my desk, Herr Feric," continued Ganz, choosing to ignore Xander. "The two chairs by the fireplace—please, gentlemen."

Slowly, Xander and Feric moved through the piles of books littering the floor, both careful to keep hands visible. At the same time, Ganz arced behind the desk, stepping gingerly in front of his own seat in order to turn on the small fringed lamp that stood atop the crepe blotter, his eyes ever trained on the smaller of the two men. All three sat at once, Ganz showing the first signs of strain as he let his arm rest momentarily on the edge of the desk. Feric shifted in his seat, prompting a sudden surge of energy from the old restorer, his gun again raised to chest level. Keeping his eyes focused on Feric's hands, Ganz spoke, "You were saying, Dr. Jaspers?"

"Emil, this man was sent to protect me."

"And why does a sixteenth-century scholar need such protection? Your work has always been interesting, but not, shall we say, dangerous."

"It's not my *work* that's dangerous, and you know it." A certain vigor had returned to his voice. "It's the eleven chapters of Eisenreich that are somewhere in this mess; otherwise, you wouldn't be pointing that gun at my friend's chest."

Ganz paused. "Two men break into my house in the middle of the night and I merely seek to defend myself."

"And you decide to make your bed before dashing into the study?" Xander surprised himself with his own composure. "I hardly think so. When was the last time you slept?"

"So you are now a detective, as well?"

"*Emil*, do you have the Eisenreich?"

Ganz looked at Jaspers, the eyes gentle as before, their warmth oddly juxtaposed against the cold reality of the gun barrel stemming from his hand. After nearly a minute, Ganz slowly lowered the gun, his hand still firm around it, letting his back release into the cushion of his chair. "Of course I have it." He rested his free hand on the desk as if to stand. Instead, he began to rub the wood, his eyes tracing the pattern of knobby fingers. Looking up from the strangely calming routine, he said, "And now I ask you the question I have been asking myself for the last two days: Why is it so important?"

Xander looked at Feric, then Ganz. "It's a great find—"

"*Don't* treat me like a child," he broke in, standing as he spoke, the first explosion of emotion he had shown. His words were angry, the movement forceful, strong. "A first edition *Dante* is a find. No one, though, prowls through your house to find it. And no one does *this*." He picked up a newspaper that had been resting on the desk and tossed it across to Xander, the sudden burst of activity making the catch somewhat awkward. Xander flipped to the front page and scanned the articles for an answer.

"No, the third page." Ganz, too, could be impatient. "At the bottom. It is from yesterday's *Algemeiner.*"

Xander opened to the page. There, staring back at him was the face of another old friend, Carlo Pescatore. The words below the picture were even more devastating. SCHOLAR FOUND IN ARNO—POLICE CONTINUE INVESTIGATION.

"It becomes even more interesting," added Ganz. "The police say that his office was broken into, that there were signs of a struggle, his computer discs tampered with, and"—he paused for effect, resting the gun on the desk—"that two unknown people were seen leaving the university courtyard the day of the break-in, one a man with a beard. That seemed an odd detail to me."

Xander started to answer, then stopped.

Ganz continued. "For how long have *you* had this beard, Doctor?"

Xander met his gaze, the eyes no longer the warm and gentle blue of moments ago. He had forgotten the hair on his face, now several days old, his immediate response to place his hand to his cheek.

"It is a recent addition," said Feric, until now quiet in his chair.

"Ah, and I am to take the word of the man with the gun?" Ganz returned to his chair, choosing not to sit. "Perhaps now you understand why I wait with a revolver? I receive the Eisenreich—mind you, only the second half—and a day later, a man to whom I have written to tell of my discovery—because he is one of a handful who will truly appreciate it—is dead. But not dead *that* day. No, he is dead at least a week earlier, about the time that London sends me its books for restoration. Coincidence? Perhaps. I am deeply disturbed by the loss of a colleague—the strange circumstances no less upsetting—but I do not yet concern myself.

"Then, the next evening, I am informed by our mutual friend Herr Tübing that the *second* man to whom I have sent a letter about the Eisenreich is arriving in Wolfenbüttel—no letter to *me* to forewarn of the visit—and that he is traveling with a companion. A *companion*. Has he ever traveled with an assistant before? No, not that I can recall, and he has always said how much he enjoys the *solitude* of research. Moreover, he calls from the train station in Göttingen, a last-minute choice for a man I know to be a meticulous planner." The interrogation continued, fatigue slowly beginning to show on the older man's face. "And now, when you *do* arrive, you break into my house with a man who has a gun, and you sporting a beard. These things I cannot view as coincidence." He picked up the revolver and raised it. "You are an old friend, but old friends do not act as you have. The Eisenreich is at the heart of this, *natürlich*. I must know why."

Xander spoke before Feric could stop him. "Because there are some very powerful and capable men who are trying to put the theory into practice."

Ganz's eyes locked on Xander's. For a long moment, he remained still; slowly, the hard stare slipped away, the blue neither gentle nor unkind as the words took hold; his gaze drifted to the desk. After nearly a minute, Ganz spoke, his voice controlled, direct, "Then it is far worse than I feared." He looked at Xander. "Trying or succeeding?" When the young scholar did not answer, Ganz nodded, glancing at Feric. "That of course explains why *you* are here. No doubt, you would have killed me for the book." Feric said nothing. "I understand. Such men must be stopped, no matter what the sacrifice. I trust you would agree, Doctor." Xander sat

silently as Ganz opened the top drawer and placed the gun inside. "Very few had the courage to make those sacrifices fifty years ago. Do not think your friend ruthless because he accepts the burden with such easy detachment. I can assure you, those who use the manuscript will act with equal indifference."

"They already have," replied Xander.

Ganz closed the drawer. "I see. The . . . *first trial*." He nodded to himself before looking up. "The manuscript makes it all quite clear." He held Xander's gaze for a moment, then turned to Feric. "You may retrieve your revolver. I do not like such things in the open." As Feric leaned forward to pick up the gun, Xander found it impossible to tear his eyes from the older man, the piercing eyes somehow more focused, more determined, a sense of purpose radiating from within. Ganz continued, his words equally forceful. "You, naturally, have the first nine chapters?"

"Yes," answered Xander.

"Which would mean there is *another* copy of the manuscript."

"Two others," corrected Xander. "One German, one Latin. The men I just mentioned have them both."

"And they, of course, are eager to have the third."

"That," said Feric, depositing the gun in his front pocket, "is something that continues to trouble me. Why should they be so concerned with the *other* copies? From what the doctor has told me, the theory is filled with broad suggestions for a process years in the planning; it does not, however, offer any substantiating detail. Only general points: what they intend to do, what they have been doing, how many men are needed, the spheres where the chaos is to occur, and so forth. But if it does not tell us exactly *how*, and, more important, *when* they intend to initiate the scheme, the manuscript is of limited value. It gives an overview, but nothing tangible, nothing to specify the essential day-to-day process we must assume they are following. They know the manuscript is incapable of giving that detail, so why would it matter if we should find any of the other copies?"

"You answer your own question, Herr Feric." The first hint of a smile graced Ganz's face. "Most assuredly, there *is* something in the manuscript that gives the detail you seek. Otherwise, as you say, there would be no reason to take such interest in the two of you, nor in our dear friend Pescatore, now would there?" Ganz swiveled in his chair, looked momentarily at Xander, and then opened a thin drawer at the bottom of the desk. He pulled out a small book, its color and binding difficult to discern in the light.

Xander sprang from his chair and took the book from the collector's hand, flipping open the cover in anticipation. His heart sank as he saw the words on the page—thick umlauted script of typewritten German. For a moment, he could only stare. *German? It should be Italian. And where's the notation of a second volume?* Xander looked at the cover again. No sign of the Medici seal. "Read the author's name," advised Ganz. "Not quite what you expected."

WOLF POINT, MONTANA, MARCH 4, 8:45 P.M. ⚔ The call had come in from New Orleans an hour ago, but it had clarified nothing; CNN had been airing pictures of the devastation since six o'clock. The old man had not moved from the television, both entranced and exasperated by the images filling the screen.

Too soon, he thought. *All of it too soon.* Fate, once again, was testing his resolve. The explosion had been designated as part of the final stage, not the first trial, its effects mitigated by its singularity. The events it had been coordinated with would not begin for another three days, the destruction of the port now little more than an arbitrary act of terrorism.

Still, it was proving instructive. Via satellite, Bernard Shaw was interviewing the trade commissioners from Argentina and Chile, two men as yet unwilling to speculate on the impact of the recent disaster.

"As I understand it," Shaw continued, "close to one-third of all trade in and out of South America finds its way through New Orleans." Both men nodded. "And with the port inaccessible to commercial shipping for at least ten days—according to earliest estimates—that raises some rather interesting questions, gentlemen. Coupled with the recent crash of the grain market. . . ."

The old man listened with only half an ear, wondering what the reactions would have been had a number of key Midwestern railway and trucking arteries also succumbed within a few hours of the port's demolition. What kind of questions might that have raised? What sort of economic panic?

But it was not to be; the timing had gone wrong. The final stage would now need reassessing, perhaps even a shift in the schedule.

An acceleration.

⚔

"*Confirmation?* What the *hell* does that mean?" Stein was the second person in the last ten hours to press Sarah with the question.

"I need some people to know what happened to me after Amman."

"You *need*—"

"They're going to get their hands on my file anyway. Trust me."

Stein shook his head. "You're telling me there's a *leak*? At most, ten people have access—"

"Trust me," she broke in. "The problem is, my *recovery assessments* are included in those reports, and they contain more information than I want our friends to have. They're psychological accounts—"

"I know what they are."

"Good. Then you won't have any trouble finding mine." She stood and moved to the bed and her overnight bag.

"No problem at all. Yours have been in my office for the last week."

Sarah's face registered a moment of surprise. "That's convenient. Should I ask why?"

"I like to know whom I'm dealing with."

Busy with one of the zippered compartments, she asked, "How many copies are in circulation?"

"None."

"Even more convenient."

"Convenient for what?" he asked, an impatience to his tone.

Sarah turned casually. "There's a list of four passages, date and hour installments that I need you to . . . get rid of. Lose them."

"*What?*"

"In their place, write whatever you want. 'Patient incapacitated,' or 'Needed to sedate. Session canceled.' Whatever they *did* write down during the days they thought it best to *restrain* me." Sarah paused momentarily, her eyes locked on an unseen point. Voices from a past broke through, images of a bed, tethered wrists, syringes filled with . . . "Anything you want just as long as it looks like there aren't any holes. Then slip them back in and return the file." She pulled out a piece of paper. "These are the dates—"

"Hold on." Stein had twisted round, his eyes following Sarah. "Not only do you want me to tamper with something I'm not even supposed to have seen, but you also want me to put it back so that someone *else* can get their hands on it?" He shook his head as he reached for the pitcher of coffee. "You're going to have to do more than smile to get me to do either one. I need answers."

"No, you don't." She zipped up the case and started back to the sofa. "There's information in those assessments that will make everything I've set up meaningless. These men have to believe I'm part of them; Votapek's already convinced. My files, as they stand now, would compromise that position."

"I see. And do I get some idea of what I'm looking for?"

Sarah placed the paper in front of him. "This is the list."

Stein shook his head, easing himself into the cushion of the sofa. "I'm sure it's fine, but that's not what I asked. Remember, I've seen the files."

Sarah stared at the analyst, her face devoid of the charm of only moments ago. "Just follow the list."

"Seven years is a long time to remember the *exact* dates you want removed."

"Trust me, Bob," she said, her tone cold, precise, "I won't have forgotten."

"Oh, I have no doubt that the dates are accurate. I'm just wondering if something might have slipped out during a *different* session. As I said, I've read those reports. I think I know what you want me to take out—"

"Then why all the questions?"

"Because I need to know *why*. You don't want to tell me what Jaspers is up to, what this manuscript has to do with anything, why Schenten is so important—fine. I can almost accept all of that because for some unknown reason, I actually believe you know what you're doing. But I *won't* be an errand boy, and I *won't* be a part of this if you don't trust me enough to give me something to work with. All I want to know is what makes the rantings of a drugged-up, half-dead, slightly psychotic operative from seven years ago cause any consternation to men like Tieg? What's in those files that I'm not seeing?"

Sarah waited, watching his eyes before responding. "Because they give the complete picture, and I can't have Eisenreich seeing that."

"Why?"

Again she waited. "All right, Bob. . . . I want them to know that I was angry, that I felt betrayed, that I was looking for . . . something to make sense of everything that had fallen apart for me. But I can't have them knowing *why*. I can't have them reading how much I hated the chaos and the structures it had led to. Pages of endless rantings. If they find that, they'll know I consider them—the Tiegs, Sedgewicks, Votapeks, and Schentens—no better than the Safads, men who think they have a right to destroy in order to make their vision of an ordered world come alive. You read the file, Bob. In those passages, I'm everything they hate and fear. I'm the voice of reason."

Stein sat silently, then spoke. "And these men are capable of creating that kind of mayhem?"

She remained by the windows. "How's Washington these days, Bob?"

"What?"

"Last week. Washington. That was their dry run. Any other questions?"

Stein stared at her for a moment, uncertain, until his eyes went wide. Sarah said nothing; he reached for the list she had left on the coffee table, scanning the numbers on the page as he spoke. "There's a Department jet flying at nine-twenty. I can be back in Washington in three and a half hours."

"That's quick."

"It flies *real* high and *real* fast."

"Thank you." The words were honest, an admission of genuine need Sarah had not allowed herself in a very long time. Maybe O'Connell wasn't the only man at COS she could trust.

Stein folded the paper and wedged it into his pocket. "I'll leave the rest with you." Sarah moved to join him as he began to shuffle the pages into neat stacks. Halfway to the sofa, she heard the muted knocking at the door. No more than a tap, the sound froze them both, heads turning as one.

Sarah lifted a finger quickly to quiet Stein. "Yes?" she answered, a calm, if impatient, response.

Two more raps.

Sarah looked down at her newfound confidant, his face having grown ashen, his hands tight around the files. Motioning him to take them out to the terrace, Sarah walked slowly toward the door. "Who's there?"

No response as she peered through the peephole, her view the empty corridor. She stepped back, waited a moment, and then quickly opened the door. Standing off to the side was a tall, strikingly handsome man, a shock of white hair combed back, revealing a high forehead, clothes impeccably well tailored, wide shoulders above a trimly built body. The gambit with the door had worked to little effect, his composure intact, Sarah only now aware of a second man farther down the hall. The man at the door glanced at her, then beyond and into the room—a look of caution masked by a practiced smile.

"Ms. Trent, I'm Laurence Sedgewick. I believe you're in town to see a friend of mine."

Xander stared at the name. *Rosenberg. Alfred Rosenberg.* Trying to place it, he turned to the next page, saw the date of publication, and instantly recalled the face. Images of the close-cropped hair at Nuremberg, the man slightly slumped in the back row of the dock flashed in Xander's mind. *Of course. Rosenberg, self-proclaimed philosopher of the Third Reich. But why?* Xander stared at Ganz, his own expression sufficient to prompt response.

"I have had this little book for nearly thirty years," said the restorer. "It was not, I should say, something I ever really took much notice of, except that I am virtually positive it is the only copy." He sat forward, indicating with a nod. "You will see that it is still in typewritten form, making it a pre-published manuscript that never quite made it to press. Evidently, Hitler did not think it worthy of printing, ironic given it is the only thing his dim-witted ideologue ever wrote that showed even the slightest coherence. I had not read it in its entirety until yesterday"—Ganz paused, pulling a second, much larger book from the drawer—"when I remembered this." He pointed to the book in Xander's hands and said, "Turn to the third page, where Rosenberg reveals the source of his Nazi wisdom. You, too, will be quite surprised."

Xander obliged, flipping through the thin pamphlet until, staring up at him, he saw the all-too-familiar name. *Eisenreich.* He looked back at Ganz.

"Yes," said the older man, "who knows how, but the manuscript must have fallen into Nazi hands. If you were to read Rosenberg's piffle, you would notice that the book is written as a sort of schedule, a detailed process whereby the Nazis, not yet in control, could create the mayhem necessary to position themselves as the only reasonable alternative. Hitler might not have published it, but he certainly took to heart a number of its suggestions. One of the last pieces of advice is the burning of the Reichstag. Hitler obliged in February of 1933, his final act before assuming full dictatorial power."

"A schedule," said Xander almost to himself.

"Pardon?" asked Ganz.

"Something I always thought it would have. A way to set the whole thing in motion." He turned to Feric. "It's what I told Sarah in New York. Then it was hypothesis. Now"—he looked at Ganz—"you're telling me that Rosenberg used the manuscript to create a how-to book for the Nazi rise to power."

"*One* possible version of that rise to power," Ganz corrected. "I do not say that the book details the precise movements between 1919 and 1933. But it is interesting how the first ten pages of a twenty-page pamphlet are devoted to the first *thirteen and a half* years of that association, whereas the entire second half discusses a period of less than *three* months. Not exactly equal space for equal time. The first half of the book is little more than a glorified history of a thoroughly deranged group of men up to the point they take control. The second half, on the other hand—it is those sections that are the schedule to which you refer, and it is those sections that Rosenberg believed he had taken from Eisenreich."

"And this other book?" asked Xander, nodding to the volume in Ganz's hand.

"Ah, yes, this other one." Ganz took a moment to smooth its cloth cover. "This one, as well as the one you are holding, were gifts from Pescatore. Years ago." He placed the book on the desk. "You should know that he was an excellent scholar, but not one to indulge the sentimentality of the books themselves. Whenever he finished with a volume, he would send it on to me. By his generosity, I amassed quite a collection"—he looked at Xander—"all of which cite Eisenreich as their source. This one is a tract written by Ireton, Cromwell's co-conspirator at the Putney debates. He, too, writes a short book on the best methods to secure the realm, and also sets out a *schedule* whereby Cromwell may assume full authority. Do you begin to see the connection?"

Xander nodded to himself, the idea gaining momentum as Ganz continued.

"Though far more lucid than Rosenberg's feeble attempt, it was, as you can imagine, also never implemented. Which brings us to this." Ganz reached into the drawer for a third time and pulled out a small leather-bound volume, the Medici crest unmistakable in the light. "I only reread the others after receiving this two days ago. I believe you have a phrase for what happened—'something clicked.' It was in the middle of the final chapter"—Ganz opened the book, flipped to the end, and read with strained eyes—" '*an exhortation to action.*' At first, I did not understand why the chapter held such fascination for me. Then I recalled the two books on the desk. In that last chapter"—he looked at Feric—"Eisenreich *does* give the detail that so interests you. In no more than a page and a half, with several examples drawn from his own period, he outlines the methods best employed during the crucial final stage, before the chaos is to erupt. A period, I might add, that is meant to last no longer than two to three months. It is incomplete, but it makes its point." He glanced at one or two passages. "Rosenberg, of course, muddled the theory. Ireton was somewhat better. Yesterday morning, I saw the connection as quite exciting.

Today"—he put the book down—"it is far more unsettling." Again, he looked at the operative. "That, Herr Feric, is why it should matter to those men if you were to find *any* copy of this book. Given what you have told me, it would seem that they, who are eager to put the theory into practice, have written their own schedule as the manuscript instructs, one that they believe Dr. Jaspers would understand if he were to find the last chapters of the Eisenreich. You would have your *how* and your *when*."

"I imagine that is true, Herr Ganz," answered Feric, "but there seems a far more likely reason why they would be concerned."

"And that would be?" asked the man at the desk.

"Not whether the doctor can piece together the schedule, but whether he is aware of it *at all*."

Ganz paused. "And why would that be so?"

"Because if Dr. Jaspers can draw the connection between *their* schedule and that of the *Nazis*, surely it is then easy enough, with what he has of the manuscript, to expose these men as nothing more than latter-day fascists."

The room was silent until, with eyes widening, Xander turned to the operative. "Of course." The point began to come clear. "It wouldn't matter if it were true, just so long as people *believed* there was a link. Get hold of their schedule, expose it as the great-grandson of Rosenberg's schedule, and the men of Eisenreich become nothing more than another neo-Nazi fringe element." The idea was picking up steam. "There'd be no need to explain the subtler parts of the theory—the autonomy, the deception, the spheres. Just connect them to something people are terrified of." Again something struck him. "That's why they've gone to all the trouble to find the extra copies—they know the link is out there. They know we could set them up."

"Exactly," replied Feric.

"I am still somewhat unclear," said Ganz.

Xander looked at the older man and continued. "All we need do is produce these few books and link them to the men who have the manuscript, and the press will do the rest. The media. Exposure—even half-baked exposure—is a dangerous thing. These men thrive on secrecy. By connecting them to these books—no matter how tenuous that connection might be—they'll have lost the two things vital to their success: deception and credibility. We find their schedule, place it side by side with the Eisenreich and Rosenberg documents, and the entire structure comes tumbling down."

Ganz picked up the two books on the desk and said, "If you are right, it means their version of these tracts is their own Achilles' heel."

The words were barely out of his mouth when the sound of a squeaking hinge tore through the darkened house. It had come from below, a reminder of the kitchen door. Feric immediately pulled the gun from his pocket and pointed for Xander and Ganz to turn out the lights. Feric sprang up, grabbed the long-backed wooden chair he had been sitting in, and pushed by Xander toward the door. Just as the footsteps reached the landing, Feric slammed the door shut and jammed the chair under the knob. The *pwit-pwit* of a silencer erupted instantly in the hallway, the immediate burst of lead on wood sending Feric back, a sharp wincing in his left arm as he fired back, his own silencer muffling the shot that seared through the now-splintered wooden door. He looked to his left, to see Xander moving to the window, the three books safely deposited in the computer satchel as the scholar stepped halfway out to the eaved roof. Ganz remained immobile in his chair, a strangely serene look on his face as the second wave of bullets pelted the door. Feric quickly covered the old man with his own body, the tiny explosions bursting all around, tearing through books and plaster. Turning again, Feric let go with another volley, the sound of a muted cry from without indication that his shot had some-how found a target. Feric stepped back, Ganz unharmed underneath. The old man rifled through the top drawer of his desk, pulling out his gun and a set of well-worn keys. He handed the chain to Feric and mouthed the word *car*, a knobby finger pointing to the window as he nodded for Feric to go. The exchange took only a second, but it was clear that the old man was not going to leave, the blue eyes now fixed firmly on the door, wait-ing for the bodies to crash through, his gun leveled, both hands grasping at the handle. *Such men must be stopped, no matter what the sacrifice.* A final act—fifty years in the waiting—a final moment of true purpose. Feric understood.

He slid over the desk to the window, looked back before stepping through to the roof; Ganz was locked in position, strong fingers letting go with a furious barrage, the unsilenced gun exploding in a thunderous wail as the first assailant smashed through the door, his body lurching back-ward, bullets tearing through his head and chest, a lifeless body tripping to the wall in a heap of crimson flesh. A moment later, a hail of gunfire strafed across Ganz's chest, bouncing his torso against the cushion of the chair, his head rolling to the side as his eyes, sapphire stones, stared off into empti-ness. For an instant, they held Feric, only the sudden crescendo of racing feet in the hall enough to tear him away.

Firing back, Feric bent through the window, his coat sleeve awash in dark red streaks, the cold air a welcome relief from the thick heat of the room. To his right, Xander had managed his way along the short projection of roof and was waiting for him. Feric watched as the academic leapt to the ground, rolling to his side, still clutching the case close to his chest. In a loud whisper, Feric barked at him from the roof, *"The car!"* as he himself turned back, let go another volley, and then jumped, a return brush of bullets whisking overhead as the sudden intrusion of hard ground buckled his knees and forced him to roll onto his shoulder. The pain in his arm was now staggering as he tore at the dirt in front of him and made his way to the car. *"Drive!"* Feric slapped the keys into Xander's chest, opened the door, and slipped into the back. Tossing the case onto the passenger seat, Xander slid in behind the wheel; a moment later, the far window shattered, lights from across the street suddenly on, all the while Xander fumbling with the chain. Somehow, he found the key, popped it into the slot, and ignited the engine.

The old Saab fired into gear, the motor screaming at the exertion as the car lunged forward, the *ping-pang* of bullets on metal keeping Xander's head just below the steering column. He looked back through the splintered rear window, to see two men jumping from the narrow roof—old acquaintances from the university. The bald titan immediately stood and fired after the car. The bearded one remained on the ground, his hands clasped to his lower leg in obvious pain. Xander watched as the standing man turned and fired two bullets into the other's head.

"Did you *see* that?" Xander gasped as he turned his attention to the road ahead, oblivious to Feric's pained expression.

"Just *drive!*" came the orders from the back, the sound of cloth tearing as Feric ripped a piece from his shirt with his teeth to bind his wound. "Find the highway." A flash of bright light rose from behind, the high beams of a car quickly gaining, blinding Xander momentarily as the shock of dazzling white stared at him from the rearview mirror. "Give me your hand."

"What?"

"Your hand! Give me your hand!"

Xander extended his hand over the seat, Feric quickly positioning two of the fingers on a segment of the ripped cloth. "Apply pressure." Xander was leaning over the wheel, his shoulder contorted in an attempt to help, the tacky warmth of blood coating his fingers as he spotted the name of a familiar road, his instinct quick enough to swerve the car and make the turn, the movement careening Feric—cloth, fingers, and blood—against the far wall.

"*Please!* Concentrate on the road." Another order from the back as Feric continued his repairs.

"This takes us out to the Autobahn. In about ten to twelve kilometers."

Feric did not answer, knotting the cloth and pulling his arm away, Xander's hand free to retake the wheel. "You have the books and computer?"

"Yes."

"Concentrate on the road."

Lights from behind now filled the small cabin of the Saab, Feric gingerly reloading his gun as the driver from the other car reached out his window and fired off a round. The rear glass shattered completely, Feric miraculously unscathed by the shards; Xander, however, felt a jagged edge drive into his right shoulder. The pain increased as Feric yanked the chip out. Not bothering to clear away the glass, Feric fired back, claiming the left front light and forcing the car to snake its way along the road. "He will now try to draw up next to us. Drive in the middle of the road."

Without thinking, Xander shifted the car over, the pain in his shoulder a dull throb, the road beginning to twist as it emerged from the residential area. He brought the car to eighty, its entire shell shaking from the strain, the constant swerve jostling Feric back and forth. Within a minute, the road straightened, a long expanse cutting through farmland, as Feric again took aim, the other car now no more than thirty feet behind.

"He will shoot for your tires. *Swerve!*"

Xander complied, the loping rhythm of the car's movement in strict counterpoint to the intermittent bursts of gunfire flying through the night sky. A jolt from behind sent Feric into the back of Xander's seat, bumper crashing into bumper, a momentary loss of acceleration but without the conviction to force the heavy Saab off the road. Xander recalled the last such trip—the hills of Florence, the black Mercedes. It seemed months ago. A sign for Kassel raced by, the Autobahn no more than a minute away. The distant haze of lights came into view as the two cars jockeyed for position on the narrow strip of highway, the road widening into four lanes, enough room for the car behind to draw alongside. As the entrance neared, Xander found himself forced to drift farther and farther away from the ramp, his only recourse against the second car now inching its way up on his left-hand side. At the last possible moment, he downshifted to third, the car screaming in agony as he spun hard on the wheel, perfectly timing the maneuver so as to drive through the entrance and leave Eisenreich no room to follow. Just then, Feric lunged forward, grabbed the wheel, and turned the car back onto the smaller road.

"*What* are you doing?" There was no reason to struggle, the ramp no longer possible, the road again narrowing, the second car tucked in neatly at the rear. "We had it. The Autobahn, and Eisenreich nowhere in sight."

"By now, or very soon, this car will be on police monitors," yelled Feric above the whine of the engine. "Plus, on the Autobahn, he would have drawn parallel, and we would not have had a chance."

Xander shifted back into fourth, momentarily putting space between the two cars; Feric aimed and shot out the second headlight. Screaming above the wind, Feric asked, "Do you know this area?"

"No," yelled Xander over his shoulder, "but we're going to run into another town in about five minutes. That's what these small roads do." At that moment, the front window streaked into a thousand fine lines, a stray bullet finding an impact point just below the mirror. Xander tried not to think how close the bullet had come to his head as he shifted again, Feric's foot suddenly thrusting past him, the sheet of glass ripping from its hasps, sliding along the hood and shattering on the road below. The burst of cold air smacked at Xander's face, a jolt of energy as the breath tightened in his nostrils. The sign for Salzgitter flew past, Xander unsure if the sign had said three kilometers or eight.

To his left, a shrill whistle blew. His head snapped in its direction, where he saw a train beginning to slow, evidently its next stop the town's station. Feric, too, had turned to his left, now leaning closer to Xander's ear, the wind racing through the car in violent streams, making communication virtually impossible. The word *station* managed to come through as Feric pointed across Xander at the train. He nodded. The question was how.

Houses began to appear, the first since Wolfenbüttel, the town growing around them at unspeakable speed. Feric again took aim at the car behind; the front-right tire exploded in a flapping of rubber, the steel wheel scraping angrily against the hard surface of road. Still, the car came on, the driver undeterred, letting go an equally debilitating shot at the Saab. The sudden crunch of the blowout bolted Xander from his seat, his head smacking against the roof as his hands momentarily left the wheel. Amid the rough-and-tumble of the descent into Salzgitter, Feric managed one final shot, its accuracy deadly. The second front tire burst in a torn heap, the car behind now unable to maintain the road, its front grille careening to the left, bouncing off several parked cars before spinning to a stop. Two hundred yards up the road, the station waited, the whistle of the standing train mercifully outdueling the clatter of the back wheel. Within thirty seconds, Xander and Feric had dislodged themselves and the computer case from the car as the train began its slow departure. In a dead sprint, the two hurdled a set of steps up to the platform and, jogging alongside the train, leapt to the outside edge of the steel landing between two of the cars. Holding on to the chain link, the two stepped over the swinging barrier and into the open air.

Within a minute, the country was sailing by at some forty-five miles an hour. Feric immediately pulled off his coat and tossed it over the side. Breathing hard, he brought forward the rucksack, still miraculously on his back, and removed two windbreakers, handing one to Xander. No words were exchanged as the two men donned the unstained jackets; within three minutes, the two were inside the fifth car of the train headed for Frankfurt, relieved to find themselves alone.

At the station, the bald man, hampered by a strained knee, limped up to the platform, eyes fixed on the receding lights of the train. He pulled a cellular phone from his pocket and dialed.

⚔

Sarah stepped back, an invitation to the room; Sedgewick nodded and moved past her. The second man, his large hands clasped at his waist, his suit bunching at the shoulders, remained in the corridor. His eyes followed her as she closed the door, a none-too-subtle message that the meager partition would prove little obstacle should he decide his presence was necessary inside. The latch clicked shut, and Sarah turned, to find Sedgewick already at home in the room, an easy smile on his lips.

"I hope I'm not interrupting, but it was the only time I could get to this part of town today. No doubt you were expecting Jonas Tieg." His self-confidence served as a natural buffer against any awkwardness the situation might suggest. Though tied to Eisenreich by the same ambition, he was clearly a far cry from Votapek, less willing to hide his conceit.

"I wasn't expecting anyone."

The smile remained. "Jonas doesn't much like going out in public these days. Difficult, given the success of his television show." He took in the room, then turned to her, his hands tucked casually in his pockets. "I didn't expect you to be alone."

He was wasting no time. Sarah returned the smile. "I wasn't aware you'd be expecting me at all."

"Ms. Trent," his tone still amiable, "the fact that you were permitted to leave the island could only mean that your next stop would be either here or New Orleans. You didn't come to see me, so I've come to you."

Sarah stared at the man. He was remarkably deft, showing no caution in the response, no need to dance around with subtle jabs. In only a passing phrase, he had defined both their positions, not afraid to reveal his role, along with hers. *"You were permitted to leave the island." Permitted.* A word that both hinted at her status as an accepted minion of Eisenreich, and made abundantly clear his ease with the threat that those not granted such privilege would not survive. Votapek had let her go. Evidently, that was endorsement enough. More startling, though, was his admission that he was keeping an eye on the activities of at least one of his compatriots.

Taking in his features, Sarah knew that, with him, it would be even more crucial to sustain the poise that had so unmanned Votapek. Sedgewick would need to see his own arrogance reflected in her. "Considering that contact is out of the question, I'll have to assume you've been keeping tabs on our island friend? Not showing a great deal of team spirit now, are we?"

The eyes momentarily flashed, the smile unchanged as Sedgewick moved toward the sofa. "You'd be surprised, Ms. Trent."

"How did you find me?" She needed to shift gears.

"It wasn't that difficult."

"Without tailing me?" Sarah shook her head as she sat. "I've been at this a long time, and either your people are superb or I missed something."

The smile grew. "I'm sure you missed nothing." Sedgewick glanced around the room. "The man I expected to find here. Who is he?"

"That doesn't answer my question. How?"

"Oh, but I think it does." He sat. "As I said, we were expecting you. What we didn't expect was him—a little frenetic and obvious, wouldn't you agree? He wasn't difficult to pick out at the airport last night, and considerably easier to keep track of than you would have been. He registered here and we waited." Sedgewick offered a rather condescending smile. "Not to worry, your talents are no doubt very much intact. Again, who is he?"

Sarah smoothed her skirt as she spoke, "You surprise me. I would have thought the *who* would be quite easy for you. It was for Votapek."

"It's those sorts of things that Anton and I don't bother to discuss, Ms. Trent." He crossed his legs, picking a piece of lint from his trousers. "And by the way, the idea that contact is forbidden"—he shook his head—"that wouldn't really make a great deal of sense, now would it?"

"Is sense really at a premium?"

Sedgewick looked directly at her and then laughed, his cheekbones creasing his eyes to thin slits. "Very good. No, not initially. Sense is the very thing we seem to be fighting against, isn't it? But then, Anton would have told you that, wouldn't he?"

"I knew that long before I had the pleasure of Mr. Votapek's island hospitality. The manuscript is rather explicit on the topic of chaos, so, too, I thought, on the restrictions on contact among—"

"The *manuscript*," he cut in, "doesn't mention anything about the grain market, but we managed that." His tone was almost self-congratulatory. "You have to be able to read *between* the lines."

Sarah contained her amazement. *The grain market.* In what to him was another well-timed phrase, he had revealed far more than he could possibly know. He had exposed another piece in the Eisenreich agenda to prove a point and, willingly or not, had offered final confirmation of her as a part of that process. He had *expected* her to have such information, had tossed it off casually because he believed he had nothing to hide. And why should he? She had played her part masterfully for Votapek and was doing the same for him. And yet it seemed too easy, too pat. Or was she seeing the surest sign of their weakness—the male ego desperate to flex its muscles so as to impress?

"The particulars don't interest me," she replied with the same even tone as before. "I was talking about the general theory."

Sedgewick's laugh had eased to an animated stare. "What a mystery you are, Ms. Trent. No wonder he chose you."

"Votapek?"

Again a muted laugh, his head tilting back as he spoke. "Anton doesn't have that kind of imagination. No, the man who . . ." Sedgewick stopped and looked across at her. "You call him Eisenreich, don't you?" He waited for her reaction. When none came, he continued. "A little theatrical, but understandable. Your exact words, I believe, were, 'I'm not being paid enough to take that sort of risk.' Am I right?"

Sarah stared back, crafting her own smile as she answered. "You *have* been keeping tabs. Any reason I should know why?"

"Who is he, Ms. Trent?" The eyes had lost all invitation. "The man who asked so many questions about you at the airport and yet who decided not to stick around and pick you up. Who is he? I don't much like loose ends."

Sarah paused. "He's unimportant—a source, a connection from my earlier days at State." She let it stand at that, allowing Sedgewick to put whatever pieces together he thought necessary.

"Earlier days?" It was the first crack in his mask. "I didn't realize your
affiliation had ended."

"It hasn't. My focus has simply changed, and I'm trusting that the men
for whom I work are equally unaware of that shift. The man you're so
interested in also works for them."

"And his reason for flying all the way out here?"

"Recent events."

"Such as?"

No subtle jabs, only instinct. "New York. An alley. They're still trying to
piece that together."

"That was a simple case of misjudgment." Sedgewick showed no hesitation in his response, as if, again, he had anticipated the topic. "I had no idea
who you were. And, of course, there was Jaspers. You understand."

I had no idea—further confirmation that Eisenreich's right hand knew
little of what its left was doing. "I didn't at first, no. I might have killed
either man. That could have complicated things immeasurably."

"Perhaps."

"And Florence?"

Sedgewick paused, his eyes narrowing for only an instant, a moment of
decision before speaking. "I didn't concern myself with Florence." His
denial spoke volumes and he knew it; he *meant* it to. He wanted her to see
that he had known all about Florence, every detail, that he had monitored
the entire Pescatore incident—no doubt from a distance.

"Tieg," she said, statement, not question.

"He's very capable. And, like me, he doesn't care for surprises."

"So you create them instead." He had played it openhanded; so, too,
would she. "The grain market—that was . . . what? A clever piece of
manipulation, or a statement of power?"

"Part of the process. An indication of control."

"*Your* control. And what about the others? Or should we be preparing
for a solo performance?"

Sedgewick remained unruffled by the obvious prod. "They have their
areas of expertise; I have mine. Uncertainty is essential to a point, Ms. Trent,
but it can become rather annoying unless one controls it. I choose to control the aspects of it I understand; they, the aspects they understand."

His sense of purpose—or perhaps vision—removed all hesitation. It was one thing to make the boast, quite another to see it through, and they had each proved themselves more than capable at every turn. Controlling uncertainty. Chaos—to a point. Chaos—as a tool. Washington and Chicago as the blueprints. It was the boldest statement of their agenda she had yet heard, and Sedgewick seemed completely at home with its truth, so much so that he could dispel its audacity with a practiced smile.

"I thought control and uncertainty were mutually exclusive," she said.

"Then you haven't been doing your reading well enough." Sedgewick glanced at his watch, uncrossed his legs. "Unfortunately, we'll have to continue these introductions later tonight."

"Introductions?" The word seemed out of place.

"You came here for *confirmation*." He pursed his lips. "Jonas and I want to be as helpful as Anton was. Shall we say in an hour, a late supper?"

Hers was obviously not the only concern he meant to settle. She was getting to the men of Eisenreich, forcing them to defend themselves. It was another sign of weakness.

"Yes. That would be lovely."

"Good. Jonas has a reasonably well-stocked wine cellar, which I trust will make up for any unpleasantness to this point." Sarah stood as Sedgewick stepped back around the sofa and walked to the door, she a few paces behind. He turned as he opened the door. "Oh, by the way," he said, indicating the man in the hall, "George will pick you up so that we can avoid any further misunderstandings." Another smile. The man was already by his side as Sedgewick nodded and moved off toward the elevators. "Until tonight, then."

A minute later, Sarah turned back into the room, the door firmly shut behind her; Bob Stein appeared on the balcony.

"God, he's smooth." Stein returned to the sofa and sat, arching his back into the cushion. "The chairs out there aren't all that comfortable."

"My apologies, but it couldn't be helped."

"I understand." He placed the files on the table. "I didn't realize I was that obvious. Frenetic, though, is going a little overboard." He turned to her. "And what was all that about the grain market? Are you telling me—"

"The plane, Bob. And the assessment reports. That's all you should be worrying about."

His eyes remained on her. "And you'll take care of *everything* else."

"Something like that."

He slowly nodded. "I just hope you know what you're doing."

⚔

On Feric's command, Xander had fallen asleep twenty minutes ago, the operative explaining that he himself was used to such situations and would manage quite well even with his arm—*"superficial, not to worry. Take your rest while you can."* Xander had wondered how much his friend was letting on, but nerves and fatigue had gotten the better of him, his eyes having lowered without much resistance. Now, after a series of anxious dreams, he awoke to the cold seat, his shoulder far less mobile, having stiffened against the icy pane of glass. Across from him, Feric sat motionless, a pair of clipped tickets wedged into the crease where seat met wall, their reflection caught in the mirrored glass of a dawning sky. The two stubs were the only indication that, somewhere, a conductor roamed the lifeless aisles. The train slowed.

"Thank you. I suppose I needed the sleep."

"Yes." Feric kept his eyes on the car door, his expression no less concentrated for the apparent lack of passengers. "We are nearing the next station, the fifth since Salzgitter."

Xander stared out the window, his eye catching the vague outline of a town in the distance, a more pronounced glow from the few lights dotting the approaching platform. The hazy lines of a small brick building grew more defined as the brakes clamped, the sound of pained steel rising throughout the car. Feric was bending for a better view of the station when he slowly stepped back. A moment later, Xander blanched, as well. There, waiting at either end of the platform stood two large men, the bald giant joined by a second, even more imposing figure.

"Get down," whispered Feric, Xander quick to obey, the operative already moving swiftly along the aisle, sliding into the windowless seat at the back—its angled perch offering a hidden view of the platform ahead— as the train glided past the first man. Xander remained on the floor, his every instinct begging him to sneak a glance but his panic fixing him firmly to the ground.

Feric continued to watch for the second man, now only three cars away, close enough to see his head turn almost imperceptibly, then lower to a gentle nod. *The signal.* Feric had seen the tactic all too often, knew the nod was meant for the man at the opposite end of the platform: Meet in the middle and trap the prey. Waiting until the man had stepped onto the train, Feric tore himself from the seat, raced down the aisle, and grabbed Xander. "We must go."

Clutching at the computer case, Xander followed him to the back of the car. Both men jostled from side to side as the train accelerated, Xander now aware that Feric's left arm had sustained far worse injury than the operative had let on. It hung at his side, useless as they pressed through door after door into empty cars, well aware that the net was tightening around them. At the fifth open vestibule, Feric suddenly stopped.

The wind, pitched at a constant scream, made conversation impossible as the door shut behind them. Feric motioned for Xander to flatten himself against the car wall, then pointed to the wrought-iron ladder leading to the roof. Xander grabbed at the link-chain guardrail and watched as Feric began the climb, left arm bunched at his side. Within a minute, he had reached the top, shouldering his head into the wind, its force nearly throwing him from the ladder, sheer will pulling him back as he hoisted his left leg onto the roof and lifted himself over. Ten seconds later, a hand appeared from above and motioned for Xander to follow. The train began to lean into a tight curve, Xander thrown forward as he gripped at the chain, its tug the only brace keeping him from losing his footing altogether. Catching his breath, he slipped past the door and began to climb.

With each step, the wind grew stronger, Xander forced like Feric to improvise with only one hand as his other clung desperately to the computer case. Within a minute, he reached the top, his head snapping back at the onslaught of air. He threw himself down on the roof, the case held firmly under his chest, his eyes glued to the door below as the wind beat down from all directions. For almost three minutes, the two lay patiently, watching for the hint of shadow to cross into the open expanse below.

A sudden release of air from below—the door pulled back—brought a massive figure into view, clutching tightly at his hat as he stepped to the platform, the wind sweeping across in a violent upsurge. For an instant, he stumbled, his hand quick to find support against the door, dwarfing the steel handle in his grip. Bending his torso through the doorway, he disappeared.

An instant later, Xander began to worm himself toward the ladder, Feric's hand swift to grab at his arm and press it to the roof. Pulling him closer, Feric lifted his head and positioned his mouth less than an inch from Xander's ear. Wind pelting from above, his words were muffled but decipherable.

"They will . . . find each other . . . at center of train . . . will be forced to retrace steps . . . each alone . . . leave only one for us."

Xander nodded as the wind swept up under the smaller man's chest, the thin body lifting above the train, his fingers clutching at the hand pipe that bordered the roof. In a moment of pure instinct, Xander flattened his shoulder into Feric's back, the movement enough to stop the operative from sliding off the side, but with enough force to reignite his own sharp pain, the recollection of a discarded shard of glass pounding in his shoulder. Feric looked back at Xander, a nod of thanks as he gave him the go-ahead to return to the ladder. Three minutes later, the two men stood at either side of the far door, waiting for their assailant to return.

For Xander, the next minutes stretched to an eternity. More than just the physical pain—his pulsing shoulder, numb ears, frozen face—he was overwhelmed by the very real possibility that he would not survive this latest attack. Never before had he been granted the time to consider *his* moves, *his* options. Never the time to think. And it was the thinking that was making it unbearable. *Just open the door! Run at me, rip at my throat, anything! Just do it now!* But the door remained fixed, silently calm to Xander's panic.

Feric had placed him to the right, an unspoken understanding that he was to be the first seen, the primary target, the lure to turn hunter into hunted. Feric would wait and attack from behind. Both men knew he would need the advantage, his left arm now of little use in combat. All around, the dawn had begun to climb to the horizon, a cold wash of orange day cutting through the thick mist and granting both men a clearer view of the platform.

The door swung open, the wind screeching into the sudden cavity as the large figure reappeared. His recognition of Xander was immediate, his arms stretching out in the pose of attack, his shoulders left free as Feric lunged from behind. But it was Feric who was surprised as the man whipped his leg back, catching the operative in the midsection and throwing him against the steel wall. With equal force, he cracked Xander across the jaw, sending him to his knees before leveling Feric with a kick to the ribs. Xander struggled to his own feet, aware that the man was landing blow after blow to Feric's chest. The train veered left, sending Xander careening into the man's back.

It was enough for him to lose his footing, grab at Feric for support as all three lurched toward the cabin door. Suddenly, the man's boot rose up, driving into Xander's groin, the instant agony forcing him to the floor, the case crashing to the platform.

Xander felt the first taste of vomit rise in his throat as he struggled to find the will to grab for the case. He was perilously close to the ledge, his hand locked tenuously to the bottom rung of the ladder. Above him, the man stood with Feric's limp body in his arms, the bloodied head dangling to the side. With one short burst, the man shifted his weight and tossed Feric into the dark vacancy. An instant later, Xander felt the steel begin to slip from his own hand.

⚔

The Range Rover had been a complete surprise. Given Sedgewick's penchant for expensive suits, Sarah had expected a limousine, or at least a well-stocked Mercedes to pull up to the hotel. Instead, George had jumped from the cab of the four-by-four to help her up to her seat. She had changed into dark pants, a simple jacket, and a linen T-shirt. If she was meant to play the loyal minion of Eisenreich—the onetime assassin recruited to do their bidding—she meant to dress the part. Elegant but practical, enough to make the right impression, enough to match the profile they had no doubt seen in her file.

Just over an hour into the ride, Sarah understood why the Rover. Driving up into the hills, the trucklike car made the steep grades and rocky terrain of the climb remarkably comfortable. They had left the main road, if that is what one could call it, not more than five minutes ago. Now Tieg's large ranch house appeared on a not-too-distant ridge, bathed in a sheet of lights. As its various levels came into view, the house began to resemble an assortment of rectangles thrown together in haphazard sequence, each buffeted by endless panes of ceiling-high glass, windows to give every corner a breathtaking view of the rolling hills to each side. To the north and west, trees reached to the edge of a gravel drive, the rest retreating down the mountain in a jagged line of leaves and branch. Tieg clearly enjoyed his privacy, his mountain retreat nearly inaccessible to uninvited guests.

They drove along the narrow lane that bordered a pristine garden of clipped grass, an obvious stamp of order on the otherwise-wild surroundings. Even here, Sarah thought, the men of Eisenreich needed to show their control.

The car came to a stop at the apex, the front door a few steps down from the driveway. George slipped out from behind the wheel, darted around the car, and extended a hand to help Sarah from her seat. An hour and a quarter, door-to-door. It seemed far more remote than that. Leaving her at the head of the steps, he returned to the wheel and drove off to an unseen garage. Standing alone, Sarah enjoyed the view for a brief moment before taking the first step down. As she did, the door opened, Sedgewick's figure appearing in the light.

"Ah, Ms. Trent," he said, pulling the door back, "taking advantage of the mountain air. It's often my first reaction, as well."

"It's beautiful up here," she answered as she moved through the doorway and past him into an open foyer, a sunken living room just beyond. The cool night air was replaced by the smell of a pinewood fire. The hearth, at the center of the room, rose like an inverted funnel to the cathedral ceiling twenty feet above. Off to the right, framed by a windowed view of a starry sky, Anton Votapek stood, his glass lifted in her direction.

"Good evening, Ms. Trent."

Before she could answer, a second man, much larger, with a wide chest and thick fingers, appeared from behind a grand piano at her left. "I'm afraid we haven't been introduced." He stepped toward the center of the room and smiled. "My name is Jonas Tieg, and I've heard a great deal about you."

✍

"What are you telling me, you *imbecile!*" The voice crackled, but it was not the transatlantic connection causing the tremor. Rage seethed from the other end, the bald man with the cellular phone pulling it from his ear as the voice thundered again. "*What* were you told to do, Paolo? To *kill* them both? *No!* This you were expressly warned against."

"Eric went over as well. They must have given him no choice—"

"Given *him* no choice? You expect me to believe that a three-hundred-pound man is *forced* to kill *them*? What kind of *stupidity* is that?" The sound of coughing sputtered on the line, a wheezing of breath before the tirade continued. "And the manuscript, the notes?"

"The manuscript?"

"The *books*, the *books*! Are you paying attention, Paolo?"

"Oh, the manuscript, the books, yes." The man spoke quickly, trying to deflect the attack. "It must have gone off the train with them. There was no sign of anything by the time I reached the car."

"*By the time you*—" Another spasm of coughing. "You were not together?"

"I . . . we . . . no, we met at the center—"

"Enough." Control returned to the tired voice. "You were meant to protect Jaspers, and now . . ." There was genuine anguish in the voice. "You have disappointed me beyond measure." The line was silent for a few seconds as the weathered voice gathered its strength and considered the next move. "I needed those notes, Paolo. I needed to know what he had. I will now have to—" He cut himself off. "Get off the train and return to Wolfenbüttel. Make sure everything has been cleaned up there."

"But what about Eric? And the other man? What of Jaspers?"

"Get off that train and do as you are told!" The venom returned. "I will send somebody to clean up your mess."

The line went dead, and Paolo Vestuti slumped back into his seat. He had never heard the old man so angry, never heard the coughing so intense. But he would do what he was told. As he always had. A week of trailing, only to lose him. Vestuti closed his eyes, the image of the two men falling from the platform—Eric's huge frame breaking through the chain barrier, Jaspers gripping at the enormous neck. The violent picture remained with him, his own futility in pulling the door open too late, peering over the side to find nothing, the wind driving him back to the safety of the car.

He would be made to atone for the sin. Of that he was certain.

⚞

Sarah stared at the unexpected face of Votapek; her eyes, however, remained controlled. She then turned to the less familiar member of the trio. "And I've heard a great deal about you, Mr. Tieg." Sedgewick was extending his hand toward the steps. "Daniel into the lion's den?" she asked.

"Daniel?" Sedgewick smiled as he followed Sarah down to the living room. "Hardly, Ms. Trent. You don't seem the type to call on the gods to save you. And we"—he stopped at the bar, lifting two champagne glasses and handing one to her—"we're not animals."

"Not *gods,* Larry," said Votapek, "*one* God. Capital *G.* That was what Daniel was willing to die for, his *one* God. Am I right, Ms. Trent?"

Sarah took the glass and smiled at the smallest of the three men. "I think he survived. That was the point of the story."

Sarah's candor had the desired effect. Votapek and Sedgewick looked at one another and laughed; Tieg, though somewhat more subdued, joined in a moment later. Sarah moved to the window. There was little doubt in her mind that the men of Eisenreich had accepted her as one of their own. The easy banter, the attempt to make a new associate feel welcome—all the trappings of self-confidence and commitment. And yet she felt a distinct uneasiness. These were the men ready to throw the country into chaos, eager to foist a new breed—a programmed breed—of children into the vacuum they would create. Light repartee and champagne hardly seemed fitting.

Sarah glanced out the window. Just below, the room jutted out beyond the scarp of the hill, the slope falling off in a tangle of trees and plants, the topmost awash in a glow emanating from an unseen column of lights. Sarah wondered whether it was meant to highlight the view or to maintain a careful watch on the most densely camouflaged access to the house.

"How often do you have these little get-togethers?" she asked as she moved toward the fire to find a well-cushioned chair.

"Those questions, I think, can wait for dinner," said Sedgewick as he topped up Votapek's glass and turned to Tieg.

"One is sufficient for me." He smiled, then turned to Sarah. "Eisenreich is always better over a nice piece of fish and some artichoke. I trust salmon is to your liking, Ms. Trent." Tieg had situated himself on a leather sofa against the far side, more window than wall, with an equally stunning view of the surrounding hills. His legs were crossed, his hands holding the glass at his knees. Sarah looked over at him, a pensive figure, a far cry from the man described in the dossier she had read earlier that evening.

"Anton is always quick to point out my little shortcomings." Sedgewick's smile elicited no reaction whatsoever. "*One* God? It seems to me the Greeks and Romans were far more sensible—they had hundreds to do their bidding."

"*Their* bidding?" Votapek laughed. "Isn't it supposed to be the other way around? We following God's commands—something like that?"

"Larry has a way of looking at things," piped in Tieg, more for Sarah's benefit than Votapek's, "that makes conventional interpretation seem somewhat naïve." Sarah noticed how different Tieg was from his television persona. No homespun aphorisms. This was a highly articulate man.

"Not naïve, Jonas. Rudimentary perhaps, but not naïve." It was Sedgewick's turn to correct. "Monotheism has managed to keep a stranglehold on us for the last two thousand years. What we've failed to remember is that religion is a tool, a means to—"

"Control." Sarah's interruption caused a momentary lull, none of the men ready with a response. Sarah kept her eyes on Tieg, the last of the triumvirate somehow more compelling than the others.

After a moment, Sedgewick smiled. "Exactly."

Tieg seemed equally fascinated by Sarah, his stare locked on her.

A pair of sliding doors suddenly opened, revealing a beautifully laid table. "We'll continue this over the fish." Sarah stood and led them up the steps. In the corner, George stood patiently.

✠

The guard waved Stein through. The exchange was the usual for the late hour, a few smiles, a passing reference to midnight oil before Bob moved down the wide corridor and into the elevator. He listened for a moment as he exited at the sixth floor to make sure the custodial staff had completed its nightly prowl. He then stepped to the left—silence as he continued past O'Connell's office, the thick sheets of matted glass that framed the door reflecting the row of halogen lamps dimmed for the late hour. Never raised to full capacity, the light cast an even more somber glow than usual on the cream-colored wall.

Arriving at his office, Bob slid the key into the lock and opened the door to the mayhem he had left behind less than eighteen hours ago. He tossed the keys onto a small leather footrest—one of the few areas not piled high with paper—and moved to the desk. Flicking on his own halogen, he crouched to his knees and began to fiddle with the combination lock of his safe, its top providing ample storage space for an odd assortment of books, coffee cups and half-filled bags of cheese balls.

The stacks of papers within were a far cry from the mess scattered around the office. Three neat piles of manila folders waited patiently; Bob began to thumb through the second stack before pulling out a thick dossier, the word *Restricted* stamped in bold type across the front. Settling himself into the desk chair, he flipped through the first pages, a recent history of Sarah—an impenetrable section on post-trauma syndrome that showed no understanding of the woman he had just met. Pausing only once, he continued to fan his way back to the earlier sessions at Langley.

He was scanning one page, turning to the next, when he realized that something was different, somehow wrong. He stared at the page, trying to see what it was, when he realized that the pages were *sticking* to one another, a sort of static cling making the peeling awkward. He flipped through the rest, the answer slowly dawning on him as he released the sheets. *Xerox. Someone's Xeroxed this file.* He was certain, the texture retaining the electrical backwash that the flash of light on glass always produces. He stopped and looked at the stacks in the safe.

Somehow, someone had gotten to the file; somehow, someone had found a way into his office, into his safe—the combination of which he changed each week—and had left everything in place, even the position of the second stack.

All thoughts of his own vulnerability quickly vanished as he remembered Sarah, the immediacy in her voice: *"In those passages, I'm everything they hate and fear. I'm the voice of reason."* He looked at his watch. Ten to three. Ten to twelve San Francisco time. She was already gone. She was with them. And he knew they had all the information they needed.

⚔

There was nothing to do but sit. His chest ached with each intake of breath, his shoulders burned from the strain, but he felt it all, the wind shoot by, the sun on his face, the clawing in his stomach where hunger had replaced fear. His left arm lay limp at his side, the right again clutching at the case, the miracle of the last ten minutes still a blur.

Xander tried to piece it together. He remembered his hand slipping from the rung, the sudden grip of an enormous hand on his forearm as he had been pulled back, his other hand finding the thick, gristly skin of the man's neck, pulling down on it, only to have the weight teeter toward him as both bodies had flown from the platform. How the chain had found his hand, he would never know, but the iron links had somehow fallen into his grip, his hand quick to clutch at them as his entire body had swung off the platform, slamming into the underbelly of the train as the large man had disappeared from sight. The speed of the train had been all that had kept Xander horizontal, his feet straddling unseen rigging, enough to keep him elevated, enough to lend him the strength to pull himself back along the chain toward the platform.

And then the real miracle. With his arms no longer able to contain the pain, Xander had felt his fingers begin to slip, the wind too much against his body. It was then that a pair of hands had reached around from the platform to pull him in. Thrust onto the ledge, Xander had looked up to see a face, a contortion of blood and flesh, the right cheek ripped, revealing shards of bone, the body a tangled amalgam of cloth and skin, chest heaving, each breath revealing the exposed wound of a broken rib. Drained of all vitality, the body had tripped back, feet collapsing underneath, head smacking against the steel of the train wall.

A dying Feric, the computer case at his side.

Now the operative sat hunched over a growing pool of blood, his mouth sucking for air as Xander began to inch his way closer.

Dragging himself across the platform, Xander reached up to the handle of the car door and pushed his back into the heavy steel. Ignoring the pain, he reached across to Feric and the case and pulled them in, the door slamming shut as he laid Feric's head on his lap. The two sat silently, the passing minutes bringing greater consciousness, the pain intense as Xander tested each limb—strains but nothing broken. Feric, however, remained still, his breath growing more and more erratic, dots of blood speckling his chin.

Xander held tightly to the small broken body of the man who had saved him once again. This time, though, he knew it would be the last. No tears. Only anger, self-loathing as Feric's breathing began to quiet, a gurgling sound rising from his throat. Hushed and staggered, the words began to form.

"Get to New York . . . Sarah . . . contact number . . . in pack." He coughed, his entire body convulsing at the shock, more blood finding the floor. "Throw me . . . from train." His back arched, the last words forced through the pain. "They will expect . . . to find me." He lifted his arm to Xander's shoulder, squeezed tightly, and then released; a moment later, his head fell lifeless.

✄

On the platform, the sun danced on steel as Xander cradled the lifeless mass to his chest. Fields raced by; the wind whipped at his face. He stepped to the ledge. Eyes staring straight ahead, he released, unwilling to watch as the small body crashed to the ground below.

Find Sarah. It was the only thought his mind would permit.

PART THREE

7

The rest, therefore, must attend to the practical.

—ON SUPREMACY, CHAPTER VII

XANDER STARED OUT at the crush of bodies, the platform beyond the window thick with the first early-morning commuters. He had lost all sense of time, the minutes since the attack frozen in tiny capsules of activity, each a disconnected strand of energy focused on necessity: retrieve the computer case; examine Feric's pack; commit the contact numbers to memory. One after another, a simple list of tasks, each performed with numb ambivalence.

And somewhere in a hazy past, he remembered having cleaned himself up within the cramped confines of the train rest room, a tiny corner insert with barely enough room for toilet and sink. A thick sweater had miraculously appeared in Feric's pack and had quickly replaced the torn windbreaker. First, though, he had forced himself to mop up the blood in the corridor, most of the paper towel consigned to the small puddle left by a dying Feric. With even, measured strokes, he had scrubbed away the last drops before rinsing the towels in the sink, the rotelike activity enough to foster a few moments of calm. But they had been short-lived, the reflection in the mirror quick to remind him of the night's events—hair blown wild, cheeks streaked with blood, eyes dazed and red. In those dark minutes, he had never felt so alone, the image of Feric fixed in his mind, fragile, broken, the contorted face resting on a bloodied shoulder, arms and legs limp in a cradling grasp. Weightless, lifeless. And then gone. *What do I do now? What can I do?*

A strange sort of vacancy had come over him, the panic of isolation finding its match in the hollow stare reflected in the mirror—eyes that had grown somber and cold, distilled of both fear and compassion. He had seen those eyes before. In a tunnel. In Florence. And they had been hers. *Sarah. Find Sarah.*

Now, as he sat alone in a first-class cabin—he had made the move an hour ago—the words echoed through his mind, an inner beacon against the bump and cluster of the early-morning crowds boarding the train.

The door slid open, the sudden noise snapping his head to the right, his grip imperceptibly tighter around the case. A tall woman popped her head through, a timid nod as she pointed to the empty seats across from him.

A week ago, he would have found his own reaction strange. Now his concern for his surroundings seemed almost second nature. He was learning. *Trace the stare of an eye, the hat pulled too far down over a face. They are the sure signs.* Feric's words.

"Sind diese frei, bitte?" The Schweitzerdeutsch accent was unmistakable.

Xander's shock passed without notice, his smile pure reflex as he nodded. She returned the smile and bustled two small boys through the door, each dressed in the gray flannels of traveling attire. Perhaps eight and ten, the boys had cheeks that revealed the puffy red of early-morning rousing, hair slick and exact under what had no doubt been a grueling comb, parts perfect to the twin cowlicks. They were impeccably well behaved, taking the two seats across from Xander as their mother sat down next to him. Removing two small books from identical satchels, they began to read, feet dangling above the carpeted floor, boots swaying in haphazard meter. They were an organized little family, silent save for the occasional flipping of a page. For a few moments, Xander allowed himself to blend into their world—ordered, kind, simple—the serenity broken only by the jolting start of the train and the coincident arrival of the conductor. Even he seemed to recognize the hushed quality to the cabin, peering over at the boys with a gentle smile, clipping tickets and returning them without a word. Sliding the door back, he moved off down the corridor, and the cabin was again silent.

For the first time in days, Xander felt protected, safe. Without thinking, he closed his eyes, his thoughts drifting to a welcome nothingness.

The dessert proved even more exquisite than the salmon, a fruit tart floating in a raspberry sauce, the taste prompting all four to purr in approval. At no time during the meal had Sarah shown the slightest hesitation in sparring with the three men around the table, egged on by the roles each took in response to her self-assurance: Sedgewick, the intellectual, finding in her a worthy adversary; Votapek, the intimate, playing up the *bond* from their first meeting; and Tieg . . . Tieg, the enigma. Sarah had yet to ascertain his role, uneasy with the detachment he maintained among such close associates.

Sedgewick was the first to resume speaking as he swept his spoon through a pool of the red confection, his cheeks flushed from several glasses of wine. "Though I hate to admit it, Marx had it right—it's a waste of time to try and define the day-to-day workings of the last stage in the process. Just set everything up, or at least allow things to move in their natural patterns so that a future is viable." He lapped at the spoon. "Of course, I'm no Marxist, but it isn't hard to pat old Karl on the back for having had the horse sense to refrain from offering some design for the future. Create the playing field. That's all one can do." He took a sip of coffee and sat back.

"It's been a long time since I read Marx," said Sarah, "but I think he had *some* idea of what he wanted—communal property, the dictatorship of the proletariat. I find it difficult to believe that 'creating the playing field' would have been sufficient."

"Actually, it was," responded Votapek, already in the middle of his second piece. "Marx *did* think it would happen on its own—capitalism would come crashing down all by itself. That's where he made his mistake." He wolfed down a healthy slab. "But you're probably right. There's no question that you have to have an idea of what's best for the people, how to get the most out of them and how to stabilize them *before* you set out to create the playing field. Anyone with an idea for the future has to know that you can't draw up the . . . let's call them *blueprints* . . . until you see the space you're going to build on. You have to clear the land before you set the foundations." *Clear the land,* thought Sarah. *Chaos at its most innocent.*

"A period of statelessness," added Sedgewick, "to make sure that the foundations are correct. That seems to me a central maxim of the manuscript."

"You have to remember," reminded Sarah, "that my familiarity with that book is far more limited than yours." She had pressed the point a number of times in the last hour. "My questions—"

"Are those that come from the onetime assassin of Jordan." All eyes turned to Tieg, who was pouring a cup of tea. He had been quiet for several minutes, his words clearly timed to elicit the most effective response. "We're well aware of that, Ms. Trent. We're also aware that you see the world from a somewhat *different* perspective." He put down the pot and looked at her. "General theories derived from a sixteenth-century manuscript aren't likely to overwhelm or impress you, are they? You like to know *how*, *when*, not *why*. Or am I misinterpreting your part in all of this?" He took a sip.

Sarah had not expected the question, nor the reference to her past. More troubling was the way Tieg looked at her, something behind the stare. "No, I think that would be a fair estimation."

"Good." He placed the cup on its saucer. "The problem is, the *how* and the *when* have never been that important to us. Don't get me wrong. The practical side is ultimately what drives us. I think we can all agree on that. But it can't be our focus." Looking at Sedgewick, he continued. "I really have no interest in what Larry is up to, nor he about me. I *trust* that when we reach a certain point, he'll have accomplished everything he needs to accomplish so that we can move forward." He looked back at Sarah. "Aside from that, our lives are brought together only by the *why*. That, with some minor variation, is the same for all three of us."

Tieg had waited for the appropriate moment to *instruct* Sarah in the ways of Eisenreich. Unlike his colleagues, he showed no need to impress with allusions to grand theories or his own exploits. Of the three, he was the one to keep his cards closest to the chest. More than that, he seemed to be testing her. Twice during the meal, he had cut Sedgewick off so as to press her further for the details of her relationship with Eisenreich. Each time, she had parried with innocuous phrases, recalling her desire to remain on the periphery when it came to details. Only now did she realize how clever he had been, timing his interruptions so as to make sure that the conversation remained focused on the abstract. Evidently, he was not inclined to permit facts to enter the debate.

"I'm not sure I'd put the *why* in those terms," added Votapek, "but I agree it's the search for permanence that ties us together." He was not willing to allow Tieg to speak for all three. Sarah knew that had the situation been reversed, the more famous member of the trio would have sat in silence, his ego secure enough to avoid such obvious flexing. It troubled her to find such strength at Eisenreich's core. "Order is about setting boundaries so as to encourage people—especially the young—to challenge their potential. That, naturally, demands structure, discipline, a bit of weeding out. Not *everyone* is capable of the potential I have in mind." Sedgewick's pretension had given way to Votapek's eugenics.

"Simply put, we have to get rid of constraints—old institutions—and throw everything into turmoil; that way, the cream can rise to the top. The great unwashed will have no choice but to recognize who their natural leaders are." Votapek lifted his cup, his eyes momentarily locked on the undulating coffee within. "Only the best are capable of taming chaos—those who can harness its power and lead the unenlightened in new directions. The rest"—he shook his head—"teach them to follow. Give them toys to play with—greed, hatred, pettiness. Then create controlled battlefields for them—bigotry, fear, that sort of thing. Focus their energy on a common hatred and you have a satisfied, manageable mass. Institutions are merely an afterthought. A few innocents may get hurt, but that's the price. With that, and with the right sort of technology, you can control them all very easily. Keep them busy and you allow real innovation to seize the day." He put the cup down and leaned toward Sarah. "Cling to old institutions, and the best you can do is erect monuments to your own limitations, because *that's* what institutions represent—our sense of *workable* boundaries. Then, when the truly remarkable *do* emerge, we stifle them because they tear at the very walls we've put up. They challenge us, and we destroy them." He sat back. "The middle ground isn't worth a thing, Ms. Trent. Our only choice—permanance through excellence."

Votapek looked at each member of the dinner party, a self-satisfied grin on his lips. There was nothing humorous, though, no conceit in the words he had spoken. Only conviction. And perhaps a sense of responsibility, a sense that these three were the men ready to bestow a gift of great value on a foundering world, a world in need of their insights. As if it were their duty to create the darkness so as to usher in a more perfect, more permanent light.

Trying to formulate a response, Sarah's thoughts were interrupted as Tieg accidentally spilled and shattered a glass of wine, George quick to come to his aid with a napkin. Without a word, the large man stepped away from the table and made his way through a swinging door, no doubt in search of a replacement.

Tieg continued to mop up the mess, removing one or two shards as he apologized. "That'll teach me to serve the expensive stuff."

"It's easily replaced." Sedgewick laughed. "We'll just have to be careful about how much we let you *drink*."

Votapek and Sedgewick broke into laughter as Tieg turned his attention to Sarah. "Now you understand why we focus on the *why*, Ms. Trent. The *how* seems to be beyond me." Again the laughter, this time Sarah joining in, the surest way to mask her astonishment at how easily the men of Eisenreich could move from tales of conquest and master races to a simple miscue with a wineglass.

Tieg folded the napkin, laying it by his plate as he sat back. "As I said, though, I'm sure it's the *how* and the *when* that intrigue you most. What you were sent to *confirm*." He looked at Votapek. "That *was* the word, wasn't it, Anton?" He had allowed each man his moment. It was time to press on.

"I believe so, yes." Votapek smiled, still intent on some fun. "I think Ms. Trent was sent to find out whether one of us might be trying to fly solo. Something about a separate agenda."

"Flying solo?" Tieg crossed his legs and looked at Sarah. "You mean if one of us was *deceiving* the others?" There was only a slight shift in his tone, his words carrying a twinge of reproach, but even Sedgewick and Votapek showed a moment's reaction. "Isn't that ironic, Ms. Trent? *Deception.*" The word now took on a harsher quality, clearly intended as accusation. "For us, it's the very cornerstone of the *how*," he added. "Not among ourselves, of course. We would *never* deceive one another because we trust one another. It's the people we intend to control—who *need* to be controlled—who are the ones we mean to . . ." He paused, eyes riveted on Sarah, "*Deceive* is such an unpleasant word, don't you agree, Ms. Trent?" She returned his stare, not once giving in to the alarm bell blaring in her head. "*Manipulate?*" he prodded. "No, that's no better, is it? *Oversee?*" Now he waited, nodding to himself, his command of the room complete, the mood strikingly different from only moments before. "Yes, *oversee.* I think that captures our intentions." His gaze remained on her. "Which brings us back to *your* intentions, Ms. Trent. Was I far off the mark when I talked about deception?" The room was suddenly quiet, Votapek and Sedgewick clearly unnerved by Tieg's insinuation.

Sarah waited. "This meal and conversation answer any misgivings I might have had about your commitment to one another."

"*Our* commitment to one another." He was baiting her.

"Yes." Simple. To the point.

"So readily convinced, Ms. Trent?" Tieg had no intention of letting it go at that, his tone and posture now far more aggressive. He began to shake his head. "It's not our deceptions that concern me, Ms. Trent—"

"*Our* deceptions?" broke in Sedgewick.

"Keep quiet, Larry." Tieg kept his eyes on Sarah.

"What do you mean, 'keep—'"

"I *said*, keep quiet." The severity in tone was enough to silence the financier. Votapek, too, held his tongue. "It's *yours*, Ms. Trent," whispered Tieg. "*That's* what's most troubling. *Your* deception. Far more subtle than a few bugged computers or a hidden taping device, wouldn't you agree?" He now turned to his comrades, their expressions proof enough of the indiscretions. As if dealing with two children, he calmly asked, "What were you thinking?" He shook his head in disbelief. "Do you have *any* idea who she is?" Sarah watched as the two men—only moments ago so pleased with themselves—began to buckle under the scrutiny. "You simply allowed yourselves to buy into the ruse." Sarah remained silent as Votapek and Sedgewick now erupted.

"What are you talking about, Jonas?" said Sedgewick, his indignant tone a futile attempt at self-command. "What ruse?"

Votapek followed with even greater incredulity. "*Impossible.* I was told we ran a thorough check. *Everything* she said was confirmed—"

"It's very easy," continued Tieg, now ignoring the two men and turning back to Sarah, "to lose sight of the obvious when you *want* to impress someone, isn't it, Ms. Trent? When you feel put up to the challenge?" A strange smile crossed his lips. "And you placed quite a clever little challenge at our feet, didn't you? That tape Larry made of your conversation with Anton. Most impressive. And very convincing. You picked your target very cleverly."

Again, Sedgewick exploded. "This is *outrageous*—"

"*No!*" This time, Tieg held nothing back. "What's outrageous is that the two of you could *ever* have let it go this far. She mentions a few names, choice tidbits from a rather checkered past, and you willingly fill in the rest for her." His frustration forced a momentary pause, his jawline taut from the tension. "We're less than a *week* away from the most crucial moment in a lifetime's worth of preparation, and you allow *this* to happen." He now turned on Sarah. "Oh, don't worry, Ms. Trent. Nothing you've done has made that moment any less certain. Nothing you *could* have done would have gotten in the way. You see, chaos is something that comes in small steps. One tiny explosion means nothing. One on top of another—now, *that* is something quite extraordinary. The actual effect is inconsequential. Only what is perceived. And that is unstoppable. *That* is what brings people to their knees." He paused, aware that he had let himself go too far. "What was it, Ms. Trent—set us on one another? Make us question one another?" His jaw tightened. "We've been doing that for years, haven't we, *boys?*" Neither answered, a forced calm returning to his expression. " '*Alison's* role.' " He shook his head as the smile reappeared. "That *was* clever. It's exactly what would frighten him most. Isn't that right, Anton? And all of that about going over the edge, your madness—all in the files. Except you left certain crucial pieces of your past out of the picture. That surprised me, Ms. Trent. Didn't you think if we had access to *one* we would have access to *all* of your files?" George reappeared at the door, accompanied by three other men. *The broken glass. The signal.* She had seen it too late.

"I have no idea what you had in mind, Ms. Trent," continued Tieg, "or why you thought you could take us on as your special project." He looked at Votapek and Sedgewick, both men unable to match his glance. "Neither does our good friend, whom she calls *Eisenreich.*" He stared at Sarah for a long moment. "You've never actually been in contact with him, have you, Ms. Trent?"

Sarah remained strangely calm. "No."

"Of course not." Tieg stood. "I would like to thank you, though, for having brought a number of things out into the open. If nothing else, you've made us aware—some of us more than others—that we're not invulnerable. What exactly you'd hoped to accomplish"—he shrugged—"that still remains a mystery." He nodded to George. "There are, as you no doubt know, certain . . . *narcotics* that will help us to fill in the gaps." George moved in behind her chair. "Keep her downstairs until I've finished here." He looked at Votapek and Tieg, then moved off into the living room. The two men rose slowly, neither returning Sarah's gaze as they followed.

George waited patiently. She stood, placed her napkin on the table, and accompanied him out into the darkened corridor.

⚔

Hydra. Drenched in an amber sky, a dry heat billowing on chest and thighs, water gliding to the small incline of his back, skin a deep brown from days on the beach. Her arm lies gentle across his stomach, sprinkles of sea held on each lash as a distant boat races by. Gently, the waves begin to lap against their bodies, hers arching at the touch of the cool swirl, he turning to see her lips, dark red, her hair, so perfect, sprayed on the powder-white sand, auburn streaks of light radiating from a thousand freckles she calls a tan. One eye pops open, a smile, the head turns and lifts, lips parched for his, rising closer, moistened by an eager tongue, his body intoxicated by her, the touch of her fingers on his chest, lips to his, and he breathes again as she slips back to her sleeping pose beside him. Fiona.

The sun beats down, a muffled voice whispers at him from somewhere behind, his head too heavy to turn, his eyes too stained by sea and sun to open, the voice more and more intense, the cool water growing less pleasant on his back, her arm somehow gone. He turns, his eyes now struggling for sight, and he sees the mouth, the face, the voice beckoning at him. Feric. Day suddenly night, sand suddenly snow, a chill coursing through him, his body airless, breathless, slipping from Feric's grasp, falling from the train, the eyes bloodied and cold. . . .

"Mein Herr, wir sind am Flughafen angekommen."

The mustachioed face of the conductor stared down at Xander, a hand to his stiffened shoulder, trying to shake the sleep from his crumpled frame. Xander's head had clamped down onto his neck, his entire side wedged deep within the seat, his knees pulled in tight for warmth. Squinting into the light, he slowly tried to straighten his neck. The pain he felt was far more than just the odd strain from sleep. Forcing himself forward on the seat, he watched the conductor move to the door, attention fixed on his pocket watch.

"The train leaves in six minutes, Mein Herr," he continued in German. "Please be certain to have all your belongings."

With that, he disappeared, Xander once again alone in the compartment. His surrogate family was now long gone, their books and satchels only a distant, fond memory. He had slept for twenty minutes, enough to infuse his brain with that disconcerting sensation of floating, his nose prickling at the cold air that was creeping through an open window. Hoisting himself up—the case still firmly in his grasp, the pack on his back—he tried to recall the dream. *Something with sand. And water. Or was it snow?* He shook the sleep from his head and started to rise. It was then that he noticed the woman.

"Did you have a good sleep, Dr. Jaspers?" She held a gun at her hip, a modest weapon, but one capable of ripping a hole through him at such close range. As she spoke, she latched the door behind her, long, thin fingers easily managing the ancient clasp. "Looks as though the reports of your death were greatly exaggerated." The accent was American, the tweed suit and raincoat English. Somehow, the small gun looked rather elegant in her hand.

Xander stared at it and then up at the woman.

"There were only two bodies from the Saltzgitter train," she explained, "neither fitting your description."

Again, he did not answer.

"Don't look so surprised. We knew you'd try to get to the airport. In fact, we had no intention of doing anything with you on the train. Just wanted to keep you tight until Frankfurt. Shame about your little friend."

She took the seat across from him, the gun aimed at his chest.

For some reason, Xander was finding the prospect of death surprisingly calming. "The train leaves in six minutes. I assume we're not getting off."

"It does, and we are," she answered. "But we're going to wait until everyone else is off. Fewer crowds. Less congestion. Much better that way."

"And then?"

"I really have no idea."

"Another loose end to take care of?"

The woman smiled. "I could have done that the moment I walked in. No, my orders are simply to get you"—she stopped and smiled again—"to get you off this train. We each play a role, Dr. Jaspers, and for the next few hours, yours will be that of the accommodating captive. It's not a difficult one, I can assure you."

Sitting, staring at her, Xander focused on the eyes. Deep brown, almost black, they sent a message of confidence, even arrogance. *Such assurance conveys truth.* It was as if Feric were by his side, explaining, cautioning. *Control requires no mask, only simplicity.* Simplicity and truth—which meant he had been granted a reprieve. She was no executioner, only a courier, an agent of Eisenreich sent to deliver him to some unknown place, unaware of the treasures hidden within his briefcase. Otherwise, she would have checked to make certain he still had the disc. It's what the manuscript would have taught: *At every level, give them only the information they need, only the role they are to play.* She had said as much.

He was learning. And knowledge granted power, power its *own* arrogance, its own role to be played. It was not difficult to understand why so many had found Eisenreich's theory so comforting.

"How old are you?" he asked. "Twenty-four? Twenty-five?" The woman did not answer. "And you've killed—"

"In one minute, you and I are going to walk out of here as a happy couple, only you'll have a gun nestled to your ribs." She had no patience for his prodding. "On the platform, we'll be arm in arm. Do you understand?"

"Three, four?" continued Xander, ignoring her question. "More? I wonder how someone makes a choice like that, at that crucial moment? How—"

"At least one." She stood. "That's all that really matters, isn't it?"

"I've no idea." His response conveyed little emotion. "I've only watched people die. I suppose killing me would be quite easy?"

"Get up, Dr. Jaspers."

"*Sie sind keine Mörderin—*"

"*Get up*, Dr. Jaspers."

The words had meant nothing to her, her eyes giving away too much in the repetition of the command. It was clear what she had expected—what she had been *told* to expect: an easily daunted academic, a man beyond panic. What she had found—what he *himself* had found—was someone quite different. He *was* learning. He had unnerved her, the German causing an instant of confusion.

As she had said, the platform was empty, no one to get in their way before the escalators leading up to the airport's sublevels and main terminal. Her grip was firm, her movement agile. Until now, he had not realized just how physically strong she was, his right arm virtually immobilized by the pincerlike hold on his elbow. Perhaps no killer, she had been trained *very* well.

At the top of the escalator, she nodded to the U-bahn, pushing him toward the track for one of Frankfurt's myriad suburbs. Following him through the turnstile, she drew up to his side as they trundled down the steps. Within a minute, she had taken them to the far end of the platform.

"We'll wait here." Her hand now became a vise. "Smile."

Xander complied, still somehow guided by the calm he had conjured on the train. Half a minute later, a burst of light flashed along the far wall, the arrival of an incoming train. As it sped past, she dug the gun deeper into his back, twisting his elbow to make her point.

"When it stops, stay calm, wait for the passengers to get off, and then step on to the train." The words were whispered, direct, hot bursts of air moistening his ear. "If I feel even the slightest bit uneasy, I'll twist your elbow right out of its socket. Do you understand, Dr. Jaspers?"

Xander nodded, the pain already reaching up to his shoulder, his mind racing for some means of escape. If it was going to happen, it would have to be in the next minute. Once inside the train, he'd be trapped, no further threats necessary, and no chance of a second reprieve at journey's end.

The train began to slow, sweat creasing his neck, the last car coming into view. To his amazement, the windows were lined with people. Somewhere, he could hear Feric telling him that crowds were a tool, a mechanism to be used. The doors peeled open, the agent of Eisenreich pressing ever tighter to his side as people poured out. He waited, certain that she could feel the tympanic throbbing in his chest.

"Just remain calm," came the voice, hers or his own, he could not tell.

And then he saw it.

Out of the corner of his eye, Xander noticed a man jump up from his seat, his hands pushing through the other passengers, the strain on his face apparent—a man about to miss his stop. Slowly, Xander stepped into the car, timing his approach as the desperate commuter darted for the door.

At the last possible moment, Xander thrust her into the man's path.

"Sie hat eine Pistole!" he yelled in German as, elbow miraculously free, he managed to push his way to the door. *"A gun!"*

Screams erupted throughout the car as people backed away, the gun in full view, the doors beginning to close. Xander leapt to the platform, she too slow, too confused to escape the now-frantic crowd in the car. The doors slammed shut and, for a moment, their eyes met through the glass, hers lost in disbelief. The realization of failure began to rise on her face, terror in her eyes as the train inched out of the station. He watched as she backed herself into a far corner, the crowds cowering in their seats, the gun still in her open palm.

Xander turned and walked away, his pace casual, his head down. It was over. *We each play our roles.* He had learned to play his.

NEW YORK, MARCH 5, 4:12 A.M. ✍ Janet Grant crept through the darkened room, a tiny flashlight bobbing along with her movements. The instructions had been curt, no detail: *"Notes, Italian, a small book. Perhaps an envelope from Europe."* The address of the brownstone on West 107th Street. Nothing more.

A long green sofa sat along the far wall, two matching chairs neatly across from it to create a small sitting room. Doilies adorned each of the armrests. Everything neat, ordered. A rather ancient record player sat atop a cabinet to the left, a row of records—Brahms, Beethoven, and Bach— nestled at its side. The most contemporary piece was the stern desk by the window, four plain legs below an equally plain top. Nineteen sixty-five, at the latest. It was a room that had not changed in thirty years.

Janet moved to the desk, the top empty save for a few old picture frames, the photographs equally dated. She sat at the chair and began to open the drawers, the bottom left locked. She removed a penlike object from her pack and threaded it through the slot. The latch released. Inside, a large manila envelope stared back at her, the stamps European. She took it from the drawer—the envelope's flap already open—and pulled out the contents.

Clara,

Hold on to these. At home. Anyone asks, you haven't received anything. I'll explain when I get back.

A. J.

Behind the letter, she discovered pages and pages of notes. All in Italian. She tucked them into her jacket, closed the drawer, and stood.

An instant later, she was on her knees.

The first blow to her back had been enough to daze her, the second to disorient. She turned, just in time to ward off the third, her instincts to lunge at the figure above her. Her gloves found flesh, a weathered neck, her grip tight enough to bring the figure to its knees. The face now came clear, an older woman, jet black hair, thick cheeks.

Clara Huber was no longer putting up a fight.

Janet stared into Huber's eyes, uncertain what she should do. There had been no instructions, no contingency plans. *"Notes, Italian, a small book."* Nothing more. For an eerie few seconds, she simply held her grip. Soon, other words began to drift into her head. *There must always be a place for sacrifice.* Words to calm her.

Without thought, Janet Grant drove her thumbs up into Clara Huber's windpipe and twisted. A single snap and the eyes glazed over.

Again, Janet looked at the face in her hands. No questions, no remorse. She placed it on the floor and checked her watch. Eight minutes.

The old man would be pleased.

✍

He had disposed of the computer in one of the terminal rest rooms—another bit of advice from Feric—and had taken the opportunity to trim his beard, wet down his hair. Now, as he stood at the American Airlines counter, he actually resembled the picture from one of the many passports Feric had kept hidden within the rucksack. With a few bills from the wad of cash he had found there as well, he bought a ticket for the twelve o'clock to New York. It would mean a stop in London, a layover of about an hour and a half, but Xander knew it was smarter to spend the time there than here. They would no doubt be returning to the airport to find out what had happened to their quarry. He had no choice but to take the earliest flight possible.

To his relief, the woman behind the counter showed no surprise at either his payment in cash or his lack of luggage, more concerned with both his good fortune at finding a seat at so late a date and his promise to be at the gate fifteen minutes before takeoff. A smile sufficed as assurance, all the while his shoulders growing less and less comfortable in the pants and turtleneck. He had been in the clothes for less than seven hours, but they were already giving off a rather distinct pong, and he had no intention of finding out how far he could stretch the limits of good taste during the ten-hour flight. More to the point, he knew it would be a good idea to alter his appearance. And remove the beard. Another cue from Feric. With just under an hour before takeoff, he had more than enough time and cash to remedy the situation.

Heading for the escalator and the stores one floor down, he suddenly remembered the second volume of the manuscript, conveniently forgotten in the mayhem of the past five hours. There had been no time, no energy to think of it. A day ago, he would never have permitted himself such a lapse. Now . . . He forced his mind to focus on the practical, Feric's dying order displacing any theoretical yearnings. *Sarah. Get back to the States and find Sarah.*

The memory of her eyes from Florence suddenly flooded back—confusion, loss. Eyes he had seen only minutes ago, this time, though, on a different woman. And yet somehow the same—the anguish, the terror. He wondered how many times *his* Sarah had been forced to kill? How often had she let one slip away? *Put it behind you!* Another internal command. *You have no time for it!*

The contact numbers began to race through his mind. Reaching the lower level, Xander headed toward a bank of phones. Once again focused, he calmly checked his surroundings and moved to the leftmost cubicle. Satisfied, he removed the receiver and punched in the first string of numbers. Every so often, he paused as instructed, dial tones and clicks ringing in the earpiece before he could enter the next set in the series. After several minutes, the sound of transatlantic static hovered on the line, a hum to accompany the final connection. Two rings later, the line engaged and a voice answered.

"There appears to be a receiver off the hook. If you are trying—"

He typed in the last four numbers and waited. Fifteen seconds later, a second recorded voice interrupted.

"Monica on the line. I trust all is well." Xander hit several buttons and waited for the message.

✄

The sign on the door had said CHAMPAGNE, the shadowed light of the basement corridor having been enough to distinguish each of the separate holding pens: German whites, French reds, roughly ten rooms, from the little Sarah had been able to see, her own cavern fitted with stool and seven or eight near-finished wine shelves propped up against a far wall—a work still in progress. For the time being, though, the room served as a makeshift cell for one. A tiny window was tucked in at the ceiling, no lock needed for an opening too narrow for any but a child to squeeze through. Even so, the gravel drive above was not exactly suited for inconspicuous escape, a good ten feet of floodlit area between house and trees. The window was *not* a possibility.

Nor was it a concern. Sitting on the stool, Sarah had given no time to studying the room around her. Instead—back against the wall, eyes fixed on a spot directly across from her—she had replayed the conversation from dinner over and over in her mind. It had been nearly an hour since Tieg's revelation, but her expression had remained unchanged, no emotion surfacing to cloud her thoughts. Only the conversation. Only Tieg's words. And with each subsequent rehashing, the strains of a once-familiar voice had grown louder and louder, echoes of a past fighting to break free from the tattered shelter of an overprotective psyche. *You should have seen them—the sudden shift in his mood, the spilled glass.* A voice that demanded control. *Seven years away have made you slow, unaware.* The words were direct. *It all happened too fast for you, the warning too late. All unacceptable.* With each rebuke, the voice gained greater command, claimed a sense of belonging. *The three of them together—you should have known; it was too easy, too . . .*

And yet, only Tieg had known. Votapek and Sedgewick had been as much in the dark as she had. *Only he had known.* It was a less severe voice that broke through, a voice that had kept the demons at bay for so long and that now reasserted itself. *Concentrate on what he said, the warning he gave.* Sarah forced herself to focus on his words. *"We're less than a week away . . . One tiny explosion means nothing. One on top of another . . . That is what brings people to their knees."* They had seen the theory play out in Washington, Chicago, ready now to extend the vision. It was enough to keep her mind occupied, to relieve her of the self-evaluation that moments of solitude and failure all too easily provoked. And yet, as she sat, other images flooded back, an eerily similar room: a guard, a bed, though no window. No slits of light seven years ago to grant even the hint of an elsewhere. Only the darkness and the shadows. And always the questions.

"*You understood the directive.*"

"*Yes.*"

"*You understood it might extend beyond Safad, to the others?*"

"*Yes . . . I—*"

"*Yes, you what?*"

"*Yes, I—*"

"*It was a contingency, and you made a choice. Certain sacrifices had to be made. In the end, you chose correctly. But it was your choice, your decision. You had to kill them, even if it meant having to let her die.*"

"*No . . . yes . . . I—*"

"*Was there another alternative?*"

"*There was a delay. I was told to wait. I could have saved her without the delay.*"

"*It was your choice to make, your responsibility in the end. The delay was irrelevant.*"

"*I . . .*"

"*The delay was irrelevant.*"

She stood, a need to shake free from the memories. *I made the choice. I took the responsibility.* A rush of anger, a venom seethed below the surface. *I can't let you back in!* She needed to find her *own* control, her *own* release. But the images were proving too much, forcing themselves to the surface with an unrelenting abandon. Unable to quell them, she swung her open fist against the face of the plaster wall, the smack of skin on cold flat stone enough to jar her senses. The pain pulsed throughout her hand, drove up through her arm. For a moment, she simply stared at her reddened palm, traced one of its threadlike lines from wrist to thumb, clenched her fist—the pain more acute—and saw the crease vanish into the folds of skin and fingers. Only then did the voice begin to recede.

And with the release, the shadows lifted from the room, her reason more acute, the ten-by-ten space the only reality she permitted. Strangely serene, Sarah drained her mind of everything but escape. They would be back for her soon enough. The operative needed to take control.

She scanned the cell, her eyes stopping at the door—keypad, no handle. Tieg had taken great pains to protect his wine, a precaution that was now paying dividends. *Something to puncture the plastic, get at the wires behind.* Her eyes lit on the group of shelves resting against the far wall; one two-by-four, ripped out and with nails still lodged within, might do the trick. She moved toward them, passing under a ceiling vent, the sound of muted voices echoing from above. Stopping, she strained to hear the words. An alternating cadence of accusation and denial indicated several speakers, but there was little else to make out. At least they were still in full lather.

The conversation suddenly broke off as a simultaneous flashing of lights invaded her near-darkened cell, the tiny window vanishing in a flurry of reds and blues. Sarah moved quickly to the stool and stepped up, only to be blinded by the onrush of headlights to her left. An instant later, the sound of footsteps rose from the corridor, a momentary pause before the door flew open, one of George's comrades bolting into the room, a gun at his side.

"You need to come with me." Sarah stared at the young face before slowly stepping down from the stool, the man quick to thrust a pair of shoes into her hands. "Put them on." A reprieve. The *narcotics* would have to wait. Very deliberately, she sat and began to lace up the shoes, an impatient gun waving in her face for encouragement. There was concern in his eyes, the butt of his silencer urging with greater insistence as he grasped her upper arm so as to *help* her to her feet. She considered attack, but instinct held her back. *Wait for the options to come to you.* Pushed out into the corridor, she came face-to-face with the two best reasons to keep herself in check—another set of well-suited minions, guns in evidence, the smaller of the two nodding for her to move down the hall. Overhead, the sound of scurrying feet followed the quartet along, the activity above in stark contrast to the silent stroll among the caverns. One in front, two at the rear, a pattering of rubber shoes along the carpeted cement leading her away from the steps to the kitchen and toward the back of the house. Within a minute, the narrow corridor brought all four to a large steel door, its thick shell unable to fully muffle the sound of a single voice issuing commands from beyond.

"Check around to the side and secure the area. I want a sweep of the entire grounds."

The three men stopped, her escort holding tightly to her arm as he looked at the other two for instruction. The smaller man shook his head, placing a finger to his lips and raising his gun, a non-too-subtle suggestion to Sarah that she keep quiet. Within half a minute, the footsteps outside faded to the distance, another voice, this time from a radio strapped to the smaller man's belt, breaking through. "You're clear." The man lowered his gun and moved to the door. Taking a key from his pocket, he unlocked a small box on the wall, punched in a sequence of numbers, and listened for the dead bolt to disengage. Ten seconds later, he slowly pushed the door open, the dank air of the subterranean corridors lifting at the invitation of a mild night outside.

Thick walls on either side shrouded the first ten feet of the ramp in darkness, creating a channel barely wide enough for two men to walk abreast. The remaining five feet rose in half shadow, just to the left of the high beams that flooded most of the grassy expanse above. Sarah tried to move, but she was held firmly at both arms. She watched as the smaller man nodded for the three to move through the door, the two at her sides sliding their guns into their belts before emerging to the night air. At the same time, the smaller man pushed past her—back to the door—pulling it shut behind him, the sound of the dead bolt reengaging a moment later as she was maneuvered up the ramp.

Once again, voices from above froze all three. In near-perfect unison, each man grabbed one of Sarah's shoulders and pressed her back up against the wall, simultaneously flattening himself at her side. The man to her left drew a knife and placed it under her throat. Silently, the trio listened to the disembodied conversation.

"I'm sure there's been some sort of mistake." It was Tieg, no hint of strain in the voice. "As you can see, I'm in no danger whatsoever. I keep these lights on as a security measure."

"We'll determine when the area is secure, sir." The words were official and smacked of law enforcement. "These lights have been on all night?"

"Yes. There's nothing back here—"

"Let *us* determine that, sir. As I said, the call came from Washington, and the Bureau's not likely to have sent us on a wild-goose chase if there wasn't reasonable cause."

"I appreciate that—"

"I'm sure you do, sir. And *we'd* appreciate it if you'd let us do our job. The other men inside—"

"As I said, close friends who prefer not to be involved."

"For whatever reasons, Washington believes you might be a target. There are enough crazies out there who think your show—"

"My television show? You're not trying to convince me some lunatic—"

"I'm not trying to convince you of *anything*, sir. My orders came from—"

"Washington. Yes, you've said that."

The agent now took a different approach. "I understand that this seems like a mistake, but I can assure you, you'll sleep much easier if you let us come to that conclusion. Even if we don't find anything, we'd still like to leave a man or two here just in case. Bureau policy."

Tieg audibly exhaled before answering. "Very well. I'll take you through the house, but I'm sure you'll see . . ." His voice grew fainter as he and the agent moved off, Sarah still pressed to the wall. It took her less than a second to realize what had happened.

Stein. Genius. It had to be Bob. Somehow he had realized she'd walked into a trap. Somehow he had known she was in trouble, and what better cavalry than federal agents to cause a little confusion? *Confusion—always the best remedy.* It was her only chance for escape. *Tieg a target. Brilliant. That's* why they had replaced their guns. *That's* why she was being shuttled out the back. They needed the house empty of any unexplained guests and, more important, they couldn't do anything that might draw attention. As the men at her sides listened for the conversation to fade to nothingness, Sarah heard another voice—an internal voice that had no intention of waiting with them.

She swung her elbow upward into the throat of the man to her right, his grip momentarily loosened, enough to leave her fingers free to tear across at the hand of the second man. Slicing her nails into his wrist, she twisted the blade away from her neck as she pushed him against the far wall. At the same time, she kicked backward, driving her foot down onto the kneecap of the first man, her heel smashing upward into his chin as he fell forward. Head snapping back, his body collapsed in a clump at the base of the ramp. The second man—only stunned—now grabbed Sarah by the hair and threw her against the wall, both of her hands tearing into his wrist, using his momentum to pull him into the wall after her, his chest careening into her raised knee, the collision forcing his body to double over. In that instant, his fingers relaxed on the knife, hers quick to grab the handle, and with one final thrust, she swung the blade up, for some reason veering it away from his chest and into his shoulder, the thick piercing of skin and sinew heavy in her hands as his face contorted from the agony. But not a sound, only a mouth gaping in anguish, eyes staring into hers as her hands released the knife and cleaved down onto his collarbone, the snap of breaking bones a momentary prelude to the drop of his body to the cement.

Sarah gasped for breath, eyes squinting shut to combat the throbbing in her head. *You wanted to kill him. You wanted it. And yet you couldn't. Why?* No tears this time, no regrets—only the relief of survival.

With her back against the wall, she scrutinized the brightly lit expanse between ramp and trees—her only means of escape. Not more than ten yards long, it remained unapproachable, men roaming the area, others no doubt positioned at the windows above to thwart any attempt. The light had to go, and it had to go in a hurry. Staring straight ahead, she saw the small locked box, keypad and electronic wires no doubt within. *Wrong choice!* The voice was adamant. *Short out the circuits? Think! Would he have been so careful with his wine and so foolish with his wiring?* There seemed only one reasonable choice. Stooping to the man whose chest now resembled a concave oval, she took his gun and began to frisk the body—one round of ammunition, wallet, credit cards, cash, and driver's license. Slipping them into her pockets, she scampered to the edge of the ramp—still in shadow—checked the silencer, and fired five shots into the high beams forty feet above her.

The response was immediate. The sudden sea of black beyond the ramp exploded in a burst of voices and movement. Sprinting from her cover, she darted across the rays of light still pouring from the living room windows, enough to provoke a storm of gunfire to her right as she zigzagged her way closer and closer to the trees. Flashlight beams began to whip across the grounds, one or two inadvertently giving her a point of reference, glancing off several branches to guide her steps. As she reached the fringe of trees, a sudden flash of light burst from behind her, dousing her in its predatory glow, able only to catch her head and neck as they slipped out of sight, her body falling willfully along the rutted slide of the muddy slope.

Her rate of descent was furious, somehow her back and legs finding a path among the gnarled stumps and trees, nothing to guide her but the mountain's natural seam. She couldn't be sure how many were following, her ears lost to the thundering brush of leaves and branches that swatted at her, her hands held as funnels to her face, knuckles battered in an unrelenting frenzy. As the gradient began to level, she slowed, enough to find her feet, arms now slashing out in front of her, the sound of water rising below enough to quicken her pace. Once again, lights from above streaked the trees around her, everything growing denser, the nooks less tangible with each step, only the sound of the water prodding her along through the clawing scrape of woods.

How many minutes passed, she couldn't tell, but her knees began to ache, her feet slipping, shoulder and side slamming to the brambled ground with a violent crash. Only the immediate arrival of another steep descent saved her head from certain impact, this time the trees less intrusive, the sudden appearance of stars and moon the first indication of clearing. The trees continued to thin as she tried to peer over her careening legs, her eyes seeing what she had hoped to find—an endless pit of black vacancy less than thirty feet in front of her. With a sudden release, she felt the ground disappear, her body tumble forward, aware for only an instant of the rush of moving water everywhere before it enfolded her.

All bearings vanished, everything in slow motion, eyes searching for the surface as her arms struggled against the current. Nearly a minute passed before she broke through the water. The full moon flooded the scene, her body twisting round to examine the walls of soil perhaps thirty yards apart that were funneling her away from the lighted beacon of Tieg's hillside perch, now a good hundred yards behind. No sign of pursuit broke the stillness, her head just above the surface, her eyes fixed on the area just below the house as flashlight beams suddenly appeared, laserlike in their probing. One or two skimmed the water, Sarah quick to duck under, waiting as long as she could before resurfacing, the lights slipping from sight as the gorge began to bend her away from the glare. Her legs, only a short while ago burning from the strain, now began to numb under the embrace of the water. Scanning the shore, she maneuvered herself to within fifteen feet of the far bank, arms and legs wading before depositing her on a bed of silt and rock. Pausing for a moment, she pulled herself to the shore, dropped to the mud, and caught her breath, the water less comfortable dripping from clothing and hair, though tempered by a mild evening breeze.

Three minutes later, she reached the plateau above, a new gathering of trees lining a more gradual incline as she silently pulled string after string of leaves from the branches. Nature's insulation. With the pile sufficiently high, she removed shirt and pants and began to wring out the excess water, nestling within the leaves for warmth. Two minutes later, she removed her underwear, slid her legs and arms into the clothes, and began to stuff shirt and pants with the foliage. Prickly, but efficient.

As she buried her underwear, she took stock of the last fifteen minutes. Belt, shoes, and wallet had miraculously survived. The gun was gone, but at least she had gotten a jump on the agents who would soon be swarming the area looking for . . . for *what*? The thought forced her to pause. A *man*? A *woman*? The question suddenly dawned on her. How much could they have possibly seen? And with how much accuracy? Those details, she knew, would all depend on Tieg and his desire to protect Eisenreich.

Which meant she could take a chance. Grabbing the leaves, she crawled up to a small furrow surrounded by a hillock of high grass. She would be safe there, hidden. A place for sleep.

⚔

The New York skyline was a welcome sight, clipped rays of light broken by an angularity of steel and glass driving upward through the early March afternoon. Xander peered through the plane's porthole and saw the city as it was—hard, distant—not as a refuge but as a reflection of himself, silent and alert, eerily calm, struggling to mask the dissonance below the surface.

But it was more than just a part of himself that now stared back. Much more. It was the chaos itself, not as the arbitrary collision of time and circumstance, but as the essential and *ongoing* tension that sustained the vitality of each force and that lay at the core of real strength. *Chaos as power's fuel, power as chaos's parameter, both meaningless without the other.* In the city, in its controlled mania, he saw the relationship that made one the lifeblood of the other. In that moment, staring out at the buildings, Xander came to understand one very basic truth, a truth he knew Eisenreich had never fully grasped. Power craves chaos as the object of its own control; chaos seeks power as the arbiter of its own limitations. Without the one, there can be no other. Each survives through that tension. Each dominates through that unity.

Xander continued to stare into the distance, more and more aware of a similar strength growing within himself, a detached self-mastery made possible only by his own inner turmoil—power as a response to that confusion. Entranced by the stark patterns below, he realized he had become more accustomed to the game, the voice inside less a command from Feric or Sarah than from himself. Slowly, he was beginning to cultivate the instinct, to create a reality that made sense of the last week, an internal will that both frightened and relieved him. The episode on the subway had made certain of that. He was discovering a strange duality of needs—one that sought to contain the mayhem, the other that looked to incite its frenzy so as to ensure a constant challenge. The last ten hours had granted a momentary respite from that struggle—even with the change of planes and the nervous few hours he had spent at Heathrow. Thirty thousand feet above the chaos, he had had time to think, to evaluate, but not in the ways he had relied on in the past. Theory had no place now. Eisenreich had made that all too clear, the last two days altering his perception completely.

And yet, there *was* the other reality, the small leather-bound books that he had forced himself to pore over during the flight, forced because he had been afraid to return to their world, to let his guard down, to recapture that simplicity. More so because he had begun to question his own capacity. Staring at them, turning their pages, he no longer saw them as relics to be admired and discussed. They each had meaning, purpose beyond the theory. Of course, he tried to convince himself that he had known it all along, that he had reveled in the impact such books could have, but the real questions remained. Had he ever truly seen *beyond* the theoretical? No. He had taken the easy way out, dismissed them as absurd, rejected them as madness, and thus ignored their truth. Even a few days ago, rifling through the texts, he had not allowed himself to believe in their application. *They're books! They offer nothing more than the thrill of discovery. Nothing else!* Somehow, he had let the truth of Eisenreich's *first trial* slip from his mind. He had allowed himself to read the theory as little more than the fuel for an academic flight of fancy. Now, staring into a vacant sky, he knew far better. Now he had witnessed their power firsthand.

And that power was no more clear than in the prescriptions set forth in the second volume. Xander once again flipped open the book, aware that he had seen its methods, its brutality, not on the pages in front of him but in a small house in Wolfenbüttel, on a train from Saltzgitter. *How to create chaos, how to build from it, how to cultivate hatred*—the three central chapters, the three most damning statements of Eisenreich's vision. Now, reading through the words again, Xander knew what the men devoted to that vision planned to unleash; Washington, the grain market—they had merely been a promise of things to come. Minor disruptions at first—perhaps not even genuine threats—but events serious enough to raise questions about security in *the simple minds of the people.* Next, they would cultivate that doubt into panic, depict the smaller episodes as symptoms of a larger problem, one that would demand drastic measures. That *problem*—the one Eisenreich had so cannily latched onto all those centuries ago—was nothing more than *moral decay*. Simple, but accurate. How better to manipulate the public than to play up to its pious indignity? How better to rouse a people than to rattle their sense of self-righteousness? And Xander knew there would be plenty of that to go around. The interest groups, the Coalitions, the majorities—they were all waiting to clean the slate of its social, political, and economic corruption. Tieg had been making certain of that. Every night for the past two years. Ten million households growing more and more restless. The answer—tear everything down and start again. Make everything *right*. It was why Eisenreich had described chaos as *"the welcome release from a general iniquity."* Chaos as savior. Chaos as moral detergent. From there, it was but a short step to control for those who wanted it. To maintain it, they would simply have to create a pariah within the state, cultivate bigotry, and thus distract the rabble. That was Eisenreich's gift. An old trick, thought Xander, but one that had worked well enough in the past. It would work again.

Xander sat back and closed his eyes as the plane banked away from the island, the image of the little monk etched in his mind. *Did you really intend all of this? Was this the vision? Was this God's will?* Xander knew there had to be more to it than the brutality Tieg and his cohorts meant to unleash. More than a tyranny of greed and power bent on stripping society of its most basic freedoms, and turning out generation after generation of mindless automatons. Yes, the theory tempted with a promise of unimagined power, but it also granted a world of order, of control. And *that* was what made it so seductive. Not its gift of supremacy. Not its harnessing of chaos. It was its dream of permanence through excellence that set it apart. A dream unthinkably violent beyond the page, yet tantalizing in its rhetoric.

A quick descent to the tar and grass of Kennedy Airport shook him back to the present. A final bump to the ground, and Xander opened his eyes. He stared at the manuscript, then slipped it into his briefcase. The moment for its beauty had passed. The game had begun again.

Five minutes later, a strange sensation washed over him as he stepped out onto the concourse. It might have been the same terminal from which he had left six days ago, but it was a very different Jaspers who now returned. He had left a part of himself behind, shed it so as to create a decipherable reality out of the madness of Eisenreich. Ganz had been right to recognize the finality, but he had seen only one side, only one part of that sacrifice. Xander, on the other hand, had come to understand a different kind of death, a death that came in stages, ripping at the soul until only the shell remained. He had seen it in Sarah. In Feric. And now in himself. Somewhere, he had lost the naïveté, the simple enthusiasm that had defined his every choice, his sense of purpose, and had always propelled him along, only to be violently stripped away, bit by bit—Florence, London, Wolfenbüttel—a devastating spiral from disbelief to panic to horror. Death at his own hands. Death as his reality. All that remained was a will to survive, a will he had learned to exercise with relative ease in the bowels of the Frankfurt airport.

It was that same will, that same intuition that was forcing him to concentrate on the simple order that Sarah—so close now—had left for him: *Tempsten, New York. The Sleepy Hollow Motel.*

⬩

"A game? And hitching doesn't break the rules?" The young man driving the pickup couldn't have been more than twenty, his thick upper body, grease-stained hands, and grimy coveralls—the name Jeff on his chest pocket—all in keeping with the logo Sarah had read on the passenger door: MICK'S AUTOWORKS—WE DO FOREIGN TOO.

"There *are* no rules," she answered. At least that much was true. *Keep it simple.* "It's just whoever gets to Tijuana first wins the bet."

"You got *money* on this?"

"Enough to keep it . . . worthwhile."

"*That* is a great idea. I mean, really great." He shook his head as he smiled. "And you say you got dumped in Claghorn Gorge last night just to slow you down? That's beautiful! They're lucky you didn't drown or something."

"Well, there is *one* rule—nothing life-threatening. And no planes. It wouldn't be fun if you could just hop the next flight south." *If anyone asks, he'll have to keep it simple.* "I got tossed in with a life jacket. I guess they figured I'd give up once I got wet."

"Beautiful! I mean that is absolutely beau-ti-ful!" He pounded an open palm on the steering wheel. "Hell, I wish I could drive you the whole way just to see those guys' expressions when you show up!" He started to shake his head again. "Leaves! I'd never've thought of that. I'd still be in those damn woods freezing my ass off."

"Maybe, maybe not." Sarah recalled the hour or so of fitful sleep she had stolen. "This blanket's a welcome relief."

"Yeah, well that's Mick's. He sometimes sleeps in the truck." Jeff shrugged. "Don't ask. Something to do with his ex-wife. Or his girlfriend.

He doesn't talk about it and . . . Anyway, you got lucky last night. Usually this time of year, it doesn't get much over fifty-five. Last night, must've been close to sixty. Maybe sixty-two."

"It didn't feel that high."

"Yeah, I guess it wouldn't have." He laughed. "You're also pretty lucky I had that job out in Presterton, or else you'd have been walking for another hour, at least."

Coming out of the curve, the young mechanic slowed and turned into a driveway, the garage logo emblazoned on a well-worn sign that swung precariously from two strands of rusted chain link. Several cars were parked on the fringe of grass separating Mick's from the main road, a strange array of expensive German and Japanese imports that seemed out of place next to the ramshackle buildings to the rear. Inside the garage, high on a hydraulic lift, a jet black Porsche was receiving expert care from the hands of an equally greasy coveralled figure.

"That's Mick. We do all the work ourselves." He brought the truck to a stop and hopped out of the cab, shouting over to his partner. "Hey, hey. It was a busted fan belt. Two seconds. The guy didn't know what was wrong. I told him next time to check it himself so he doesn't have to pay us an arm and a leg." Mick nodded from under the car, only now aware of Sarah, who was stepping to the gravel. "And she wants to know if she can rent a car." Jeff moved off toward the small office.

"Rent?" Mick stepped out of the garage, wiping the grease from his hands. "We don't rent. You know that."

"Yeah, yeah, but listen to this," Jeff shouted through the door as he rang up the bill for the fan belt. "She's got some kind of bet going, see who can get to Mexico first, and last night she ends up in Claghorn with a little help from two of her bettin' buddies. Sounds like fun, huh?"

"Yeah." Mick continued to cross the gravel drive, the cloth working a patch on his neck. He kept his eyes on Sarah. "Mexico. What's in Mexico?"

"Tijuana," answered Sarah.

"Yeah . . . well, I don't rent, and I don't sell. I just fix. Best I can do is have Jeff run you into Glendon. That's about twenty minutes. You can catch a bus there, or a train into San Francisco. About an hour and a half, I guess. Plenty of places there to rent a car."

"Thanks," said Sarah, watching Mick step into the office. A moment later, she heard traces of a hushed exchange before Mick reemerged. He kept his eyes on the ground as he stepped to the drive and dug the rag deep into his back pocket. Sarah expected to see Jeff behind him, but the office remained strangely quiet. Watching Mick move, she sensed something odd in his walk, the gait somehow too deliberate, too casual. *He can't look at me.* Something was out of place, something Mick was trying to hide, the reason he was keeping his eyes low.

Every instinct told her she had to move. Stepping back to the truck, Sarah slowly opened the door and tossed the blanket in, discreetly sliding herself into the driver's seat. With a minimum of movement, she reached for the keys that still hung from the ignition, all the while her focus on the tall mechanic. She waited until he had disappeared into the garage and then fired up the engine, shifting the truck into reverse.

Behind her, a black sedan screeched to a stop and blocked the exit, forcing her to slam on the brakes. Her entire body jerked forward, her chin and shoulder colliding from the near impact. Slightly dazed, she waited, the car behind idling, only its smoke-glazed windows quivering from the vibration. Sarah expected her captors to fly out, guns at the ready. But none came. The doors remained strangely silent. Only the hum of the engine. A minute might have passed before the sound of footsteps broke through. Even and slow, they approached from the office. She began to turn.

"Hello, Sarah."

The voice tore through her, its impact like a hammer to her skull.

8

One man must stand behind the three to guide them with subtle suggestion and wise counsel.

—*On Supremacy*, chapter **VI**

HER GAZE REMAINED frozen on the long angular face not ten feet from her, its thick gray eyebrows hovering above a pair of sunken eyes. There was no expression on the face, save for a slight squinting that tucked the pale green orbs even deeper within their sockets. It had been seven years since she had seen him, seven years since she had stared into the cold eyes.

"*It was your choice to make, your responsibility in the end. The delay was irrelevant.*"

"*I . . .*"

"*The delay was irrelevant.*"

Pritchard.

"Shall we walk?" he asked.

Sarah waited, then opened the door, the movement enough to provoke a sudden swirl of motion from the car behind. Almost simultaneously, three men sprang out, each in a dark suit and thin black tie, a shake of the head from Pritchard enough to stop each in his tracks. COS's director wanted it quite clear that he would handle her himself. Even so, she sensed the hesitation on his face as she stepped from the truck. Without waiting, she moved off along the driveway; five seconds later, Pritchard was at her side. Only the sound of gravel churning underfoot interrupted the silence.

"You look well," he said. "Better than when last I saw you."

"Yes."

"Then again, anything would have been better than that."

"Well, at least this time round you avoid any pangs of conscience."

"There were none last time." Pritchard's expression remained unchanged.

"The escort's new. Not usually your style."

"More of a nuisance than anything else, but it seemed the best choice, given the contact."

"The contact?"

"You. They've been told I'm an NSC negotiator—brokering information out of Nicaragua. You've been cast as the reluctant liaison. They believe you're rather dangerous. You might even be a threat to my safety."

"At least that part's accurate."

"Yes, I'm sure it is," he answered.

"And they won't make a fuss?"

"Not unless you do." It was a recommendation rather than a response. He tucked his hands into his coat pockets. "You need to come in."

"I thought we'd been through this?"

"Things change. You need to come in."

Sarah ignored the request. "You tracked me through Stein?"

"He was sloppy. The charade at Tieg's was put together at the last minute. Not that Bob had much of a choice, but he handed us the location. We simply had to wait for you to emerge. Not exactly a needle in a haystack."

"The fan belt in Presterton?"

"One has to work with what one's given."

"A mechanic's truck"—she nodded to herself—"on a lonely country road."

"Innocent enough—it seemed as good a choice as any. And your grease monkey . . . well, he was ideal for the role. You were bound to come out downstream. We just didn't know how far."

"Why not just pick me up yourself?"

Pritchard allowed himself a smile. "Highly unlikely you'd willingly step into a government issue with me in the backseat. We needed to keep your options to a minimum. Mr. Mick was the most appropriate choice."

"It's his first name," corrected Sarah.

"I'm sure it is."

The drive began to curve round to the back of the garage, a sudden gust of wind driving up from a distant copse of trees. Pritchard pulled his coat closer around his chest.

"So," continued Sarah, "I now willingly step into that car with you and your three friends—no struggle, no questions?"

"I think so. Yes."

"Because my options are *considerably* limited. A few witnesses. A convenient story that explains everything they need to know about me."

"Something like that." Pritchard was stating facts. "Yes."

"It still leaves one loose end—*you.* Why does Arthur Pritchard need to put in an appearance? Why not simply send the boys? The result would have been the same. Or am I missing something on current COS policy?"

"The policy," he replied, pulling a handkerchief from his pocket to wipe his nose, "is the same as it has always been. To be blunt, some of the channels are not as *secure* as we would like them to be."

"Meaning?"

Pritchard continued in silence, his eyes squinting against the haze.

"Funny"—Sarah nodded—"Stein said the same thing. Doesn't give me much reason to trust *any* of you."

Again, he smiled. "Was that ever really part of your repertoire?"

"You still haven't answered my question. Why you?"

"Because *I* need to know what you have."

"And you couldn't coax it out of Bob?" They had reached the edge of the driveway, open field directly in front of them. Sarah stopped. "I find that hard to believe."

"Unfortunately, our friend Stein has disappeared." Pritchard continued to walk, leaving Sarah behind. "I never really thought he had it in him."

"What? An autonomous will?"

Pritchard now stopped, his eyes fixed on a small bird coasting to an outstretched branch, his back still to her. "Not surprisingly, all the relevant files are missing with him."

"I *am* sorry to hear that."

"Yes, I thought you might be." Again, the handkerchief appeared, his gaze still on the bird. "Meanwhile, things have taken a decided turn for the worse for your Dr. Jaspers."

"Really?" The word was spoken without emotion.

"It seems he's been implicated in the death of a book dealer in Germany."

"That's absurd."

"Perhaps."

"Implicated how?"

"Newspaper articles. Police reports. The usual sort of thing." He was busy folding the handkerchief into neat squares as he turned to her. "It all happened about sixteen hours ago in a town called Wolfenbüttel." He looked up. "I don't suppose you would know why Doctor Jaspers was there?"

"Evidently to kill—"

"Yes, I'm sure that was it." He deposited the handkerchief in his pocket. "You might be interested to know that Jaspers wasn't working alone, a fact that raises some very interesting questions. All of which lead to you."

"Now, that *is* a surprise." Sarah smiled. "But isn't that what you've wanted all along? Send me out, ruffle a few feathers, then see what turns up? And if a few people need to be eliminated—well, then you've got the perfect tool. Touch all the right buttons—drag in a few innocent lives—and the little doll will take all the responsibility. Dive right back in because she can't live with herself if she lets the same mistakes happen all over again."

"One might even see it as a last chance for her to ease her conscience."

"You bastard."

"Perhaps, but all in a good cause, Sarah. This has been a rather nasty business."

"Really?" Sarah let the moment pass. "The problem is, from my vantage point, it doesn't look like it's worked out the way you'd hoped. Otherwise, I don't think we'd be having this nice little chat on such a lovely morning."

"I need to know what you have. Things could get very . . . *messy*."

"For whom? For *me?*" Sarah pressed her hands deeper into her pockets. "Messy would be a step up." The gust picked up again, blowing through the open area and bringing a chill to her shoulders.

"You must be cold after last night," he said. "We should head back." Pritchard started toward the gravel.

"Your concern is overwhelming," she answered as she drew up to his side.

"No, I'm afraid it's not."

They walked in silence until they were once again in full view of the men by the car. Pritchard looked over at the three and nodded once, the signal to start the engine. "I sent you out for a purpose, and that purpose has been served. I have no intention of letting the Amman fiasco repeat itself. I'm simply here to make sure we don't run into the same problem again."

Sarah started to reply, then stopped, her eyes fixed on Pritchard. "I thought you were here because certain *channels* couldn't be trusted?"

He had moved ahead and now stopped, his back to her. After a few moments, he turned and answered. "I would have thought you'd be more than happy to disentangle yourself from all of this."

"All of *what*, Arthur?"

"That's why we're having this little chat, isn't it?" Pritchard squinted and added, "You've done all I expected of you; it's time to step aside."

"That simple?" Sarah shook her head. "They know who I am, where I come from, and what I know about them. It's not likely they'll let it go at that."

"You might be surprised."

"And what is that supposed to mean?"

Again he paused. "Do you really want me to answer that?" He let the words sink in. "You have very few choices right now. Best to be smart."

"Jaspers has been set up, and you know it."

"Yes, I believe you're right. But he's either dead or a wanted killer. Such are the sacrifices we make." Without waiting for a response, he turned and headed for the car.

Sarah watched him go, his confidence apparent in the easy gait; a second nod, and two of the men started toward her. She had less than a minute, time enough to think, unpack the hesitation she had seen in his face. *Best to be smart.* He had said almost nothing, little more than catch phrases in a game of cat and mouse, but she had heard it, exposed the inconsistency. *Do you really want me to answer that?* What *he* wanted was her out, and it didn't matter how—a trumped-up conspiracy at COS, the fear of a re-creation of Amman. How many other options had he discarded before bringing the message in person? What was it that he thought she had? Inconsistency and hesitation.

The sound of an engine tore through the morning air, a jarring prelude to the sight that appeared from behind the garage. Four tires—each nearly five feet tall—pummeled the gravel beneath, axels, driveshafts, and exhaust pipes in full view below the small four-by-four cabin. MENACE was painted across the doors, the vaulted M rising like a wave in metallic red and blue. At the wheel, a grinning Jeff looked down at Sarah, his invitation unheard over the sound of feverish revving. Pritchard's men began to run, hands reaching to inside jacket pockets. Without thinking, Sarah raced around to the passenger side, pulled open the door, and jumped up to the red leather seat. The bite of the engine rocked the car from side to side, Jeff releasing the clutch, the gravel steaming from the burst of acceleration. Sarah reached out for the door—the road beneath a wild blur—summoning all her strength to swing the large frame toward her. A moment later, safe within the speeding cabin, she looked over at the boy who had saved her.

"Did you see their faces!" His grin was all teeth. "I mean, did you *see* their faces! Especially the old guy. What a rush!"

"What a rush," she repeated, her eyes searching through the rear window for the dark sedan. The men were just now slamming doors as the car tried to make chase, its tiny shell a good hundred yards behind and losing ground with each passing second. Whatever Jeff had concocted under the hood, it was more than a match for the government car. Sarah shifted forward and watched the enormous wheels tear along the tarmac, the ride remarkably smooth given the snaking curves of the road.

"You're full of surprises," she said.

"Yeah, well that old guy was a little too smart for his own good. *Government business.* Like I wasn't going to see right through *that* one? He's one of those guys in the bet, right?"

"Right . . . he's one of those guys," nodded Sarah.

"I knew it!" Both hands pounded down on the steering wheel in triumph. "And Mick acting so official with him. *God,* that old guy got him good! You should've seen Mick's expression, all serious, like I couldn't understand what was going on. You should've heard what he said, telling me to sit in the back room till they were gone. Yeah, like I was going to let him have all the fun."

"I'm glad you—"

A sudden turn to the right stopped Sarah short, her arm quickly finding the dashboard for support. The car had left the main road and was now careening down what could at best be described as a trail, brambles and stray logs scattered along the path. The four-by-four was having little difficulty, although the ride had become far less comfortable. Bouncing along, Jeff turned to Sarah.

"This cuts off about twelve miles. No little sedan's going to have a chance taking it. There's no way they catch up. Sorry about the ride."

Sarah adjusted her seat belt and kept her arm on the dashboard. Whatever had inspired her young friend to go to such lengths on her behalf, she wasn't going to question his enthusiasm or his methods. "No, no. This is great."

Four minutes later, they emerged to a paved road, Jeff firing up the engine to bring them to a cruising speed of nearly eighty miles an hour.

"So," he asked, "where to? Tijuana?"

Sarah sat back. *How about upstate New York—ever met a senator?* "It just feels good to be moving again. Let's see where it takes us."

Jeff smiled and brought the car to ninety.

Votapek stepped away from the bar, his fourth vodka and tonic clasped firmly in his fingers, the effects of the alcohol apparent in the bloated red of his cheeks. His free hand toyed with the lobe of his ear as he returned to his seat by the piano. Sedgewick was having trouble with a phrase from a Chopin etude, the passage somehow repeating itself in an endless arpeggial loop.

"The C is *natural* in the left hand," blurted out Votapek as his fingers worked angrily on the few stray hairs growing from his ear. "*Natural.* Why can't you get it right?"

"You have your refuge, Anton," replied Sedgewick, unable to extricate himself from the loop, "I have mine. That one should be your last."

"I'll thank you *not* to tell me what to do." Votapek downed the drink in one gulp and placed the glass on the side table to his right. He then sat back, folded his arms to his chest, and closed his eyes. "You know it's wrong," he said as he began to shake gently back and forth. "I can't let him do it. I just can't."

"She compromised us," answered Sedgewick, finally moving on to the next phrase. "Ah, there it is. You're right, the C *is* natural."

"Did you hear what I said?"

"Yes. You can't let him do it. I don't think you have much of a choice. She's too dangerous with the Trent woman still on the loose. Even at this stage." He began to play with greater insistence, eager for the end of the piece. "It still puzzles me, though, how she found her—"

"How can you say that? She's a child. She never really recovered. You know she didn't know any better *then*. How could she know any better *now*? It's that Trent woman. She has a way, a way of—"

"We both know what she has a way of doing." Sedgewick was somehow back in the loop, his frustration forcing him to stop. He continued to stare at the keys as he added, "We were very foolish, you and I." None of the usual bravura tinged his words; he slowly lowered the piano lid and looked up. "Not that it'll make much of a difference. Alison, I'm afraid, doesn't know what to believe now. *Whom* to believe. Stable or not, she has a great deal of information that could be very damaging. Ms. Trent has made her a liability."

"I see," said Votapek. "We destroy her life thirty years ago, and now we simply take it. Just like that." The words were those of a defeated man. "Is that what we've wanted all along?"

"Only so that we can build something that has real meaning, that—"

"Oh, stop it, Larry!" Votapek stood. "She's a *part* of us, the reason we started all of this in the first place. And now—"

"The reason *you* started all of this." Tieg had appeared at the steps leading down to the living room. "She's forfeited our trust."

"I tell you she didn't *know*—"

"Irrelevant," Tieg continued. "This issue should have been resolved a long time ago."

"Resolved!" Votapek began to shake his head wildly. "Is that how we talk about our own, about the children who sacrificed—"

" 'Sentiment is weakness,' " Tieg broke in. "How many times have I heard you say that? Well, it's time to recognize it as a reality, Anton, not as some abstract theory that serves a pedagogic turn in your classroom."

"Fine," replied Votapek. "I *also* know that no one would believe her."

"*No* one will have the chance," answered Tieg. "Larry, try and explain that to our conscience-laden colleague."

Sedgewick had moved to the bar, a club soda in hand. Trying to soothe, he said, "You know he's right, Anton. As long as she showed commitment, she was a liability we could live with. We could understand your feelings—"

"*Thank you!*" barked Votapek, standing and moving to the window. "Thank you both *very much* for your condescension!"

"Anton," continued Sedgewick, "she *knows* who was there; she *knows* about Pembroke; she *knows* about the children we managed to salvage from Tempsten. She saw it all happening, and she can fill in a lot of holes. As long as she didn't know any better, she was a reminder of how things can go terribly, terribly wrong. Now she's confused. And she's no longer alone. If, for some reason, Ms. Trent were to convince her to come forward with that information, too many links would be made public—regardless of their source. Do you want to drag her through that? We can't have any of it, Anton, and you know it. Trent, Alison—"

"And now our friend from Washington." A tired voice, silent to this moment, cut off Sedgewick. The old man, nestled in a corner, shifted in his chair, the strain of the last week scrawled in deep lines across his face. He shook his head, more to himself than to the others. "That, I am afraid, cannot be helped. He has left us no choice." He coughed. "Such *ego*." The word carried only disappointment. "Never content to play his role. *Always* more, *always* second-guessing. And now this foolishness. Did he ever understand?" The old man did not expect an answer. "So be it. I have found another to replace him. You must act quickly with him. He will be very dangerous now. He will be willing to do anything to save himself."

"It's being taken care of," answered Sedgewick, who turned to Votapek. "You know the same applies to Alison now."

"That is entirely untrue. *He* knew what he was doing," said Votapek. "He knew *exactly* what he was doing."

"Yes, but the rationale is the same. *Any* connection among us and the entire agenda blows up in our faces." Sedgewick paused. "Not all of us care to wait *another* thirty years before getting the chance to try again."

"And I suppose you mean Tempsten was all *my* fault—"

"I don't mean *anything*. All I'm saying is that we can't take any chances this time. We leave her out there and we could very well sacrifice what we're on the verge of creating. Wittingly or not, Alison could draw those connections. Would you choose her over that future?"

Votapek remained by the window, not bothering to look at the other men in the room. "Would you let me?"

⚔

They had backtracked a good twenty miles, cutting through roads that Jeff had promised were too obscure even for the local police. Sarah had told him that her *friends* would no doubt try the same sort of ruse they had plotted in Glendon, and she had therefore convinced him to travel north, away from the city, so that she could avoid another run-in. At first, the mechanic had been reluctant, insisting that he drive her all the way to Mexico, but, after careful explanation, she had made it quite clear that Menace—though a fine piece of machinery—was perhaps a shade too conspicuous to make it all the way south of the border without further interruptions. A few minutes of silent consideration had brought Jeff to the same conclusion. He had turned off the road and opted for the more scenic approach to the town of Palametto.

Now, about a mile outside the village, still safe within the cover of a backwoods trail, Sarah asked him to stop. Opening the door, she stepped down from the cab.

"You're gonna *what*?" he said, snapping his head in her direction to emphasize his amazement. "It's over a *mile* from here. Maybe two. There's no reason for you to walk. I said it's *no* problem for me—"

"I'd like to get into town without too much of an entrance. You know, slip in, slip out. That kind of thing. Catch the next train."

"*Jeez*, you guys take this game seriously. You know he's halfway to Carmel by now, and you're gonna start walking?"

"Trust me," answered Sarah, "I've played with him before." *Such are the sacrifices we make.* Ever the rationale. Ever Pritchard's modus operandi. And now he wanted her out. Why? Or had that been part of the ruse? Another prod to make certain she would see it through to the end. To Tempsten and Senator Schenten. She recalled a phrase from Feric's message: *"cut off the head and the whole thing falls apart."* Again, Pritchard had left her so few choices. Disappear now and ensure the sacrifice. Or become the assassin. It was the only way she knew to save Xander.

"Hey, it's your thing," answered Jeff. She could tell his interest was waning, speed a vital component to his enthusiasm. He revved the car. "Just thought you might want the help."

She nodded. "You've been really great." She reached into her pocket and pulled a hundred-dollar bill from the wallet she had taken from Tieg's man. "I want you to have this."

"*What* the—"

"It's . . . your share if I win," she explained. "I wouldn't feel right winning the five thousand knowing I'd still be at the garage if not for you." The boy's eyes responded a moment later, his cheeks a little flushed as he coyly reached across the seat.

"Five thousand?" His eyes widened. "Well . . . I guess that's okay, then. And we did outgun that little sedan."

"We sure did," replied Sarah. "Oh, and I'd really appreciate it if you didn't get back to Mick's until, say, late this afternoon. You know, just in case my friends are there and want to know where I headed."

Jeff was busy cramming the hundred into his pocket. "Right, right," he nodded. "Get yourself a head start. I can understand that. I'll drive out to a friend's, play some vid. I can handle that."

"And Mick won't mind?"

"Nah, we're slow right now. Two Beemers by next Friday. Nothing much. Hey, it'll serve him right for treating me like an idiot." He smiled and reached over to pull the door shut. "A hundred bucks and some great driving. I should be thanking you. . . ." He stopped and looked at Sarah through the window. "I don't even know your name."

"Susan," she said.

"Cool, Susan. Hope you win." With that, he gunned the engine and tore off down the trail, his hand waving out the window as Menace disappeared around a curve. Sarah waited a minute and then headed for town.

☆

Twenty minutes later, she stood in the ladies' room of the Palametto station, a tiny cubicle about halfway down the platform. The train had been her only option—no way quicker or less obtrusive to the Sacramento airport. If all went well, she would be on the first flight to points east within the next hour, then a connector to upstate New York. And Schenten.

And somehow she knew Jaspers would be there. He *had* to be. She needed him there, *needed* to see that he had survived, more for her own sake than for his. The gentle, decent man who had tried to reach out to her, who had seen her lose herself in those tunnels, and whom she had sent out into the madness. And all with just a smile. *Don't let me down, Feric.*

The question now was whether they would recognize *her* once she arrived. In a short leather skirt, silk blouse, and suede jacket, she was a far cry from the Firenzan Signora Fabrizzi. The tight-fitting ensemble had come courtesy of The Fashion Plate, Palametto's only women's clothing store, and duly stocked with all the latest styles—or so the sign had said. Exactly whose idea of style, though, remained something of a mystery. The new clothes—including a pair of dark green kneesocks, a rather daring pair of lace bikini underwear, and a set of climbing boots—had transformed Sarah into a poster child for northern California chic.

Now, standing in front of yet another mirror, Sarah was making the most of the few items she had picked up at the local pharmacy to finish the job. With slow, even strokes, she was carefully smoothing a few dollops of Ultra-Tan into her face and neck. Bathing her hands, forearms, and thighs in the oily concoction, she decided not to worry about the aftereffects. All that mattered were the few age lines and scrapes from her tumble down Tieg's hillside. Within a minute, they were gone, and with them a good seven years, transporting Sarah to somewhere in her mid-twenties. *All right, late twenties. The clothes would have to work a little overtime.* Next came the clippers, to make quick work of her hair, cropped to chin length and trimmed to as straight a line as possible. She hoped the six hours of flying time—and several packets of blond dye—would be enough to damage the hair to perfection. If nothing else, her costume was sufficient to get her as far as the airport.

With one final check in the mirror, she pulled the door open, only to be met by two discrete sounds in the distance. The first was the train's horn, a blaring burst to inform everyone in Ballard county that the 9:40 had arrived two minutes ahead of schedule. The second was the rumble of an oversized engine, its familiar groan causing Sarah to step back. It was eerily familiar, the hiccup in the engine unmistakable. She had heard it too many times while barreling along overgrown trails not to recognize the sound of the four-by-four.

They had found Jeff. *Had Pritchard been clever enough to place a homing device on the truck?* It was a foolish question; Sarah knew those were exactly the sorts of details he never missed. And now, because of that, Menace was somewhere behind her, stalking the streets of Palametto.

The train screeched to a stop, momentarily returning her focus to the platform. Almost in unison, the car let out a final growl. Sarah froze, expecting to hear steps, the soft pitter-pat of prowling feet. But nothing. Only silence. A moment later, a few leaves swirled overhead as the train doors slid open, the intrusion snapping her head up, the empty cabin beckoning not ten feet in front of her. And still only silence. *Think! Consider the options!* For nearly half a minute, she waited, until, springing from her alcove, she darted across the platform and into the cabin just as the doors slid shut behind her. Seconds later, the platform began to slip by as she moved to the window, trying to catch a glimpse of her would-be pursuers. All she saw was an empty cement strip glide by. She stepped away as a swath of wooded countryside swept up in front of her, leaves and branches tunneling the train along through an arc of greens and browns. *Where are they?*

And then it dawned on her. They were on the train.

⬟

Bob Stein ran his hand along the bed frame, the dust cascading to the pillow in a cloud of gray mist. Across the room, O'Connell—until only minutes ago buried in the bed's yellowed sheets—swung his head from tap to tap, cold then hot, in a strange ritual of midafternoon rousing. The shirt he wore was sleeveless, ribbed at the chest, and in equal need of a good wash. As to his pants, they were too short, too wide at the ankle, too tight at the stomach. Stein had seen him like this only once before. After Amman. The sight was enough to force Bob to look around the room, take in the dilapidated space, its chipped plaster, crumbling Sheetrock scattered all about. As O'Connell stepped away to dry himself, the sink came into view, its pipes straining against the wall, its entire metal heft threatening to plummet to the floor with the least bit of prodding. All in all, it was a squalid little hole that conjured images of the worst of the Third World. Hard to believe it could be rented for a week at a time less than three blocks south of Union Square in New York.

It hadn't been hard to track him. In fact, O'Connell had left a rather obvious trail—a fact that had comforted Bob. As with Sarah, he seemed to have been asking to be found. Naturally, Bob had complied.

A mucal cough brought his attention back to O'Connell, who had draped the towel around his neck and who was now busy with the cap on the bottle.

"It's a fine stock, Bobby," he said, the voice still hampered by sleep. "Only the best for you." The Irish lilt had grown somehow more exaggerated.

"I'll pass," answered Stein. "Maybe later." O'Connell shrugged his mammoth shoulders and took a long swig of the chestnut liquid. "How many of those do you go through in a day?"

"A day?" O'Connell laughed, cut off by another eruption of phlegm in his throat. He spat in no particular direction and settled onto a short metal stool by the door. "An *hour*, Bobby. An *hour*. When I'm good, it's two. When I'm not . . ." He winked and smiled. "What do you want? As you can see, I'm very busy. Not much time for the likes of you. A meeting at Rock Center for tea and crumpets." He laughed and took another drink.

"You left the trail. I just followed it," answered Stein. "You're usually quicker than this, Gael. It's beginning to look a little sloppy."

"I'm sure it is, Mr. Stein. I'm sure it is." He thought about another swig, then stopped the bottle halfway to his lips. "But what's a few days between friends?" The smile disappeared. The bottle continued up, the liquid rushing down along the glass. O'Connell wiped his mouth against his bare shoulder. "Sometimes, though, you need a little . . . privacy. A little time to think the great thoughts." Again, he drank.

"I didn't know you had any."

O'Connell winked, the smile returning. "At least you're honest."

Watching him drink, Stein continued. "I've never understood why you do this. They pay you enough—"

"Worth every penny," he broke in, raising the bottle in a mock toast.

"Yes, every penny," agreed Stein, "but why this? Why not Maryland, the farm? Why not do your thinking there? See the pooch—"

"Shut the fuck up, Bobby." The words carried no malice. "I do my thinking where I choose." He took another drink, his eyes blinking in a slow, unconnected rhythm. "The dog's dead. Did you know that? Yah, some fuckin' kid. Driving a truck or something. I told them to keep her inside at night—simplest fuckin' thing to do—but you can't trust any of them, stupid bastards. They let a fuckin' dog run wild in the dark. Served the old bitch right anyway." He finished off the bottle and tossed it against the far wall. It refused to break, landing with a thud on the wooden floor.

"I hadn't heard." Stein took in a deep breath and slid a girlie magazine out from under the pillow. Flipping through the pages, he added, "Then again, she wasn't going to live that much longer anyway."

Gael smiled, his chin dropping to his chest, elbows on knees for support. "Fuck you, Bobby. She wasn't as old as your fat ass."

"I need you to dry out." Stein tossed the magazine onto the far side of the bed and placed his hands on the soft mattress. "Sarah's in trouble and it looks like you're the only one she trusts."

"And that surprises you?"

"Maybe, maybe not."

For a few seconds, O'Connell's eyes seemed to clear before slipping back into the easy drunk. He looked away, his hand fiddling with a loose piece of plaster. "Yah, well . . . how is our little Miss Trent?"

"They've gotten hold of her files," replied Stein. "*Everything*. And Arthur's been . . . unreachable."

At the mention of Pritchard's name, O'Connell's face suddenly became tight, the eyes narrower as they sought out Stein. "The ever-popular Arthur C. Pritchard."

"No *C*," he corrected. "That's Clarke. Ours has no middle initial."

"Fuck you, Bobby." O'Connell stood and walked across to the sink. He turned on the faucet and scooped up a mouthful of water. Swallowing, he added, "You have no idea what's going on, do you?" He laughed to himself. "He promised, you know. She was gone, out. His solemn word." He slammed his hand into the wall and screamed, "Yah, well, *fuck* you, Arthur Pritchard!" He turned to Stein. "Said she was done. Except, he didn't have to go in after her, did he? He didn't have to scrape those bastard boys off the street, see her standing in that hotel room, her hand so tight around that gun, you'd have . . . I don't know." He shut his eyes and dropped his head back. "She was a good kid, you know that?" The voice was almost a whisper. "And a great shot. Cool. That's what she was." He opened his eyes and looked at Stein. "Thought she could get back for the girl, you know that? As if she'd had a choice." Again he laughed to himself, then drifted back to the stool, taking a deep breath as he sat. "She blamed herself, and he brought her back. Why'd he do that, Bob? Why?" Once more, he let his chin drop to his chest. Then, with no kindness in his eyes, he stared up at his colleague. "We should've known better. We should've left her alone. We should've seen it."

Stein waited for him to sink deeper into the chair. "Not my call."

"That's good, Bobby. You believe that." The bitterness now boiled up. "Pass the buck. *Good* for you, Bobby. *Good for you.*"

"You really think that's what I wanted?" Again he paused. "Then you can go straight to hell. This isn't about Arthur; this is about her."

The onetime operative blinked several times. After a minute, he sat up, took in another deep breath, and then rubbed his hands through his hair and over his face. He stretched his neck and coughed. "Ya, well, I'm not as bad as I look. Not more than half a bottle a day. Tops."

"You never could hold this stuff."

A different smile returned. "Don't push your luck, Mr. Stein."

"I need you to walk out of here with me tonight."

O'Connell tried to shake the booze from his head. "And into what?"

"That," he replied, "depends on you."

The Irishman looked up. "Where is she, Bobby? And where, by the way, *is* our Mr. Pritchard? Or wouldn't you know that?"

Stein stared at O'Connell. "Is there something I should know?"

"Little problem of whom you can trust." O'Connell stood and again moved to the sink, flipping the tap before gulping down several handfuls of water.

"Meaning?"

He doused his head before speaking. "So they know who she is. Where?"

"Tieg's. San Francisco."

"When?"

"Within the last twelve hours."

O'Connell turned off the faucet and looked back at Stein, patting the towel against his neck and face. "And she's still there?"

Stein shook his head. "I . . . I'm not sure."

"That's not good, Bobby. That's not good at all."

⚑

Sarah scanned the aisle in front of her, the fifteen or so rows mercifully full, a few empty pockets here and there, but enough bodies to offer some semblance of cover. Behind her, an equally dense collection of commuters and vacationers sat side by side, several lost in papers, others in conversations, most, she noticed, in identical ties and scarves. On closer inspection, she discovered that the pants and skirts were similarly coordinated, neatly creased gray flannels, everyone in loafers or pumps. *So much for blending in.* That notwithstanding, she ventured to her left, steadying herself against the edge of the seats as she moved farther into the cabin. With each new row came another set of ties, another flock of pants and skirts to add to the mystery. The aisle, though, remained clear of any other noncostumed arrivals. If Pritchard's men were on the train, they had yet to make it to the clone car.

Swaying from side to side, Sarah caught sight of a single empty space in the last row of seats, a pair of loafers from an unseen passenger resting comfortably on the vacant spot. To their left, a man in his late thirties—also in full attire—slouched over a crossword puzzle, the cap of his pen weathering the worst of a gnawing concentration. *By the window, back up against the wall.* Half a minute later, Sarah politely slid past him, watched as the shoes on her seat found the floor, and sat, her bag at her side.

After a minute or so, the man across from her nodded over his shoulder and said, "Must be quite a sight." He, too, was in his mid-thirties, an eager grin on his face. "The uniform, I mean. Must be quite a sight all in a row."

"Yes," she said distractedly, her peripheral vision intent on the rest of the car.

"Not the most original, but respectable."

Sarah smiled again.

"You must be wondering what this is all about?"

This time, she merely raised her eyebrows before looking down the aisle as if for a friend.

"We're the Savoy Singers." He pressed on, undeterred by her less than subtle brush-off. "Gilbert and Sullivan. You know, *Pirates of Penzance, Pinafore.* We do concerts, clubs, that sort of thing. Big one tonight."

"*Pinafore.*" She nodded out of kindness, her thoughts still elsewhere, although she did remember a performance years ago, a tinny soprano voice that had required several trips to an open bar. "Something about sisters and cousins?" she added offhandedly, instantly sorry for having shown even the slightest bit of interest.

The man's face lit up. "Sisters, cousins, and *aunts*," he corrected, at once breaking into song. "'*And we are his sisters, and his cousins and his aunts,/*'" the two others in the foursome immediately joined in: "'*His sisters and his* cousins / *Whom he reckons up by dozens / And his aunts.*'" Without so much as a pause, the man with the crossword jumped to his feet and in a deeply felt baritone poured forth with "*'For he is an English man.*'" A moment later, three-quarters of the cabin were on their feet, swaying to the train's steady rhythm and chiming in with the chorus in full glee. "*'For he himself has said it / and it's greatly to his credit / that he is an Englishman, that he i-s a-n E-E-E-E-E-E-E-Englishman.*'" Sitting quietly, Sarah tried her best at a smile, wondering how wise a choice the seat had been, vantage point or not. A moment later, the cabin burst into great waves of laughter as everyone retook their seats, another chorus—this one an ode to poetry, as far as she could tell—picking up where *Pinafore* had left off. Remembering there were some ten to twelve operettas in the canon, Sarah knew she was in for a long ride.

It was only then, as she was settling back into her chair, that she noticed one of Pritchard's associates at the far end of the car, his eyes scanning the passengers as if looking for a seat. *The dark suit, the thin black tie.* He, too, seemed somewhat perplexed by the regularity of the uniform, less so by the singing, clearly interested only in the few women who, like Sarah, had inadvertently stumbled into the chorus car. One of those unfortunate few had evidently had enough and was politely disentangling herself from another foursome halfway down the cabin, her smile one of relief as she moved past Pritchard's man on her way to the far door. For a moment, the agent looked as though he might follow, but then decided against it, quick to return to his surveillance. *Too short,* guessed Sarah. *Still, he took the time to make sure. He was being careful.* Of course, there was the chance that he wouldn't recognize her. She remembered him as the one by the car, the one who had stayed too far back to get an accurate picture of her face. And what with her clothes, hair, even the color of her skin thoroughly altered since their last encounter, it seemed unlikely that he would be able to pick her out. Then again, it was those very changes that were now making her so conspicuous among the rest of the tuneful little troupe. He *would* scrutinize her. That much was clear. Which meant she needed to create a distraction.

With that in mind, Sarah turned toward the baritone and began to mouth the few words she could make out—always half a beat behind—swaying her head back and forth. Immediately, he nodded in encouragement. As she had anticipated, the movement was enough to draw the agent's attention. *Good,* she thought, *enjoy the show.* Sarah felt his gaze on her face, waited until he had begun to move toward them and then, very slowly, began to spread her legs. The short skirt inched up her thighs. Soon, her knees were far enough apart to offer a generous view of the upper leg and beyond for any interested parties. And Pritchard's man was interested. From the corner of her eye, she saw him stop, his glance drift downward, his eyes eagerly begin to trace along the curve of her inner thigh, ever upward, enrapt by her flesh and panties for several long moments. Sarah waited, allowing him to indulge his appetite.

And then, without warning, she abruptly pulled her knees together. Her eyes were already locked on his, her expression one of shock and reproach—the wounded female having caught her violator in the act. His response was all too predictable. His face flushed, his eyes darted about before he offered a feeble smile and turned. A moment later, he was retreating in awkward haste, his hands digging into the seats for support. Sarah watched him sway from side to side, certain that, even now, he was trying to force her face from his mind. What else could he do? He had felt only the humiliation, had seen only the accusation in her eyes, not the woman behind them. And for that reason alone, she knew he would not return. He could not allow himself to believe she had been the woman he sought. His ego would never permit it.

Before Pritchard's agent had slipped from sight, the door to her left suddenly flew open, the sound of wheels and wind bellowing through to drown out the choristers. Looking up, Sarah nearly flinched. There, standing less than three feet from her was the stocky escort from Tieg's cellar, the man who had led her to the ramp some ten hours ago. *Tieg?* She stared in utter disbelief, her momentary triumph over Pritchard all but forgotten. The man had stopped and was looking straight ahead, undistracted by the resurgence of music. Sarah inched closer to her singing partner, an attempt to obscure the man's view should he turn, but his gaze remained on the aisle, his eyes fixed on something farther down the car. Unlike his predecessor, he showed no need to scan the seats. Somewhere beyond her view, he had targeted his prey.

Very quietly, Sarah sat back, puzzled less by his appearance than by the message his expression conveyed—he was *not* looking for her. That much was clear. In fact, it seemed as though he might not even be *aware* that she was on the train. *Then what was he doing here?* A rather disturbing thought sprang to mind. *Pritchard's boy.* But why? Before she could speculate, Tieg's man was already halfway to the far door. Sarah slowly got up. Without so much as a nod of good-bye, she began to follow.

Keeping well back, she trailed Tieg's man through the next three cars, at each successive door staying far enough behind so as to see him stop, size up his quarry, and then move on, never close enough, though, to catch sight of the prey herself. Only when she dared to narrow the distance between them did she finally discover whom he was tailing—*Eager Eyes*. Granted, Pritchard's man was the only logical choice, but the question remained: Whose logic? Why would he be showing even the *slightest* interest in the boy from Washington? Why be aware of him at all? Insecure channels aside, the target made no sense. She knew they would have been after *her*. *Should* have been after her.

The questions quickly slipped from her mind as the strange game of cat, mouse, and cat began to pick up, the ensuing minutes transforming Sarah from hunted into hunter. Gliding down the aisles, she could feel her heartbeat quicken, her senses grow more acute—textures, sights, smells—everything on the train pass with an amplified clarity. And with that intensity came a sense of relief. For the first time in weeks, perhaps years, she felt in control, the voices within momentarily at peace. The chase—so simple, so much a part of herself. For three cars, she kept both men within eyeshot until, nearing the fourth, she was forced to stop on the small ledge between cars. Pritchard's man had found his two comrades, the three in hushed conference midway through the cabin. Tieg's man had likewise been forced to stop, taking the first available seat before pulling a small radio from his jacket pocket, his eyes never once straying from the trio. Meanwhile, Sarah had stepped into the shadows of the open-air vestibule, her reflection eclipsed within the glare of the sun-glazed window.

The three from Washington remained surprisingly unaware of the dual surveillance, each clearly wrapped up in his own inability to locate their common target. As Sarah had expected, her voyeur showed no signs of recounting his recent misadventure, shaking his head and shrugging along with the others, his failure, so it seemed, as complete as their own. It was only when all three seemed to stop simultaneously that Sarah realized they had not been explaining their exploits to one another. Instead, they were listening intently, their joint focus on the seat directly to their left. It was then that she noticed the shock of gray hair rising above the headrest, the familiar coat draping out into the aisle. *Pritchard.* He, too, was evidently less than pleased, his fingers darting above the seat to punctuate each of his frustrations. One point was clear. He had taken an interest in her—a very *personal* interest—and one that was forcing him to play an active role in an arena he understood only in the abstract. *So why was he taking the chance?*

Pritchard stood, his tirade ended, his expression one of disappointment, perhaps even irritation, but never without the arrogance, never at a loss for the presumption. *He* would lead them on a sweep of the train—his posture said as much as he moved down the aisle. Until he suddenly stopped. For a frightening moment, Sarah thought he had seen her through the glass, but his eyes told her otherwise. It was Tieg's man who held his attention, not her. Both men stared at each other, Pritchard frozen, his cheeks ashen in a flash of shocked recognition. A palpable fear began to wash across his face. *Fear?* She had never once seen even the slightest trace of emotion penetrate those stony eyes. Now, she saw terror, a wave of real panic rise up to stifle all motion. Gazing into his weathered face, she tried to understand, tried to answer her own confusion, but she could find nothing. For several seconds, she felt trapped by his gaze, floating in an absolute stillness, until, quite accidentally, she let her brow graze across the glass—its chill enough to release her from her stupor. And in that moment, in that instant of clarity, she sensed it—the truth, distant at first, but there in all its incongruity. He was a part of it, a part of the madness. Pritchard had given himself to the men of Eisenreich. And somehow, he had betrayed that trust.

That was why Tieg's men were here. As Pritchard had traced her, so they had traced him. She wondered how long they had been looking for him, not bothering to question her own good fortune at having avoided the trap.

Pritchard stepped back, inadvertently bumping into one of his agents. The man awkwardly moved aside, unclear as to the sudden change of direction. But there was to be no change. George—Sarah's erstwhile chauffeur—had arrived at the far door to discourage any further thoughts of escape. Evidently, they knew how to keep options to a minimum as well. Pritchard turned again, and for a few long seconds simply stood gazing down the aisle. Very slowly, he sank to the nearest armrest. His three minions, meanwhile, remained blissfully unaware of what was happening around them. They continued to watch as Pritchard steadied himself against the seat, each exchanging a bewildered look before the pieces began to drop into place. But it was too late. Tieg's men had already drawn near, their hands wedged deep within their coat pockets, the first with his mouth to the radio once again. He began to nod. Only then did Sarah realize what he was doing. He was calling for backup.

She quickly glanced through the window behind her and saw several large bodies approaching down the aisle. Stepping from the shadows, she very calmly pulled back the door and entered the cabin, heading straight for them. She kept her head up. None seemed to recognize her, the first slowing as she sidled into a vacant space so as to let them pass. Each nodded his thanks, the last of the four even offering a smile before moving past her and leaving the aisle free. She stepped out and continued to walk away from them, her gait casual, until she heard the door click shut behind her. They were through. She could turn. As if having forgotten something, she let out an audible sigh and spun around. None of the other passengers seemed to take any notice. Half a minute later, she was back at her perch, the scene within completely different. The men from Eisenreich had surrounded Pritchard and his cohorts, cleverly enough so that only someone looking for it would have recognized the tactic as encirclement. Those on the outer ring kept one hand within the folds of their jackets. Likewise, the men inside had clearly been instructed to keep their hands visible, jackets open, eyes on the ground. As Sarah scanned the inner three, she noticed that one of them had not given in without a struggle. He held his left forearm close to his chest, his limp hand the evident sign of a shattered wrist. The message was clear—no signals, no coordinated attacks, no further attempts to break up the happy little get-together. At center stood Pritchard, eyes shut, defeated.

"Alderton, two minutes," the crackled voice penetrated even to the open-air ledge. "Two minutes to Alderton."

The train began to slow, a few passengers showing signs of life, several standing in order to retrieve packs and briefcases. Fingers fiddled with buttons; suitcases dropped to the floor. All the while, the group at center remained comfortably detached from the growing activity. Within a minute, the train had pulled into the station, a final screech of brakes to signal the arrival. Doors opened, and the cluster of agents was on the platform, a single unit heading for the stairs at the far end. Sarah pushed open the door and entered the car, maneuvering through the newly boarded passengers, never once taking her eyes from the train's windows and the group beyond. Sliding into a vacant seat, she watched as the men from Eisenreich led their captives to several waiting sedans, the boys from Washington immediately separated from Pritchard. No doubt, the three would be forced to answer certain questions before meeting their individual fates—a bullet to the head, perhaps a garrote. But all of that would come later. For now, they remained useful.

Pritchard, however, had lost all such value; he would merit no delays. Even now, as the train pulled out, Sarah knew he was already dead.

⚓

Xander flicked on his lights and tried to concentrate on the center line, the dip and turn of the backwoods road growing less manageable under a spreading dusk. He had been on the road for nearly two hours, the map showing Tempsten another seventy miles on. Five hours ago, he had opted for a bus from the airport, happier to let someone else make the decisions. But the sleep he had wanted had never come, his mind too restless to permit such luxuries. There had been nothing to distract him, no girl with revolver, no unread manuscript. Alone only with his thoughts. Not pleasant. And yet, for a few moments, the prospect of seeing Sarah had managed to ease his mind. He had not asked why.

Instead, he had left the bus at one of the small towns along the Hudson and had bought a car—a used Rabbit—with the money Feric had left him. Driving as diversion. The dealer had explained that the transmission might need work, the alignment might tug to the right, but Xander knew he wouldn't be keeping it long enough to find out. It's sole purpose was to get him to the Sleepy Hollow without drawing attention. No rental decals, and no out-of-state license plates. The dealer had been more than happy with cash.

Xander had kept to country roads, at first for security's sake, even though he knew Eisenreich would need several hours to trace the bus, the dealership, and whatever else they could find to ferret him out. Now, as he made his way from town to town, he realized his unconscious mind had been at work as well. Several miles back, he had begun to recognize something of the familiar in his surroundings. It was while passing through the tiny hamlet of Yardley that he had understood why. Somewhere nearby— ten, twenty miles to the west, he couldn't quite recall—he remembered Mrs. Grier's, an inn that had been his home for several long weekends during that first winter teaching at Columbia, when he had considered throwing it all in. His writing had been going poorly, his work called outlandish; there had even been talk of terminating his appointment. And, of course, there had been Fiona. Lundsdorf had recommended the three-story house, said it would revive his enthusiasm for the work. And he had been right. The fireplace, the odd assortment of guests at the evening meals, one Carlo Pescatore, slightly more quirky than the rest, but certainly always the most entertaining. An instant friendship. And his room on the third floor, a windowed alcove that had helped him to recall how much he cherished his work. Articles, books, notes scattered everywhere. How much a part of himself they would always be.

And now, fate was being kind again. It was allowing him to remember.

Other thoughts began to creep in as the sun slipped to the horizon, not the least of which was how far he had let himself stray from what he knew best. From what he *loved*. Somehow, he had learned to destroy with his hands, deceive with his eyes, grow numb to his own fear and anger, but he knew such weapons had only limited use. Their aim was to keep him alive, nothing more, and he had grown tired of mere survival. Too reliant on them, he had forgotten himself. True, the idealist was gone, but the thinker remained. And if Eisenreich could manipulate ideas so as to wreak havoc, why not he? Why not create a little chaos of his own? It was an idea that had been gaining momentum ever since the purchase of the car. The manuscript, the role of the different spheres, the parallels borne out in the words of Ireton and Rosenberg—*these* were his resources, his tools to expose and defeat the men of Eisenreich. He knew he had been foolish to look elsewhere for answers, blind not to see how to put them to use.

It was why he was looking for a place to stop. He was tired, hungry, but, more than that, he needed to put his thoughts to paper. He needed to tie together everything he had seen, everything he had read, so as to create his own weapon. He had few facts, but all the theory, and at this point, he knew it would be enough. The details would come later—the Tempsten Project, the schedule, the linchpin, and whatever else Sarah had discovered. He had to believe that she would have the proof necessary to give the memo conviction. For now, he would create the shell; he would explain in dry academic prose how a sixteenth-century manuscript could translate into a twentieth-century conspiracy. And he would do it with the detachment necessary to lend his thesis credibility. Hypothesis, argument, conclusion—a series of ever-widening assertions, built on evidence, verified through interpretation, all designed to lead to one irrefutable conclusion. An exposé to bring Eisenreich to its knees. It was what he knew, what others would believe.

A winter rain began to spit at the windshield as he drove into the town of Creighton, the lights along its main street standing in a neat row. Halfway down the block, he noticed a stationer's shop, a small diner two or three doors beyond. Again, fate. Fifteen minutes later, he sat in the last booth, coffee, soup, and a small pad at his side. He would get to the books later. For now, it was enough simply to write.

⚔

It was five to seven when she landed, 7:15 by the time she walked across the tarmac, the cold rain on her face a welcome relief after six hours of flying. She had slept for the first few, the stopover in Chicago allowing her time to pick up more packets of dye, along with a second mirror and hair dryer so as to rectify the miscues from the Palametto station. Sarah had managed it all with several trips to the airplane rest room, a series of fitful naps in between, each filled with too many disquieting memories to make the sleep even mildly restorative. Pritchard himself had crept into her dreams—his face draped in despair, eyes darting about, spying her through the door, yelling to Tieg's men that she was there, behind them, his finger pointing in a desperate attempt to barter for his own life.

She had awakened to the sound of her own screams ringing in her ears even as she had realized that no such terror had passed her lips. Only silence to accompany the strange feeling of pity she felt for a man who had never shown her the least bit of kindness.

She reached the terminal. Within ten minutes, she had purchased three sets of black pants, turtlenecks, ski masks, and gloves. They would come later. She then rented a car from the same young man she had patronzied just yesterday—no hint that he recognized the blond, suntanned woman as a onetime redhead—and was soon back on the road to Tempsten. The highway would be quickest, a more circuitous route safer. She opted for the latter, soon putting the bright lights of the airport behind her.

One hour. Yesterday, she had made the same trip in order to gather information, to find a link to the horrors that had turned children into time bombs, innocents into killers. Then, it had been speculation. Now, she knew far more. Vice President Pembroke, Senator Schenten, Pritchard—other players, other roles. She knew about the schools, about the children who were learning to hate all over again, and about the prototypes from thirty years ago who had grown up to become an army of devoted minions, capable of unleashing untold chaos. More than that, though, she knew the strategy—less than a week, and then explosion after explosion. Washington, Chicago, New Orleans on a grand scale. Alone, the information was meaningless, a series of disjointed facts. She needed more. She needed the connections.

She needed Jaspers. Somehow, more than she wanted to admit.

⬩

He had written for nearly two hours, half the pages of the small pad filled with his familiar scrawl, the first few neater than the rest—a short-lived attempt to make the paragraphs legible. But his mind had raced too fast for careful penmanship, his need to set down the initial statements on state theory too overpowering to leave time for presentation. Those first eight pages, a dizzying array of academic logic, had formed the shell, a series of assertions couched in the starkest of terms so as to leave no room for misunderstanding. One point following the next, a rigorous patterning of reasoned argument. It was what he had been trained to do, what he knew best—to synthesize what others could not see.

With that in mind, he had turned to the texts themselves in order to lend the theory pragmatic force. Spreading the books out on the table, he had cross-referenced the corresponding passages from among them, explained away the discrepancies as misinterpretation, and identified their common purpose—to place power in the hands of three men, each controlling a separate sphere, each distinct in the public eye, and each bent on coordinated manipulation so as to ensure the ultimate prize: stability in the abstract, iron domination in reality. The price, individual freedom. The tools, chaos and hatred. From Eisenreich to Ireton to Rosenberg—a clear progression. Then, citing what little he could recall from the files, he had extended the lineage to Votapek, Sedgewick, Tieg, and the overseer. Only then had the abstract taken on a human face, more so when he had forced himself to recount his own experiences—the depravity beyond the men themselves— ever careful to maintain an academic objectivity despite his own outrage. Perhaps the least comprehensive, they were the most compelling statements within the document; they alone specified the meeting point of theory and practice. Turning conjecture into reality.

He had put the pen down half an hour ago, eager to get back on the road. He had made a copy of everything—including the manuscript—and had sent it to Mrs. Huber, again for safekeeping. Granted, holes peppered his argument—theories without evidence. Whether they would be enough, though, remained to be seen. That would depend on Sarah. So much, now, depended on Sarah.

The car hitched as he pulled into the Sleepy Hollow, the transmission living up to all the dealer had promised. It was a classic single-level motel, eight to ten rooms directly on the driveway, each with its own parking space. He eased the car into one of the spots, grabbed the backpack, and started for the small office, its VACANCY sign somewhat redundant, given his was the only car within two miles. At the front desk, the little bell emitted a high-pitched twang.

"Just a second." The voice came from beyond a curtained doorway, the sound of a television quickly turned off before a woman appeared. She was wiping her hands on an apron. "All right, all right, here we are."

"I'll need a room," said Xander.

"Yes, I should think so," she replied, reaching for the registration book. She slid it toward him and asked, "You wouldn't be Mr. Terni, would you?"

Xander started to shake his head, then stopped as the word sunk in. *Terni. Ternistato. Iron state. Eisenreich.* The clue to Carlo's notes. *Clever girl!* Xander smiled. "Then she *did* call ahead. I'm so pleased."

"Made the reservation yesterday." The woman was reaching behind for a key. "She said it would be either today or tomorrow, so I suppose your conference ended early."

"Not a minute too soon," he answered, signing the book. He pocketed the key and moved to the door. "Thank you."

"Paid up through Monday. It's the fifth one down."

The key took a moment to find the lock before he pushed open the door, the smell of pine unmistakable. He stepped in and fumbled for the light switch, tossing the pack onto the bed before he heard something move on the far side of the room. The light came on.

A young woman sat on the floor, her back against the wall, her eyes veiled in terror.

"Please, don't hurt me," she said, a gun in her lap.

⚔

Xander stood motionless, aware that she was shaking, her hands held firmly under her knees, eyes locked on the edge of the bed. In his own confusion, he managed to find the words to comfort. "I won't hurt you."

He let the door shut, careful to keep his movement to a minimum. Alison Krogh sat rigidly, her long hair, draped in her lap, oddly caressing the barrel of the gun.

"She told me to stay here," whispered Alison. "She said I would be safe. That they wouldn't find me." She suddenly looked up at him. "You won't hurt me, will you?"

"No, I won't hurt you." He removed his cap and placed it on the floor as he sat, his back against the door. "Did *Sarah* tell you to stay here?"

She nodded her head, a single jerked motion.

Xander watched as her eyes welled up. "Has Sarah been here?" he asked.

She shook her head. "She said she would come back. And that you would come. And someone else. That's what she said."

"It's just me."

"Yes." She now looked at him, wiping the tears away. "We'll wait for Sarah." She placed her hand on the gun and nodded. "We'll turn off the lights and wait for Sarah. That's what we'll do."

⚔

O'Connell sat at the end of the bar. He'd been nursing a double whiskey for the last ten minutes, waiting for the damn phone to ring. It was an odd sensation, anticipating the contact, a voice now no longer faceless. And yet, it felt strangely familiar. Too familiar. Seven years had evidently done little to dull his senses. Everything fit in perfectly.

Except the waiting. It always felt like a setup. The phone rang.

"Sorry to keep you waiting." Stein sounded tired.

"I've been firing up the furnace. Getting the blood running again. You didn't tell me how cold it could get in these woods."

"Didn't think I'd have to. Any sign of her?"

"None. Nor her young professor."

"Any unusual activity at the house?" Stein's voice conveyed a confidence O'Connell had never heard before, an authority obviously reserved for those in the field. It was a pleasant surprise.

"No. Looks like the senator is taking the time to recuperate. His 'illness' has prompted a few more guards on the fence at night, but I suspect that's just an old man's weakness showing itself. No unexpected guests, if that's what you're asking."

"There will be, trust me."

"And why are we so certain of that?"

"Because he ties in, and Sarah knows it. Schenten hasn't taken a sick leave in nearly thirty years. Why now?"

"Setup?"

"That's why you need to spend a few more nights in the cold, Gael. Make sure they're not that clever."

"And then what? Bring her in?"

"I don't know." It was an honest admission. "I don't know what she has. I don't know what *either* of them have, if Jaspers is even back in the country. The Germans lost him. They're convinced he didn't get out, or at least not to the States. Our young professor has a hell of an instinct for survival."

"That is if he hasn't been given up already."

"Keep your distance. If we move too fast, we could give them both up."

"If the boy's not dead, my guess is that he soon will be."

"Don't count on it. He's obviously got something they want."

"So how long do I keep watch?"

"The program's changed," said Stein. "Pritchard's dead."

There was a pause on the line before O'Connell answered. "That doesn't answer my question. How long?"

"Just keep watch. Timing's always been one of your stronger points."

✍

It was almost an hour later when the beams from a pair of headlights swept across the far wall. The woman remained motionless, unaware, save for a hand gently stroking the barrel of the gun. Xander listened as the car pulled up outside the room; a moment later, the light gone, the engine silent. He began to inch his way to the far corner. Footsteps followed, the sound of a key in the lock, all the while the woman staring into an unseen distance. He stood, his body masked in darkness; she looked up, the gun now gripped tightly in her hands as the door opened.

In shadowed profile, Sarah stepped into the room.

"Hello, Alison." Her voice was hushed. "You can put the gun down."

Slowly, the woman lowered the barrel to the carpet, her expression unchanged. "Hello, Sarah. I'm glad you came back." Xander watched as Sarah closed the door, stepped to the night table, and flicked on the lamp. Only then did she see him, her eyes distant at first. For a moment, they stared at each other, he squinting against the light, both unable to speak.

"You look tired," she said, breaking the silence. Xander nodded. She remained by the bed, tossing her bags on the blanket. She began to fumble with her hair. "Tired . . . but well."

Again, he nodded. "You, too. . . . Blond, tanned. That's a change." She smiled, and, for the briefest of moments, he thought he sensed— perhaps *wanted* to sense—something beneath the self-control, a tenderness. It forced him to stop, to let his guard down. "It's good to see you, Sarah."

"Yes." The room became quiet again before she spoke. "I see you've met Alison . . . who must be very tired." The woman had not taken her eyes from Sarah. "The room next door is safe," she explained. "Would you like to sleep in there?" Alison nodded and stood, then looked at Xander.

"Thank you for waiting with me."

Xander smiled and watched as Sarah walked her out into the rain. A few minutes later, Sarah reappeared, tossing the two sets of keys onto the bed. She closed the door and leaned up against it.

"She'll sleep for a while. I told her everything would be all right."

"Promise?" he asked.

Sarah smiled and let her head drop back. "I'll do the best I can. If you're wondering, she's the girl who killed the boys thirty years ago. Here in Tempsten. The little girl whose name never quite made it to the papers."

Xander tried to respond but could only shake his head.

"Yes," she agreed. "I found her yesterday. Set her up here. They've kept her in town for some reason. Probably think she's harmless." She looked at him. "She isn't. Strangely enough, she thinks Votapek's her father."

"Jesus Christ."

"No, that's who Tieg thinks *he* is." She pushed off from the door and headed for the bathroom. "We have a lot of catching up to do." She stopped before disappearing. "Where's Feric?" The question caught Xander off guard. Somehow, he had managed to forget. He stared at her for an instant, an instant too long.

"When?" she asked.

It took him a moment to answer. "Outside of Frankfurt . . . he saved—"

She nodded, another twinge of tenderness in her eyes. She held his gaze for a moment and then slipped out of the room.

"I'm sorry." It was all he could offer. "I wouldn't have found the manuscript without him. He was . . ."

She reemerged, a towel in her hands. "Yes, he was." Again they stared at each other. After several long moments, she tossed the towel to the chair and asked, "Does it tie any of this together?"

"Tie . . . Oh, the manuscript. Yes. Yes, it does." Xander stepped to the bed and pulled the manila envelope from the backpack. Handing the package across to her, he said, "I think that's what you want."

They talked for nearly an hour, he first, recounting everything that had happened since Florence—the madness at the Institute, the insanity at Ganz's, the train, Feric's death, every minor detail so that she could understand. Through it all, he spoke with a strange objectivity, as if relaying a long-forgotten history he himself had never witnessed. Sarah sensed the detachment, heard the distance in his voice, but said nothing. Only once did she see the pain beyond it. Only once did he let her in.

"You know, he seemed so light in my arms. . . . I don't know why. Doesn't really make sense, but I remember the sun being very hot, almost scorching my cheeks. . . . Freezing, early morning, sun barely above the trees, and yet all I could feel was that hot sun, and how light Feric was in my arms." He shook his head. "I dropped him, you know. Just . . . let him go. That's what he said I should do. Strange, but it didn't feel all that different without him." His voice seemed to trail off. "I don't think I moved after that. I think I just stood out there . . . all the way to Frankfurt." He looked over at her. "Maybe not. I don't really remember."

Thereafter, he spoke with little feeling. He ran through the rest of the story, focused on the hours he had spent with the books, the pieces that had begun to fall into place. Only when he mentioned the schedule did he seem to regain himself.

"And you think they have one?" asked Sarah.

"It would make the most sense. If they've followed the manuscript to this point, they'll have concocted something that spells out—with dates, locations, and methods—how they intend to create the chaos beyond the first trial. All we have to do is find that schedule and use the information in it to pull the rug out from under them."

"You mean connecting them to Rosenberg and the Nazis."

"Trust me, the media's the media. They'll do the damage."

"If they have the time."

Xander looked at her. "I don't understand."

"Less than a week," she answered.

"What?"

"Less than a week," she repeated, "until they get that chance. That's what Tieg said."

"*What?*" His eyes went wide. "Less than a *week*? That doesn't make any sense. The manuscript talks in terms of *months*. That would mean—"

"Yes," she added, "that every*thing* and every*one* is in place. They're ready to push the buttons."

"It's *supposed* to be months. They'd—" He stopped and looked at her. "Oh God. *How* could I have been so stupid? We do things today in a few hours that would have taken Eisenreich weeks, months. . . ." He took the envelope from her and pulled out the pages he had written that afternoon. "If it's that quick, I don't know if this will be of any use."

"This?" she asked. "You mean this isn't the manuscript?"

"It's something that goes a good deal beyond it."

He began to explain, she leafing through the pages with him as he tried to pinpoint the areas where she could give him the detail he needed—*they* needed. Soon, it was she who was instructing, recalling the documents she had taken from Justice, the violent history of the Learning Center with its esteemed graduates Pembroke, Grant, and Eggart—the latter two, she reminded him, conspicuous in the recent killing of the Dutch diplomats. He listened with wide eyes, amazed at the names and events she was bringing together. She recounted her first meeting with Alison, the frightened woman who remained the only real link to a devastating past, but who could no more recall her part in the death of the two boys than relieve herself of the guilt she kept tucked deep within. Sarah then told him of her visit to Votapek, the first hint that the men of Eisenreich were vulnerable, dinner at Tieg's, the wild diatribes on conquest, eugenics, power. She even told him about Pritchard, the Committee, hinted at her own involvement to underscore the full extent of Eisenreich's grasp. And finally, she gave him Schenten.

"It's why I came back here," she said. "It's where I can bring this to a close."

"Bring this to a close—how?" She didn't answer. "I see."

"You see," she repeated. "Do you really?" She stood and moved away from him. "What do you want me to say? I'd found the linchpin. You wouldn't need the connection to Rosenberg. Cut off the head and kill the beast." He said nothing. She turned to him. "Does it surprise you? Does it fail on the erudition scale—no footnotes, no cross-references? Well, I'm sorry, but now I know it's why I was chosen. Why they wanted me in the field in the first place." She paused. "I kill—that's what I do. It's not what you do."

"That's *not* why they chose you." Xander stood and moved to her. "This Pritchard—he wanted something, you said so yourself. He didn't think—"

"*Pritchard?* Pritchard had nothing—"

"Of course he did. Why do you think Tieg wanted him dead?"

"Pritchard's not important."

"He needed something from you, something he kept from the others."

"I said it's not important."

"Why? Why won't you admit there was something else?"

She turned to face him. "Why are you pressing this?"

"Does this have to do with the tunnel," he said, ignoring her question, "in Florence—"

"Let's just drop this, okay?"

"No." He took her arm as she tried to move past him. "Not okay." Their eyes locked. "Do you know how close to the edge I am here? Have you let yourself see that at all? You're talking about killing, and I've . . . shut down just so I can keep what little sanity I have left. The problem is, it's not working. I guess I'm not strong enough to carry all of this around inside me. But I don't think I'm alone. Maybe you've been trained to do something else, act with absolute control, but I don't think that makes any difference. I'm asking what happened to you because *I* need the help. Do you understand that? I'm asking because when everything went crazy in Germany, I had nothing else but you. *Find Sarah.* That's what I was told to do. . . . No, that's what I *needed* to do. I need *you*, not the assassin you think you are. Because you're not. You can't be. I need you to be as frightened as I am and as close to the edge, to be so much stronger, so much more in control, and . . . I don't know." He let go of her arm. "I need you to need *me*." He moved to the bed. Lying down, he looked to the ceiling. "Sorry, Feric. I guess I didn't learn that lesson too well."

Sarah stood alone, suddenly cold by the window. She looked at his long frame draped across the blankets, his eyes shutting out the pain. Slowly, she moved to the bed. Slowly, she sat and laid her hand on his chest. Tears crept down her cheek as she gently stroked his hair. "I'm sorry," she whispered. "I'm *so* sorry." Soon, they were side by side, his face nestled in her neck, their bodies tight together, rocking back and forth, she trying to quiet him through her own tears. "I *do* need you. More than you could possibly know."

"Why?" he whispered.

"Because . . ." She held him even more tightly, her tears falling to his cheek, her voice fragile. "I let someone die once. Someone like you. And I can't live with that again. I can't. . . ."

He took her in his arms, rocking her back and forth.

They fell asleep, clasped in each other's arms.

⚔

They awoke an hour later, she first, then he, neither willing to rejoin the stark world beyond them. Together, they remained safe, protected. Minutes passed before she found the energy to pull herself up on an elbow, her other arm not ready to release his chest. She stared down into his eyes and, without thinking, lowered her lips to his. Soft, simple, the tenderness of a first kiss, the velvet of her tongue gently playing with his. She stopped and looked at him. He began to speak, but she dipped low to him again. She then sat up, stretching the sleep from her shoulders. "I know. I wasn't expecting that, either." She turned and caressed his cheek.

"It wasn't your fault, Sarah. Amman . . . it wasn't your fault."

She stared into his eyes and again drew her fingers across his cheek. Another kiss and she stood, moving toward the bathroom. At the door, she asked, "Do you think Schenten has the schedule?"

It took Xander a moment to shift gears. "Schenten?" he answered, his legs swinging off the bed as he pulled himself to a sitting position. "Yes. I would guess as overseer, he probably wrote it."

Sarah popped her head out, her eyebrows thick with soap. "Overseer?"

"It's what Eisenreich called the ringleader, the linchpin." She nodded and returned to the sink. Xander tucked his hands under his thighs. "Will you have to kill him?"

The water fell silent, Sarah reappearing a moment later with a towel. "Why ask?" Xander said nothing. "If we can find the schedule without him, no. No one would have to die." She placed the towel by the window. "Is that what you wanted me to say?"

"I don't know." He released his hands and reached for the envelope. "A great many people have died already. A few more won't make that much of a difference." He placed the loose pages inside and looked at her. "It's not why you were chosen. I won't believe that."

"I'm glad you have so much faith in me."

"I have to. You've left me little choice."

She allowed herself a smile and moved to him on the bed. Cupping his cheek in her hand, she drew him to her. This time, though, no kiss, only his gaze. She pulled away. "We need to get in there tonight," she said, reaching for her bag. "His house is about a twenty-minute drive from here. The last two miles will have to be on foot."

"And the girl?"

"She'll sleep. She's safe." She handed him a pair of black pants and a dark turtleneck. "You take her gun."

Xander picked up the pack. "Was it loaded?"

"No."

"Then I'll need some bullets."

⚔

Moonlight crept through the leafless branches, speckling the ground in pale shadows of shimmering white. Sarah led, hidden beneath the dark contours of her clothing, Xander behind, his eyes fixed on her. In and out of the slats of light they moved, carefully, urgently, without a sound.

They had left the road over a mile ago, finding stray branches to cover the car. Not once had she said a word, pressing ahead even when he had become entangled in the brambles of an unseen bush—her message clear: *You're here for the schedule, to identify it. If it's not there, I will kill him. If you fall behind, I will kill him.* Her gun remained at her side as she pushed through the branches, its silencer once or twice catching the moon's reflection before she was forced to slide it into the small of her back. He had done the same.

At the next turn, a clearing came into view, beyond it a wire fence, farther still the vague outline of Schenten's mansion, the house dark save for a single light shining from a room on the third floor. The old man was awake. They would have to be careful. The moon had mercifully ducked behind the cloud cover, shrouding the approach in blackness. Sarah stopped, Xander at her side, both crouching in the undergrowth. She was staring at the western end of the fence, tapping her thumb against her thigh, waiting, watching. A minute into the count, a figure appeared, his gait slow, relaxed. Sarah kept her eyes trained on the man as he neared the other end. She then waited another cycle. When he had slipped from view a second time, she darted out, no word to Xander, no warning. He followed.

A moment later, she was sliding toward the fence. Dragging himself along the grass at breakneck speed, Xander felt the strain in his shoulders. His upper arms were also aching; he was letting his chest drag. Shutting out the pain, he pulled himself to the wire and sucked in as big a breath as his lungs would allow. He then watched as she positioned a pair of clippers on the wire and began to snip, just enough for one body to slide under and through. A minute later, they were ten feet beyond the fence and making their way toward one of the first-floor windows.

Within half a minute, both stood flattened against the wall of the house, Sarah tracing her fingers along the sill of the window. She peered up and around the frame until she located the wire. The alarm system. Taking little time, she crosscut the wires, attaching an extra large loop of coil at two points—sufficient to open the window without breaking the connection—and snipped. The lock proved far less demanding, a minor obstacle to their arrival in what looked to be a sitting room—love seat, lamps, and chairs all facing a small brick fireplace. She turned and shut the window.

It would not be here; they both knew that. They needed to find the study, the place Schenten kept things of value. Sarah moved to the sliding doors, quietly pulled one to the side and stepped into the foyer, its green marble floor agleam even in the relative darkness. Directly across from them, another set of doors stood ajar, a quick perusal revealing the dining room. The other doors were equally unkind, opening to the music room, living room, but not the library. Xander pointed up and moved toward the stairway. Sarah scampered past him, leading them up to another foyer, another set of four doors, three of which opened easily; the pair on the far left, however, did not. A moment with the lock, and Sarah led them into the study, a simple room, even in shadow, with a touch of personality. Chairs sat thick with books and newspapers, a half-drunk cup of tea visible on one of the end tables. Sarah checked the cup—ice-cold—as Xander headed for the desk, a sturdy block of oak somehow neater amid the surrounding clutter. She then pulled two fine-beam flashlights from her pack and handed one to him. The beam was less than half an inch wide, enough to light objects within a three-inch radius, but not enough to cast a glow. He had told her to look for a diary.

For ten minutes, they pored through anything that might hold the schedule. This time, though, there was no Augustine to keep it hidden, no clever little codes from which to work. All they had was instinct, a sense that it was here, in the room, waiting to be found. Two minutes into the search, Sarah discovered a safe behind one of the paintings, the voice-activated lock, how-ever, too much for her primitive tools. She had not anticipated such high-tech equipment from the senator.

"Very good, Ms. Trent." The lights came on around them, Schenten alone at the door, bathrobe and slippers his attire. "That is, in fact, where I keep it." In his hand, he held a small black book. "Tonight, though, it's been on my night table. A bit of reading before bed."

9

Once leaders drive invention and ingenuity from men's hearts and minds, the people can pose no threat to stability.

—*On Supremacy*, CHAPTER XVIII

SARAH DREW HER GUN and aimed it at Schenten. His eyes, however, had moved to Xander.

"You surprise me, Dr. Jaspers. I wasn't aware you were so quick with a pistol. Even quicker, it seems, than our young lady friend."

Sarah turned and saw Xander's gun leveled at Schenten's chest, both hands gripped tightly around the trigger. The senator, meanwhile, had raised his arms in mock surrender. "You can see I'm alone. Nothing with me except this book, and I have no interest in forcing your hand, as it were." He began to move forward, then stopped. "May I come into my library?"

Sarah motioned for Schenten to take the chair in front of the desk. She then moved to the side of the window and peered out into the darkness.

"If you're concerned with the guards, don't be," said Schenten, shifting a pillow as he sat. "I told them I was coming down to the library. They weren't looking for you."

"Who, then?" asked Xander.

"Who indeed?" he replied, then paused. "The answer might come as something of a surprise."

"Try me."

274

Again, Schenten waited before speaking. "What if I were to say the very same men who've been so interested in you?"

"I wouldn't believe you," he answered.

"Would you, Ms. Trent?" Schenten kept his eyes on Xander. "No, I don't suppose you would." He reached toward the desk, Xander quick to bring the gun even with the older man's eyes. Schenten immediately stopped, pointed to a gold box, and said, "They're cigarettes. You can take a look, if you like."

Xander pulled the box across the desk and flipped it open; several rows of neatly packed Rothmans stared up at him. Sliding the case to Schenten, he asked, "You want us to believe you're afraid of your own people?"

Schenten laughed, pulling a lighter from the pocket of his dressing gown. "Nothing of the kind." A moment later, smoke streamed from his nostrils as he sat back. "Can you see the inscription, Doctor? In the case— it's on the bottom of the lid. . . . No, please, take a look." He waited for Xander to locate the tiny writing, then asked, "Would you mind reading it aloud so Ms. Trent can hear? I'm sure your French is passable enough to make sense of it."

Xander studied the man's weathered face. "I don't think—"

"Please, Doctor," insisted Schenten. "Humor me."

Xander looked at Sarah, then pulled the box closer. Translating, he read, " 'with a love that is ours alone, I am forever with you—Jean.' " He stared a moment at the words before looking up at Schenten. "Lovely. I'm sure you and your wife are—"

"It's not from my wife," he interrupted.

"My mistake," corrected Xander. "I'm sure you and your *mistress*—"

"Wrong again," said the senator.

Xander shut the lid. "Look . . . *whoever* she is—"

"Strike three," said Schenten, staring directly into his captor's eyes. He drew the cigarette to his lips and slowly inhaled. "*French*, Doctor," he said, smoke billowing from his mouth, "French, where Jean is a *he*. Jeanne, I believe, is the feminine, as in Jeanne d'Arc. Believe me, my Jean was no saint."

"What are you saying?"

Schenten sat back and smiled. "Is it that difficult to believe?" He turned his head to Sarah. "Have I lost you as well, Ms. Trent?"

"He was your lover," she answered coldly.

"*Very* good. And?"

"And"—she dropped the curtain, her eyes on Xander—"senators aren't supposed to have skeletons in their closets."

"An interesting choice of words, but yes." He now looked at Xander. "She's very intuitive, you know. Much better at this than you are." He continued to stare across the desk. "*And*, Ms. Trent?"

"And," Xander responded, no small amount of cynicism in his tone, "you've decided to lash out at a world that's never understood you—"

"That would be ludicrous." The smile remained on Schenten's face. "Don't you agree, Ms. Trent?"

"Look," continued Xander, "your sexual history is fascinating, but that's not what we're here—"

"That is *exactly* what you're here for," he answered icily. "As Ms. Trent pointed out, it's the sort of thing that can put someone like me in a rather vulnerable position." The smile had disappeared. "A potent weapon, information. Used properly, it can turn even the most powerful into puppets, make them appear to be things that they're not." He sat back, smoke once again cascading from his nose. "You begin to see my point, I'm sure."

Xander slowly sat forward. "Are you telling me—"

"I think you know exactly what I'm telling you." He spat a stray piece of tobacco from his lips. "Wouldn't it be nice if everyone could be as open-minded as you? What a lovely world that would be. Sadly, old bulldogs aren't meant to blur the distinctions between decency and depravity; we're not meant to raise unpleasant questions in the minds of our self-righteous constituents. Just smile and project an image that at worst makes them admire, at best makes them revere." Another long draw, more smoke. "As you know, there isn't a great deal of introspection on the part of those who associate themselves with the grassroots conservative Right, but what can you do? That's the reason we can lead them around like a group of mindless idiots. They're not very clever, but they do have their limits. Stray from the image and influence disappears. So as you see, Doctor, my sexual history can make a *great* deal of difference, especially when it's used as a bargaining chip."

"And Eisenreich has that chip," he whispered.

"That," answered the senator, "is the reason we're sitting here."

"This is incredible."

"For how long?" asked Sarah, moving to the desk.

"About two and a half years," he replied. "You had no idea, did you?"

"Why?"

"Why?" The word was spoken in mock disbelief. "Because they *could.* What other reason did they need?" He shook his head. "This is a complete surprise to you, isn't it?" Neither answered. "I'm amazed. . . . That, and the fact that I wasn't interested in what they were selling." He inhaled deeply. "Their response . . . photocopies of several letters—far more detailed than the inscription you just read—sent to my office some three weeks later."

"They approached you," said Sarah. "How?"

"Does that really matter?" He began to crush out the cigarette, taking time to play with the ash. "A few meetings. Something like that."

"And you have records of those meetings?" asked Sarah.

"I did. Somehow, they managed to . . . *disappear* at the same time the photocopies began arriving." He lit up another. "Funny that."

"And you have no idea who delivered the copies," asked Sarah, "or who had access to your records?"

"It's the United States government, Ms. Trent. Bureaucracy doesn't lend itself to a great deal of accountability."

"But why?" asked Xander, unconvinced. "Why would they have told you anything if you weren't interested?"

"Ah, but I *was* interested . . . for a time. That proved most informative. They showed me bits and pieces of a manuscript, set up meetings with Messrs. Votapek, Tieg, and Sedgewick—and believe me, at the outset, I was very enthusiastic. I genuinely believed they had uncovered something that—how should I put this?—that could control the electorate without appearing to put a stranglehold on rights? Yes, I think that's right. Something that would allow us the room to create effective policy without having to cater to public sentiment. That is, after all, the only way to get anything done." He stopped. "My opinion troubles you, Doctor, doesn't it?" His eyes squinted as his lips creased around the cigarette. "I offer no apologies. That, my young academic, is the simplest truth of politics. You won't find it in any of your books." He exhaled and laid the cigarette in the ashtray. "And so, when they came to me with their plans, I didn't look horrified; I didn't stand appalled by the deceptions they were ready to unleash. I embraced them." He smiled. "Do you *honestly* think we tell you everything we do in Washington? Do you honestly think you would *understand* why certain compromises have to be made? The *people*—the myth you hold so dear—are, on the whole, indifferent, uninformed, and stupid. So why put them in the loop at all? Do you really think it was designed to be a *democracy*? Don't be ridiculous. It was meant to be a *republic*, a system where the most capable represent the desires of the rest—whether that rest realizes what's good for it or not. Without a little bit of deception, you're doomed to mediocrity—"

"Obviously," interrupted Sarah, "you and Votapek took the same correspondence course."

"You might not like my politics, Ms. Trent, but you know I'm right."

"Your politics," broke in Xander, "are supposed to be about *dismantling* big government, giving power *back* to the people, or have I missed the point? It seems to me you folks on the Right are the ones who don't want to tell the people what's good for them, even when they don't realize it themselves."

"It's a wonderful tactic, isn't it?" Schenten nodded as he reached for the cigarette. "But do you think we're giving up power by doing that? We're simply letting the states deal with the petty quarrels. 'Get government out of your backyard.' It's a clever slogan, isn't it? Keeps them preoccupied with the minutiae. Actually, we're taking their minds off the federal government, giving them something smaller to play with so that they leave us alone to handle the larger issues."

"Such as?"

"Let government do what it's best designed for—turn a maximum profit without having to worry about the few who can't make it on their own. The more we focus the *people's* interest on state government, the less they focus on the federal, the less they get in our way. Once you create a thoroughly disjointed electorate—a group of people concerned only with their own backyards—you can achieve great things."

"So why weren't you buying?" asked Xander. "Eisenreich makes all of that possible."

"To a point. The difference is, I trust in the republic."

"I find that hard to believe."

"Why? I might be an elitist, I might even insist that a modicum of deception can be quite useful, but I still believe in a balance of power—a *real* balance—among the few who truly understand the issues. Naturally, that means the people shouldn't be allowed to poke their noses in at every turn. But it also means that the few who *do* run things must do so with an honest end in mind. A republic must be accountable to stability, permanence, progress, not to the whims of the poorly educated. Eisenreich eliminates the people, but unfortunately, he also eliminates the balance. In its place, he offers Star Chamber hidden beneath a veneer of republican virtue.

Deception is one thing, Doctor, tyranny through cultivated bigotry quite another. I chose not to ally myself with that."

"A dash of John Stuart Mill with a hint of Machiavelli." Xander nodded. "A strange pairing, to say the least, as the cornerstones of the modern conservative movement."

"Think what you will," he answered. "It's what's best for this country."

"So they blackmailed you," said Sarah. "Why? Why not kill you?"

"Because, my dear Ms. Trent, at that point I had nothing that could harm them. I was never alone with the manuscript, never had time to make copies of my own, and never had any proof to link them to it. Moreover, they needed me . . . or rather, they found some rather clever ways to *use* me. My summer home in Montana has become a frequent spot for meetings, among other things."

"Other things?"

"It's where, I believe, they are organizing all of this. A compound of some sort, another school for those ready to turn the vision into reality. I haven't been allowed back in over a year. Whatever it was, I became a very convenient subterfuge should anyone take an interest in Tieg, Votapek, and Sedgewick. Even the location of *this* house makes me a prime candidate for association with the Tempsten school. I often wonder if that's what they had in mind all along. Throw people like you off the track. Evidently, it worked." He paused. "That, however, seemed rather unfair." He placed a small black book on the table. "So I took something of theirs."

"The schedule," said Xander. "When? How?"

"Very good, Doctor." Schenten slid it across the desk. "It came into my hands about a month ago; how . . . how isn't all that important, is it?" He watched as Xander began to flip through the pages. "According to the dates, the real fireworks begin in less than three days. I'm sure you're aware that what happened in Washington and with the grain market was designed merely to test the waters. New Orleans, I believe, was a mistake. It wasn't supposed to happen for another three days—part of something far more comprehensive."

"Why haven't you done anything to stop them?" asked Sarah. "If you knew we were out there, why didn't you contact us? Three days isn't—"

"Because, Ms. Trent, the moment I would have tried—the moment I would have shown even the *slightest* inclination—I would have been dead. Contact *you*? What a ludicrous thought. And where was I supposed to start looking? I knew you were involved. Beyond that . . . no, it had to be the other way round. As you'll see, it's all far too extensive, far too intricate to disrupt without striking at the core. I'd never have gotten that close." He shifted the pillow higher up his back. "Somehow, you two have managed to elude them. I'm simply counting on the fact that you will continue to do so. You were careful breaking in, no one aware. You will be equally diligent on your way out. I therefore give you the schedule and wish you Godspeed."

"The core?" asked Xander insistently. "You mean there *is* an overseer, one man behind it all?"

"Of course," answered Schenten. "It is, no doubt, why you were chosen, Doctor. Why you—"

Glass shattered all around, lights extinguished in a hail of bullets. Xander lunged across the desk for Schenten, only to find himself grabbed and thrown to the floor between the wall and desk. Sarah crouched next to him, her gun an inch from her face, the book clutched in her hand as the library once again fell silent. Seconds passed before they heard it. Distant at first, then deafening, the sound of a helicopter erupting within the room, a spotlight tearing through the madly flapping curtains, its beam coming to rest on the heaving body of Schenten, his arms drooped to the side, his mouth wide in convulsions, blood blotted on his chest. A moment later, the light slid from the room, rotors retreating, the telltale sound of landing. Sarah pulled Xander to his feet and ran to the door.

There was no time to think, no time to consider the man or his words—*"It's why you were chosen"*—only time to follow, to match her stride for stride, first to the stairs, then the sitting room, the sounds of rifle fire echoing from the front of the house as they leapt through the window to the grass below. Schenten's guards were holding the men of Eisenreich at bay, giving their own lives for a man only minutes away from death, their sacrifice granting still others a chance for escape. Sarah raced ahead, Xander after, the woods rising like a vacuum drawing them ever nearer. It was only when he saw Sarah dive to the ground that he remembered the fence. Tumbling forward, he careened into her back, ramming both of them to within an inch of the metal spikes. She pushed him aside and removed the clippers. He snapped his head toward the house and gazed at its darkened facade, the calm exterior masking the violence within. *"It's why you were chosen."* The words battered at him.

Light suddenly burst forth from every window as Sarah grabbed his neck and pulled him toward the fence. She had cut through.

The next minutes passed without thought, the back of her head leading him through the trees, a path where there was none, direction where he had lost all sense. The world behind them vanished, the questions faded, only darkness—endless and unrelenting—until, in the distance, the road appeared, a final dash for the car, the branches tossed to the side, doors slammed before the bite of the engine tore through the silence.

"Drive." Grass turned to road as the car sped into the night.

O'Connell sprang from his perch, his gun held to his chest as he pushed his way through the branches, feet nimble on the rooted floor below. For a large man, he showed remarkable dexterity.

It had happened quickly, as he had known it would. Sarah and Jaspers had approached the fence, unaware of the two men racing out from behind the house, rifles at the ready. Within five seconds, the men had spotted their targets; within eight, each had dropped to a knee and was taking aim. But it had been O'Connell who had fired first, two pinpoint shots of his own, the silencer muffling all but the *thwit-thwit,* both men eliminated in less than three seconds. Their bodies had collapsed on each other, forming an odd triangle in the middle of the open field.

Now he was running, aware that others would soon be in pursuit, he more concerned with the two he had been sent to protect. The *two.* Jaspers had made it. There *was* an instinct there; Stein had been right.

Up ahead, a diesel engine ignited and O'Connell quickened his pace. Two minutes later, he emerged to the road, dashed across the pressed gravel, and pulled a small motorcycle from a makeshift pile of pine and wood he had built some five hours earlier. He heard the engine to his left; within fifteen seconds, his 250 cc rumbled in response. Sliding the gun into his jacket, O'Connell mounted his bike and released the clutch. The wind slapped at his face as he searched the night for taillights.

Sarah leaned out the window, her ears intent on any sound other than the gnawing cough of the Rabbit's straining motor. At the same time, she scanned the sky, certain that the helicopter would appear, waiting for its searchlight to bounce along the tree line before targeting the car and its cargo. But nothing came, no sudden intrusions, only the hollow whistle of air beating against her face. She continued to search, uneasy with the silence, until the wail of a distant siren brought her attention back to the road. She pulled her head inside and glanced at the speedometer. It hovered at eighty, Xander's hands white-knuckled on the wheel.

"Slow down," she yelled over the wind, "and try to find a turnoff."

Xander did as he was told, bringing the car down to a reasonable speed as they both hunted for an opening. The sirens grew louder and louder, a hint of flashing light beyond the next hill, when Sarah pointed to an almost-invisible breach in the wall of trees to their right. Xander shifted the car into second gear, its frame buckling at the deceleration, and turned the wheel sharply, lurching the Rabbit down the steep slope. After thirty yards of back-wrenching bumps, he flipped off the beams and cut the engine. Above, the screech of the siren continued to mount as reflections of red and blue danced along distant trees, ever closer, until, in a near-blinding flash, the lights cascaded overhead and then gone. Xander reached for the keys, but Sarah was quick to stop him as the sound of a second siren broke through; again, reflected blues and reds flew by. Waiting for complete silence, she dropped her hand and nodded. The wheels churned through the dirt as the car inched its way back to the road, the rutted ascent no less jarring in reverse. Within half a minute, they were tearing along at eighty.

"You'll wait in the car while I go in for her," said Sarah, her eyes once more searching the sky through the windshield. Xander muscled the car around a curve, his eyes fixed on the limits of the high beams. "Did you hear me?"

"I wait; you go." The words were spoken in rote monotone. "Yes."

For the next mile, they traveled in silence.

"She should be able to sleep in the back," explained Sarah. "I don't think she'll be too much of a bother."

"Fine." Again silence.

Sarah turned to him. "What?"

He continued to stare at the road.

"Is it the schedule, Schenten, what?" She stared into his face, saw the tension in his jaw. "Does this have to do with what happened at the motel?"

"Doesn't it strike you as odd," he asked, clearly oblivious to her questions, "that I've managed to survive through all of this?"

It took her a moment to answer. "I hadn't really thought about it. I guess I'm just grateful."

He looked over at her, then turned and took the car to ninety.

Another minute passed before she spoke. "What happened back there?"

He laughed in disbelief. "Happened? A man was killed. That's what happened. A man just like Carlo, or Emil, or Feric. Schenten was just another to be sacrificed." A controlled rage laced his words. "And, yet, through it all, I somehow manage to remain unscathed. Now, that's *strange*, isn't it? How do we explain that?"

She tried to understand. "What are you asking me?"

"I'm not asking *you*. . . . I'm simply asking. Yesterday, an hour ago, I would have been too frightened, too relieved to think of anything but my own survival. Then again," the self-mockery more apparent, "I did write that *neat* little memo that gives me a purpose in all of this, didn't I? That's high on the *erudition scale*, isn't it? Problem is, it doesn't really count. Theory won't explain why I've managed to survive to this point."

"*What* are you talking about?"

"You want to believe you're a killer—fine. You want to believe that in all of this, that's your *purpose*, the reason you were *chosen*—"

"Slow down," she broke in, uncomfortable with his tone.

" '*It's why you were chosen*,' " he barked. "Didn't you hear what Schenten said, what he said about *me*?" He glanced over at her. "Don't you get it? You're not the only one who's been handpicked to take part in all of this."

"You think—"

"I don't *think*," he cut her off, his focus again the road. "I heard it, saw it in his eyes. Even he seemed surprised to find out that I had no idea."

"No idea about what?"

"I *don't* know. How I tie in. Why I was chosen. *My* purpose."

"Chosen for what?" she asked. "By whom?" She started to reach for him, then stopped, her shoulders inching away. "You mean *me*?"

He glanced over at her. "*What?*"

"You said 'chosen.' I was the one who got in touch with you. That would seem to say that—"

"What?" For a moment, the anger and confusion faded from his eyes. "That's not it at all. You're the only reason I'm still holding on. I've told you that."

"Then what *do* you mean?" she asked defensively.

He looked back at the road. "I don't know." The motel sign appeared on the left. Xander slowed and pulled the car into the driveway. "I stay. You go." His tone was again distant. She stared at him, then opened the door.

O'Connell cut the engine and coasted to the top of the hill, guiding the bike onto the shoulder and the relative cover of the tree line. A hundred yards below, the Rabbit sat idling in the drive of a roadside motel, the passenger door open. He inched himself tighter against the trees, stopped, and pulled out a pair of binoculars as the sound of a helicopter rose from somewhere off to his right. But it was Sarah who drew his attention as she emerged from one of the rooms, a second figure at her side, bundled within blankets and pillows. He watched as both stooped and slid into the car, Sarah slamming the door as the VW accelerated to the road. An instant later, a set of giant rotors appeared hovering just above the trees. The copter banked to the right and swung low, its high beams lighting up the back of the speeding Rabbit, which now serpentined across both lanes. Rifle fire exploded from above.

O'Connell fired up the engine and surged out onto the road. With his right hand, he pulled a gun from his jacket, this one far larger than the small precision piece he had used to compromise the two men in the field. He squeezed the throttle and brought the motorcycle to within twenty yards of the bird, whose nose was edging ever closer to its prey. The rear rotor, however, was riding high and exposed, a position all too vulnerable to someone with a trained eye. Leaning into the wind, O'Connell raised his gun and fired.

The recoil from the shot forced him to swerve, the grassy ledge of the shoulder coming precariously close before he straightened himself out and regained the center line. Meanwhile, the helicopter had banked high, his bullets evidently having missed their mark, a second high beam now appearing to target him in its blinding attack. Shots cascaded from above, peppering the road around him and forcing him to careen from side to side, both his hands essential to the task. With another burst of speed, he raced to the bird's underbelly, zigzagging with it so as to maintain his position directly beneath, the huge bulk unable to shake him. Again, he drew his gun. Again, he fired. This time, his aim was true. Smoke billowed from the fuselage as the rear rotor began to jump haphazardly from side to side. He slowed and let off several more shots. As if caught in a sudden updraft, the helicopter bounced high in the air, twisting on itself like a giant top out of control. She was going down. She would be forced to land.

He swung out wide on the narrow road, taking the motorcycle to its limits so as to slip past the dying bird. Once beyond her, he tried to reaccustom his eyes to the darkened road; even so, he could find no trace of the two red dots he had been following for the last half hour. Over his shoulder, he saw the results of his handiwork, four or five bodies leaping from the smoke, several of them spraying the carcass in an attempt to keep the helicopter from exploding. But no Rabbit. As he shifted forward, however, he caught sight of something off to his right, something flickering through the trees, mirroring his own movement. It took less than a second to recognize it—taillights. There, deep within the woods, the VW bounced defiantly, its driver somehow having found an inroad to the dense cover. *Bloody brilliant.*

O'Connell slowed and allowed the car to move farther ahead. For nearly a mile, they ran in tandem, until the main road began to bank away from the trees, the car's lights growing distant. O'Connell drove the bike off of the shoulder, weaving his way through the branches and trunks, several saplings falling prey to the teeth of his spokes and tires. But it was his face and hands that were getting the worst of it, angry limbs tearing at them as he pushed his way through. Reaching the trail, he wiped the blood from his face and accelerated on the rooted floor. The car had already dipped out of sight.

"I don't *know!*" yelled Sarah, "I don't see anything. You must have lost him."

"Where the hell did he come from?" Xander was doing everything he could to keep control of the jerking wheel. "Absolutely clear, then— wham!—the helicopter arrives, Evel Knievel arrives—"

"He was obviously trying to help us."

"Help us," shouted Xander, "or keep us alive?"

"What's the difference?"

"The *difference* is what Schenten said. Did you hear what I said before? There's a reason to keep me alive."

"I don't think that's what the boys in the helicopter had in mind," she said. "*They* were firing at us. Those weren't warning shots."

Xander saw the opening to his left and slammed on the brakes, bouncing all three high off the seats as he made the turn. "You're right. They *were* trying to kill us. That doesn't mean Mr. Motorcycle was necessarily friendly."

"Oh, I don't know," she replied sharply, "anyone who keeps me from getting shot usually strikes me as a friend."

The car emerged from the trees, wheels sliding on the grass before the tires found the smooth surface of the highway. Xander swung the wheel to the right, shifted into third, and brought the VW to sixty. The chassis nearly sprang from the road at the sudden thrust of power. "The transmission's holding up better than I thought," he said, his tone no less strident.

Sarah did not respond, her eyes dead still against the sweep of the road.

"It might even get us as far as Montana," he added.

She looked at him, her expression unchanged.

☄

Dawn came with Sarah at the wheel, Xander pressed against the window, his head resting on his chest and rising in the even rhythm of sleep. He had dropped off less than an hour ago, reluctant to give in to the exhaustion. So she had insisted. It had been their only conversation since Tempsten, no more discussion of Schenten, of an unknown motorcyclist—the miles slipping by in silence, save for a quick driving changeover on a deserted strip of road just before the Pennsylvania line. Xander had been right. Montana was the only choice. The senator had confirmed everything Stein had shown her in the Committee files. The training area. The compound. Wolf Point, Montana.

The Canadian route would have been quicker but more dangerous. Border guards. Instead, she found Route 90, settled the car in at eighty, and watched Cleveland, Lakewood, and any number of unknown towns pass with the quiet forgetfulness of a 5:00 A.M. sky. Now, half an hour from Indiana, she noticed the fuel gauge hovering precariously close to empty. It was a relief. She needed coffee. And maybe a short nap. *Sleep—the vital weapon. Without it, all others cease to function.*

The sign read a mile to the next rest stop. Sarah accelerated and swung the car into the right-hand lane. She glanced back at Alison; a smile had crept up the sleeping face.

☄

His head against the stone wall, his back too badly bruised to mind the minor discomfort, Bob Stein sat in utter darkness. His hands had been chained to either end of a bed, how many hours, days ago, he could only guess, his mind still woozy from the drugs—a narcotic whose aftereffects were proving far worse than its punch. At least then, he had been unconscious. Now he had the distinct displeasure to experience every moment of wakeful recovery.

To combat the discomfort, he had begun to piece together the moments that had led to his current condition, the last salient event a brief exchange at State with the duty guard. After that, Stein could remember only a sharp stabbing in his neck, followed by a stinging in his backside, spinning lights, a siren, and then the darkness to which he had awoken. It wasn't hard to fill in the early gaps. The guard had alerted someone, then an injection, a trumped-up ambulance ride, and this. It was the later gaps—or better yet, one large hole—that disturbed him. How much had he told them? More bewildering, why was he still alive?

A sliding segment of the door suddenly opened, a burst of light battering at his eyes from above, Bob quick to bury his head in his shoulder. He heard words before a lock disengaged, the door pulled back unleashing a torrent of pulsating white light into the room. Blinking through his sleeve, Stein tried to focus on the figure at the door, but his eyes would not see. He tried to speak but could produce only a muffled whelp, his lips and tongue still held in the control of the narcotic. Then, as quickly as it had come, the light from outside vanished, the door still open, a figure now in its frame. Bob looked up again, the silhouette of the body clearer than before, the outline of the room coming into focus as he peered to his right and left. As best he could tell, the room was roughly ten by ten, high ceilings, completely bare, no windows. Day or night, Bob had no way of telling.

"I apologize for the chains," said the man in the door. It was an old man's voice, European. "They are for your own protection. They tell me the drugs can make one rather violent. I trust you understand."

Bob tried to speak, but again he produced little more than an animal's moan.

"Ah, yes. Another aftereffect, regrettable but necessary. You have my further apologies. Your voice will return within the hour. For the time being, though, all you need do is listen." From behind, a woman entered and placed a chair at the center of the room, the smell of perfume momentarily eclipsing the stale air in the cell. The man sat. "You have told us a great deal. I am not much in favor of such methods, but the drugs can be quite useful, and with Mr. O'Connell back in the field . . . well, we needed certain questions answered." He paused. "You might be interested to know that your recovery will be easier than most, as you put up little resistance. I hope that is of some comfort to you." He whispered something to the woman. A moment later, she was gone, Stein alone with his inquisitor. "What is most interesting, however, is the information you offered *without* questioning. I was not aware the drugs worked in that way, but I am no expert in such things. An added bonus—for us all." He coughed before continuing. "I must say, you are a rather remarkable young man, Mr. Stein. I had no idea." His breath was short, the words punctuated by intermittent wheezing. "Trust me, I am a *very* good judge of character and of, shall we say, possibility. You show a considerable penchant for both. All in all, you are a very nice surprise. *Very* nice indeed." He cleared his throat. "To be candid, had you not shown those qualities, it is very likely you would no longer be alive. But I do not like to dwell on such things. I am here to give you an opportunity." Bob began to see a few wisps of hair on the man's head, though the face remained in shadow.

"I think it is fair to say you are aware of what we are, what we intend to do—or at least you have a rudimentary understanding of what is to come, if the drugs are accurate." Again, a short coughing spell, far more muted than the first. "*You,* to your credit, have an agile mind, a sense for the epic, for the grand scheme. This I find most agreeable. Coupled with that is the fact that you are in a position—how shall I put it?—of substantial *breadth.* We are, as you can imagine, not without a certain number of men in government. Few, though, show your talents. A man with your ability, with your access can be quite useful. Chained to a bed, the use goes to waste. You see what I am saying?"

If only to please, Bob nodded.

"Good, because in just over a week, this conversation will have no meaning." The man shifted in his chair; a moment later, Bob felt an ice-cold hand on his knee. "They say that time waits for no man, Mr. Stein. I would add that chaos is equally uncompromising. Today, there is time for you to think. That time, though, is running out." He removed his hand as another fit of coughing erupted. "'Never before,'" he continued, trying to stifle the spasm, "'has so much conspired to offer so propitious a setting and so great an impetus for a change in the wielding of power.' Never. Remarkable words, are they not? Written over four hundred years ago by an equally remarkable man. And as true today as they were then." His tone became less animated, though no less pointed. "Unfortunately, no one took that man seriously. A great pity. Eight days from now, no one will have a choice." He paused. "I am giving *you* such a choice. One few have been given. I trust you will not be foolish." The old man rose to his feet. "Eight days, Mr. Stein. After that . . ." He shook his head, turned, and slowly walked to the door. A moment later, the pitch-black returned, the bolt reengaged.

⚹

Jonas Tieg dimmed the desk lamp and sat silently for a few moments. The sound of feet on the stairs had prompted him to place the telephone receiver to his chest. As expected, his wife popped her head around the door a moment later. Her eyes were heavy with sleep. "Sweetheart, you need your rest. Come upstairs. What time is it?"

"Late, my love," he answered. "You go. I'll be up in a little while, I promise. I have to take care of this."

"Oh, Jonas," she said, finding her watch, "it's quarter to five in the *morning*. This is ridiculous."

"I know, dear. Ridiculous. You go. I'll be there in two minutes." He kissed the air, smiled, and nodded as she yawned through her own tired kisses and closed the door. At the sound of the ever-familiar creaking third step, he placed the phone to his ear and spoke. "You'll have to repeat that. . . . No, I don't care what you've been told since then; *I* am telling you *now*. There was no mistake. You were to shoot to kill. . . . *Yes*, both of them . . . including Jaspers. Are you having trouble hearing me? . . . Then put the license number on the wire. . . . Because within the next few hours, state police from Ohio to California will be looking for them. . . . That's not your concern. . . . What? . . . *Disabled* the helicopter? How is that . . . What do you mean you have *no* idea who? Someone simply appeared—" Tieg listened closely. "I see." He paused, then spoke, his words precise. "You are to eliminate anything that gets in your way, is that understood? . . . Good. . . . Yes, I'm sure that will be the case."

He hung up and turned off the lamp. Again, he sat in silence, all too aware of the tightness in his shoulders. He knew he would have to wake her, as he always did. And she would take him, caress his back, rub her strong, thick hands along his thighs, drive him to climax and then let him drift off in her arms. For thirty years, he had wanted no other, had found salvation in no other. She had always understood. She would understand again.

⚹

Laurence Sedgewick sat in the limousine, eyes riveted to the screen in front of him. A Mozart horn concerto filled the space, strangely incongruous with the images he watched. Bodies lay strapped to stretchers, others as yet untended sprawled across the grass and mud, eyes open, deathly still against the constant movement around the house. Police were everywhere, cordoning off windows, doors, a collection of guns they had assembled between two patrol cars. Cameras also dotted the landscape, network teams busy with questions, early-morning reports dispatched to stations around the country. A cameraman transmitting to a private car drew no special attention.

Senator George Maxwell Schenten was dead, shot to death in his upstate home, signs of an extensive battle in evidence. Already, the newspeople were raising questions about foreign involvement—a reaction to the senator's policy on a united Europe? An extremist fed up with Schenten's open criticism of Islamic fundamentalism? Or was it somehow connected to the events that had been occurring across the country? The police declined to speculate.

The phone rang.

"Yes." Sedgewick continued to watch the screen.

"They've begun to match fingerprints. They should have Jaspers and Trent within five minutes."

"And the records?"

"Updated to indicate connections to the killings in Germany and Italy. We're also ready to leak her history in Jordan."

"Good. A slow drip, I hope."

"An unnamed official, excerpts from a confidential file. Acceptable?"

"Difficult to acquire."

"But not impossible. The reference should be enough."

"Agreed. Naturally, you'll let the boys from Washington put the pieces together themselves. We wouldn't want any of them to think that they've been handed their suspects."

"Of course. Do we pursue?"

"Only if asked," answered Sedgewick. "We'll be in touch."

Anton Votapek tramped across the open field, the few clumps of brown grass underfoot the last vestiges of a once-lush soccer pitch. The rest was a mass of petrified mud, shaped by the spiked soles of eager cleats, hardened to rigid mounds of soil by chilled Montana nights. Beyond the goalpost stood a single building. Votapek mounted its steps and opened the door. The fire across the room beckoned, as did a pair of leather chairs planted comfortably by the blaze. He sat and picked up the receiver on the small side table.

"Hello."

"Anton." The voice was tired but alert. He did not like to be kept waiting. "You said it was urgent when you called before."

"Yes," answered Votapek. "I was hoping not to wake you, but I didn't think it could wait."

"I am sure you are right. Especially given recent events."

Votapek waited, then spoke. "Alison's missing." His eyes remained fixed on the blaze.

"I see."

"It's impossible to say when. Sometime in the last two days."

There was a pause. "Laurence told you this?"

"Yes."

"And he is concerned?"

"Yes."

"Why was this permitted to happen?"

"We can only assume—"

"The Trent woman," interrupted the old man, his voice no less steady.

"Yes."

"I find it hard to understand why she is proving to be so difficult. She was on the train with Pritchard—that is what we were told by that boy from the NSC. And you mean to say no one recognized her, that no one realized there could be only one reason for Arthur to be on that train?"

"It wasn't their priority—"

"'Their *priority*'? What could be more pressing than a woman who is utterly determined to undermine everything we have been working for? I have made it quite clear. Alone, she poses no threat, but with Alison . . . who is to say what might be believed? We have no place for such distractions."

"I agree. Alison is of the utmost importance—"

"We have been through this, Anton. Personal sentiment only gets in the way. Your feelings for the girl, however strong they may be—"

"Then why do you continue to protect Jaspers?" A log shifted, flames darting through the tumbled recess.

For a moment, the old man remained silent; when he spoke, the words were simple, direct. "That has nothing to do with sentiment."

"You really believe that?"

"You think you understand, Anton? You understand *nothing*." He had little patience for Votapek's goading. "Was Jaspers at Schenten's home?"

"Yes."

"And the conversation is on tape?"

"Yes. They knew about the schedule even before Schenten brought it up."

"And they were eager to find it."

"Very." Votapek began to fiddle with a stray piece of thread dangling from the chair's arm. Trying his best to sound casual, he added, "Schenten also told him that he had been . . . *selected.* That the overseer—I assume he meant you—had chosen him. We didn't understand what that meant."

"Did the senator mention my name?"

Votapek waited before answering. "Our men arrived before he could say anything." He dropped the thread. "His explanation would have been—"

"Of no consequence."

"Laurence and Jonas think otherwise."

Votapek heard the deep breath. "And what does that mean, Anton?"

"It means," he said, a slight waver in his voice, "that they find Schenten's remarks a little puzzling. We've all been under the impression that Jaspers stumbled onto all of this *accidentally.* If it's otherwise . . ."

"*Yes,* Anton?" Impatience now turned to irritation. "What would *that* mean? What would Laurence and Jonas have to say about *that*?"

"I . . . I don't know." Silence.

"Of course you do not know, because you speak without thinking— Jonas the worst of you, his belief that he is somehow cleverer than the rest. Perhaps that is why it was clear from such an early age that he belonged in politics. But you, Anton, you were smarter than that. I always hoped it would pass, that you and Laurence would see his prattling for what it was."

"He said we needed to eliminate the problem."

"*Miss Trent* is the problem, Anton."

With as much courage as he could muster, Votapek answered, "That's not what Jonas said."

Again, he paused before answering. "I see. And what *did* he say?"

Votapek remained silent.

"What have you done, Anton?" The words were almost a whisper. "My God, what have the three of you *done*?"

☒

Sarah sat across from Xander, her second refill nearly gone, the waitress too busy to take any notice of the empty cup. Instead, she was chatting with a driver, a young man whose interests clearly lay in more than just coffee and pancakes. He had even removed the meshed baseball cap from his head, smoothing back the greasy blond curls in an attempt to make himself more presentable; it was having the desired effect, the young woman's lips peeling up to her gums in a frighteningly toothy smile. Sarah couldn't help but stare, her gaze fixed on the large yellow teeth, her fatigue stripping her of the will to turn away. No thoughts. Only smile, teeth, gums. Even Xander slipped from her mind, his complete self-absorption in the book lost to her fixation. He flipped a page, the movement enough to draw her attention.

She watched him, elbows firm on the table, right hand clenched in a thick tuft of hair as his eyes flew through the words on the page. If he was tired, he was doing his best to fight it, his knee shaking with nervous intensity. All thoughts of Schenten had clearly been set aside. For the moment, the scholar was back at work. Sarah sipped at her coffee and continued to watch. It was good to have him so close again.

"They've got to have an army of people to do all of this," said Xander, not bothering to look up from the page. "Rapid-fire disruptions, phases to be carried out by different groups of people—one to plant the explosives, another to position them, still others to set them off. Where Eisenreich took weeks to instigate his chaos, they're taking days, sometimes hours. Plus, they've got things going on all across the country, timed out to the minute."

"How long a period are we talking about?" asked Sarah.

"Eight days. *Eight* days of sequential terror. The irony is that very few things in here could be described as catastrophic. The first one on the list"—he flipped back a few pages—"reaches completion in two days." He looked up. "At least we have some time before they start by bombing the Capitol."

"And that doesn't strike you as catastrophic?"

"Symbolically, yes. As a means to social upheaval, no. Look at Oklahoma three years ago. It was despicable, tragic—however else you want to describe it. And for two weeks, every militia in the country got ten minutes on *Nightline*. But that was it. We were all horrified, outraged, but then we happily forgot about it. By itself, that bomb didn't create the kind of panic our friends want." He flipped a few pages ahead.

"Which is?"

"Suppose something else had happened that day—a systemwide failure of the computer network at Southwestern Bell, or every tunnel and bridge leading into Manhattan out of commission, all in less than five hours? Then it would have been a little more frightening, a little more overwhelming."

"And that's what they're planning to do?"

"Replace Oklahoma with the Capitol and you have numbers one, eight, and seventeen on their list. The first raises the question of national security, perhaps even foreign involvement; the others confirm those fears and heighten panic. It's what they did in Washington and Chicago writ large. You put those little events together, making sure that their timing is precise, and you can create the sort of chaos that makes the big events seem much larger than they are. It's right out of the manuscript."

One on top of another, on top of another. Tieg's words. "How many?"

"Forty-eight. The grand finale is the assassination of the president."

Sarah shook her head. "How original."

"It's not the killing that's important to them."

"*That's* reassuring."

"It's the way people will *see* it that will make the difference."

"I don't follow."

"Think about it. When JFK was shot, people talked about conspiracy, but most of them regarded it as the act of a deranged gunman. Sorrow, betrayal, anger—those were the prevailing sentiments."

"Not mass hysteria."

"Exactly. When they kill Wainwright, his death won't be an isolated incident, but the ultimate act in a sequence of battering blows against the republic, a sign that the country has become too weak or too corrupt to maintain order. Whether it's seen as a conspiracy won't matter. All people will feel is despair, a sense that everything has fallen apart."

"Enter Pembroke"—Sarah nodded—"and you have an antidote to the chaos."

"From the looks of it, they plan to play up to every major fear in the book during the buildup—sharp declines in the market, foreign terrorism, urban crime—nothing new, and nothing startling by itself, but now it's all going to happen in a matter of *eight* days."

"Tieg's going to have a field day with the media."

"Of course."

"How many groups are we talking about?" she asked, pulling the book across the table and glancing at the chart on the inside back cover.

"About thirty. Each assignment is divided up into four separate phases, one cell or team—"

"Per phase," she cut in, the words spoken almost to herself, her eyes now scanning the page with greater intensity.

"Right," he agreed, concerned by the sudden change in her expression. "What is it?"

She continued to read, ignoring the question. "Jump rotations, redundancy cells"—she nodded—"and, naturally, separate stagings."

"What do you mean, 'naturally'? What are you talking about?"

She looked up. "This is . . . I'm familiar with this design. It's a—"

"Pritchard matrix," came a voice from behind her, its sudden intrusion shocking them both into silence. "Number of cells, assignments, the overlap. Finish one job, wait for instructions for the next." The voice paused before adding, "But it's the staging that gives it away, isn't that right, Sarah?"

The Irish lilt, the clipped words. She turned and looked at the man. He had slid to the corner of his booth and was staring directly at her.

"O'Connell?"

"Gaelin Patrick at your service." He smiled and looked at Xander. "The good doctor, I presume?" Xander could only nod. "You've had a nasty time of it, but you seem to be in one piece. As for you, you're looking remarkably blond. I preferred the deep auburn, but, then again, you know my tastes."

"How did you—"

"The lady's going to ask me how I found you." He winked at Xander. "And I'm going to tell her that another friend of ours thought it best to keep an eye on the two of you. A man with an appalling taste for cheese balls."

A loud gasp at the counter forced all three to turn; a woman was staring at the television affixed to the far wall. On screen, a reporter stood silhouetted in flames.

"In what appears to be a return to the madness of last week, a bomb exploded just after six A.M., engulfing the western wing of the Capitol in flames. Washington has awoken, once again stunned as firefighters. . . ."

"It changes nothing," answered O'Connell. They were outside by the VW, Alison seated on the passenger side. "Either they've gone ahead of schedule or something snafued. How much time before the next one?"

Xander scanned the chart. "There's a gap of about fourteen hours before number two—the kidnapping and execution of the English ambassador. In fact, the first six events are spread out over a two-and-a-half-day period. After that, it picks up considerably, something every four to five hours."

"That's Pritchard." He nodded. "First few events to make sure things are playing clean. A mock-up. Then acceleration. It gives us time—not a lot—but it gives us time. By the way," he added, "I was expecting *two*. You haven't introduced me to the red-haired beauty."

Sarah knelt by Alison and took her hand. "This is a friend, Alison. His name is Gael."

A blank stare, then a smile. "Hello, Gael," she said. "You have a pretty name."

The Irishman seemed caught off guard by the comment. He looked at Sarah, then at Alison. "Thank you. I'm . . . rather fond of it myself."

Sarah motioned for him to join her on the other side of the car. In a hushed voice, he said, "You'll have to tell me what that was all about."

Fifteen minutes later, O'Connell sat on the lip of the hood, arms crossed at his chest. He'd heard enough. "It's a hell of lot more than Bob was letting on. He doesn't even know about the redhead." He looked at Alison through the windshield. "Jesus, no wonder she's . . ." He shook his head.

"It'll have to be quick, a small strike," said Sarah. "Shut it down from the center. If we blow up the site, my guess is they'll have a fail-safe on the computers. Any interference and the signals on the accelerated stage will go out automatically. We need to dismantle the system from the inside."

"Agreed," he said. "Probably six to eight men to get into the compound."

"And we'll need a few pictures detailing the house—layouts, numbers."

"The details are not a problem."

"Details?" interrupted Xander, exasperated by their rapid-fire exchange. "What do you mean dismantling? We know what they're targeting—it's all in the schedule. All we have to do is take that information—and Alison—to someone who can stop them. Set up security at the various attack points—"

"And allow them to crawl back under a rock once they realize they've been exposed?" Sarah shook her head. "They've been waiting thirty years. If they see anything out of the ordinary, they'll pull back and draft another schedule. No, we have to go now. If we don't, I can assure you that none of us, including Alison, will be around to stop them the next time they try."

"Wait a minute," insisted Xander, "you're telling me that not *one* of your *all-powerful* government organizations could race in, save the day—"

"And create the kind of panic that we're trying to avoid?" Again, Sarah shook her head. "You send out an alert like that, with the National Guard swooping down on God knows how many places—people will get *very* concerned. Remember Waco? They create the martyrs while Tieg plays up the anxiety. Abuse of power. Government paranoia. And six months from now, they fire up—"

"Another schedule," interrupted the Irishman. "Unfortunately, it's not an option either of you has anymore."

Xander turned to O'Connell. "What does that mean?"

"Back there, that was the first news you'd seen today?" Both of them nodded. "I thought so. Since about six, they've been talking about nothing but the Schenten assassination. You've both been implicated."

"What!"

"It gets better." He stopped and brought his hands to his lap. "It seems, Doctor, that you're also wanted for questioning in the deaths of a man in Italy, another in Germany, and a woman in New York . . . a Mrs. Huber—"

"Oh my God!"

"She was found in your office. It's not a pretty picture—of either of you. The crazed academic and the former assassin." He looked at Sarah, hesitating before he spoke. "They've leaked Amman. They're saying . . . you were responsible for the death of the ambassador's daughter. I don't know how they got the information, but there you have it." He saw the reaction in Sarah's eyes. "Descriptions of the two of you, the car—it's all over the wire. That's why I had to make contact."

Xander sat on the hood, head tilted back. "Did they say how she died?"

O'Connell waited before answering. "You can't let yourself worry about that, son."

"I'd sent her Carlo's notes, everything. I didn't think—"

"You couldn't have," said Sarah, revelations about her own past pushed aside for the moment. "And Gael's right. You *can't* think about it. You have to think about the men who killed her—who are so desperate that they're willing to use the police to try and stop you." She took his arms. "And they *are* trying to stop you, whatever Schenten might have said."

Xander brought his head forward, eyes on Sarah. He nodded slowly.

She turned to O'Connell. "It means we can't risk flying. And we can't use this car. I'll have to take it into the woods, cover it up."

"I'm one step ahead of you. Give me half an hour." He slid off the hood and placed a hand on Xander's knee. "You're in good hands, son. Sometime, I'd like to know how you got yourself out of Germany."

"Sometime," answered the academic, "I'd like to tell you."

O'Connell winked and headed for his bike. A minute later, Xander and Sarah were seated in the VW, its engine purring in loud diesel overtones.

"He's a nice man." It was Alison who spoke as she stared through the window at the Irishman's back. "A very nice man."

✄

"Do you *realize* how difficult it will be to undo what you have done!" In three different states, three men winced at the voice screaming at them over the telephone. Each conjured his own image of the old man as the sound of coughing erupted on the line. His fits were occurring with greater frequency, thought Tieg. It wouldn't be long now. Still, he had survived this long. "Fifty years—*fifty years*—you think you know what to expect; you think that somehow they will rise above themselves and act as they have been *taught* to act. But time and time again, you realize you are wrong, that they remain children, that you have chosen unwisely, and that they are no more now than what they were when you first found them." He paused, the sound of breathing filling the line. " '*The burden shall be his to choose his pupils wisely.*' Perhaps mine was too great a burden." Again the sound of breathing. "Can any of you explain why you have made Jaspers a pariah, a criminal . . . a madman?"

The line was quiet. Tieg was the first to speak. "Because there were no other alternatives."

"The voice of reason." The old man made no attempt to hide his disdain. "You were all in agreement, then, that this was the only course for Jaspers?"

"We all discussed it—"

"I am not asking you, Jonas," he cut in. "I am asking Laurence and Anton. Or have they ceded that role to you as well?"

Again a pause; Sedgewick: "The recording from Schenten's made it very clear to *all* of us that both Jaspers and the Trent woman are now in possession of a rather damaging document."

"And to you, there is no difference between this assassin and Jaspers?"

"At this point, no. We might not get to them before they have a chance to pass on that information."

"You think he would run to the police? You think they would take him seriously?" The old man waited. "You agreed with this, Anton?"

"I . . . yes. He is a . . . a liability. He had to be . . . resolved."

"You would have made a very poor actor, Anton. Next time, Jonas, take more care when you teach him his lines."

"He's a grown man," answered Tieg. "He makes his own decisions. We *all* make our own decisions."

"Ah," said the tired voice, "so at last we come to it. At last we see why all the private plotting has become so important. It has nothing to do with Jaspers, or Alison, or even Miss Trent, does it, Jonas? It has to do with who makes the *decisions,* who has the *control.*" He waited, hoping for an answer. When none came, he continued. "You stupid, *stupid* man! *You* are concerned with decisions; *you* know how this will all fit together. You know *nothing*! Do you think I do not understand you, Jonas? Do you think I am so old or so foolish as to have been blind to what you have wanted all along? Chaos, naturally. It is what we *all* want. That, though, is where we part company. Am I right? Chaos is as far as you wish to go. Order bores you, permanence and stability—merely secondary concerns for a man like you. You prefer the freedom that chaos brings, the unlimited possibilities." His words were laced with contempt. "You think I do not know, that it is not obvious? It has been *obvious* from the beginning, the reason I chose you—your egoism, so vital to the task. Why do you think I have kept the leash so tight these last few years? Perhaps I was foolish to think you would not pull at it from time to time. It was my mistake. I shall not make it again."

The line fell silent. Finally, Tieg spoke, his words controlled, precise, clearly masking the fury beneath. "Did you choose Jaspers?"

"You ask for information that is of no concern to you."

"I have made it my concern, *old man*! Did you choose him?"

"You will *not* speak to me in that tone! Is that understood?" Silence. Is that *understood,* Jonas?"

The words carried a long-forgotten fire, a venom that seemed to transport all four back to a cabin, to the Italian sand and sea, to three young boys sitting in a corner, terrified, as the old man bore down on his oldest pupil.

"Tell me, Jonas, why do you try to deceive me? Why do you not tell me that it was you who forced Anton into the water?" He slapped his hand across the boy's face, the force enough to send the young body to the floor. Jonas pulled himself to the stool, no tears, only the slight shaking of his head. Again, the man struck; again, the boy fell, this time blood trickling from his lip. "Why do you deceive me?"

"I didn't—"

"You will not speak to me in that tone!" he screamed, sending his open fist into the boy's brow, the head smacking back into the wooden wall, a torrent of tears following, uncontrolled, wild. "You are nothing. Nothing! But I will make of you a great conqueror. All of you—great conquerors. Do you understand this?"

Head down, his entire body shaking, he nodded. "Yes," he sputtered. "I deceived you."

The man reached out and caressed the boy's hair. "You are a good boy, Jonas," he said, looking at the other two. "Now go and wash up."

"Yes," answered Tieg, his voice trapped in the memory.

"Good. . . . Anton, tomorrow you will dismiss the students for their late-winter recess and then take your own holiday on the island. Make certain that the staff is prepared for my arrival. I will be flying in before noon. Laurence, you will remain in New Orleans. And Jonas"—he paused, expecting no answer—"you will be in San Francisco. Is everything clear?"

As one, the voices responded. "Yes."

"Good. I will correct the mistake you have made. Do not put me in this position again. I am getting far to old to clean up after you."

⚔

O'Connell stepped from the driver's seat, the wagon a far cry from what Sarah expected. Clearly past its prime, the car sported a strip of wood paneling, an odd touch given its dark green color. At the back, the window was a wild menagerie of college and high school stickers, the bumper a collection of strange warnings and even stranger messages, sometimes the two commingling in a single effort: WATCH OUT FOR THE LORD—HE DON'T NEED NO FLASHING LIGHTS. Alison stood rapt, reading each one with a certain deference, as if she had gleaned a more subtle meaning beneath the clutter. O'Connell tossed the keys to Xander and moved toward her.

"The bike's about a fifteen-minute drive from here," he said. "I'll need a lift." He drew up next to Alison and joined in the perusal. "It's an odd mix, that's for certain." She continued to stare. "All this and that, and not much to tie it together. Still, it makes for a nice bit of reading."

She turned to him, a smile creasing her lips. He started to move toward the open door, she quick to grab his arm, the smile no less genuine, the eyes no less gentle. For a moment, O'Connell stared at her, uncertain as to how he should react. Then, very slowly, he placed his hand on hers and said, "Why don't you come sit with me. We'll ride together. How about that?"

The smile grew on her lips, the eyes brighter still.

"Good." He winked and brought her to the door.

Twelve minutes later, Xander began to slow along an isolated strip of road leading toward the town of Bryan, O'Connell giving instructions from the backseat. The bike was off in the woods; he would manage it himself.

"Use the number I've given you as a contact point," he added. "I can probably have the men together in eighteen hours. It's open country, so find a place within about seventy-five miles of the—"

"I know the drill," said Sarah. "We'll be lucky if we get there by tomorrow morning. We'll have to watch ourselves, especially with Alison—"

"I'd like to go with him," said the girl, her voice quiet but clear. All three turned at once, Sarah the first to respond.

"That might be a little difficult, Alison." She tried her best to reassure. "Gael only has a motorcycle—"

"I know." The voice was no less direct. "I would like to go with him."

Sarah looked at her onetime associate. The expression on his face was anything but what she expected. He was grinning.

"Might not be such a bad idea," said the Irishman. "Me taking her." The idea seemed to gain momentum, the smile growing. "In fact, it might be the best thing to split them up, just in case. . . ." He looked at Sarah. "You've got your charge—no offense, Professor—"

"None taken," answered Xander.

"And I've got mine. All the easier to keep them both out of harm's way."

Sarah was not convinced. "It's nearly fifteen hundred miles to the compound, Gael. Plus, you'll be—"

"Might be a bit blowy," he said, turning back to Alison and ignoring Sarah. "And there won't be much time for sleep." Alison continued to stare at him. "Well"—he nodded to himself—"I suppose that's that, then." He opened the door and stepped outside, reaching his hand back to help Alison from the car. A few seconds later, he ducked his head in, grabbed her heavy coat, and said, "We'll see the two of you outside of Wolf Point. Safe journey." And with that, he slammed the door and headed for the woods.

Sarah turned to Xander, astonishment etched across her face. He was smiling.

"What?" she asked.

He shook his head.

"What?"

"She'll be fine," he answered. "Probably do her some good."

"It's not her I'm worried about."

⚜

The twin-engined Packer dipped comfortably over the secluded airfield, its landing lights flashing along the ground in bloodred intervals. A few patches of snow remained, but none to blemish the stark black line that cut through the expanse, a strip of tar amid a pale sea of rock and earth. Seated beside the pilot in the cockpit, the old man clutched at his armrest, the plane already in middescent. As the ground approached, his thoughts drifted.

There had been nothing from Stein—now sleeping comfortably in the back of the plane—nothing that might indicate that the intelligence officer had come to the right decision, a fact that troubled the old man only in that he now realized how useful his "guest" could be, given the situation with Jaspers. A few words to the appropriate people and the entire mess in Europe would be forgotten. Likewise, the connection to Schenten. Unfortunately, the young man was proving far less amenable to the project than had his predecessor. *His predecessor,* he thought. *Pritchard.* How eager he had been to join Eisenreich. How certain, how committed. Stein, however, was showing no such enthusiasm. Chains evidently lacked the necessary allure. But he was a smart boy. He would recognize the inevitability of it all. And he had shown a surprising concern for the young professor while under the narcotic. That, at least, was encouraging.

Within twenty minutes, they had reached the turnoff for the compound, a half mile of chewed gravel that lent the place a rustic quality, perhaps even a hint of dilapidation should anyone venture beyond the NO TRESPASSING signs plastered along the trees on either side. A seemingly cosmetic wooden gate stood at the end of the winding road, a quaint reminder that the cluster of cabins beyond were private property. Schenten's onetime sanctuary. How much had changed, he thought, in only a few short years.

As the car pulled to a stop at the gate, a squirrel ventured across its path, the animal stopping to sniff at the post. It was a mistake the little creature would not soon forget. Its tiny body lurched into spasms, the shock lasting only seconds, but enough to indicate that all was not as it seemed. The men in the car watched as the squirrel fell to its side, its twitching less and less animated, until, finding its feet again, it slowly limped into the woods. The system had been designed so that the larger the animal, the greater the shock. A moment later, the gate opened, and the large Mercedes continued through, lumbering past a set of cabins and up toward a ranch-style building set off from the rest. A tall, bald man stood waiting at the door.

"How many are we, Paolo?" The old man shifted his weight forward and stepped from the car without so much as a nod of thanks for the extended hand.

"Twelve. Not including those assigned to the house and the lab."

"Excellent. I will take a nap, some lunch, after which time I would like to see how everything is proceeding. You will then join me." The man nodded. "I trust we have put Wolfenbüttel behind us." He did not wait for an answer.

At the top of the steps, an attractive woman in a calf-length skirt and white blouse extended her arm. The old man refused it and moved past her into the house. "It's good to have you back, sir."

"You will come with me to my room, Ms. Palmerston."

He was halfway down the hall before she turned to follow.

By 4:30, he was ready to assess the linkups with the satellites. Two of the tracking specialists had put in an appearance at lunch, each to assure him that everything was in order—codes, transmission sequencing—anything that required an expertise in software. They had returned to the lab while he had phoned his three prefects with last-minute instructions, after which time he had retreated to the bedroom for another visit with Ms. Palmerston. He had always required a certain attention at times of greatest intellectual excitement. For a man his age, he possessed a remarkable eagerness; happily for both, he managed to sustain it with an equally vibrant stamina.

She was asleep as he left the room, her legs draped lazily across the bed, the single white sheet brushing coyly over her perfectly rounded rump. He lingered at the door for a moment and then shut it, moving down the corridor toward the waiting elevator.

The ride to the subterranean lab took nearly four minutes, a slow descent to a depth of almost a hundred feet. Monitored at all times by heat-sensitive cameras, the elevator was fitted with an automatic disabling device should the temperature rise above a certain level without prior authorization. The snail-like pace was simply an added precaution to give those below time to prepare should anyone manage to circumvent the system. The doors opened and he stepped out to the bright lights of a corridor, newly carpeted since his last visit. Paolo stood directly across from him, a glass of water in one hand, several pills in the other. The old man smiled and shook his head.

"You are determined to keep me healthy," he said, taking the pills, then tossing the water back with an exaggerated snap of his head. He returned the glass and started down the hall, the temperature dropping several degrees as he neared a steel archway, its metallic sheen jarring against the pristine white of the surrounding walls. Beyond it, the corridor became a balcony some fifteen feet long, a ledge that extended over a large open area, the space below filled with computer equipment. Nothing overly elaborate—keyboards, terminals, one ceiling-high screen covering the far wall—all relatively quiet save for the purring of various plastic boxes, all of which he admired from a distance. Such things were beyond him, a choice he had made long ago. Others understood them and that was enough. He took his time with the steps before reaching the lower level, whereupon Paolo began the introductions.

"This is Angela Duciens," he said. "She is—"

"A marvelous field hocky player," the old man cut in. "Yes of course. At the school in California. I seem to recall a match in which you scored— what was it, six, seven goals? Wonderful play."

The young woman flushed. "It was eight, actually."

"Of course." He smiled, his hands raised in the air in absolute delight. "Eight. How could I have forgotten? Eight indeed. And against a rather formidable defense, if memory serves." The woman nodded modestly. "Still, I should have remembered. You will forgive an old man."

So went all the introductions, eased by the notes Paolo had prepared for him less than an hour ago; still, the tactic was having the desired effect. It was also allowing him to scan the large screen on the far wall, a map of the United States, peppered with small blue dots. The final stage.

Chaos was at hand.

⚔

She was reluctant at first. Stopping would be dangerous. The quicker to Montana, the better. Then again, they had made remarkable time, twelve hours of uninterrupted speed, a slight delay around Chicago for the late-morning rush hour, and then open road for nearly nine hundred miles.

Even then, it had been a temporary diversion. Perhaps Xander was right. Perhaps they could afford to stop. *Sleep—the vital weapon.* Just beyond the last tourist signs for Bald Hill Dam, she took them off Route 94. Xander said the fates were being kind. Sarah knew better.

Six miles from the highway, however, his mood changed dramatically, the relative calm of the drive all but forgotten once they stepped inside the room. It was a near carbon copy of the Tempsten accommodations—small sofa and a bed, a lamp whose shade had seen better days. Sarah had little trouble identifying the source of his awkwardness.

"No, no, no," he said quickly, "you use the bathroom first. You've been driving. It's only fair."

She peered over at him. "Fine," she answered, a smile in her eyes, "if it's only fair." She slipped past him and moved to the bathroom. Half a minute later, she reemerged, to find him bedded down on the sofa, a pillow missing from under the bedspread. His back was to her.

Staring across at his long body under the blanket, she couldn't help but smile. Quietly, she let her jeans slip to the floor, her T-shirt loose at her thighs. She then flicked off the light and walked over to the sofa. Without a word, she slowly slid in beside him.

He nearly jumped, pressing his back against the back of the sofa and taking the covers with him. "What are you doing?"

"It's a little cozy, but—"

"No, I mean *what* are you doing?" He tried not to stare at her legs. "I . . . I left you the bed." He tossed the blanket on top of her. "I thought . . . I thought you'd want the bed."

"I suppose it would be a little more comfortable, yes." Their faces were less than six inches from each other. "But you wanted to be here," she said playfully, "so this is where we'll sleep."

He tried to get up but realized it would mean having to slide over her. "This . . . this isn't going to work."

"It was your choice."

"No. You don't . . ." His awkwardness was turning to genuine anxiety. "Look, I don't think this is—"

"Is what?" For the first time, Sarah felt uncomfortable.

"Is . . . what we should be doing."

She stared at him for a moment. "I see." She slowly sat up, her back to him. "What exactly *is* it that we shouldn't be doing?" She waited. "I'm not asking you to sleep with me, Xander, if that's what you're worried about."

"No," he said defensively. "That's not what I thought. It's just that I . . . I don't know. . . ."

"You don't know what?"

It took him a moment to answer. "I don't know . . . if I can do this."

She looked at him. "Do what?" Again, she turned away. "I thought we could be with each other. Hold each other for a while. That's all." There was a caring in her voice. "I meant what I said yesterday."

"So did I."

"Then why are you doing this?"

For a few moments, neither said a word, his cheek somehow closer to her neck, his chest all too conscious of the touch of her back. "It's been . . ." He struggled to find the words. "I lost my wife a few years ago. She was . . . she made everything right. And then she was gone." Tears began to fill his throat. "And then yesterday, I held you." She could feel his breath on her neck, "which was . . . remarkable."

"For me, too," she whispered.

Again silence. "Sarah . . . it's been a long time since I let myself—" He stopped.

She remained still. "I understand. I do." She started to get up.

"No," he said, taking her arm and keeping her on the sofa. "I don't *want* you to have to understand. Holding you was . . . I never thought I'd be able even to do that again. Maybe it's because of what's been going on. . . . I just haven't felt like that."

She could sense his lips near her neck, her body suddenly frail, small. She felt his arm slowly begin to trace around her waist, pulling her closer, pressing her to him. "Like what?" she whispered.

His arm began to tremble; his lips brushed across her neck, the very touch enough to shorten her breath, her lungs tighten with air. "To be held." She turned to him, everything suddenly numb, eyes lost to one another. And he lifted her up, his hands cradling her in their grasp, the bed, her head on the pillow, his breath colliding with hers, the sweet taste of lilac on his tongue. They kissed, tenderly at first, each a quiet exploration, innocent desire mingling with the anguish of first touch. Soon, the heat of her body seemed to envelop him, his hands drawn to the flesh of her back, his mouth swallowing the nape of her neck, down to her breasts, the eager curve of her thigh, all semblance of covering thrown from the bed. She, too, fell into him, driving her fingers through his hair, forcing him onto his back and riding up on top of him, her tongue gliding through the ridge of his chest, her lips bathing him in an unleashed longing.

She pulled him inside of her, thighs clenched around his waist, driving upward with each thrust. He grabbed at her back, brought his chest to hers, pressing her breasts against him as they continued to surge into one another. No sound save for the gasping for air. Suddenly, she was on her back, his arms engulfing her, his desire rising, her fingers tearing into him—back, thighs—pulling him in deeper, deeper, until in an anguished release, they climaxed, arms clenched so tightly around each other, they could hardly breathe.

Unable to let go, they fell asleep, naked in each other's arms.

⚔

The first explosion bolted them upright; the second forced her to the edge of the bed, flames from outside rising and falling in reflection through the paper-thin blinds. She looked back at him but could find no words. He, too, was silent. Their reprieve was over. The world outside had returned.

She stood and grabbed for her clothes, he frozen, his back rigid against the wall. Pulling her jeans to her waist, she moved to the window and peeled back a corner of the blind. Outside, rain pelted at the glass, hardly enough, though, to blur the source of the explosion. There, in the most distant part of the parking lot, she saw the engine of a small truck in flames, its meaning clear. An invitation. An invitation to *her.* Sarah pulled on her shirt and peered out again, the handle of her gun wedged tightly in her fingers. She looked back at Xander; he had not taken his eyes from her. She slowly opened the door and stepped out into the downpour.

The rain was cold, at first jarring, then a relief, shocking her senses into wakefulness. A number of the motel's guests had also ventured out, the owner of the truck all too obvious among them, a man lost in utter disbelief, pacing a few yards from the fire. Several others worked extinguishers in an attempt to tame the worst of the blaze, but they were only a diversion, a means, she realized, to get her out of the room. *What other reason could there be?* Somewhere among the faces, she knew a pair of eyes was watching, waiting for her to emerge. She could sense them, feel them on her.

This time, the men of Eisenreich had been clever. This time, they had forced her hand. Searching the rooms would have left too much to chance.

Too many options. A wrong choice and they would have left themselves open. Better to draw her out.

She spotted the man among the guests. He was making no attempt to blend in with the growing crowd. Rather, he stood a few paces off to the right, staring directly at her, an obese woman clutched at his side. Etched across the woman's face was the look of abject terror. Sarah understood. He was going to kill someone. Whom that might be would all depend on her. Either way, it would not be here. Death in the open would be foolish. Too many witnesses. He was playing it well.

Certain that she had seen him, the man moved off toward the trees across from the motel, his arm held firmly around the bait. Sarah watched as they disappeared. She then turned and whispered through the open door to Xander.

"Get some clothes on, grab your gun and pack, and get outside. I want you to work your way into the crowd by the fire." He started to answer. "Just do it!" Before he could say anything, she was gone.

⚔

Xander threw the blanket from his legs and pawed the carpet for his pants and shirt. Half a minute later, he emerged from the room, the rain battering at his face as he tried to find her. There had been something in her voice, something he had never heard before. *So quickly back to this.* He wanted to cry out, to pull her close to him, but there was no place, no time for such thoughts. They had stolen a few hours. Nothing more.

He looked to his left—the fire. He peered into the rain—a darting figure across the road. And then he heard the sirens. Police. They would ask questions. He shut the door and raced toward the woods.

⚔

Sarah slipped through the trees, her gun drawn. The rain had begun to come down in torrents, lashing at her face from all sides and forcing her hand to her eyes with greater frequency. Visibility was next to nil; any hopes of hearing them up ahead were lost to the percussive hammering of water on a frozen ground. But they were there. She knew that. He had set the trap, and he would be waiting.

A shadow skimmed across a tree not ten feet in front of her; then, from nowhere, the body of the screaming woman came barreling through the darkness, arms flailing, a useless piece of bait discarded before the attack. Sarah braced for the impact, expecting to feel the huge frame collapse into her arms, but it was not to be. Instead, the woman stopped. For the briefest of moments, they stared at each other. And in that instant, Sarah knew. She saw it in the woman's expression, in the angle of her head. There had never been any bait. There had never been any terror. But it was too late. The woman crashed her hand down onto Sarah's gun, leveling her foot into Sarah's chest and careening her into the grasp of an outstreched branch. As she fell, Sarah tried to find her footing, but the ground was too slick. Almost at once, the woman was on top of her, two hundred pounds of flesh slamming them both to the ground, her massive arms and thighs straddling Sarah in a viselike grip.

She felt the crack first, then the pain, a searing bolt of agony through her chest. Her ribs. How many had been broken, she could only guess. Thick fingers began to tear into her neck, knuckles grind into her trachea, thumbs dig deeply into the soft flesh just below her chin. Coughing for breath, Sarah felt her head lighten, the scene around her grow dark, consciousness ebb. Only the pain in her chest kept her alert, enough to thrust her knee into the woman's back, the rolls of flesh cushioning the blow, the attack only spurring the woman to claw more furiously into Sarah's neck.

But the woman was too eager, her rabid desire forcing her to shift her knee ever so slightly so as to gain greater leverage. It was all Sarah needed. Sensing the pressure lift from her forearm, Sarah ripped her hand from its prison and forced her fingers to the woman's head. In an act of brutal desperation, she drove her nails down into the woman's scalp, flesh and hair clawed at in savage frenzy. The woman lurched back, her hands releasing Sarah's neck. The darkness at once receding, air again filling her lungs. It was less than a second before the huge frame again bore down on her, but this time Sarah was prepared. As the woman leaned forward, Sarah lifted both her knees into the woman's back, using the woman's own weight to propel the lunging body forward, too fast to control, arms forced to reach beyond Sarah's head, thighs forced to release so as to steady themselves. With a quick burst, Sarah grabbed at the woman's crotch and pulled herself through the thick legs, twisting the soft genitalia as she gained her feet. The woman screamed, Sarah still scorching her nails up into the hairy flesh, scraping at the tender mound, the woman's mammoth frame dropping to the ground. She tried to flip over, but Sarah grabbed her arm and twisted it, wrenching it until the shoulder pulled from its socket. Without hesitation, she then dug her fingers into the woman's neck, hoisted the upper torso a few inches from the ground, and, with her knee, hammered down into the base of the woman's spine. The sound of a single snap told her it was over.

The pile of flesh twitched once as Sarah doubled over, the pain in her chest unforgiving, pulsating through her body with each gasp for breath. Her mind had gone blank, only now thoughts returning—the man, the fire . . . *Xander!* She bolted upright, suddenly aware of what had happened, the reason she had been lured to the trees. *How could I have been so stupid!* She began to run, her body bent to one side, her arm pulled in tightly so as to stifle the pain. *Xander.* It had been him all along, everything else a diversion. Images of Amman flashed through her mind. She needed him to be alive, to be safe. *Not again! Please be by the fire! Please!*

"Sarah."

The muted whisper tore through, the voice somewhere up ahead.

⚔

Xander crept through the trees, the gun at his side clutched in both hands. He had heard something off to his left, the pounding of the rain making it impossible to determine the source. He stopped, waited, then whispered.

"Sarah."

Again the sound, and he turned, his gun raised.

⚔

Sarah pulled herself to a tree, able to make out a figure no more than fifteen yards ahead of her. It was Xander, the silhouette unmistakable. He stood with his gun drawn, unaware of the man who now appeared behind him.

"Xander!" she screamed.

But it was too late. The man crashed the butt of his gun down into Xander's neck, a moment later hoisting the unconscious body to his shoulder as he began to weave his way through the trees. Sarah followed, but with each step, the man slipped farther and farther from sight. She had nothing—no gun, no knife—only her will to stop him. But the pain had grown unbearable.

Staying within the shadows, she turned to her left and caught sight of the man now thirty yards ahead of her, his pace remarkable given Xander's weight on his back. He, too, had kept to the edge of the trees and was showing no signs of slowing. Sarah tried to run, but her ribs would not permit it as she watched the man slip behind a curve in the road. Seconds later, the reflection of taillights bled out into the darkness. She propelled herself forward and staggered to the bend, only to see the car vanish from sight.

She stood and stared into the darkness as the rain whipped through her. Minutes passed before she dropped to her knees, her face lost in tears.

For herself, for him—she did not know.

10

Few men have the courage to . . . [s]eize the moment and dare to alter the very name of supremacy.

—*On Supremacy*, dedicatory letter

She had driven through the night, a torn sheet wrapped tightly around her chest to give some support to her ribs. Even so, the stiffness was making it difficult to breathe. She knew there had been no point in going after them. It had taken too long to get back to the motel, too many minutes spent peeling off the pants, knifing through the shirt to avoid further agony. Two, maybe three ribs were broken. One would have been enough. She had tossed the soaking clothes into the center of the room, a minute later collapsing into a tub of steaming water. Lying in the darkness, she had rethought every move, every moment. *By the fire! I will come back for you.* All she had wanted was to protect him, to keep him safe. A chance to make things right.

More than the lapse, though, the minutes of silence had forced her to confront an equally damning truth. She had taken a life. *Willfully* taken a life. This time, there had been no swerve of the blade, no choice—conscious or not—to disable rather than to destroy. With quiet deliberation, she had snapped a woman's back in two. Assassin. *"That's not why they chose you,"* he'd said. How little he had understood. How close she had come to believing him.

She had put the call through to O'Connell just the other side of the Montana border.

"We've been waiting to hear from you." His voice was tired.

"We?" she asked.

"I've been a bit quicker than I'd originally planned. Most of the boys are in place. We've set up camp—"

"I've lost Jaspers."

"*What?*"

"I . . . I let them take him."

He had heard that same tone in her voice only once before. In Amman. "Take it easy, Sarah. How?" He waited for an answer. When none came, he continued hesitantly. "Is he—"

"Lost, not dead. At least I don't think he is. . . ."

"How much does this complicate things?" O'Connell needed to focus her.

". . . I don't know."

Again, he waited. "Then what's the problem?"

The line was silent; she spoke. "Why *didn't* they kill him?"

"What?"

"They had him out in the open, close enough to finish it with a knife. Easy, noiseless, safe. Why take him?"

"I don't follow."

"He's not a bargaining chip. Christ, they know we'd let him die if it meant shutting them down. So why take him?"

O'Connell inhaled deeply before responding. "These aren't the questions we need to be hearing at this point."

"Xan . . . Jaspers was convinced he'd been *chosen.*"

"You'll have to explain that one."

"He thought there was a reason he was involved with all of this. It's something Schenten said before he died. Does that make any sense to you?"

"*Chosen?* Chosen for what?"

"I don't know. I *don't* know. But they've never hesitated in trying to kill *me,* so why not *him?*" She could hear Xander asking the same question, see him pounding at the wheel as they had sped through the open road—anger in his voice, uncertainty. And she had promised to protect him. . . .

"And you agree with him?" O'Connell's tone had changed.

". . . I don't know."

"I see." He paused. "The question is, would it make any difference? I assume the schedule went with the good doctor." The silence on the other end of the line was answer enough. "Well, they're following it. The English ambassador is all over the news."

That conversation had ended two hours ago. Just before dawn.

Now, razored strips of bloodred copper breached the morning sky as she pulled to a stop. A motorcycle stood patiently by the small cabin, still hidden from a hesitant sun. Sarah watched as the light crept over the edge of the canyon; like a wave, it swept along, swallowing O'Connell as he neared.

※

Xander slowly opened his eyes, a dull throbbing in his neck and the taste of vomit in his throat, the scent enough to rekindle a moment of nausea. Not that he had any memory of the act itself. In fact, he had *no* memory at all. Nothing. Only shadows, images flying through his head like the streaks of light glistening somewhere beyond him. He tried to think back, to recall the instant before the blackout, but he saw only snatches, disparate pieces of the last week colliding in disarray. All without sequence, without order. He wanted to focus, to find the source of the light, hoping that it would free his thoughts from their confusion, but the haze persisted—violence and terror fusing with the soft caress of a woman's hand.

He swallowed—a burning in his throat—and blinked several times, the pain slowly bringing objects into view. His senses of smell and touch were somehow more acute—the scent of freshly washed linen, the feel of crisp sheets pulled tightly over him—each helping to rouse him from his stupor. But his head wouldn't move. It felt compressed to the pillow, weighted down, so much so that he needed all his strength to turn ever so slightly toward the light. Patterns began to appear, flowers along a distant wall, soon the shape of a bureau beneath them, a small wooden chair placed at its side. He forced himself to concentrate on the objects, to imagine the iron coldness of the brass handles, all in an attempt to regain himself.

A window proved to be the source of the light, cotton drapes billowing in the breeze. The rest of the room was empty, save for an oval throw rug placed at the side of the bed. Everything neat, simple.

He lay still for a few minutes. A certain peace returned, an order to the memories, but soon, far more disquieting images began to flood his mind, muffled exchanges as if from within a fog. A voice, *his* voice but not his voice, all of it dreamlike, yet real. Figures standing over him, blinding light

searing into his eyes, thick fingers probing his face, stabbing pain throughout his body, then nausea and darkness. He tried to hold on, maintain contact, but the more he struggled, the more they faded to obscurity.

The smell of coffee momentarily distracted him, his first inclination to sit
up. Immediately, a jolt of pain in his shoulder advised otherwise and he fell
back to the bed. With considerable effort, he moved a hand to his neck and
began to probe the area with his fingers. The swelling was sizable, the skin
still tender to the touch. More startling, though, was the sight of a small
bandage on his forearm, a square piece of gauze held in place by a narrow
strip of adhesive. He released his neck and held his arm out straight. The
area around the bandage was horribly discolored, slivers of vein coursing
through a mound of black-and-blue flesh. He reached over and gently slid
his fingers along the edge of the wound. It, too, was remarkably tender.

With a quick pull, he yanked the adhesive off and stared at the small hole
in his arm, a red dot where a needle had entered. *A needle?* The tiny
reminder drove the memories back into his conscious mind—the room, the
bed, the voice, *his* voice but not his voice, and the blinding light. . . .

They had drugged him. They had violated his mind and had stolen his
will to resist.

But why? What could they have gained? He struggled for an answer. They
had the disc; they had the document he had put together. And the schedule. There was no question that they would have found them. *It's what they
were looking for all along.* So what else could they have wanted?

The sound of footsteps outside interrupted. Xander placed his arms
underneath the blanket and waited. Within a few seconds, the door cracked
open, a tuft of hair inching its way in, two brown eyes peeking through.
Seeing him awake, the eyes disappeared, the door once again shut. Xander
expected to hear a key in the lock, a bolt reengage, but there was nothing,
only the sound of footsteps fading to the distance. He looked over at the
window, it, too, free of bars, not even a latch to keep him from the grounds
beyond. And for the first time, he noticed his clothes lying neatly on the
chair, his shoes tucked in by the bureau. All readily accessible. Whatever he
had told them, they clearly had felt no need to restrain him.

Unwilling to wait any longer, he propped himself up and brought his
feet to the wooden floor, his shoulder no more obliging than it had been a
few minutes before. The silk pajama bottoms hung loosely on his legs as he
shuffled toward the window, a cautious breeze gliding across his chest as he
neared the drapes. The light from outside forced him to shield his eyes

behind an open palm. Even so, the sun felt good. A relief. He stood for a few minutes, his eyes soon accustomed to the light, his skin chilled but refreshed by the nip in the air. The door opened and he turned.

There, in beige cardigan, a pair of corduroy pants hanging on his slender frame, stood Herman Lundsdorf. He held Xander's manuscript in one hand; in the other, he clutched a mug, the smell of coffee filling the room.

"Good heavens!" said Lundsdorf, marching toward Xander, "in front of an open window, and with no shirt on. Really!" The old man reached past him and pulled the window shut. "Have you lost all sense?" Lundsdorf then turned and stared up into his pupil's eyes. "I have gone to a great deal of trouble to keep you alive. If you were to go and catch pneumonia now, I would look very foolish. Very foolish indeed." He smiled.

Xander hadn't heard a word.

⤜

"He asked him *what?*" Tieg continued to stare out at the bay, the receiver pressed to his ear, his eyes lost to the horizon.

"It wasn't so much questions," answered the Italian, "as . . . *suggestions.* The professor seemed more eager to explain than to gain information from Jaspers. Under the narcotic, the responses were very confused."

"What exactly was he trying to explain? I need details, Paolo."

"There *were* no details. It was more a lesson. Dr. Lundsdorf was speaking in very abstract terms—'the essence of authority, the role of the overseer.' Those I remember coming up several times."

"And?"

"Jaspers would agree, then not agree—it would go back and forth. At one point, they began to speak in German. I couldn't follow after that."

"And he asked him nothing about the Trent woman, nothing about the people she's contacted?"

"We believe she is dead."

"*Believe?* That's very reassuring. You're telling me he pumped Jaspers with God knows what and didn't ask him a thing?"

"Nothing that seemed relevant. As I said, it was as if he wanted to convince him of something. I can't explain it any better than that."

"And was he convinced?"

"I suppose. . . . I couldn't say. I've tried to do what you asked—"

"And you've done a superb job, as usual," countered Tieg. "That's not the issue. Where is he now?"

"Jaspers? Asleep. In one of the guest rooms."

"And you have no idea what the old man intends to do with him before he initiates the next stage."

"I've been told nothing."

"Of course." Tieg realized he had only one choice. "I'll be flying in within the next few hours."

"*Flying in?* . . . I thought—"

"The situation has changed. Meet me at the airstrip—two o'clock."

"I don't understand. We've been given express orders not to leave—"

"Then make sure no one sees you." He paused. "Do I make myself clear?"

The response was immediate. "Perfectly."

Twenty minutes later, Tieg sat in the backseat of his limousine, a phone pressed to his ear.

"And if you're *not* back?" The voice on the other end was Amy Chandler's. "You're getting much too hot, Jonas, to pull one of your disappearing acts. A rerun at this point could seriously threaten our momentum."

"As I said, I'll be back. If not—"

"No *if nots.* Last night alone we had over twelve thousand faxes and E-mails, not to mention the Web site—which was packed. Jonas, this is as close as you get to a sure thing."

"I'm well aware of that. There's a tape in my desk—something I put together last week. Just me and the camera. It runs about forty-five—"

"*What?* You put something together? Hello, Jonas, remember me? Remember Amy, the *producer.*"

"Amy . . . dear . . . I was going to show it to you this afternoon. I had it in mind for next week, but it'll be just as effective tonight. Or would you prefer a rerun?"

She paused before answering. "What's on the tape?"

"I suggest you take a look."

Again silence. "I don't like when you do this, Jonas."

"I said I'll be back."

"I don't have a choice, do I?"

"Not really, no."

"I didn't think so. I suppose you know there's a rumor going around that you're thinking of jumping ship, a political move. Tell me it's not true, Jonas. Tell me that's not what I'll be seeing on the tape tonight."

This time, he waited. "Come now, Amy, would I risk a sure thing?"

He cut the line as the car pulled up to the terminal.

✄

"A nice piece of work. Remarkable, given the conditions under which you wrote it." Lundsdorf had taken a seat on the bed, the document at his side. "A few holes here and there, but the theory is sound." There was a knock at the door. "Come."

A woman appeared, a glass of deep purple liquid in her hand. She extended the glass to Xander.

"Take it," advised Lundsdorf. "I am told it will relieve the knot in your stomach, reduce the nausea. Primarily beets, a carrot or two, some turnips. Nothing mysterious." Xander took the glass and sipped at the concoction. The woman was gone by the time he drained the glass. "Last night was no doubt . . . unpleasant," continued Lundsdorf. "You have my apologies."

"Why?" whispered Xander.

"We had to make certain that the information—"

"No," he broke in, his eyes riveted on the old man. "Why you?"

Lundsdorf looked at Xander, then spoke. "Because I knew what the manuscript had to offer. Because I could bring it to life."

"I see."

"Do you?" He waited before continuing. "You see the responsibility, the burden such a discovery places on one's shoulders? Long ago, I saw beyond the theory, beyond the words. I saw the reality of order, of permanence, of an end to mediocrity. In such instances, there is no choice."

"Really." Xander nodded, more to himself than to the old man. "How brave of you." He placed the empty glass on the bureau and added, "At least now I know why I've managed to stay alive."

"That was miscommunication, nothing more."

"The men in Salzgitter, the train? They seemed pretty clear on what they had in mind."

"As I said, miscommunication. Luckily, you were not harmed."

Xander let his eyes wander to the window.

"Is that all you see?" asked Lundsdorf.

Xander couldn't tell if it was the aftereffects of the drug or simply the shock of the last two minutes, but he suddenly felt weak. He pushed the clothes to the floor and sat. "I'd always counted you among the sane."

"And now you question that?" The old man placed the mug on the side table and picked up the papers. "You have read the manuscript."

"Of course."

"A third copy," nodded Lundsdorf. "That was a surprise. No matter. I trust you understood it."

"If you mean did I understand its madness, yes—"

"Madness? What do you know of madness?" Lundsdorf held the papers high in his hand. "This?" He shook his head. "A week trying to piece together what I have been scrutinizing for over half a lifetime, and you tell me it is *madness*? That, my young colleague, is either extraordinary presumption or mindless stupidity."

"Thank you," replied Xander. "I'm glad to hear my choices are so numerous."

"It has nothing to do with choice." Lundsdorf stopped. "You have been put through a great deal in the last week, experiences that have colored your perception." He leafed through the document. "Yet even in your few pages, I sense you see beyond the brutality." Lundsdorf waited for their eyes to meet. "Yes, there is violence, deception, perhaps even a disregard for human compassion. But we both know they are merely by-products of something far purer, far more insightful. Our monk was far cleverer than that. His methods are sometimes unsavory, but it is the result that matters."

"By-product?" For the first time, an energy infused Xander's words. "How can you expect me to believe that? You of all people?"

"Because it is true. And because you *do* believe it."

"My God, talk about presumption! Is that what that book gives you—a way to justify Carlo and Ganz, and who knows how many others? Have you seen your star pupil from Tempsten lately? Is that what you mean by a *by-product*?"

"The two men were a misfortune, I will not argue with you, the girl ill-chosen. For that I am to blame, as well. But I will take the blame willingly if it means we can achieve something greater than ourselves."

"And what exactly does that mean?" Xander stood, supporting himself on the bureau. "'Order, permanence, something greater than ourselves.' How can you bear to hear yourself say those things? You know as well as I those terms are meaningless without definition, far more dangerous once defined. Who, may I ask, decides what constitutes a *good order*? Who determines the limits of reasonable sacrifice—all, no doubt, in the name of some ideal vision? Is it you? Have you discovered some Truth that the rest of us aren't quite clever enough to see? No, that would be too much ego, wouldn't it? Instead, you give that role to our friend Eisenreich—cede the responsibility to a man who had no conception of human dignity or freedom, and who had an equally disturbing understanding of the *greater good,* if in fact such a thing exists."

"Oh, it exists," answered Lundsdorf, "of that, there is no question. And we both know Eisenreich saw it at its purest. Do not tell me you believe we are limited to a world of relative choice, where we may never achieve anything of ultimate worth? How frightening men of vision must look to you."

"Men of *vision?*" Xander began to shake his head, unable to find the words. He then looked at Lundsdorf. "Like the ones you ran from in 1936?"

"Please," replied Lundsdorf. "The Nazis are a child's comparison. Talk of power and the name Hitler rushes to the mind. Talk of permanence and the word fascism is not far behind. How utterly simplistic. Really, Xander, I expected more of you. Are we to have every grand vision contaminated by the memory of those twelve years? They were fools. If you want, I will even call them evil. What I ran away from was stupidity, nothing else. What I sought was the means to release us from such mediocrity."

"I see. So you picked Votapek, Tieg, and Sedgewick. Geniuses all."

The old man looked at Xander for a moment and then, without the slightest warning, burst into laughter. "Touché," he said. "I will not pretend that they do not leave something to be desired in that quarter. Then again, we both know they are not stupid men—far from it. They simply need guidance. They allow petty detail to cloud the mind."

"And you, of course, have the *vision* to guide them."

"You say it with such cynicism." Lundsdorf stopped and peered over at his onetime student. "How different from last night."

". . . Last night?"

"When we spoke." Lundsdorf's tone was far more cordial. "You were far more interesting then."

"Last night," repeated Xander, "I was drugged."

"Exactly. What better time to speak the truth?"

"The truth? The truth about what?"

"Chaos, power, the role of deception. You were quite candid, quite supportive."

The impact of his words was immediate. "I don't believe you."

"Believe what?" answered Lundsdorf casually. "I have said nothing. I am merely recalling what you said last night. Perhaps it is *you* who knows that we do not think so differently?"

Xander turned to the window. "Trust me, I could never think like you."

"Is that so?" Lundsdorf reached into his cardigan pocket and pulled out a small tape player. He placed it on the side table and asked, "Would you like to hear something from last night?" Without waiting for an answer, he pressed the play button and sat back. A moment later, Xander listened as his own voice filled the room.

The words were heavy, slurred, but the voice was clearly his own. A second voice began to ask questions. Lundsdorf. At first meaningless banter; then the conversation turned to the theory. And with each new question, Xander heard himself—reluctant at first—agree with Lundsdorf, accept his construct of order, authority, even sacrifice.

Lundsdorf: "So you agree that there are a select few who have the vigilance, the integrity, the wisdom to rule—surely they also have the responsibility to do so?"

"If they—"

"Yes or no? Should we cede them responsibility?"

"Yes, if—"

"So it would be best to permit them to guide the rest so that the balance may be maintained?"

"Yes, but you're assuming—"

"Only what you have told me. They possess vigilance and integrity; they promote the primary functions of the state; they will make the mediocre better than they are."

"Yes . . . but I—"

"And their methods are justified by the end they seek—the balance, the permanence and progress of the state and its people."

"Yes . . . but you—"

"They have the wisdom, the integrity. You have said so yourself. Surely they know better than the rest?"

"Yes . . . but they—"

"Surely they know better than the rest."

"Yes! Yes! Yes!"

Xander sat amazed, his faith in himself slipping further and further as each minute passed, the voice of Lundsdorf leading on, memories of long-ago discussions, mentor and apprentice—the younger ever more eager to please. Soon, he began to hear enthusiasm creep into his own voice.

"Turn it off." It was Xander who spoke.

"But some of the most intriguing dialogue is yet to come," Lundsdorf replied. "You—"

"Turn it off."

The old man smiled and picked up the tape player, pressing down on the button as he did so; Xander remained by the window. "Are you surprised?"

"Surprised by what?"

"Come now, you readily admitted that there are those who are born to lead, that they have vision—"

"Your word, not mine."

"Semantics."

"Whatever condition I was in—whatever condition you *put* me in—I was speaking theoretically. Not practically. You were putting words in my mouth. None of it had to do with Eisenreich."

"It had *everything* to do with Eisenreich." Lundsdorf paused. "If it was all theory, why did it provoke such hesitation at first?"

"I was disoriented—"

"Really? Why, then, are you so eager to stop listening now? As you say, it was merely an academic exercise. What is the harm in that?"

"I have no interest in—"

"Or shall I play you an excerpt from our discussion of the overseer where you explain the intricate relationship between knowledge and deception? Or perhaps the exchange in which you offer solutions for some of the more troubling sections of the manuscript? Your remarks are quite convincing."

"Why are you doing this?" asked Xander. Lundsdorf said nothing. "Pang of conscience? Is that what this is—you need to hear that everything you've done is acceptable, noble, that we should all thank you for taking on the responsibility? Sorry. You won't get confirmation from the ivory tower—"

"I do not seek your approval."

"Then why?"

Lundsdorf placed the tape player in his pocket. "As you said, men are fallible."

"That's not an answer."

"I, too, am concerned about my three 'geniuses.' They will, of course, have to be replaced at some point. Perhaps sooner than later. Three others will be chosen, groomed, made ready."

"I'm sure you've got the next little trio already picked out."

"No," said Lundsdorf, a look of fond recollection in his eyes. "I have played my part." He peered over at Xander. "There, someone else must take the reins." The two men stared at one another. "How did Eisenreich put it? A man with the insight of Aurelius, the self-command of Cincinnatus."

Lundsdorf picked up the papers. "A man with the wisdom and integrity to sustain the vision." He turned again to Xander. "I know of only one."

The room fell silent. Xander stood absolutely still, suddenly numb to the breeze on his back.

⚔

Votapek began to backtrack. It was half a mile to the turnoff, another half mile to the gate. He had been careful, more so than usual. An assumed name on the airline ticket, several connections along the way, three separate drivers for the last hundred miles of the trip. He had thought about calling to explain his arrival, but he knew the old man would only have convinced him otherwise. *The old man.* It seemed strange to think of him as such. They were all old men, now. A lifetime spent in the pursuit of . . . what? It had become far more difficult to explain of late. Perhaps Jonas was right. Perhaps they had been under the yoke long enough.

The future, however, was not the reason Votapek had made the trip. He had come for her. About that, there would be no discussion.

⚔

It was 3:11 when the last of them arrived, a small, fine-featured man with a razor-thin beard. He looked no more than twenty, his hands wedged deep within the pockets of a coat a good two sizes too large for him. He remained by the door of the cabin as O'Connell moved from behind the table to greet him. Introductions were kept to a minimum. His name, Tobias Pierson; his passion, computers. And, from his appearance, he looked completely out of place among the six men and two women who nodded in welcome.

"This," said O'Connell, "is the special package we'll be taking into the compound. If it's got a keyboard, Toby here can play it. He's a virtuoso."

Pierson rocked back and forth on his heels but said nothing. The others turned back to the charts, O'Connell taking his place at the head of the table. Only Sarah continued to stare at the strangely unobtrusive specialist, his demeanor a complete surprise. Cool to a fault—almost indifferent to the surroundings—he glanced around the room, clearly uninterested in the group at center. The sight of the refrigerator, however, prompted a momentary raising of the eyebrow, and within seconds he was at the door, examining the contents within. From the expression on his face, Sarah could see he was not pleased. After several near choices, he reached in and pulled out a can.

"Nothing that's not diet?" he asked, expecting someone at the table to acknowledge him. When no one answered, he shrugged. It was then that he noticed Sarah. "I don't like diet," he said. "It tastes kind of gray. You know, like washed-out carpets."

Sarah stared at him for a moment, then nodded. What else was there to do? Evidently, their computer expert lived in his own little world. Better not to disturb him. In that respect, she realized how well he fit in with the others in the room. Sarah knew three of the six, all men who belonged to a select group of onetime Pritchard operatives, each, for reasons unknown, having fallen from grace. Their stories were familiar. Cut adrift, hunted for a time by the men who had trained them, each had managed to survive to become independent contractors. Men without allegiance, men beyond malice. Now all that mattered was the price. She knew O'Connell had been right to choose them. COS had been compromised; only those outside its reach could be trusted. Only those at home in their own little worlds. For some reason, the image of Xander flashed through her mind.

"These," O'Connell began, "are the original plans for the building. The layout of the grounds, the fence—they're exactly as you see them here. One difference is that they did some work on the place about a year and a half ago. Trouble is, we don't know what that entailed. A lot of material, but not a single change to the main frame—no extra rooms or floors. Which leaves only one option. All those nice little additions must have taken place underground. So, gents, getting inside is only half the job. We're going to have to make sure that the access to the lower level remains open. In other words, we're going to have to make our way in *very* quietly. Good news is, there's no sign of animals; bad news . . . well, you know the bad news. It'll be trip wires most of the way up. Once inside the house, it's anybody's guess." He paused again and then nodded toward Sarah. "Our female colleague here will take charge of young Toby. Hold his hand, as it were."

Still rummaging through the refrigerator, Pierson popped his head out and said, "Just as long as she's holding it on the way out."

"We go at seven," said O'Connell, his attention back on those around the table. "You've each got copies of the prints—that includes you, too," he said over his shoulder to Pierson. O'Connell then looked at his watch. "Let's say an hour. Familiarized and with specific options." The group dispersed, and O'Connell made his way to the door, nodding to Sarah to join him. A minute later, they were outside.

"How are the ribs?" he asked.

"Stiff, but I'll survive."

"You've had worse." He sat on the ledge of the porch. "You don't have to do this, you know. You can monitor it from here." Her silence sufficed as response. "It's a motley crew," he continued, "but worth every penny. They'll get us in and out."

"If we can find some nondiet soda," answered Sarah. She sat.

"Ah, yes, Toby. Met him in Benghazi. Good lad. Couldn't understand why he was roaming around a city that barely had enough electricity to boil water; then I found he'd met someone who was interested in a Mossad tracking system. A certain Colonel." O'Connell squinted, trying to remember. "I think he made Toby a lieutenant. Might have been a major. Toby just liked the hat."

Sarah laughed, then stopped.

"You can't worry about him," added the Irishman.

"It's not our computer friend I'm worried about."

"I know," he answered. "They had a clear shot and they didn't take it." Sarah said nothing. "Chances are, Jaspers is still alive."

"But for how long?" she asked.

"That's why we're going in quiet." O'Connell paused. "Now, you don't think I'd tell that lot in there about it, would I? You've got Toby. I'll take care of the professor."

Sarah smiled. "Alison was right. You're a nice man, Gaelin. A very nice man."

⚔

The two academics had barely begun to talk when a woman appeared at the door.

"What?" Lundsdorf had barked, his irritation apparent.

"I'm sorry to disturb you—"

"Yes, yes. What is it?"

"Mr. Tieg has just arrived."

Xander had seen the momentary look of surprise in the old man's eyes, though Lundsdorf had been quick to recover. "Thank you, Ms. Palmerston. Tell him I will be with him presently." Turning to Xander, he had added, "Nothing you need concern yourself with. In fact, some time alone might give you the opportunity to consider your . . . position."

That had been nearly two hours ago. Since then, Xander had showered, shaved, and dressed, venturing out into the maze of hallways for a tour of the house. Not once, though, had he stopped thinking about Lundsdorf's words, the enormity of their implication. *"I knew from the start, from those first days with your dissertation."* Lundsdorf had spoken with absolute certainty. *"Here was the mind I had been waiting for. Here was the spirit to sustain the vision. It was simply a question of when to introduce you to it."* Xander had stood in utter disbelief. *"You are the one to succeed me. You are the one who must take the reins."* Even now, having been ushered into a small dining room to face a plate of poached halibut, Xander found it hard to summon an appetite, despite the gnawing pit in his stomach.

As if on cue, Lundsdorf entered, a second man just behind him at the door. "I see they have gotten something for you to eat. Splendid. I trust you are feeling up to it?"

"Not much of an appetite, no."

"Understandable," Lundsdorf said as he sat across from Xander, "but you would do well to try a few mouthfuls. Recover your strength." The second man remained by the door.

"I hear Votapek's arrived," said Xander. "Another unexpected guest?"

Lundsdorf smiled. "Try the hollandaise. It is really quite good."

Xander stared at him. "Have you told them?"

"Told—ah, you mean about our conversation."

"I'll save you the trouble. I've considered the 'position.' I decline."

For a moment, Lundsdorf said nothing; then, in his most comforting voice, he spoke. "What a strain this past week must have placed on you. I, too, was hesitant at first. But, as I said, in such matters, there is no choice. Such things demand more of us than perhaps we are able to see. In a less disoriented state, you will look on it quite differently."

"I see. Read the manuscript and become a disciple?" Xander pushed the plate to the middle of the table. "You seem to forget. I *did* read it; and I *didn't* convert. I'm sure, though, you can find someone equally *spirited* from within the ranks. Isn't that what those schools are all about?"

"What you read was a piece of theory written over four hundred years ago. And we both know your mind and heart were not exactly in the right place to appreciate it. You read from the standpoint of uncertainty, from fear. It is not, to say the least, the best position to be in when passing judgment."

"My judgment—"

"As to choosing from within the ranks," he continued, "that was never a possibility. After Tempsten, we were forced to revise the curriculum, concentrate on the more immediate goals. We designed schools to produce soldiers, individuals who could carry out the tasks set before them."

"Mindless automatons."

"No, that would be unfair. Each of them recognizes the larger end, albeit on a somewhat rudimentary level. It will be another generation before we can produce the types of leaders from whom to choose an overseer. Even now, the new curriculum is showing remarkable results. The past eighteen hours are a testament to that."

"Very reassuring."

"*Xander*," there was a fatherly tone to his voice, "you have *so much* to offer. Not just your mind but your compassion, your ability to make people better than they are, to force them to see their own excellence; I have seen it time and again with your students. It is remarkable. And it is *that* gift you will bring to the theory, *that* quality which will allow you to temper Eisenreich's brutal side. The chance to take what is already in place and make *even* it better than it is." Lundsdorf paused. "I am giving you the opportunity to improve on what *I* have created."

Xander did not answer for a moment. "And you expect me to thank you."

"To lead during the most crucial period in the entire process? Yes."

"I see." Xander seemed to nod in agreement. "So crucial that you didn't think it necessary to explain any of this to me beforehand? What were you afraid of—that I'd find implementing the theory lunatic even if I hadn't stumbled onto it myself? Or am I talking in terms of *choice* again?"

"I was afraid of nothing. If you were thinking a bit more clearly, you would see that as well."

"So when exactly were you planning to introduce me to the manuscript? You discovered my *extraordinary* gifts fifteen years ago. What took so long?"

"Actually, it was to have been four years ago." Lundsdorf reached over and took a spear of asparagus. "When you first showed an interest. That article you wrote on the myth of Eisenreich was quite inventive, especially given your limited resources. But then Fiona fell ill. It was not the time. Understandably, you associated anything to do with Eisenreich with her. It was very difficult, I can assure you."

Xander waited, then spoke. "I'm sorry Fiona's death was such an inconvenience for you."

Lundsdorf remained silent for a long moment. "I can understand—"

"No, you can't." There was no emotion in his voice. "Please don't mention her again."

Neither said a word. Xander was the first to break the silence. "So when did you intend to bring me into the fold?"

"A great irony, that." Lundsdorf dipped his finger into the hollandaise and sampled the sauce. "No doubt Miss Trent told you about Arthur Pritchard."

"Yes."

"Unfortunately, I misjudged his curiosity, or perhaps, I should say, his ambition. He was not content with the role I had given him. Hence Miss Trent. He thought she could find him the manuscript, explain his future place. When she would not, he exposed her to us, no doubt thinking— given her past—that she would try to eliminate me, thus leaving him free to become overseer. Had she not arrived at your door, you and I would have sat down with the manuscript on your return from Milan. Fortuna, however, had other plans. In that regard, Signore Machiavelli might very well have been right."

"A week before? That's when you were going to tell me?"

"Oh, I might not have told you at all . . . but then Pescatore began to publish his articles, and it became imperative that you and I talk. I knew you would speak with him in Florence. He told me so himself. It seemed an appropriate moment." He took another spear. "There would have been time."

"Why kill Carlo?"

"Again with Pescatore." Lundsdorf looked genuinely surprised by the remark. "Was he such a friend that you feel the need to press this point?"

"Just a man's life," answered Xander, "that's all."

"Oh, I see," nodded Lundsdorf. "And the life *you* took was justified? The man on the train from Frankfurt?"

"If you can't see the difference . . . I was protecting myself."

"And *I* was protecting something far greater than one life. How easily you have taken on the role of moralist. I do not think it suits you."

"Perhaps because it's not in keeping with your usual company."

The smile disappeared. Lundsdorf returned to the asparagus.

"And the same for Ganz and Clara?"

"By then, it was a matter of security, but yes. I needed to know what you had found. Mrs. Huber was . . . the most obvious choice. I knew you would send it to her. Her death was . . . a mistake. You might find some solace in knowing that the woman responsible is no longer capable of such things."

"I don't."

"Pity."

Xander waited before speaking. "So once again, everything had to be just right for me to *appreciate* the manuscript. So much for my 'genius' if you thought you had to hold my hand while I read it."

"Not at all. I have known you for fifteen years, Xander. I have seen your mind develop, have helped to guide it in that development. You can be assured, I know *exactly* what it is that compels you."

"You *always* thought you knew what I wanted. *That* was the problem."

Lundsdorf pulled the rubber-banded Machiavelli from his pocket and placed it on the table. "I, too, have always been rather fond of our Italian friend. The tapes from last night only confirm what I have known all along. Even now, you are growing more and more intrigued—"

"I've formed my opinion of your 'vision,' whatever you think those tapes tell you, and no amount of intellectual jousting is going to change that."

"Xander"—Lundsdorf again in gentler tone—"when the chaos has run its course, you will understand why the manuscript is our only hope for a future. You will embrace its promise of permanence."

"Along with its promise of manipulation, brutality, hatred?"

"*Tame* the theory, Xander. Temper it. You alone can do this. We both know that men will never abandon their aggression, nor their penchant for hatred. If, on the other hand, we can find a way to direct those appetites to a *positive* end, then we must accept the responsibility to do so. You have spoken of choices—I agree. I am telling you that chaos is inevitable. The question arises: If *we* do not step in, then who? The military? It is, as you know, the most likely response. Foist chaos on a people and you have but limited time before they run to their generals for protection. Would you prefer that?" He paused. "Remember Cincinnatus. He had no love of power, no desire to rule, but Rome called him to serve, and he obeyed. Sadly, he abandoned his post too soon, and the generals returned. *You* will have the power, Xander, you *alone* to shape the process whereby we may tame the worst that is within us. Surely you can see the nobility in that."

"In the same way that Votapek, Sedgewick, and Tieg do?" Xander watched as the warmth slipped from Lundsdorf's eyes. "How foolish of me to think that it's the promise of *power* that draws them, not their 'nobility.' " Something suddenly struck him. "That's why they're here, isn't it? That's why the surprise visits. It's time to see who's in control."

"I said that need not concern you."

"Are they as eager for me to take the reins as you are?"

"It is of no consequence."

Xander smiled. For the first time in days, he smiled. "You really think you can control all of this, don't you? Me, Votapek, Tieg—the manuscript says it *must* be so, and therefore it *will* be so. One virtuous man to make the world right. One man to make a virtue of brutality and deception."

"You are not thinking clearly."

"Things have never been clearer." Xander paused. "*Theory*—that's all it is." He picked up the Machiavelli. "All *this* is. All it can ever be."

"No, Xander, you know—"

"What I *know*—what *you* have taught me—is that to see it any other way is madness. No matter how seductive. And I will have nothing to do with it."

"You *will*—"

"You'll have to kill me, you know that, don't you?" Lundsdorf did not answer. "Tieg? Votapek? Have they disappointed you as well? Oh, but then who will lead us out of the chaos? Now there's a *practical* dilemma."

"You need time—"

"There *is* no time. You've seen to that, for the past eighteen hours."

"*No!*" Lundsdorf barked, the first hint of frustration in his voice. "I will not permit you to do this. When the time comes, you will accept your role. You must take the time to consider more carefully."

Calmly, Xander pushed back his chair and stood. "No. That's not going to happen." He tossed the Machiavelli onto the table and moved to the door.

"You *will* reconsider," answered Lundsdorf, regaining his control. Busy with the asparagus, he added, "Oh, yes, I meant to tell you. There will be no last-minute attempts to interfere. Miss Trent is dead."

Xander stopped for a moment, his back to Lundsdorf. If nothing else, he had no intention of giving Lundsdorf the pleasure of a reaction. Slowly, he stepped past the guard, only to notice a second man off in the shadows, thin to the point of frailty, a set of nervous eyes trying to avoid contact. Xander recognized him instantly. Anton Votapek. And he knew he had heard every word. Without acknowledging him, Xander continued down the corridor.

The first car left at 7:07, the second eight minutes later. Only Alison had remained at the cabin. O'Connell had mentioned another woman, someone who would arrive to take care of her. He had not explained; Sarah had not asked.

Each operative wore a turtleneck and black wool hat, the clothing pulled to the limits so as to leave a minimum of flesh revealed. And each carried a revolver fitted with a silencer, strapped tightly in a holster at the waist. Knives hung on the side of the belt, garroting wire coiled innocently through an open loop—the usual fare for such expeditions, worn with the familiarity of men well schooled in the art of infiltration. Sarah felt strangely at ease in her own gear, although her ribs made it impossible to carry anything on her shoulder, even the weight of a pack too much to sustain. Toby had taken hers without too much of a fuss.

It was 7:57 when the first car pulled to a stop along a stretch of road half a mile from the compound. The three men and Sarah got out and waited while O'Connell drove into the gulley between highway and wood; five minutes later, the car lay hidden under branches and foliage, plastic reflector caps from the lights tossed into the trees. In single file, they began to walk.

⚔

Jonas Tieg entered the study, an all-too-familiar knot in his stomach. The pain had grown less acute over the years, but it had remained an essential part of the ritual, a connection to a past beyond which he had never quite moved. Willingly or not, Tieg became the frightened twelve-year-old all over again, the old man behind the desk aware of his pupil, never choosing to acknowledge him. Tonight, however, that would change.

Without looking up from his book, Lundsdorf spoke. "I thought you were leaving, Jonas. You should be in California for the next few days. Or does your television show not need you?"

"I can leave in the morning," answered Tieg, taking the chair across from Lundsdorf.

"I would prefer it if you were to leave tonight." Only now did the old man look up. "I will be closing off access to the lab within the next hour or so. Again, it would be best if you were not here when that occurs."

"I was hoping to—"

"I have heard your concerns, and I trust you understood my answer. Do I make myself clear?"

"Absolutely," answered Tieg, "except you forgot to tell me how important Jaspers will be in our future." He spoke with little emotion. "Obviously, my insecurities weren't as far-fetched as you led me to believe."

Lundsdorf placed the book on the desk and sat back, his hands clasped in his lap. "You have been listening to things that do not concern you."

"I'm a little tired of being treated like a child."

"And I am tired of treating you as such, but you rarely leave me any other choice. This business with Jaspers—"

"Is unacceptable," Tieg cut in. "He must be eliminated."

"Really? To soothe your ego?"

"To make certain that an old man's fantasy doesn't get in the way of fifty years of work."

"Fantasy?" Lundsdorf smiled. "Tell me, Jonas, when I am gone, will you understand how to coordinate the three spheres—"

Now Tieg began to laugh. It was a response Lundsdorf never expected, enough to silence him. "The three spheres?" continued Tieg, no humor in his voice. For some reason, the knot in his stomach had disappeared. "I'm *already* coordinating the three of us, or weren't you aware of that? Larry doesn't make a move without me, and Anton . . . well, Anton, as you know, does what he's told. So there's really no need for Professor Jaspers, is there? As I understand it, even he realizes that, whatever motives he might have for declining your *generous* proposition. Unfortunately, it isn't yours to offer anymore."

"I see," he replied. "And you have had this planned for some time, yes?"

"Actually, no. Unlike you, I recognize a certain unpredictability when it comes to fate. There are things we can control and things we can't. Those we can't are the ones—like Dr. Jaspers—to which we simply have to react. That's what I'm doing now."

"And if Jaspers had not appeared?"

"Who knows? I might never have—how do you always put it?—*questioned my role*. Strange how your need to control everything—even after you're dead—is the very thing that keeps you from seeing it all work out."

"Your role has not changed."

"Oh, I think it has." Tieg removed a gun from his pocket and aimed it at Lundsdorf. "You have the codes to initialize the final stage. I need them."

"And you think I will give them to you so that you may kill me."

"I think your ego couldn't bear the thought of being so close and never having had the chance to push the button, no matter what the outcome."

"Why not wait for me to input the codes, and then kill me? Surely that would have been easier?"

"We both know you'd never let me into the lab. And we both know that, given my feelings for Jaspers, there's little chance I'd live much beyond the next eight days. You'd be only too happy with Pembroke as your political prefect. So I die and become a martyr, one more tragedy within all the chaos, a fact that only makes my army of viewers all the more ready to do your bidding. No. I need the codes now. And you're going to give them to me."

A muffled shot rang out from beneath the desk. Tieg lurched backward, for a moment uncertain what had happened. He then looked down at his stomach and watched as a growing circle of red began to spread across his shirt. A second shot fired, jolting him back as his gun fell to the floor. He began to cough blood, his instinct to stand, but his legs would not support him. From the shadows, Paolo appeared.

"I was hoping it would not come to this, Jonas," said Lundsdorf, calmly lifting his hand from his lap and placing the gun on the desk. "Hoping you would see beyond yourself to the future. Sadly, that is not to be." He watched as Tieg coughed up more blood. "By the way, you are quite right. The vice president—or should I say *president*—will make a fine prefect, and yes, we will make certain that your death elicits the proper response from all your many devotees. As to Anton, again you are most perceptive. He does what he is told, especially when he is promised that Alison is not to be harmed. That, of course, is untrue, but he is somewhat too believing when it comes to that young woman. Nonetheless, he was quite clear as to your intentions." Tieg reached for the desk, only to have Paolo's hand clasp his shoulder and press him to the chair. "And, of course, Paolo." Lundsdorf nodded. "His penance for Wolfenbüttel has been most helpful." Lundsdorf pushed back his chair and stood. "You know, I did not anticipate this. So you see, I, too, know when it is necessary simply to . . . *react.*" He stepped around the desk and, in a strangely affectionate gesture, placed his hand on Tieg's cheek. "You played your role as best you could, Jonas. Take comfort in that."

A minute later, Tieg's head fell to the side, his eyes frozen in death.

✠

O'Connell had led most of the way, angling the quintet through the trees, the two men behind, followed by Toby and Sarah. Twenty yards from the gate, he raised his hand and dropped to his knees. The others did the same, save for the taller of the two hired hands, who continued on, prone to the ground, snaking his way through the underbrush on his arms.

They watched as he positioned himself about halfway between the gate's wooden pilaster and the first fence post some eight feet farther down. Two pieces of strip wood lay horizontally between the two columns, the picture of a simple country fence designed to keep out only the largest of animals.

To the party crouched in the trees, however, it was anything but simple. They continued to watch as the man removed a small box from his pack and placed it on a two-foot tripod about eighteen inches from the lower rail. A second box, then a third appeared, each placed at specific points between the two posts in a triangular formation. The man then seated himself within the triangle, removed yet another device—this one no larger than his palm—and aimed it at the first of the three boxes. No sooner had he done so than a thin strip of light seemed to jump from the gate to the first box, then to the second, then to the third, and finally to the far post, a razor-thin beam dancing two feet off the ground. He then placed the device under his hood and squeezed himself through the two pieces of strip wood. He was inside. No alarms. No jolts of electricity. He pulled the device from his hood, disengaged the beam, and signaled for O'Connell to take his position. One by one, they each entered the triangle; and one by one, they waited for the beam before breaching the fence. Though considerably more advanced, it was nothing more than a slip loop, much like the one Sarah had used to gain access to Schenten's house. Within three minutes, they all lay prone inside the grounds of the compound.

Directly in front of them, the grass rose on an incline to a flat, open area; a cluster of five cabins dotted the far horizon and formed a strange pattern against the deep black of the sky. The main house stood apart, off to the left on another raised plain, though nearer than any of the cabins. Light from inside spilled out onto the grass, creating a gentle aura around the building. It was on that hill that they knew they would find the trip wires.

O'Connell checked his watch. He nodded to the second man, who immediately dashed up to the summit. Crouching, he pulled a set of lenses from his pack and began to scan the grounds. Infrareds. Less than halfway through his sweep, he suddenly pulled the glasses from his eyes and reached back to his holster. In the same motion, he signaled to the group below to flatten themselves on the grass. Pressed to the cold ground, Sarah heard the sound of a single *thwit* break through the silence. A moment later, she looked up. The man had moved off. O'Connell nodded for the rest to follow as Sarah took up the rear behind Toby.

Bending into the hill, she felt the first strain on her ribs. Up to this point, she had been able to put the pain from her thoughts; now it became a constant reminder. Reaching the top, she took a moment to readjust the bandage that O'Connell had wrapped tightly around her torso. As she did so, she saw the lone figure of a guard—rifle still in hand—lying faceup not more than twenty feet from her. Blood trickled from the side of his neck, a pinpoint shot to ensure a silent death. Almost immediately, three more *thwits* tore through the night air somewhere off to her left. Sarah crawled after the others, her gun now in hand, her ribs momentarily forgotten. As she drew up behind Toby, she saw the second and third victims of the point man. They lay some sixty yards apart from each other, at either end of the base of the hill leading up to the house. It had been their misfortune to appear at the same moment. The victim of the third shot, however, was nowhere to be seen.

"Spread wide," came the whispered command from O'Connell, the signal that the approach was clear. O'Connell and the two men darted about halfway up the incline, where they were met by the other trio, the men from the first car, who had secured the approach from the back of the house. All six flanked out along the hill, each donning a pair of infrared glasses. As one, they began to crawl to the summit, Sarah noticing the electronics wizard from the fence placing a series of small boxes in his wake. The pace was excruciatingly slow, Toby more than once shifting nervously next to her. "Patience," she whispered, as much to herself as to him. A minute and a half later, the sextet had made it to within ten yards of the house, keeping well back of the light shining from the windows. The man from the fence once again pulled the device from his hood, aimed it; this time, two thin beams of light appeared, forming a narrow path up the hill. Wide enough for one person. They had discussed it beforehand. Neither Toby nor Sarah, with her broken ribs, could be expected to wriggle under the trip wires. Too many risks. Instead, they would wait for the electronic path while the others split into teams of two, each pair targeting a window on one side of the house. By the time Sarah and Toby reached the top, the men were gone. She picked up the device, disengaged the path, and crouched in the grass.

"Remove the lock, Paolo." The Italian did as he was told, then opened the door for Lundsdorf. Inside, Xander lay on a bed, his arm pulled over his eyes in the pose of sleep. Paolo waited by the door as the old man entered.

"You have had some rest, I trust," said Lundsdorf. "You will need it. Put on your shoes and come with me."

Within a minute, the three were in the hallway, Lundsdorf followed by Xander, Paolo a few paces behind. Xander glanced over his shoulder at the

Italian; he recognized the bald head at once. "Did you enjoy Germany," he asked, "or was London more to your liking?" No response save for a quick adjustment of the gun in his hand. The message was clear. However much Lundsdorf might be willing to trust his onetime protégé, Paolo clearly had no such illusions. Anything amiss and he would shoot, perhaps not to kill, but certainly to incapacitate. Xander knew it would be but a short reprieve. Soon enough, the old man would recognize the truth. In some strange way, though, the threat of death was once again having a calming effect. As with the woman in Frankfurt, Xander felt quite at peace. Somehow he knew it would make the violence to come less jarring.

They reached the elevator and waited for the door to open. Lundsdorf motioned for Xander to enter, then Paolo; he then stepped inside himself and tapped the button, all three in quiet darkness as the small chamber descended. Very gently, Paolo slid his hand under Xander's elbow, a move Lundsdorf failed to notice. The two younger men exchanged a glance. Another subtle reminder.

"We have managed all the stages from below," began Lundsdorf. "The first trial in Washington and Chicago, the—what did Arthur call the business with the Capitol, the ambassador, and so forth, Paolo?"

"The mock-up," answered the Italian.

"Quite right. The mock-up. And now the third stage—the acceleration. As with all things great, always in threes. A shame he will not be able to see the best part." He turned to Xander. "But you shall. You will see how things must be, how you must take your place, how destiny must play its part."

Destiny. Lying awake, Xander had not been able to deny with complete certainty the force of the manuscript's logic. Perhaps even its practical application—order, social perfection, permanence. The tapes from last night had made that all too clear. The question remained: If the chaos were to come, would he be able to find the strength, the will to reject the theory? Would he become as blinded by it as Lundsdorf?

Xander stared at the small man standing in front of him. And he knew. He knew that one of them would have to die to make certain that the chaos would never come. An hour ago, he had justified the decision as an answer to Sarah's death. Then, pure brutality had inspired him; now a colder rationale guided his thoughts. Somehow, the line had blurred. Perhaps Lundsdorf had been right to dismiss it as moral indulgence. *"I kill, that's what I do."* Her words came back to him. It would simply be a question of how.

The doors opened and the old man stepped out without a word. Paolo gestured with his head for Xander to follow just as the fluorescent strips above flicked off, replaced by the dim glow of blue lights, the sound of an alarm echoing throughout the hallway. Lundsdorf stopped at once and turned to Paolo. Before Xander could take advantage of the moment, however, he felt the clasp of thick fingers on his upper arm, iron spikes driving into his flesh. Again, Lundsdorf did not seem to notice. A woman appeared behind Paolo.

"Disengage the elevator!" barked Lundsdorf to no one in particular.

Paolo turned to the woman and spoke, maintaining his grip on Xander. "Seal the house, and make sure you open up the secondary vents for the lab." Xander remained silent as several others appeared in the hall, Paolo quick to shout out orders. Lundsdorf, meanwhile, had moved to the lab, undeterred by the events; as the alarm stopped chirping, the lights returning to normal.

Lundsdorf was talking with a technician below when Paolo appeared on the balcony, Xander in tow. "Where do you want Jaspers?"

Preoccupied with the technician, Lundsdorf replied, "That depends on whether he means to behave himself." He now looked up, an odd smile on his lips. "Truly exhilarating down here, would you not agree? Everything but a moment away. I cannot imagine that you would want to miss it, but that, of course, is up to you. For the time being."

Xander said nothing. "I could put him with the other one," suggested Paolo. "Let him think about it."

Lundsdorf slowly began to nod. "Yes. Excellent. He started to move off, then turned back to Xander. "Use the time wisely."

Several mazelike corridors later, Xander found himself in a darkened room, enough light to make out a figure in the far corner.

Silence. Then a voice. "You must be Jaspers."

"Yes," he answered, still trying to gain his eyes. "Who—"

"Stein. Bob Stein. Today must be the open house."

The outline of a bed off to the left began to come clear. "I don't understand," said Xander.

Stein moved away from the wall, toward the bed. A moment later, he pulled back the sheet. "This one arrived about half an hour ago."

Xander stepped slowly to the bed and stared at the face. A lifeless Jonas Tieg peered up at him.

The house went black. Toby turned to Sarah, but she was already crouching her way to the near wall, signaling for him to stay where he was. They both knew this had not been part of the plan. Silently, back flat against the wall, she inched closer to the window; then, raising her head just above the sill, she peered into the darkness. Nothing. Toby was suddenly by her side.

"What the *hell* is going on?" he whispered.

"Quiet!" she said, not bothering to explain. Instead, she watched as a mist began to collect on the inside pane, thousands of gray specks frosting the glass. It took her less than a second to realize what was happening. *Gas.* Sarah reached for her gun so as to shatter the window, only to stop as the sound of a motor broke through the silence. Before she could react, a steel door, the height of the window, began to slide across the sill. It was only then that she spotted the narrow runner guiding the door to the far wall. Turning to Toby, she grabbed the pack, hunting for the canisters of liquid Mace she had placed inside less than two hours ago. The size of beer cans, the canisters were pressurized and made of reinforced metal, dense enough to slow the door's progress. She pulled out the three cans and positioned them lengthwise on the sill. She then removed two gas·masks from the pack.

"Put this on!" she ordered. Hers was already in place when the sliding door met the first canister, the door's motor grinding more angrily, her gun smashing into the glass an instant later, a wave of gray smoke pouring out as she hoisted herself to the ledge and forced her way through the shards of glass. She then reached out and pulled Toby to the sill as the first canister began to let off a high-pitched squeal, the sound of imminent explosion. Without prompting, Toby tossed the pack through and dove in, his pants leg ripping on an errant piece of glass. Sarah yanked him free as the strain on the can reached critical, both of them falling into the room before the can exploded. A moment later, the other two canisters spun harmlessly from their perch as the steel door slid shut against the wall.

A harsh residue of gas hung in the air, biting at their unprotected skin, both of them quick to pull their turtlenecks higher on their cheeks. Sarah found a flashlight in her pack and flicked it on, watching as a thin beam cut through the dusted air. The room seemed to shimmer, tiny flecks of moisture spinning from the ceiling in strands of fine wire. She handed the pack to Toby and pulled her gun from its holster. Without a sound, she eased the door open. The hallway stood dark and empty, a heavy mist settling on its wooden floor. Sarah darted out, stopping some twenty feet down in front of a second door; she motioned for Toby to stay back. She reached for the handle.

From nowhere, an arm reached out and grabbed her gun, the strength of the grip enough to pull her into the room. Her flashlight streaked to a distant wall; somehow, she managed to hold on to the weapon, discharging two bursts in the direction of her assailant. The shots flew wild as a figure appeared out of the darkness, its massive frame outlined in a strange glow.

"*Don't shoot, Toby!*" the command echoed in her mask. It was O'Connell. Sarah peered around the Irishman and saw Toby kneeling in the doorway, his gun raised. Two other men from the team now appeared, one quick to take the gun and place it in Toby's holster. The other signaled all was clear. Within a minute, all five were moving along the corridor, the point man raising his hand as they approached an archway, the living room beyond. Inside, three others waited. The gas, Sarah realized, had been a blessing in disguise. It had forced Eisenreich to take shelter below.

"Trace the corridors for anything that might get us downstairs. Let's be quick about it, lads." Turning to Sarah, O'Connell added, "You and Toby stay here." Sarah watched as the five men disappeared through the various archways. Three minutes later, a voice broke the silence.

"We have an elevator in the eastern corridor. Steel door. Sealed. We also have six or seven people who didn't quite make it out before the gas."

"Move them," it was O'Connell, "but don't touch the elevator. We'll be right there."

☖

Lundsdorf sat at a desk, the area slightly elevated, though tucked under the balcony and secured behind thick glass walls, his eyes closed, his hands folded gently in his lap. A message flashed across the large screen. Five minutes to code initialization. Votapek sat at a smaller desk to Lundsdorf's left, far less comfortable amid the preparations.

"And if they *do* find a way through?"

"They will not," answered Lundsdorf. "There *are* no other ways through, except for the elevator, and that has been disconnected and sealed."

"Yes, but—"

"Even if they do come, Anton, they will be too late." A curious smile spread across his lips as his eyes opened. "It is quite possible that both you and I will be killed. Oh, yes. It is often the response of the violent to lash out when they are forced to recognize their own failure." He turned to Votapek. "And yet they would not touch Xander. They would save him"— the smile grew wide—"thus forcing him to witness the chaos to come. Only then would he be granted his treasured choice: watch a world destroy itself, or make use of the structure I have set in place. Ironic, no? By saving him, it is *they* who will have made the choice for him. In the end, he will not be able to deny the force of the manuscript. This I know, Anton. And for this I am willing to die." Votapek could only nod, unable to find the words. Lundsdorf glanced at the clock on the wall. "Four minutes before the final codes." He looked back at Votapek. "Mark my words. Xander will thank me. One day, he will thank me."

The smallest of the five men crouched by the elevator, pressing his thumbs into a thick claylike mound, making sure to smear the entire lower-right-hand corner of the door with the substance. He then pulled a thin metal strip no bigger than a stick of gum from his pocket, shaped a tiny hillock within the mound, and wedged the strip into it. "Step back," he said.

Sarah watched as the mound began to heat up, soon bubbling into a red mass, a lick of a flame at its center. In a sudden flash, a spark ignited and began to race up the length of the elevator, a fuse seemingly in search of explosives; halfway to the ceiling, the spark darted right, momentarily gone, then reappeared as a pulsing dot coursing behind the wall's plaster.

"Locates the source of power," said O'Connell. "All very much in the experimental stages."

About three feet from the door, the dot flared bright and then vanished, the man already at the point of implosion to chisel out a section of the wall. The sound of steel on steel forced him to stop; he began to apply another wad of clay to the area, this time, though, much thicker. The man worked far more delicately, careful to leave a thin border of steel untouched. He then pulled several wafer-thin strips of something resembling dried mud from his pack and placed each one in the mound in a little rectangle. Again, he produced a strip of metal, sunk it into the clay, and stepped back. This time, there was no spark, only intense heat, a blue flame that literally ate into the steel. Within seconds, it had cut through to open air; almost at once, the flame fizzled out, for some reason uninterested in the wires it had just revealed. Scraping out the excess with his knife, he explained, "Only eats through metals."

The electronics man now stepped in and stripped the casing from the wires; he pulled what looked to be a voltage meter from his pack and tested each line. Then, removing yet another box, he clamped it to two of the exposed wires and flicked a switch on its side; a moment later, the elevator door released and slid about two inches from the wall. "Magnetics reversed," he said. Immediately, the man with the clay wedged two cylinders into the opening, placing them about four inches from the ceiling and floor. Very slowly, the tiny objects began to expand, pushing the door farther and farther from the wall; locking in placing, they created just enough room for a single body to slip through. O'Connell peered down the shaft.

"It's about a hundred feet," he said, scrutinizing the area with his flashlight. "Bad news is, the cables have been cut."

He stepped to the side as two of the other men now removed long coils of nylon line, clipped them to the top cylinder, and tossed the lines into the shaft. One by one they rappelled down. The remaining six watched as the cords stretched taut, twin lines beating out the descent in contrapuntal intervals. Half a minute passed before a voice came through. "Solid steel, boys, the whole way down." The twang was Deep South. "No chance of gettin' into that car. It looks like we're goin' to have to go huntin' for hollows." Sarah turned to O'Connell for explanation.

"Ducts or vents behind the shaft," he answered. "Another toy we're using these days. A little device that sends out a high-pitched tone, then checks for resonance. Determines location and size. We'll see if we get lucky."

Two minutes into the search, he had his answer. "We got us one about twenty feet from the base," came the voice from below. "By the sound of it, might even be wide enough for you, O'Connell." No sooner had the information piped through than the man with the clay reached for a line and disappeared into the shaft. Within a minute, a blue glow began to emanate from the darkness.

It wasn't long before the southerner once again broke the silence. "We got us an openin', folks. Time to go huntin'."

※

"Reverse the last two in the sequence, then reenter," said Lundsdorf, his eyes scanning the three terminals directly in front of him. He removed his finger from the intercom and sat back. "You see how simple it is, Anton. How simple a thing it is to alter the very name of supremacy."

"Yes, I . . . can see that," answered Votapek. He had grown far less comfortable in the last four minutes. "I thought Jonas would be joining us. And Alison. That everything had been . . . cleared up."

"Do you think we should have Jaspers here when it engages?" Votapek said nothing. "You know, it suddenly strikes me, Anton, Xander has never seen all three of the manuscripts together." Lundsdorf caressed the ancient volumes on the desk in front of him. "What a treat that will be." He pressed down on the intercom. "Paolo, would you be so kind as to fetch Dr. Jaspers?"

There was a pause before the Italian responded. "Do you think that would be . . . wise, to have him out in the open while—"

"Are you questioning me, Paolo?" Lundsdorf waited. "Good. Then bring him." He turned again to Votapek, a quizzical smile in his eyes. "You look troubled, Anton. Am I wrong to think you would prefer not to be here? Is the prospect of death so frightening?" Votapek remained silent. Lundsdorf nodded. "Perhaps you are right. Perhaps you should go." Lundsdorf reached under the desk. Before Votapek could react, a door cracked open behind the old man, a sudden burst of cold air streaming into the booth. "So you see, there was another way through. Paolo's idea. I never understood, but now, of course, I see it does serve a purpose. A tunnel. A car waits at the other end." Votapek hesitated, then stood. "Do not run too far away, Anton. I will need you in the weeks to come." Votapek moved to the door. "What a shame, though. To have come all this way and to miss such a perfect moment."

※

Sarah was the last into the vent, the aluminum casing leaving her about four inches to maneuver on either side. To make things easier, the man at the front had been greasing the duct as he went; even so, she could feel each metal seam as she pulled herself along, her ribs throbbing. The grease, though, had been more for O'Connell, the Irishman having taken several stabs at entry before squeezing himself in. Amused by it all, Toby had chosen that moment to describe his strict aversion to tight spaces, prompting O'Connell to say something about *other* tight spaces. Toby had quickly taken the line, hoisted himself up, and had slipped quietly into the vent.

About thirty feet in, the small convoy stopped. "It splits off," said the lead man. "Looks like six different tunnels."

"Slice out a look," ordered O'Connell, his breathing already heavy from the jaunt. Lying on her stomach, Sarah pressed her fingers into the metallic walls and understood what he had meant. A sharp knife would be able to penetrate the casing and give the man a view of the area below.

"It's insulation strips and a lot of wiring," came the response, "most of it heading along one of the left-hand branches, back the way we came."

"Is there any green coiled wire?" It was Toby who spoke, his tone more serious than Sarah expected. "Anything that looks . . . like a thick Slinky?"

Silence. "Yeah. Wrapped in something like Saran Wrap. It runs separately, but in the same direction as most of the wires."

"That's it," answered Toby. "It's what they're using for the satellite hookups. Whichever way it goes, that's where you'll find the op center."

"Then we go the other way," O'Connell cut in. "Some place nice and quiet to get out of these vents. Pick another tunnel, then move your ass."

⋌

Paolo clutched Xander's arm as he led him down the corridor, neither saying a word, no explanations of Stein or Tieg. The request had been curt, the gun an unnecessary inducement. Now, as they neared the elevator, the Italian suddenly stopped. No warning as the grip on Xander's arm grew tighter. For a moment, Paolo stared into the distance; he then cocked his head to the left, eyes lost in concentration. He spun quickly to his right, his expression far more animated as he began to sniff at the air. A moment later, the radio was at his lips. As the Italian spoke, he stared at his captive.

"Professor. . . . Yes, I have him. . . . No, but traces of the gas are coming in through the vents. . . . Exactly. I suggest— Yes, of course." Paolo pulled the radio from his mouth, flicked a switch on its side, and spoke again. "Seal the vents. . . . Fine, then open up the auxiliaries. I'm also going to need men. . . . No, they could be anywhere. . . . Start wide, pull to the center. . . . And lock down the lab. I'll be with the professor." Paolo returned the radio to his belt and ushered Xander down the hall. A moment later, the fluorescents disappeared and the blue lights reengaged, Paolo's grip on his arm having grown considerably tighter. "Your friends are making this more entertaining than I expected. Don't worry. The fun's about to come to an end."

⚔

Sarah was the last to jump from the vent to the cement floor, a storage room with boxes piled high. "Toss the masks," said O'Connell as he knelt at the door and drew his gun. He tried the handle—no luck. Moving away, he nodded for the man with the clay to take care of the lock. A minute later, O'Connell pulled back the door and slowly edged his face out into the blue light. No sooner had he done so than he raised his gun and fired.

The point man quickly darted out into the hall, only to return with a dead woman in his arms. He placed her on one of the crates, drew his gun, and nodded for the others to follow. Five seconds later, O'Connell and the electronics man slipped out, then three more, and finally Toby and Sarah.

She found herself scurrying through an open area, a space perhaps twenty-five feet by thirty, six numbered doors along each wall. The only exit stood in the middle of the far wall, the point man leading them toward it and—according to Toby's green-wire theory—the operation center. Weaving her way through tables and chairs, Sarah noticed a pool table and television set on opposite ends of a galley kitchen—all the trappings of living quarters for those planning to spend an extended period of time underground. *A bunker,* she thought. *How appropriate.* At the exit, she heard the sound of a snap. Like the others, she stopped. The man at the front was cautiously edging his way around a distant corner, a second snap moments later to indicate all was clear. Once again, they started moving in pairs. Sarah matched Toby stride for stride until another snap, another junction of corridors. She watched as the point man and O'Connell spoke, both of them nodding before O'Connell turned to the team and strapped on a second set of lenses they all carried. The rest did the same, Sarah unsure what he had seen to warrant the change. He then disappeared around the corner, Sarah the last to make the turn.

Instantly, she knew they had made a mistake. The corridor was too long, too narrow, and with no place for them to take cover. Instinct screamed at her to pull Toby back, but before she could turn, men had appeared at either end of the hall, guns drawn. The next few seconds were the longest she had ever known as she waited for the icy lance of bullets to drive into her flesh; instead, a bright flash exploded all around her, her sight momentarily lost, gunfire everywhere, no time to ask why she was still alive. She scrambled to her left, firing behind her wildly, her eyes clearing to reveal the men of Eisenreich scattering in confusion. She watched as they groped for the walls, for one another, for some way out of the darkness; then she understood.

The flash had blinded them.

O'Connell had known, and he had been ready. He had baited them out, and they had come. Within fifteen seconds, the corridor had fallen silent again.

Seven men lay dead, one wounded, none from the team who now pulled the lenses from their eyes. O'Connell moved to the wounded man and hoisted him to his feet, pressing his fingers into the soft flesh of the man's throat.

"You're the lucky one, aren't you?" he whispered. "So I'm going to ask you once, and then not again. You may choose to answer, or you may choose to die." O'Connell drove his fingers deeper into the skin. "Where are the computers, and how much security?"

The man shook his head once.

Without hesitation, O'Connell aimed the silencer and shot the man in the kneecap, all the while holding on to his throat so as to stifle the scream. Saliva dripped from the man's mouth, his entire body shaking. "I didn't say *how* I'd kill you," added the Irishman, "but now that's *my* choice, isn't it?"

"Third corridor . . . left," came the choked response, "vault door . . . ten technicians . . . unarmed—"

O'Connell swung his gun across the man's chin and let the body fall to the ground. Two minutes later, the team passed the elevator and stopped ten feet from the steel door that guarded the entrance to the lab.

"I don't think I trust our friend back there," said O'Connell, the demolitions expert already at the door. "Not likely they'll be unarmed. Keep Toby back. And put on the lenses." He turned to the computer man. "We wouldn't want to lose you this late in the game, now would we, Toby?"

Half a minute later, the air lock on the door released, leaving a space wide enough for two more of the small cylinders, this pair far more powerful than their predecessors. The sound of voices and running feet spilled from the lab, the movement in stark contrast to the easy posture of the man at the door; he calmly removed two canisters, twisted the tops of each, and tossed them through the ever-expanding gap. Bracing for the explosion, he turned away as a series of blinding flashes erupted beyond the door. Then, dropping to a crouch, he spun through the opening and into the lab, four others from the team quickly behind him. O'Connell followed. Sarah waited until her old friend was through the opening and then slipped past the door, Toby in tow.

The scene from the balcony was unreal, men and women below fumbling along the floor, others against the wall, hands and fingers trying to give direction to their sightless eyes. Still others sat in front of terminals, staring aimlessly into screens they could no longer see. A few guns lay scattered here and there, dropped or lost at the instant of blinding explosion, none a threat to the men who cautiously descended the stairs. Sarah scanned the faces for Xander, the team already tying up its captives, O'Connell pulling explosives from his pack. As she reached the bottom step, a hollow pain rose in her stomach—too easy. And there was still no sign of Xander.

"Welcome." A voice boomed from an unseen monitor; almost at once, a series of steel slats snapped open from underneath the balcony, revealing a glass-encased booth. Inside, Xander stood at center, his arm in the grasp of a second man, still another man seated to their left, behind a desk. It took Sarah a moment to recognize the face. "Ah, Miss Trent," continued Lundsdorf, "you are alive. How interesting. One of these others, no doubt, is our mysterious motorcyclist—perhaps the large fellow with the explosives?" Sarah kept her eyes on the glassed-in trio. "No matter," he added. "As you can see, Dr. Jaspers is here with *me;* together, we have just witnessed a most remarkable moment. Can you guess, Miss Trent?" He paused. "Quite right. The codes—*all* transmitted. You and your friends are naturally free to tie up my staff, but it would appear that you have come a bit too late. The final stage cannot be reversed."

Sarah looked at Xander. His face showed no emotion, no reaction to Lundsdorf's words, only a vacant stare. For several seconds, all movement seemed to stop, until Xander turned toward the glass, his gaze fixed on her, his expression unchanged. "Blow it up," he said, his voice as distant as his eyes. "I'm dead anyway. Just—"

"That would not make any difference," interrupted Lundsdorf. "What Dr. Jaspers does not realize is that any attempt to do so would only trigger an . . . *automatic pilot.* . . . I believe that is what Arthur called it. Something to do with satellites and stored information, that sort of thing. You may, of course, do what you will with your devices, but you should know that even an explosion here in the lab would have little impact. True, our ability to monitor the teams over the next few days would be severely limited, but the overall results would be the same. A little less control for me, but one learns to adapt as one grows older." He smiled again and looked at Jaspers. "Does that surprise you, Xander?"

Jaspers said nothing; O'Connell turned to his computer man. "Is what he is saying true?"

"I . . . don't know," answered Toby. "I'd have to—" He stopped and looked up at the booth.

"Go right ahead, young man," said Lundsdorf. "See for yourself."

Toby turned to the nearest terminal and typed in a few words. "I don't know. These are substations, secondary terminals. They process information only when they're hooked into the mainframe. Otherwise, they stay dormant. Right now, they're off. Until I see the big boy, I can't be sure."

"Oh, you can be sure, my young friend," answered Lundsdorf.

Sarah had kept her focus on Xander throughout the exchange, drawn by the strange detachment in his eyes, a look she had seen only once before— at the motel when he had recalled Feric's death. Now, however, she sensed something behind the stare, a strength. It seemed to grow, focus his thoughts, until, with a sudden explosion of movement, he lunged across the desk at Lundsdorf.

Immediately, Paolo was on him, a gun pressed deep into his neck. The Italian pulled Xander to his feet and lowered the gun to his ribs.

The surprise in Lundsdorf's eyes was all too apparent; Xander's expression, however, remained unmoved. "Put that away, Paolo," ordered Lundsdorf as he adjusted himself in the chair.

"Why?" asked Xander, his voice quiet. "Why wait? You killed Tieg; you're going to kill me. Why not be done with it?"

"I *said*, put it away."

"You even have an audience," he continued. "Doesn't that excite your—"

"Enough," said Lundsdorf, a pronounced anger in his tone.

"Paolo knows I'm right, don't you, Paolo?"

The Italian looked at Lundsdorf. The old man spoke. "Put it down."

Paolo hesitated. "He'll never do what you ask of him."

"Put it down, Paolo! You do not understand. I will not tolerate another Wolfenbüttel." Lundsdorf looked at Xander. "Stop this foolishness at once."

"What do you think, Paolo?" prodded Xander. "*Do* you understand?"

"Let me finish it," insisted the Italian. "He's not worth—"

"Has no one *heard* me!" roared Lundsdorf. "You think I do not know what you are doing, *Dr.* Jaspers? You think I cannot see through this little ruse? It is a very dangerous gamble you take."

Xander stared into the Italian's eyes. "Do it, Paolo. Save us all the time. Pull the trigger."

The Italian looked again at Lundsdorf, then at Xander. His jaw tensed; a moment later, the sound of a single shot rang out inside the booth. For several seconds, nothing seemed to move. Then, very slowly, Paolo dropped to his knees, his eyes wide in disbelief. He fell, his head smacking against the floor. "He would have done what you asked," said Lundsdorf, his voice once again controlled, a small pistol in his hands. "I could not permit that."

Sarah and the others watched as the bizarre scene played out, Xander now moving to the desk, reaching over and taking the gun from the old man.

"But you knew that," smiled Lundsdorf, his expression almost childlike. "And now, you will kill me. How well you have managed the situation."

Xander remained strangely calm, the gun held between them. "No," he answered, "you're going to tell me how to stop all of this; somehow, I don't believe it's as irreversible as you say."

"Trust me," answered Lundsdorf, "there is nothing you can do."

"Really?" Xander aimed the gun at his own chest. "What happens if I use this on myself?" He paused. "Where would that leave you and your *destiny?*"

The old man's smile slowly fell from his face. "You would not do that."

Xander stared into Lundsdorf's eyes. "Do you really believe that?"

Neither moved for nearly half a minute. Then, very slowly, Lundsdorf leaned forward as if to say something. For an instant, Xander relaxed. The old man grabbed at the gun, pulled it to his own chest, and squeezed the trigger. A momentary tremor in his shoulders, and he slumped back in the chair. Lundsdorf stared up at Xander, a weak smile on his face.

"The question, it would appear," he whispered, "is, What will *you* do?" He coughed once. "The generals or the manuscript? Violence or order? Chaos or permanence?" Blood appeared on his lip. "The owl of Minerva has taken wing. And now, there is no choice. There never *was* one." Lundsdorf's head fell to the side, the smile imprinted on his face.

Xander stared helplessly at the lifeless body, the gun still in his own hands. He spun toward the glass, threw the gun into the corner of the booth, and stared at Sarah. "*Find* me a choice. Get your damn computer expert in here and *find me a choice!*" He pressed a button on the desk and a door opened under the stairs.

Toby was the first through, eager to take a seat in front of one of the keyboards; within seconds, the sound of rapid-fire typing filled the space as O'Connell entered the booth. Xander had moved to the glass wall, his arms folded at his chest, his eyes fixed on the ground. There was nothing he could do now. The typing stopped and he looked up. O'Connell had moved to Toby's side, both scanning the various screens for any hint of how to disarm the programming. It was then that Xander saw Sarah at the door. Their eyes met; neither said a word. The typing resumed and she moved toward him.

"They told me you were dead," he said, his hands clenched even tighter at his chest. "I—"

"A few broken ribs. I'll survive."

He nodded just as Toby's frustration took focus.

"*Jesus,* what the hell do they have in here?" He continued to stare at the screens as Xander and Sarah turned to him. "The old guy wasn't lying. There's no way to reverse what they've sent out. If I try to recall any of these command codes, the system'll lock me out. The whole thing'll shut down, and the computers will take over the tracking. I can't even get inside the compiler to try to reroute it in binary."

"So there's nothing you can do?" asked Sarah, now at the desk.

"No." He started to gnaw at his thumbnail. "It's just that we might be here awhile."

"What about names?" asked O'Connell. "There has to be a list of who's out there. We get that, we can stop them before they get their relays."

"Been there, done that," answered Toby. "I almost got frozen out of the terminal. These guys weren't fooling around. They knew exactly what they were doing."

The booth became very quiet. "What about Pritchard?" The three at the desk looked up. It was Xander who spoke.

"Excuse me?" said Toby, unwilling to hide his irritation.

"Didn't you say it looked like a . . . Pritchard matrix?" Xander continued, ignoring the computer expert. "Wouldn't that give you some idea—"

"Pritchard." O'Connell nodded. "Nice point, Professor. He'd have put something inside, wouldn't he?"

"Hello." Toby was beyond frustration. *"What* are you talking about?"

O'Connell ignored him and turned to Sarah. "Well?"

"I don't know." Her eyes began to wander. "It could be any number of—"

"Would Stein know?"

Again, all three turned to Jaspers. O'Connell spoke. "Bob Stein?"

"He's here. Could he help?"

O'Connell continued to stare at Jaspers. The Irishman nodded slowly. "If it's computers and Arthur—"

Two minutes later, a slightly disoriented Stein sat in the chair next to Toby, Sarah and O'Connell speaking at him in quick bursts.

"Override relays," Bob said softly. Both stopped and stared at him. No one answered. "Remember?" Sarah shook her head. "The *delay* commands in Amman?" He paused. "Arthur had a thing for override relays."

Sarah's eyes slowly went wide. "The delays came from *Pritchard*?"

"Yes." Stein nodded.

The confirmation only seemed to add to her confusion. "Wait a second. So that would mean—"

"Yes," he answered. "It's why you couldn't have saved her." Stein was looking directly at Sarah. "I went back and checked. Pritchard created the delay because he needed the girl as bait. The longer he kept her as a target, the easier it would be for you to get at Safad. You never had a chance to save her. He gave you no choice." Bob let the words settle, then turned to O'Connell. "Arthur had a thing for timing. He had to have complete control over each phase of an operation. That's what he would have put into the system—the one thing that would circumvent the lockouts."

"Would someone mind explaining to *me* what the hell you're talking about?" Toby piped in. "Or does the computer guy not need to be in on this?"

"A delay command," answered Stein. "It won't allow you to establish new directives, but it will let you delay the ones that have been transmitted—*indefinitely*."

"A delay command?" repeated Toby. "Meaning . . ."

"Arthur liked the timing to be perfect," he answered. "If anything was off cue, he'd send out a delay until he could bring everything into line. He'd have buried some sort of delay command deep in the programming."

"So you'd just sit there," asked Toby, turning to Sarah, "and wait for the next series of commands after the delay? What if nothing came?"

"Then nothing came," she answered, more to herself, eyes still distant, the memory growing clearer.

"You'd wait for contact," added Stein, "and, if and when it *did* come, it was always prompted by a different set of codes."

"So we're talking a delay pattern with altered sequencing." Toby was back in his element.

Again he began to type, fingers and eyes working at breakneck speed as myriad screens appeared and disappeared, all filled with strange symbols.

For the first time in the last minute, Sarah looked up. She gazed at Xander. Neither said a word.

After a very long three minutes, Toby stopped and sat back.

"Nice pop." He nodded at the screen. "You're looking at your back door. A simple delay switch. Two problems, though. At this point, I can't be sure that the command to delay would reach each team."

"Meaning what?" It was O'Connell who spoke.

"Meaning you might not be able to stop the first few relays."

"How many?" asked Sarah, once again fully focused.

"I don't know."

"*Guess,*" prodded O'Connell.

"Anything that would take place, say, within the next six hours."

"That's at most three more events," he said. "I can live with that. And the second problem?"

"According to this, I send out the delay and everything gets erased."

"Correct," Bob agreed. "That was why the codes were different in Amman."

"Where he'd be forced to reinitialize the system in order to send out the new relays." Toby smiled, wrapped up in the banter. "An op reinterface: new relays, new codes."

"The software lesson aside," asked O'Connell, "what do you mean, 'erased'?"

"I mean *every* last byte of info gets flushed, wiped clean. Zippo."

"There's nothing you can do about it," nodded Stein.

"It means," added Toby, "whoever set this thing up didn't want anyone to send out the delay without a pretty good reason. It also means that it was designed so that if anybody were to find the back door—like us—they don't get to look in the cupboard once they've broken in."

"We lose everything?" asked Sarah.

"Am I not being clear here?" answered Toby. "Nada. Nothing. Not even a cursor. You won't need any explosives because there won't be anything worth blowing up." No one spoke. "So what's it going to be, folks? Delay or not?"

For several moments, no one said a word.

"There are going to be a lot of people sitting around waiting to hear from Eisenreich," said Sarah, "and we won't know who they are." She looked at O'Connell. "We also won't know how many schools are out there training a whole new generation of disciples."

"And the *other* alternatives?" broke in Xander. "If we don't send it out, we'll know *exactly* who they are—they'll be the ones turning this country upside down during the next eight days."

"So we just let them disappear into the woodwork?" asked O'Connell.

"They're already out there," Xander explained. "Waiting. So we'll tell them to wait a bit longer. Let's not forget how Eisenreich set it up, what the manuscript stipulates: role playing. With Lundsdorf dead, where's the source? Who'll send out the new codes? Votapek? Sedgewick? I'm sure those are exactly the kinds of *loose ends* one of your national security agencies can eliminate." Xander looked at O'Connell, then at Sarah. "The best we can do is let the boys and girls of Eisenreich wait for an order that never comes."

"And when they grow up?" she asked.

"Without the manuscript, without someone spoon-feeding them *'the word according to Eisenreich,'* they won't do anything. They need to be told what to do, and there won't be anybody around to do that."

O'Connell took in a long breath. "You're putting a lot of faith in a four-hundred-year-old theory, Professor."

"No. I'm putting my faith in the men who followed that theory to the letter. They wanted to create disciples, not leaders. We just have to hope they were successful." He turned to Toby. "Send the delay. Tell them . . . to remain patient."

Toby looked at O'Connell, who looked at Sarah. She nodded. A moment later, every screen in the lab went blank.

✄

Toby had been right, almost to the minute. For six hours, the nation lived through a series of near tragedies. First, the attempted assassination of Lung Tse Pao, senior member of the Chinese trade delegation. Luckily, the gunmen had been discovered only minutes before her televised speech, both killed, no names released. Questions, however, remained. Where had security been? Was this somehow connected to the ongoing incidents in Washington? New Orleans? The ambassador? Two hours later, computer malfunctions at LAX only fueled speculation. There, too, last-minute heroics prevented certain disaster; even so, a sense of disbelief, perhaps hints of panic, began to flood radio and television news programs. Were the police and other agencies helpless? Had the United States finally fallen prey to worldwide terrorism? Still other, equally jarring stories continued to trickle in—the worst, the near meltdown at Southwestern Bell—each uncovered in time to prevent catastrophe, yet each only adding to the already-high levels of anxiety. So many threats in so short a time. Were things spinning out of control?

News of real tragedy, however, came just as the evening news programs were airing. The body of Vice President Pembroke had been discovered in his office, the cause of death heart failure. In an address to the nation, President Wainwright spoke of the great sadness his friend's sudden death had brought to the entire country. A man in perfect health only a few months before, the forty-five-year-old Pembroke had succumbed to an unknown virus evidently contracted during a recent trip to Malaysia. Doctors at the Hopkins Center for Viral Disease could offer little more by way of explanation.

The president then turned to the more disturbing matters of the day. He spoke with the easy familiarity that had long ago endeared him to his public.

"Over the last week, we have witnessed an unspeakable series of attacks, each meant to shake our spirit. And yet, at each turn, we have triumphed. At each turn, we have thwarted those who would seek to lay siege to our peace of mind, to a way of life we have come to cherish. And though—I have no doubt—there were moments of fear, perhaps panic, not once did we give in to those threats. No. We saw them for what they were—a banner by which to make clear to a watching world the resilience and courage of the American people. These attacks were mad, outlandish, but we must grant them no more than their due, and we must recognize how they most certainly pale when compared to the real loss of this day—the death of Walter Pembroke.

"We grieve at the tragedy, we accept its truth, and yet, we also learn from it. The death of the vice president must help us to put into perspective the bizarre events of the last week. They did *not* shake us. They did *not* undermine our trust. The country is strong, safe—safe to mourn the one *real* tragedy of the day. We must now look to ourselves and put our apprehensions to rest. It is, I know, what Walter Pembroke would have wanted."

By week's end, few questioned the president's sage advice.

⚔

Sadly, tragedy did strike again two days later when Tieg Telecom announced the death of their inspiration, their shining light, Jonas Tieg. He, too, had fallen prey to heart failure, and though his adoring public mourned his loss—and Amy Chandler his ratings—they were all far too caught up in the aftermath of recent events to take more than passing notice. There were some questions about the strangely prophetic program aired on the night before his death, the tape on which Tieg seemed to anticipate several of the near tragedies that had occurred the following day. Amid all the confusion, however, discussion of the show quickly faded. Articles were written, a retrospective on his life aired, but within a few weeks, a new, rising star appeared on another network—more abusive, more abrasive. And the Tieg phenomenon slipped easily into a forgotten past.

⚔

That same week, news of Laurence Sedgewick's mysterious disappearance made it to the back pages of several national papers. His bank accounts untouched, files intact at his offices in New Orleans, it looked as though he had once again been caught with his hand in the till.

⚔

Not quite the same attention was given to the death of a rather esteemed, if obscure, political theorist, whose passing managed only a few lines in the *New York Times*. Herman Lundsdorf had died in his sleep, so they reported, at the age of eighty-six. A solitary man, his books remained his only legacy.

⚔

Few of the articles, however, elicited more than a moment's perusal from the residents of a small farm in Maryland. They were too busy with other things. The owner, an Irishman somewhat famous among the locals for his reclusiveness, had begun to show real signs of life, chatting up customers at the town market, and even inviting one or two out to the house. Most of the gentry attributed the sudden change in O'Connell to the young woman who seemed to be always at his side. She, too, was flowering, more and more at ease with each passing week. Haiden Dalgliesh, the grounds-keeper at the farm, had even started up a pool—how soon before the Irish-man would make an honest woman of young Alison. Not usually a betting man, Gaelin had put a fiver on a date in late September.

Epilogue

PATCHES OF SNOW peppered the wide expanse of manicured grass. The augurs had promised it would be the last of the season; the clear sky seemed to be proving them right.

Xander and Sarah sat on a bench a good distance from the grave, neither much interested in the inscription, neither absolutely sure why they had made the trip. He had phoned and asked her to come, the first time they had spoken in several weeks. The time apart had been particularly hard on him, the strange good-bye, the sudden aimlessness, but he had known it was for the best. She had said she needed to spend time on her own, start again, find her way back. He should try to do the same. The week on Hydra, however, had done little to help. Only memories of Fiona. Still, it had been time away.

Now, sitting side by side, they peered at the name Lundsdorf. Perhaps they needed to see it for themselves. Together, one last time.

They had both missed the funeral—or rather, they had been *unavailable* that weekend, sequestered at a small house somewhere in the Virginia countryside. The debriefing specialists had been rather unhappy to learn that there were no names or files to help them mop up the loose ends. Manuscripts and documents were evidently not to their liking. Xander had pleaded with them to destroy everything. They, in turn, had assured him that they would "handle the material with the utmost sensitivity." *Not* good enough, he had explained. *Not* his concern, they had answered. It was only when the president had called to offer his personal guarantee that everything would be *fully* secured that Xander had backed down. What else could he do? There was still the small matter of the charges connecting the two of them to Schenten's assassination, Huber's death, and whatever else had cropped up along the way. "You let us take care of this, Doctor, and we'll forget about all of that," the president had said. "Of course, if there's anything else . . ."

Bob Stein had been a bit more helpful, but even he had admitted that the boys at Langley didn't like to share, even with the folks who had started the ball rolling. Pritchard's role had placed COS in a rather delicate position; they would need a little time to win back the skeptics. Until then, everyone would have to trust that the manuscript was in safe hands, or at least that it had been locked away somewhere. For the time being, though, he would be cleaning house. That is, of course, after some well-earned vacation time. Two days chained to a bed had left a few scars. The Bahamas, Bob had heard, were especially nice this time of year. He'd be in touch.

That had been two weeks ago.

"What are you thinking," asked Sarah, arcing her back to relieve the strain in her ribs.

"I don't know. Votapek, Sedgewick. I'd like to know that they've been handled with the 'utmost sensitivity.'" He continued to stare out at the undulating rows of stones. "Feric . . ." He looked at her. "Anyway. Are those better?"

"They will be." She smiled. "As long as I keep them out of air vents and computer labs. They'll be fine. Just like everything else." She turned to him and took his hand. "Xander, I came here because I need you to know that. Things will begin to make sense. They always do."

He nodded. "So once again, I have no choice but to trust you, do I?"

"You have to let it go. It's never going to leave on its own, so *you* have to let it go."

"And do what?" He took in a long strain of air. "Academia isn't exactly the most appealing place right now. Not that they'd have me back. Even exonerated assassins don't really fit in."

"Then look to what you know."

He paused, then turned to her. "Right now, Sarah, that would be you."

She squeezed his hand tenderly. "I wish it were that easy."

"So do I," he answered. "So do I."

She waited and then pulled an envelope from her bag. She placed it on his lap.

"What's this?"

"Notes. A manuscript." She looked at him. "I took it from Lundsdorf's lair, buried it before we were picked up. Maybe you can start there. I thought someone who understood it should have it."

Xander slowly opened the flap and stared at the pages inside. The Italian version. He then looked at her. "You should have burned this."

She shook her head and smiled. "That's up to you." She then let out a deep breath and stood. "Have we seen what we came to see?"

"I suppose." He closed the envelope. "I'm still not exactly sure what that was."

"A beginning." She looked out over the expanse and then turned back to him. "There's an eight o'clock flight out of Kennedy. I'd like to try and make it."

He looked up at her, nodded. "I understand. I'll give you a lift." He stood; they began to walk.

Very gently, she slipped her arm through his. "Have you ever been to Florence in the early spring, Professor? I hear it's quite beautiful."

"That's what they say."

"I've only been once. I was very lucky, though. I had a charming guide. I was thinking . . . it would be nice to find him again."

Xander stopped. He turned to her and peered into her eyes. "Are you asking me along, Ms. Trent?"

She smiled. "It does look that way, doesn't it?"

"On doctor's orders?"

"Intuition." She took his hand. "Let's just call it a beginning. Right now, I think that's the best either of us can do."

A light rain began to fall. She pulled him to her side and they started to walk.

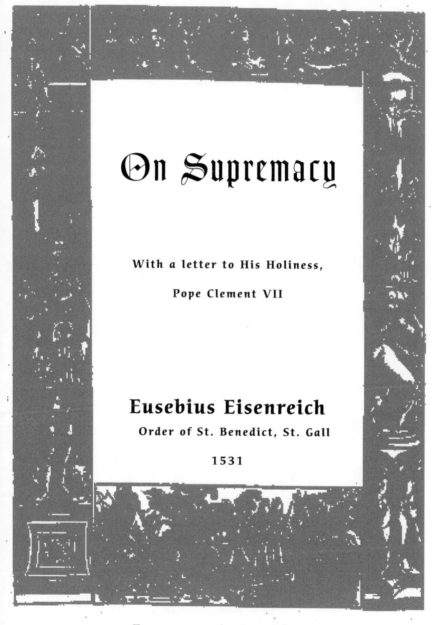

On Supremacy

With a letter to His Holiness,

Pope Clement VII

Eusebius Eisenreich

Order of St. Benedict, St. Gall

1531

Translated by Alexander Jaspers
Institute of Cultural Research
Columbia University

From Eusebius Iacobus Eisenreich to His Holiness, the Most Holy Father, Pope Clement VII

It is now the preferred course for men who seek patronage to offer some gift of inestimable worth to those of great dominion, some token that expresses both deference and ambition. Men bestow lands, jewels, even daughters in the hopes of currying favor with one of high station. But such things have fleeting value, and all too often serve only to quell a passing fancy. The true gift must stand the test of time.

Sadly, lands deteriorate, stones lose their luster, and young girls grow to be wives. But the practice of shrewd statehood, the proper wielding of sovereignty, never strays from our minds. The noblest gift, then, must take as its principal concern the stability and longevity of states; and in so doing, it must prescribe the methods most proficient for maintaining and enhancing sovereign power.

I will not waste words extolling the virtues of the small book I send to Your Holiness; nor will I indulge the current habit of fawning that humble men tend to indulge when addressing men of your exalted station. I offer only my experience as practitioner and perceiver of politics, my understanding of subtle commerce, and my insights to the nature of men and their disposition in a commonwealth as proof of my merit.

The book contains no lofty ideals or artful flourishes. It is a simple and frank treatise of the sort only one other has dared to write. The limitations of Messer Niccolò's tract are now revealed so that the true nature of power and its capacity may be set before you. In your wisdom, Holiness, do not shy away from the brutal truths that lie in the pages before you. Do not be as Plato's cave dwellers, who, fearing the light from outside, return to the darkness within, happy to hide from a power they cannot understand.

Find within these pages the tools whereby you may achieve the greatness that fortune and your genius make all but certain. Few men have the opportunity to turn the very course of history. Few men have the courage to act in those singular moments. Such a moment is now present. It is my greatest desire that you, most devoted servant of God and man, seize the moment and dare to alter the very name of supremacy.

Contents

I. That sovereignty is a many-headed creature

II. That the true nature of sovereignty remains unknown

III. How to achieve stability

IV. The third way to stable government

V. Why the nature of men and the nature of power are so well suited

VI. Those components which make up the state

VII. Why it is vital to maintain the appearance of separation among the three realms

VIII. How a state may be made ready for true supremacy

IX. The roads to chaos

X. The road to political chaos

XI. The road to economic chaos

XII. The road to social chaos

XIII. How the three realms together create chaos

XIV. How to build from chaos

XV. Why it is important to cultivate hatred

XVI. Why the state must be the only competitor

XVII. The military

XVIII. The law

XIX. The ideal form of government

XX. An exhortation to action

n Supremacy

I. THAT SOVEREIGNTY IS A MANY-HEADED CREATURE

 For most observers of states, there seem but two choices in sovereignty. Either one man must rule on his own or there must be division among many. In the first case, birthright, victory, or usurpation gives authority its force; in the latter, legislation institutes a sovereign body to act as a collective. The Empire of Rome under the Emperors and the Republic illustrates well the distinctions between the two forms.

But men are fools who choose only from the choices they are given. In truth, sovereignty is nothing more than a courtier's word for power, and it is unwise indeed for those who wield such power to claim that they know how to limit it. Sovereignty is neither the handmaid of the virtuous or crafty prince nor the entitlement of a justly formed body of lawmakers. It is a prize to be won and ridden; ridden by those who can at one moment exert a princely autonomy and at the next appear models of republican virtue. To choose to rule by one form of sovereignty is to lose sight of sovereignty's caprice, its whim. Power seeks not those who hope to tame it. Power clings to those who recognize its discord and who can turn that discord to dominance.

II. THAT THE TRUE NATURE OF SOVEREIGNTY REMAINS UNKNOWN

 If the nature of sovereignty is as I describe, I shall have no easy task giving examples of its proper use. For I would claim that none to this point in the long history of men's affairs has dared to recognize the true nature of such power. And thus none have put it to practice. I can offer no gripping tales of deceit and cunning, no moral stories of compassion to illustrate to the full this unleashed and changeable power. In that respect, Messer Niccolò's Prince shows a greater reverence for the past than do my few pages.

Yet history is of little concern to men with vision. That states have risen and fallen, have sired great leaders and vicious tyrants, in no way grants that past a wisdom in the practice of politics today. No doubt some men of learning will say that I am the fool; that those who fail to see in history their own future have only themselves to blame for untold misery. Perhaps. But I would answer that these so-called scholars do little more than find solace in any number of outmoded stratagems that promise order in a cyclical process of political life. Polybius' is certainly the most frequently evoked—that from Kingship stems Aristocracy, from Aristocracy Oligarchy, from Oligarchy Democracy, Democracy Tyranny, and from Tyranny Kingship once again.

If only the ways of politics were so simple, so well defined, so easily arranged as these great men would have us believe. Then, perhaps, the past would truly stand as a prescient guide to all possible occurrences in the governing of men and states. But such is not the case, nor is it likely to be so. Power is like a restless child who does not wear easily the clothes of the democrat or the oligarch. He pulls at the sleeves, rips at the cuffs, struggles to make the cloth conform to his measurements. Nor is the child likely to abide the constraints of one single-minded course. Rather, he chooses the democrat's program in the morning, that of the oligarch in the afternoon, and the tyrant's in the evening. Consistency is no friend of power (although the appearance of it is surely essential). Power must set its own course and wear the different suits as it fancies.

It follows, then, that power cannot set its goal on the meager conquest of one city, one land, one country. History is a pitiful tale of men's provincial view of their own capacity. Too many princes, tyrants, and even religious Fathers, have quenched their thirst with a drink from a small pond when there are oceans to be swallowed. Security—the safety of small pieces of territory, the struggles of an Emperor, a Florentine, or even a Pope—is a minor concern when compared to the larger goal of this ill-dressed, ill-tempered child. He takes all cities, all lands, all countries as his domain, as his birthright. And the men who ride him with reverence and boldness understand that his way is the only way to true stability.

I write not for those who wish to remain mired in the false dream of a classical ideal and who are content to travel in circles rather than upward toward the mountaintop. For such as these: leave off now and waste no more time with this book. There are small ponds aplenty; you may drink from them in false security until the tide from the deep washes you away. The counsel set down here will only anger and arouse you because it will defy your complacence. Pray, lay the book down before it becomes too heavy in your hands.

For those daring enough to read on, however, I shall now begin to dig deeper into the mysteries of our theme. Be warned. There will be no place along the way for turning back.

III. HOW TO ACHIEVE STABILITY

 Stability of the state is the aim of every leader, and, except for the inept, longevity as well. There are three ways by which long-lasting stability may be achieved: first, by rigorous isolation; next, by the accumulation of alliances and friendships; and third, by continued expansion through the arts of aggression and deception.

The first of these may prove useful in providing stability for a time, but it cannot maintain the state's well-being for any durable period. This is true for three reasons. First, states that practice isolation are built on fear, fear of external force and interference. No government remains long that takes fear as its bedrock. Second, lands and resources are limited within a single state. Without trade, no state can survive, and trade is anathema to those who choose isolation. Third, only the wretched state, which decays from its own corruption, avoids the aggression of others. The prosperous state, even if built in isolation, becomes the prey of those hungry to possess it. Then the state must either lie down before its conqueror or enter the fray. As men in general seek war, so there is little hope that they will remain in isolation long.

Melos was a fine example of a state too eager to maintain its isolation and, because of that shortsightedness, fell prey to the ravages of an Athenian leviathan. An island of importance to both Sparta and Athens, Melos contented itself with neutrality during the first fifteen years of the Peloponnesian War. And so it prospered. But no prize sits long unobserved. (If only the small island had cultivated its wretchedness, then perhaps it would have escaped the greedy Athenian eye! But such is not the way in statecraft.) Athens demanded tribute, the Melians sought mediation, and soon the once proud island was brought to ruin in death and slavery. No state is an island, whether surrounded by waters or not. And no people may rely solely on the sweet words of politic men to save them. In short, isolation is but an invitation to slavery.

The second path to stability relies on the good intentions of all states; that each honors its word and abides by the agreements laid down in a few pieces of paper. Why do I say that all must be virtuous? Because if even one state chooses to play the rascal, then all others are in jeopardy. And because it is difficult, if not impossible, to determine the future attitude of each state, it is equally impossible to extend trust to any such states over a long time.

It may be true, however, that a group of states could arrive at a pact so as to protect themselves from the one miscreant who threatens the overall peace. The most powerful of recent memory was that which united the five great states of Italy. Each, for a time, laid aside their petty disputes, eager for the rewards their Treaty of Lodi could bring them. Soon, however, Lodovico Sforza saw the gains to be won for his own Milan by inviting Charles of France to Italy. And so ended the temporary friendships, proving that such alliances help little the cause of long-lasting stability. The momentary success of the treaty was due more to the chance concurrence of self-interest among the five states than to the nature of the treaty itself. Private interests ultimately tear such treaties apart. Thus we find that while friendships and alliances are pleasant things, they do not reflect the deeper parts of men's souls.

IV. THE THIRD WAY TO STABLE GOVERNMENT

 Thus, neither fear nor friendship can lead to long-lasting stability. Men are anxious animals who crave change and challenge as surely as they crave bread. They are not content to work so that things remain as they are. Isolation and alliance rely on such meekness. The only alternative is to feed the human desire to move forward, the need to assert one will over another. The longevity of any state thus rests on its ability to cater to the aggressive desires of its people. Stability is no companion of tranquillity.

Any student of human nature will see in the preceding lines a prescription for self-indulgence that, to some degree, may lead to happiness. But the shrewder observer will ask how such practice can hope to achieve stability within a state. Allowing a mob to light upon policy based on whim is surely the quickest way to anarchy. We are forced to admit that, while aggression is vital to longevity, the vast majority of men are unable to see how to put this power to proper use. Men are dim-witted, gullible creatures who are as likely to follow a Saint as a serpent. They can be coddled and flattered, bullied and beaten, and, for a time, will go where they are told.

But only for a time. Then they will feel the lure of change, the need to put their private wills onto the stage. So they will destroy all that has been built up for them by men of learning in order that their own aggression may come forth. Such is the calamity of history. Such is the work of men in politics.

This is the central lesson that too many men of politics fail to grasp. It is not enough to sweep away the danger and set in its place a government reich of one man or many. Again, Messer Niccolò wants us to believe that his prince will build a strong authority from the chaos, and that his bold leader will then yield his power to a republican body that will endure throughout the ages.* Granted, at the outset the people will live in awe of so mighty a warrior who arouses within them pride, virtù, and the like. And they will follow him as long as he displays his power. Truly, the prince is a man to be reckoned with. His ability to anticipate his own future, his strength and daring to overcome the vagaries of fortune (that all-powerful goddess), his willingness to play both demon and angel in the practice of politics are all traits to be esteemed and sought. But most men are incapable of such qualities. Yet, once this quasi-deity has served his purpose and set a strong foundation for political authority, he becomes unnecessary (perhaps even dangerous), and it is at this point, we are told, that the people take the reins from him with a wisdom and understanding of statecraft that will ensure long-lasting, stable governance.

But do men's hearts change? Do their desires wane because they have lived under so formidable a prince? Do they learn how to wield proper authority because power has been granted them? And, most important, do they cease to seek diversion and change? Certainly not. Like children, they need constant distraction, constant entertainment. Too long with any one form of government and they become bored, restless. That is why they do not suffer princes (even those of inestimable quality) for

---

* Although Machiavelli does not expressly detail this transition, Eisenreich is right to conclude that to make such an argument is perhaps the surest way to find consistency between Machiavelli's *Prince* and *Discourses*.

any lengthy period of time. No matter how strong the initial authority, no matter how firmly a prince sets the foundation, it is no match for men's aggressive talents.

Unless, of course, men are taught otherwise; that is, unless their leaders make education a vital part of ruling, whereby men's souls are constantly shaped, altered, and adapted to suit political and commercial expedience. It is not enough for leaders to wield political power. Nor is it sufficient for them to hold sway in matters of trade and commerce. Even together, these two strongholds are not enough. They must be joined by a third, no less vital: Men must choose to follow their leaders along the bold path that makes aggression the core of stability. And the people must follow not only willingly but with enthusiasm. Thus, men must be led, but they must not be aware that the leash pulls them along. Education accomplishes both ends and at the same time breeds enthusiasm for the course chosen. It can turn aggression to fervor, obstinacy to commitment, and volatility to passion. A well-designed education both teaches men to have free choice and at the same time convinces them that they have chosen freely. The latter, of course, should never be the case.

Plato understood this essential quality of education and thus built his model republic around strong schooling. Had he but recognized that lessons change, that ways of thinking reflect circumstances, then perhaps he would have given us a piece of writing for the ages. But Plato could conceive only a singular Truth under which he set the boundaries of all learning. Justice. A sweet word, but little more. And in making Justice his standard, Plato turned a practical idea into an ideal. The astute student of human nature realizes that no such Truth, no overarching Good guides men in their actions or in their understanding of themselves. Or if it does, men are not keen enough to follow its dictates. Thus, such Goods and Truths hold no sway in political and commercial matters.

That is not to say that leaders may not direct a populace through an education that has a clear end in mind. But they may do so only as long as that end enhances overall stability. When education begins to create individuals who look beyond the confines of political and commercial life, the institution becomes obsolete. A given approach might last for centuries, as it did in ancient Sparta, but that had as much to do with brutality as it did expedience. Suffice it to say, those who hope to maintain power must keep a vigilant eye on education so that its lessons always conform to the political and commercial needs of the day. To educate is to contrive by stealth. This must be a central maxim of leadership.

Furthermore, the aggressive wish men have for change will be well monitored through education, speeded during one period, held in check during another. And that wish must always be allowed to flourish. This is an unswerving truth, for if the people ever feel that their aggression has limits, they will begin to tear at the very fabric of government in the same way a wild beast claws at its cage. The people must be permitted their whims, their passions, their arbitrary pursuits within the bounds of social stability. But they must never sense the walls around them. It is the task of government and education to maintain that delicate balance.

Yet we might ask, Is not aggression the very seed of upheaval? How will control of the pupil help to keep the father from rebelliousness? For those who understand revolt, this question is easily dismissed on several counts. First, upheaval is forged through generations; teach the child well and loyalty leaves no room for doubt. Next, upheaval is the product of a hidden resentment that bubbles up so as to destroy peace; allow that hostility considered expression and it ceases to threaten. And third, the cry of the malcontent is against exclusion, mistreatment, or injustice; such harsh expressions take years to develop and can thus be quelled within the young long before such excitements grow to dangerous proportions. And this is all I shall say on the presumed dangers of rebellion.

V. WHY THE NATURE OF MEN AND THE NATURE OF POWER ARE SO WELL SUITED

 Likewise, leaders must pay close attention to the subtle changes in attitude that hint at discontent. And it is for that reason that governments must be willing to play different roles as time dictates. As the restlessness of a people begins to show itself, so the government must have the skill to change its very face both to appease and to distract the volatile crowd. The change may be only superficial (and more often than not is best served through deception), but its effect can be momentous. Would that there were examples from the past to illustrate this policy. But none with opportunity have yet dared to implement it.

One reason that governments have been unwilling or unable to master this technique is because they have believed falsely that all peoples seek liberty at all times, and that a mob is most content either under a republic or a democracy. But why should men choose to live under one constant form of sovereignty when they themselves exhibit no such consistency within their souls? If all men were infused with the republican spirit at all times, then truly a republic would be the government of choice. But men are not such creatures. Nor should they strive to be. It is no secret that there are moments when men covet even tyranny, openly or not. He who claims otherwise is either a liar or a fool. Why has the world seen so many tyrants if not for the very reason that every man has a secret longing to be one? That is, to wield ultimate control; to assert his will over all others. And just as men seek such power for themselves, so they esteem it in others. To live under an empire-building tyranny, to witness its power over self and others, can sate the private tyrannical need in all men.

As I have said, men are children. And it is not uncommon for children to seek out the strong hand of authority from a ruling parent. As with all passions, however, the child grows tired of this one in time. But it is a wise parent, like a wise government, who knows when to play the bully, when the coddler. Power reflects the desires of the people; and the people are most content when catering to the whims of power. Tyranny, which is often little more than monarchy disliked, does, at times, satisfy a human passion.

Here, then, is where the nature of men and the nature of power join hands. Power does not suffer well the shackles of quietude; neither do men. Power follows caprice; so, too, do men. Power sates its thirst through far-reaching, if not limitless, conquest; so, too, do men find distraction and entertainment in political expansion. Thus do the ways of power and the needs of men suit one another to perfection.

VI. THOSE COMPONENTS WHICH MAKE UP THE STATE

 Thus far, I have spoken in general terms. I have explained that men must be left free to act upon their aggressive desires (within certain limits of which they are unaware); that power is a driving, capricious force that extends far beyond the confines of the sort imposed by democracies, oligarchies, and the like; and that, where governance is concerned, men and power seek the same end. It remains for us to ask the central question: How is that end met?

From here, I will confine my observations to those who wield authority. I have said enough about the people. They remain a concern, but only in so far as they follow the few who lead. To understand the aggressive desires of the general crowd is a necessary step in leadership. To contrive by stealth a change in their desires so that a state may thrive is the more difficult task.

Success in that endeavor requires a keen understanding of the nature of the state. It is no longer wise to describe the state as a single realm, as an inseparable entity. I do not mean to make the obvious point that sovereignty is divisible. The Roman Republic is proof enough, what with its Senate and Consuls and Tribunes, that such division is not only possible but perhaps even advantageous to stability. No. I mean to assert that states are made up of three separate realms, each of which plays a distinct role in the relations of leaders and people. These realms are the politic, the economic, and the social.*

---

* This was by far the most difficult term in the translation. Eisenreich uses the words *communitas* and *humanitas,* sometimes together, often interchangeably when describing this realm. It is difficult to believe that he would have recognized this as a "social sphere" in the modern sense, but he is certainly hinting at it. I have chosen the word *social* because it seems to capture the expansiveness of his usage. Moreover, the term is consistent with the realm he describes—one where educational and cultural manipulation take place. That the term as we know it only appears in works of political philosophy 250 years later should only confirm Eisenreich's extraordinary talents as a student of statecraft.

The first is the most easily defined, the most tangible of the three because so much ink has been used in its exploration. The second is, if modesty allows, a designation of my own meant to define those activities of trade and commerce within and without the state. For centuries, the term has designated the maintenance of households. Thus Aristotle's numerous references to "oeconomia" throughout his *Politics* and *Nichomachean Ethics.* But is not the state a household writ large? It is, therefore, only logical that we treat the maintenance of states as we treat the upkeep of households and thus develop a more expansive notion of economy. As to the third, it is the most abstract of the three. For now, I will simply remind the reader that education is at the heart of the social realm, and I will leave more detailed discussion for later.

Heretofore, writers of theories, both practical and impractical, have thrown these three realms together, more often than not taking the political as the central governing force. Economy and society have appeared as little more than echoes of political power. This approach, though oft of use, fails to reveal the truly complex nature of the state. Those who take this path are like the simple diner who, upon tasting the stew, remarks that the beef is of good quality, and that consequently the entire dish is satisfactory. But it is the epicurean who notices the subtle flavor of the potatoes, the leeks, the carrots, and the broth who truly appreciates the dish, and who knows how to maintain its delicate balance. Should the stew fail to please the simple diner the next time round, he will look only to the beef as cause for his displeasure. The epicurean has subtler tastes, a more discreet sense for the ingredients, and he knows where to investigate when the stew no longer satisfies. So, too, in states, leaders must recognize the different ingredients of the politic, economic, and social, and balance them well so as to maintain stability.

And as there are different cooks for different dishes, so, too, there must be separate Prefects for the separate realms within the state: one man who understands political relations, another who rules the economic realm, and another who decides social policy. And because each must remain solely in his own realm, he must take no heed of the designs set down by those of equal authority within the other realms. The demands of each realm are so severe that, for those who lead, there is no time to attend to anything but their own tasks.

How, then, do they bring their efforts into accord? That is, how, if each gives care only to his own realm, will the designs in each serve the best interests of the state as a whole? Surely, without some principal agent overseeing all actions within each realm, we shall have anarchy. Therefore, one man must stand behind the three to guide them with subtle suggestion and wise counsel. This single individual need not be well versed in the dealings within the separate realms. Rather, he must tend a larger vision—with the insight of an Aurelius, the self-command of a Cincinnatus—a capacity to enable the rivalries between the realms to strengthen the bonds among them all. He is no prince, no sovereign king whose single authority dictates the path of the state. Only at certain moments does he assert such power. At all other times, he sits and observes, happy to remain above the fray. He is not hungry for power, yet he can harness it when the occasion calls upon him to do so. For him, supremacy is but a reflection of stability, and he knows that such stability rests upon the push and pull of the realms that he oversees.

A short digression is needed to consider the character of this man whom I shall call the Overseer hereafter. Only one man from the past has displayed the proper disposition of the Overseer. Cincinnatus, summoned from the plow during the Minucian consulship so as to fight back the Aequi, accepted the post of Roman Dictator with the single purpose of restoring order to the Empire; having done so, he returned to his plow in six months. His ambition rested solely in bringing stability to the Empire, not in securing his own authority. Our Overseer is no plowman, nor could he ever leave the central halls of authority, but his use of power must show the selflessness and narrow aim that Cincinnatus upheld.

The relations among the three Prefects and the Overseer will determine the well-being of the state and, as important, the control of the people. Each realm must maintain autonomy. Or at least such separateness must seem real to the people. That is, men will rarely need to learn of the Overseer, who keeps the three realms in harmony. To the simple crowd, the politic, the economic, and the social will be guided by separate hands, each in some way a check to the ambitions of the other two. In this way, republican virtue will blanket the government because power will seem divided among the many. The neat appearance of limits and balances (to borrow again from Polybius) will satisfy the whim of the people.

They will also be convinced at all times that the form of the state meets their desire. When, for example, the crowd cries out for aristocracy, the social realm will dominate. When those same voices beg for oligarchy, the economic realm will hold sway. And when, capricious yet again, they shout for a prince, the political leader will emerge. Thus will the face of government change with the winds of public interest and enthusiasm in order to keep the people diverted and satisfied. And thus will the aggressive desire of the people never have cause to tear at the fabric of a state that slakes their thirst for change.

These alterations, it will be apparent, are built more on deception than reality. For if a state were, in all truth, to assume the trappings of a democracy one day and a tyranny the next, it would be no state at all. Consistency must be the watchword of its leaders. As many have remarked, a state is much like a ship. But the metaphor has little to do with the role of the captain or his sailors, and even less with the difficult question of who controls the wheel. Rather, the similarity lies in the design of the whole. To keep itself afloat, to weather any swell, to remain stable during the turbulence of battle or revolt, a ship relies on a solitary device, hidden from all eyes. The keel. The keel remains constant at all times. Perhaps the ship takes new sails, a higher mast, a larger crew—such changes appear to alter its form, but the foundation remains the same. That which keeps it stable never varies. So it is within a state.

VII. WHY IT IS VITAL TO MAINTAIN THE APPEARANCE OF SEPARATION AMONG THE THREE REALMS

 It follows, then, that the unwavering arrangement of Overseer and Prefects must remain always at the core of government. Their roles never change in relation to one another, only in relation to the people and to other states. That is, the apparent superiority of one realm over another at any given time depends on circumstance, whether the state must seem more politically dominant, economically forceful, and so forth. And it is the unseen element, the Overseer, that makes possible all the transformations a state will endure. It is his hidden relationship with the Prefects within each realm that grants the state its much prized stability.

That is not to say that the four act in alliance with one another, each aware of the detailed actions required for success within the separate realms. No. Only at certain moments do their efforts unite. The real power of the Prefects rests in their unfailing devotion to their particular realms, together with their knowledge of the unity they must observe under the Overseer, a unity unseen by all others. A second maxim of leadership is therefore: To rule effectively, men must see to their own tasks, outwardly alone in their pursuits, but with the hidden understanding of common fellowship. In this way, the full extent of their power remains masked through feigned indifference to one another. True supremacy will thus emerge through concealed association.

To this point, were this a book of ideas alone, I could be well satisfied for having explained the essence of supremacy and the nature of stability. But what a hollow victory it would be if I fail to offer even a single word on the means whereby shrewd leaders may be able to achieve this end. It now remains to see how a state (as I have described it) may come into being, and how it may flourish. Many before me have written on this subject, but most have done so with the fanciful intent of describing states as they ought to be and not as they are. And they have thus relied on equally fanciful notions of virtue, strength, courage, and the like to ensure stability within these imagined realms. Even Messer Niccolò, with his desire to represent reality, has given us a prince who seems to appear from the mists of providence, his boldness and cunning intact long before we meet him. Likewise, this prince has fortune to thank for creating chaos within the state so that he may exhibit his virtù. As Messer Niccolò himself admits, his heroes from the past and present slip away all too quickly—even those as revered as Cesare Borgia—unable to maintain their arrogance, their steadfastness, their foresight for any long period of time. Is this prince, then, any more practical to the practitioner of statecraft than Plato's philosopher king or the virtuous princes we find in the writings of Salutati, Guarino, or Poggio? No. They are pure fantasy. In short, my small book will be no more useful than theirs should I stop here. The rest, therefore, must attend to the practical. And for that, we must again start with a clean sheet so as to determine how we might build a state for the ages.

VIII. HOW A STATE MAY BE MADE READY FOR TRUE SUPREMACY

 Men are governed by their own wills and by the will of fortune, and it is the battle that rages between these two that determines the well-being of states. The extent to which one of these wills may dominate is of central importance to us. Messer Niccolò would have us believe that the two fight an equal battle. To be fair, he is the first to give men an honest chance in the struggle, even if, by his own examples, he proves all too well that fortune is history's victor. Even he must admit, though, that men cannot win because they cannot adapt with sufficient speed to the demands of time. Long-lasting stability (the core of true supremacy) remains a golden dream.

But certain men are more capable than we might believe, even more capable than Messer Niccolò's prince. Their capacity lies not in their virtù or Thesian cunning. Unlike Messer Niccolò's prince, these men need have no superhuman quality. Nor do they do battle with fortune as their single nemesis. Rather, their strength lies in their faith in the state itself, in the state's capacity to achieve permanence in the face of fortune's whim. Underneath all its many changes, the state keeps an enduring quality, an immortality. Yet most men are unaware of this durability. For this reason, they are reluctant to tear down the faulty structures on which the state rests for fear that they will be left with nothing but anarchy. So great is their fear that they choose to amend the flawed structure and produce the same errors over and over again rather than attempt to build something of worth. What they fail to grasp is that only in the chaos of destruction can strong foundations be established. And only those who place their trust in the capacity of states (and not of men) understand how stability may be achieved.

It follows, then, that leaders who wish to create a stable and long-lasting state must first be willing to throw the present state into chaos. In short, there must always be a place for sacrifice. My purpose here is not to shock but to reveal plain truths. Messer Niccolò certainly understood this point, albeit less completely. His prince reached the heights of power because he knew how to take advantage of a situation mired in chaos. Yet the prince had no cause to know how to instigate such chaos. That task was left to the caprice of fortune. In that way, Messer Niccolò yielded greater power to fortune than to men. But those willing to take the bolder step and to send the state into the chasm wrest such power from the fickle goddess and thus shape their own destinies.

The choice is not so drastic as it might appear. Take, for example, the mathematician who struggles to create an indisputable proof. He clutters the slate with theorem upon theorem, axiom upon axiom, but to no avail. His calculations do not lead to certainty. And so he cleans the slate, save for the one or two statements he considers absolutely necessary for the ultimate proof. And yet, over and over again he arrives at uncertainty. What can he do? His fellow scholars believe that the few statements he has kept are essential to the task. Without these basic statements, they argue, he would not know where to begin. But he is wiser than they and has real vision. And so he wipes the slate clean and begins unencumbered by their outmoded wisdom. He trusts the science and not the men, thus showing his courage to plumb the depths into which the others dare not venture.

So is it with states. To elicit real change, leaders must be willing to tear down every structure that has been built on faulty foundations. For two thousand years, men have erected and destroyed cities, states, even civilizations in the hopes of constructing one perfect realm. But their efforts have been in vain for the simple reason that they have never had the courage, nor the insight, to begin from nothing. The slate must be clean if the new state is to be unaffected by the cankers and disease of the previous regime. It is not enough to replace a tyrant with a legislature, a mob with a king. The facade may be different, but the core remains the same. A smooth transformation from one form of governance to another merely reveals the underlying decay. To put it slightly differently, it is but a stay of execution. That which eroded the first regime lingers to undermine the next, and the next, and the next.

The problem is due to men's lack of imagination. They cannot see beyond the walls of the past, and thus find security only in what has come before them. Yet real courage asserts itself when faced with possible failure. The unknown provides such a test. To retreat to a flawed but well-tried structure displays only a weak will and an utter resignation to mediocrity.

There can be no easy way to the state I have described. For I have asked that leaders see not only themselves but the state they hope to rule in an entirely new fashion. There is nothing from history to which they might cling so as to make the change more palatable. Nor is there anything from the past that can explain how they might establish the realms and the Overseer. As with all things novel, attack is the best path. It follows that those who hope to rule must seek the total destruction of the standing regime.

But only at a certain moment. It would be folly to create chaos if these leaders were not prepared to build new structures to replace the old, to fill the void created by the destruction they themselves will have caused. I need pause only briefly to explain the craft of such a tactic. It is difficult, if not impossible, to provoke sweeping change in a state that has but the slightest residue of comfort and familiarity; that is, in one that reeks of the same mediocrity for decade after decade. Eliminate quietude and complacence and the specters of uncertainty and disorder will rush the people eagerly into the arms of a new leadership. In that way, the bold few will contrive a vacuum that they can fill with their own brand of supremacy so as to replace the vanquished regime.

The task is not as Herculean as it might appear, for much of the preparation will depend merely on four men; one above all who has the wisdom both to instruct and to choose his three disciples so that they have access to the three realms. I will not deny that this is the longest and hardest portion of the process: the three men must be plucked up at an early age, when their minds are open to innovation, and when they do not shy away from that which seems impossible. Aristotle's tutelage of Alexander proves that, if given sufficient direction from an early age, and if inspired with a passion for innovation, young men can grow to conquerors. The world has not seen the likes of an Alexander since, nor have there been such tutors as Aristotle to set down the course for such remarkable invention. But if a select few are given a glimpse of what might be, a glimpse into the limitless power to be won through a strict division of the realms, it will not be hard for the Overseer to gain their undying commitment. The burden shall be his to choose his pupils wisely.

Furthermore, the Overseer need not worry that each of these boys will be overwhelmed by the vastness of the ultimate task, because each will be limited only to that field, that realm which is to be his domain when the new state emerges. At the same time, though, each will be aware of the larger goal, confident that his two colleagues have engaged themselves as rigorously as he. The finer details of this initial stage will be determined by the way the Overseer interprets the few words of counsel I have set down here. For that reason, I will not attempt to describe the course of that training. I cannot anticipate circumstances, nor can I determine the future demands of any of the realms. Suffice it to say, each man must become an expert in his given realm, so much so that he is in a position of considerable influence when the moment to provoke chaos arrives. That the Overseer should choose from men who have the capacity to arrive at such positions is obvious. Yet certain aspects of the instruction will become clearer as I depict the later stages of this enterprise.

IX. THE ROADS TO CHAOS

 Any one of the realms can, by itself, plunge a state into chaos. Political upheaval due to rebellion or assassination, economic ruin caused by failed ventures or a drain on goods, or social disorder prompted by plague, famine, or other disasters can cause temporary havoc. Events in England of the past eighty years are sufficient illustration of how political intrigue can shake the very foundations of a state. The various murders and plots before the arrival of Henry Tudor brought chaos to England on more than one occasion, the worst after Richard Plantagenet's accession to the throne. The country was at war with itself, and in the end found salvation in a conquering prince. But did the English make the most of that chaos? Did they seek to expunge from the state those traits that had made all the devastation possible? Probably not. The Tudors have restored a peace, but one must wonder how long lasting that security will be, since the current Henry has no male heir. Will these battered English be forced to fight the same battles once again?

As to economic ruin, you will recall that following its war with the Numantines, the Roman Republic experienced vast difficulties brought about by the thousands of peasant workers who were unable to find land to till. Food began to grow scarce, with only corn brought from abroad warding off rebellion. So great was the economic strain that the tribunes led popular agitation against the senate and consuls. The danger began to spread to the military, and the entire state, already descending toward chaos, seemed on the brink of total collapse. Had it not been for Tiberius and Gaius Gracchus, men of extraordinary gifts, whose reforms restored order to commerce and agriculture, Rome might very well have fallen long before any scheming dictator could bring her to her knees.

For social disasters I need only remind the reader of the plague in Athens as evidence of the devastation of such phenomena.

In each of these cases, the advent of chaos did not suffice to dissuade men from erecting the same institutions that had made the state so weak in the first place. Thus, for chaos to serve its proper end, all three realms must erupt together. The question naturally arises: How? In the examples we have cited, the catastrophes were not wished for, nor were they the product of human design. Perhaps Richard Plantagenet recognized the usefulness of the chaos his actions provoked, but it would be foolhardy to ascribe a human cause to the economic failure in Rome, and blasphemous to do so in the case of the Plague. Yet if a stable state is to emerge, the few must take it upon themselves to create chaos; they must destroy all power so as to create power.

X. THE ROAD TO POLITICAL CHAOS

 The roles of each realm are distinct and any one may lead the way in the move toward chaos. Yet it would be wise to explain how difficulties are most likely to arise in each realm before we consider their united efforts. For the political realm, there are three roads to chaos: first, by assassination; next, by military or foreign threat; and third, by a popular demagogue. History is too full of instances of the first to warrant long discussion, but a few stand out among the many. The most obvious is Caesar, whose death at the hands of the twenty-two left Rome in the midst of a bloody civil war, which ended with the loss of the Republic and the rise of Imperial rule. The few years of confusion and uncertainty as Brutus and Octavian fought for dominion were the immediate consequence of the assassination. A less effective example, but one which occurred within the memory of our own fathers, was the partially successful attempt upon the lives of Guiliano and Lorenzo de' Medici. The Pazzi conspired to rid the city of its two leading citizens and, during the holy Easter Mass, set upon the two brothers, killing the first but allowing the second to flee with his life. Until word of Lorenzo's escape became known, a panic flew throughout the city and, had it not been for a few words of assurance on the steps of the Cathedral from the young Lorenzo, the Medici might have seen all order abandon Florence. So cunning a member of that illustrious family was Lorenzo that he turned the failed attempt to his advantage, making changes that strengthened his control over the government. But in truth, such an outcome is highly uncommon, and resulted more from Lorenzo's own qualities than from his circumstances after the attempted assassination.

Even when successful, assassination places states only temporarily into chaos, from which an altered, though equally weak sovereignty emerges. For those who win sovereignty through conspiracy and assassination, there is little to look forward to save fear, envy, and the terrifying possibility of revenge. Princes raised by assassination inspire others to seize power in the same way, and thus soon fall prey to the very means that brought them to the fore. To build a government on such foundations is to condemn the state to retribution upon retribution. While such events will bring cities into a continuous state of chaos, it is not a chaos from which true supremacy may emerge.

The second road may lead to more stable leadership than the first, but it is equally suspect, and far more difficult to follow. For military men (of whom I will speak in greater detail) are not easy to control, nor are they likely to yield sovereignty to a leader once they themselves have tasted the sweet fruits of power. Too much has been made of the loyalty of such armies for their generals, and for the leaders who direct those generals. In a time of true heroism, perhaps such esteem held sway. But we live in an age of mercenary troops who fight for a day's pay, no matter who holds the purse strings. Soldiers switch sides in the heat of battle if they are given sufficient reward. To trust military men—even those of a city's own militia (again Messer Niccolò displays an unsuspected naïveté)—is to allow a fickle crowd to determine the course of events. Loyalty is no match for power's subtle lure. Thus, to create political chaos through military force is to doom the state to martial law (no matter how sweetly that law be imposed). It cannot be denied that military rule offers some stability, but only for a while. Ambition is the driving quality of all soldiers and too many have the means (a regiment here, a garrison there) to seize power. No state stands long that must endure the constant struggles of military intrigue.

Foreign threat is even more difficult to predict and nearly impossible to control. Furthermore, the only men in history who have won power through conquests made by others have been spies and traitors. These are the worst sorts of men and deserve any and all vengeful reprisals that fall upon them. There is nothing more to say on the possibilities created by foreign threats.

The first two roads to political upheaval share a basic shortcoming: Neither takes seriously the need to contrive with stealth the opinion of the people. Assassination is alone a tool of the few or of the lunatic. Military upheaval takes place in a small portion of the state. Those who follow either of these two roads fail to recognize that, although incapable of rule on their own, the people are the most powerful force in a state, and thus any change in power must ride upon the wave of their passions. The people would not willingly bring the state into chaos, but they must be led to do so. There is but one way to accomplish that end: A demagogue must rise who captures their devotion and who recognizes the need to catapult the state into ruin so that he (and others) may create stability from the rubble.

Once again, Florence provides a fitting example in the person of Savonarola, who became the city's leading citizen during the last days of its first republic. Only last year, Signore Michelangelo Buonarroti told me that to this day, thirty years later, he could still hear the sound of Savonarola's voice as he preached. Driven by his desire for sweeping change both in the church and in his fellow citizens, Savonarola filled his sermons with prophecies of the purifying scourge ready to descend upon Italy. When his prophecy was given truth by the invasion of the French in the year of our Lord 1494, he won control of the city and the opportunity to create his holy realm out of the upheaval. But he was a man of narrow vision, who desired little more than a strengthened republic guided by the motto "Christ King in Florence." His body soon burned on a pyre in the Piazza della Signoria, a testament both to his influence and to his limits.

Among the many demagogues over the centuries few (if any) have taken this role with the sort of foresight necessary to prepare for the state I envision. Our demagogue must be a man ready to take the reins within the political realm once chaos erupts. Therefore, he must be well aware of the other realms, and see his role as one of limited importance. It is crucial that he play the demagogue, rather than be one. For if he were to take on all of the attributes of such a leader, he would never be able to slake his own thirst once the new foundations of the state were set. Thus he must not appear on the political stage simply by happenstance; that is, by the good fortune of a few ringing sermons. No. He must study the temper of the people, understand what they crave or disparage in the current state, and then use that knowledge to cater to their desires. He must speak as if he speaks for them all. He must be a shrewd observer of men, and he must know when to enter the fray. He need not strike with a bold blow; but rather, he should build slowly from small beginnings. Let word of his deeds and of his opinions give rise to his popularity. Let the people call on him, not he on them. Then, when the moment is right, when the Overseer has counseled a sudden movement from all realms, let him take his people into chaos. They will not flinch. They will have given him their trust and their devotion. It will take time to conjure such loyalty, and it will be the circumstances that determine his progress. But all that is required of both demagogue (the political Prefect) and Overseer is that they be able to read men's hearts, a skill honed through years of study.

XI. THE ROAD TO ECONOMIC CHAOS

 Such are the paths to upheaval in the political realm. Within the economic realm, there are also three paths: first, by natural depletion; next, by foreign blockade; and third, by designed ill-use. The first is most likely to cause strife among the various groups within a state; that is, setting the landed wealthy against artisans and merchants, and against the peasants and the poor. When goods are insufficient to meet the needs of each group, those who are deprived will find cause to revolt and send the state toward ruin. Oft the fault lies with the peasantry, for they are unable to recognize the ebb and flow of commerce and trade. When food or other necessities are scarce, they blame the landed, who are no more to blame than the peasants themselves, for it is nature, not greed, that causes the dearth of grain, wood, metals, and the like.

Nowhere has this farce been more common than in the German states of the last one hundred years. Guildsmen fought against merchants, peasants against lords, weavers and miners against merchants, until, with a sudden explosion, the Peasant wars erupted, leaving behind the rule of dictators throughout the German region. The chaos created by the economic discontent did naught but return the old rulers to power with even greater control than before. Natural depletion was ill-suited to send the state in a new direction.

As foreign military threat is difficult to control and equally difficult to cause, so, too, is foreign blockade. If any have been foolish enough to encourage a threat from abroad so that they might reap the benefits such chaos allows, they are indeed the worst sorts of fools, for there is little room for sweeping change once the blockade serves its end. Too often the besieged turn with sunken cheeks to their vanquishers, happy to accept any rule that promises bread. The few who have led the starving mob may insist that all choose death rather than submission. But men are inclined more by their stomachs than by honor or loyalty. The only change such action breeds is the rule of conquerors. And for those who ally themselves with the new rulers, they have only to look to history to see the fate of such traitors.

We are left with one choice: designed ill-use. Leaders cannot wait for a natural decline in trade and commerce to cause a panic; nor should they place their fate in the hands of a foreigner or an enemy. Instead, they must choose one area within the world of buying and selling that is susceptible to severe disturbance. Do not be fooled that this action must be of the most drastic sort. Those who wish to cause mayhem need not burn all the grain, nor ravage all the land. All they need provoke is one event that will shake the confidence of the people; one area where a sudden change will cause the crowd to doubt the security of all. This has happened more by fault than design throughout history, but the lesson is the same.

We may look to Milan for illustration. When a certain duke of that fair city, a devotee of the Guelfs (I shall spare his memory the indignity of giving his name), secretly ordered one of his own ships to be sunk, for fear that both friends and enemies would discover his mistress, a woman of the Ghibellines, to be on board, he mistakenly sent a vast quantity of wool and silk to the bottom with her. The duke's actions may have prevented a nasty dispute between the two warring factions, but he created far more trouble by arousing the wrath of the merchants and weavers than if he had let the ship reach port. The silk and cloth manufacturers feared that their losses from the downed shipment would send their entire trades into ruin. Without goods or payment, they reasoned, how could they hope to continue? To limit the damage, they thought it wise to shut down almost half the shops throughout the city. The people, quick to take fright, concluded that the trouble would soon spread to all other areas of commerce. The ensuing panic forced the duke to offer large privileges to members of every guild, draining his coffers, and weakening his position with the Ghibellines. And all because of one small ship and a few rolls of silk and wool!

The duke had no intent to cause such alarm, but the lesson is clear: Those who willingly cause such mayhem can reap the greatest rewards, for they control when and how such eruptions occur, and they are able to anticipate the people's response. The Overseer, together with the Prefect of the economic realm, must therefore determine a single area within trade and commerce that can bring the same response as the wool and silk trade in Milan. As the demagogue must read the hearts of men, so this Prefect must understand the natural vicissitudes of economy, using that knowledge to master one small area of trade. And like the demagogue, this Prefect will need years of experience and training to make this decision. Thus, while the demagogue gathers his followers, so the economist (again, a word of my own making) establishes himself within the most powerful circles of commerce. When the moment is right—that is, when the moment meets the demands of the other realms—it will not be difficult to send the state into economic panic.

XII. THE ROAD TO SOCIAL CHAOS

 But what of the social realm? How might a Prefect create havoc there? The few examples I have been able to collect from history lie entirely on the side of fortune (or God's will), and have nothing to do with the plans of men. Certainly none but the Almighty rains pestilence and plague upon humanity, and no matter how clever and wise men become in the ways of disease and death, it is unlikely that they will ever seek to create such afflictions. Yet there is a subtler way to prepare the social ground for a new state; a way that calls for drastic change and thus might well be likened to a sort of chaos.

I have explained that this realm finds its base in education: to control education is to hold the social realm in one's hands. Thus, the change must occur within the halls of learning. It follows that, for this change to have any influence over the populace, the educational institution that imparts its message must be widespread. Unfortunately, we must admit that at this moment no such institution exists.

Unless we look to the most holy Catholic Church as a beacon of learning. Within its sacred walls, men's hearts may be altered, directed, and encouraged to reshape the world. Were it not for the mighty institution that emanates from Rome, it would take decades, if not centuries, to set in place a means to touch so many hearts and minds. And within those halls, an upheaval of sorts must take place. The Church must expand its vision so that it may guide men not only toward eternal salvation but also toward an enduring state here on earth. I would not be so forthright, nor would I risk the brand of impiety, were there no other institution so well suited to the demands of longevity and stability. Perhaps in days to come, some such educational institution may arise to release the Church from this heavy burden. Until that day, however, Rome must take up the reins and lead with an iron fist. Beat back the heretics and muster the strength of her faithful. To do so, she must revitalize her means of guiding the people and develop a new way of learning, a way to inspire passion and devotion to a well-dictated stability.

I do not speak without just cause. We need only look to any number of German states to understand the imminent peril. Already, a great danger has appeared in the form of a rebel priest, a man who strives to wrest authority from its rightful place. If a single man may turn the wills of so many to heresy, imagine the strength of the true Church to determine the actions of men.

It is well understood that the ways to Heaven and the ways to a stable state require separate instruction. Yet Rome must recognize that such instruction may come from the same source. It would be blasphemy to claim that the Church was meant to take as its mission the affairs of this world. But I do not make such a claim. Rather, I believe that a stable state in no way contravenes the higher end of eternal salvation and that the Church may counsel both without contradiction. The words of Aquinas, William of Occam, Duns Scotus, Peter Lombard—these schoolmen gave shape to this mission centuries ago. For them, reason and faith fight an eternal battle. Therefore the universities, Cathedral schools, and monasteries devoted themselves to questions surrounding that struggle; a struggle that continues today and that remains the test of men's devotion to the Holy Spirit.

But now a new topic sits atop the table and demands equal consideration: power, whose own struggles test men's resolve in the political and economic realms.

One educator must, therefore, develop this new area of teaching and alter certain institutions within the Church. The care of the Spirit should remain in the hands of the larger Church. But reverence for political and economic expedience should become the domain of this new area. It should not be difficult to see how the educator may serve the Church at large without threat. Indeed, when men live secure in a stable and long-lasting earthly peace, they should have all the more passion to devote to the achievement of eternal bliss.

Is this, then, a call for chaos within the social realm? Will there come a moment when the Overseer counsels a sudden movement, a lightning action to topple the existing realm? No. It would be difficult to liken the change within the social realm to those required within the political and economic realms. The moment of upheaval here comes much earlier, at the very instant one man determines to take control of education in the name of supremacy. At its onset, this new venture will seem aberrant to those who take any notice of it. Yet they will dismiss it, see nothing in it to cause alarm, for it will appear to have limited influence. Much like the heretical sects that arise from time to time, the new schools will at first seem to pose no threat. Imagine the people's surprise when, propelled into chaos by the political and economic realms, they see a small army of young men fully trained to take the state in an entirely new direction. Then these unenlightened ones will have no choice but to embrace the new way much in the way a drowning man reaches for a single piece of driftwood to escape the clutches of death.

XIII. HOW THE THREE REALMS TOGETHER CREATE CHAOS

 Before describing how the three realms may work together to create chaos, I must insist that there may be no need to combine such upheavals. I have noted that panic in one realm is not likely to create the proper conditions from which to build a stable state. But there will be those rare occasions, those singular events that place leaders in a position of uncommon opportunity. Much like Messer Niccolò's prince, these leaders will have fortune to thank for their circumstances. For those who sit well with fate (and who have prepared themselves within the three realms), they need only browse through the pages that follow, for they stand ready to build.

For those not so fortunate, we must recall that one or two of the realms may take the lead when instigating chaos. The social realm usually acts to stabilize, rather than to stir chaos. Yet all three must place their efforts together; otherwise, the singular act in one realm will prove fruitless to the well-being of the state in general. Before any action can be taken, therefore, all three Prefects must be in a position to rule the course of events within their own realms. Much of the preparation of these men will have occurred individually over a long period of tutelage, but the closer they come to the moment of eruption, the more they must act together with one another.

At that moment, it is best to begin with an economic upheaval, for men are most concerned with their own pockets and often lose their reason when property is at risk. To repeat: the upheaval need not be of vast proportions, but only sufficient to raise questions in the simple minds of the people. Once doubt is present, it will not be difficult for the demagogue to nurture that uncertainty among his followers, who will breed an indignant panic among the entire community. Why indignant? Because the demagogue will have taught his pupils to think ill of the current regime even during times of relative calm. Failures to appease factions within the state, failures to establish profitable trade with foreign states, failures to explore possibilities for expansion, failures to secure economic prosperity—these are but a few of the shortcomings that the demagogue will have brought to the people's attention, and that will now serve to stir passions. Once they witness the economic upheaval, they will convince themselves and others that they have just cause to overturn the regime.

These failures, however, will not be sufficient on their own to cause a total abandonment of the prevailing polity. There must be an underlying affliction, of which such failures are merely the outward signs. And it will be around this canker that the demagogue musters his troops. The surest choice is moral decay. Nothing suits men's instincts more than a sense of pious indignity. Let the demagogue paint all the ills of society as reflections of poor moral guidance by a regime incapable of setting men on the right course. The economic upheaval will thus appear as the final misdeed of a state mired in immoral deeds. How better to convince a grumbling crowd that the slate must be cleaned entirely than to call on its self-righteousness? Men are quick to praise their own sanctimony. Let them believe it best to cleanse the state so as to cleanse themselves. Chaos will become the welcome release from a general iniquity.

XIV. HOW TO BUILD FROM CHAOS

 And where better to look for redemption than to the realm of education, which recognizes the worth of stability? Where better to wash away the decay than in a school wrapped in the arms of the Church? The people, if well directed, will eagerly abandon all that reminds them of their affliction, all that rests on faulty foundations, and rush to commend their collective fate into the hands of the Prefects. In that way, they will willingly venture into the unknown, but an unknown that seems firmly rooted in a commitment to virtuous and long-lasting governance. It is therefore vital that the institutions of schooling be in place; or if not in place entirely, then at least to a degree that will excite and appease the querulous mob. For the people will need a safe haven in which to stand as they watch their champions tear down the old institutions.

With the educational realm reshaped, the first task of a new state must be to rid itself of the most hardy elements from the previous regime. What I mean here is men. Reeling from the chaos, these enemies of the state will be in precarious positions, but it will be for the new leaders to make examples of them. Set them before the people as authors of the corruption and decay and let them, as goats to the desert, carry all the sins of the past to their graves. Much should be made of this cleansing so that all men may feel that they have had a hand in the resurrection of the state. Furthermore, such acts will encourage a self-restraint within the people as a whole.

To be sure, it is a worthy aim to instill fear in the hearts of men. Take heed, though. Excessive displays of brutality will raise fear to dangerous levels. Fear can be an elixir that, if meted out in proper doses, may rouse enthusiasm. But given in too large a quantity, it turns to dread, dread to rage, and rage to hatred. And, as Messer Niccolò counsels well, that sort of hatred is a beast without master. Power sits uneasy when hatred prowls the streets. Therefore, the Prefects must make certain that the cleansing process suits the circumstances of the day and feeds but a part of the vicious hunger of the mob. Their aggressive passion will always cry for more blood. But be warned. Do not sate this desire fully. Keep the people hungry. Such is the way to turn fear to excitement and aggression to fervor.

The story of Raphael Ormetti teaches well this lesson. Friedrich von Keslau, a man of extraordinary gifts in the ways of establishing new states, won control for a time of Hamburg, eliminating many of his enemies in the city, and hanging their bodies in the central square both to delight and frighten the people. Von Keslau could not have known that his actions would unleash a wild passion within the people who screamed for more blood. Soon the city was infested with roving bands of cutthroats. In order to regain control of these mad men of Hamburg, von Keslau sent Ormetti to the city so as to pacify the mob by whatever methods necessary. This Raphael was a man for whom cruelty was married to efficiency, and in a short time, he had brought the people to their knees. But cruelty has its limits, as von Keslau well knew. Not wanting to incur the hatred of his newly won people, and wanting no blame for the brutalities inflicted by Raphael, von Keslau sent a second emissary to dispose of Ormetti, whose body appeared one morning cut into separate pieces, each piece impaled on one of several spears directly in front of the castle of Adolph III. This act both won von Keslau praise as a savior and inspired in the people of Hamburg a healthy fear of their new master. Alas, his reign lasted only a few months, until Lbeck again regained control of the city, whereupon von Keslau's body joined that of his brutal, if unfortunate, disciple.

Yet cleansing the state need not be a singular act. From time to time, as circumstances dictate, the political Prefect should find cause to eliminate other enemies, those who threaten the stable core of obedience and expansion that the three realms promote. There are several ways to determine who shall live and who shall die, but it is best if there is some reasonable cause for choosing victims. Acts of arbitrary will serve no useful end. Thus, he must light on a particular group that, whether in truth or not, poses a threat to the order of the state. Furthermore, the people must believe that this one group stands in the way of perfect stability. And the mob must grow to despise these outcasts. The best choices would no doubt be members of certain religious sects or citizens of foreign nations who reside in the new state.

XV. WHY IT IS IMPORTANT TO CULTIVATE HATRED

 Once again, Messer Niccolò fails to consider the animal passions that drive men's souls. Leaders must assuredly avoid being hated by their people. But hatred, if directed properly, is a powerful tool for control of the people. To good effect, the Romans persecuted the Christians, the Greeks limited the freedom of all noncitizens, and many have taken the Jews as ready targets. Keep the people preoccupied with a common enemy, and their aggressive passions (served best by a pointed hatred) will strengthen the bonds of the state. The demagogue must, therefore, cultivate this malice within the people, a malice that best serves stability when it reflects the moral righteousness that prompts the first upheaval.

To build from chaos, then, it is vital to hold public gatherings, games, and festivals that ridicule and mistreat those selected for abuse. Such events are not foreign to men. The spectacle of lions tearing into the flesh of unarmed Christians, the pageantry of public executions, even the simple puppet shows in which the old Jew is beaten to death for his usury sate a basic human desire. Furthermore, they present vengeance in its most basic guise. That is, such shows are never more than what they appear to be. No hidden meaning lies below the surface; no complexity to confuse or agitate a people. In short, these gatherings and exhibitions cultivate a passion for simple answers, which, in turn, makes the people docile and unimaginative.

The rewards of this policy are many. First, it is always more beneficial to rally a people around a common aversion than around a common love. Men seek fellowship with those who share their aggression, and nothing serves that common desire more than a single enemy. No one would be foolish to claim that anything more than their loathing of French and Spanish invaders holds the loose confederation of Florentine cities together. If a foreign threat can unite these factious peoples, imagine how well a state would maintain its unity if there were a common enemy within. Second, as long as the people direct their venom toward a small group, they will have no cause to vent their aggression on the leaders within the separate realms. Fear of popular uprising, or even of high levels of dissatisfaction, will become things of the past. Keep the people preoccupied and they will have little concern for the power that is theirs to wield. And third, any malcontent may be branded a member of the outcast group, whether he be one or not. It is then easy enough to dispose of him, as long as the people believe he is a threat to the security of the state.

Perhaps most important, this malice knows no limits and can ultimately take the people beyond their own borders. There will come a time when the tide of men's hatred runs dry within the state, when all members of the odious sect have been eliminated. At that moment, the demagogue (through pamphlets, agitators, and the like) may invent a new threat in the guise of yet another group; or, more prudently, he may determine that the threat has merely stolen away to another state, one which therefore needs cleansing.

How perfectly suited to human nature is this tactic. Men are wretched creatures, pompous, weak, and greedy, with less reason than brutish desire to guide them in their wayward lives. Allow them their aggression and they will cause little harm. Limit the reach of their claws, however, and they will destroy everything about them. So the demagogue must focus that aggression, unleash it beyond the state, and in so doing enhance the state. Expansion, fed by hatred, is the surest means to security.

It should be clear that the group accused of endangering stability is but an invention of the Overseer and the Prefects. No single sect could possibly determine the life or death of a state. But reality is not a concern for those who seek a well-ordered realm. All that is necessary is that they convince the people that the peril is real. And where better to teach the people how to direct their hatred than in a school that claims to fight moral corruption? What, then, should be the lessons? Cultivate distrust, and the people will seek out those who pose even the smallest threat to the state. Cultivate righteousness, and the people will attack all enemies with vigor. Cultivate simple answers and aggression, and the people will vanquish evil beyond their own walls, feeding power's lust for conquest in the name of virtue. In that way, education and aggression work hand in hand to assure stability.

XVI. WHY THE STATE MUST BE THE ONLY COMPETITOR

 To build from chaos in the economic realm requires almost no contact with the people. Instead, the Prefect here must, for a time, take full control of all commerce, trade, and exchange. The people will offer little resistance. Ill at ease from the sudden explosion of chaos, and well directed by the demagogue, they will recognize and accept the need for drastic measures. Only the economist will stand as an incorruptible force. Furthermore, as long as food appears on their plates, the people will consent to all efforts to cleanse the state of corruption. All lands will become the jurisdiction of the state. All guilds will yield power to the state. Those who resist will find themselves labeled enemies, a name to which the people will not take kindly.

If any doubt that one man, with the people's consent, may seize considerable authority in a single economic area, think only of the upstart Henry in England. It is no secret that he intends to take all Church lands within that realm for himself should Rome not resolve to his liking the question of his divorce of Catherine. This king well knows that the people will pose no obstacle to his desires, for he has convinced them that he is ridding England of a corrupt institution; that is, the most sacred, holy Catholic Church. Even the threat of excommunication is no match for his heretical designs and his people's prideful sanctimony.

Overarching control is thus vital if the economist is to use the institutions of trade and commerce in the service of the other two realms. Equally important, as enterprises come under the command of the Prefect, so the state as a whole will become like a single trader, with the full force of the state's economic power behind it during negotiations with others. The state will then find expansion an easy task. In time, the economist may delegate control of the realm to smaller traders, manufacturers, and the like. But should he desire fuller control in the future, he need only raise the specter of corruption by the outcast sect in order once again to restore control to his own hands. Thus will expansion and stability reflect well the natural ebb and flow of commerce and trade.

In short, to build from chaos requires ample control within each of the realms. To eliminate enemies and foster a pointed hatred is to control the political realm; to remove all competition within the state so as to dominate competition with those in other states is to control the economic realm; and to cultivate aggression and righteousness through education is to control the social realm. Expansion will be the natural outgrowth of such control and will ensure long-lasting stability.

XVII. THE MILITARY

 I would do no disservice to the enterprise of this small book were I now to conclude, well satisfied that I have offered both in ideas and in practice the means to secure a stable state. Yet there remain two topics that demand more ink. The first is the military, to which Messer Niccolò devotes almost half of his small tract. Whether he is condemning the use of mercenaries or extolling the virtù of one of his many heroes, Messer Niccolò describes statecraft in terms of military preparedness and cunning. Indeed, he claims that states need only have good arms and good laws to achieve stability. And this may be true. He offers myriad examples of the proper and ill-use of military men in securing boundaries, establishing empires, and so forth. He therefore insists that the art of war (and thus the control of the military) rests firmly in the hands of the prince.

Yet Messer Niccolò seems strangely unaware that without so appealing and cunning a figure to lead them, armies tend to become roving bands of cutthroats and drunkards who would as soon defile the daughter of an ally as that of an enemy.

He seems equally reluctant to admit that soldiers are averse to good sense and are more inclined to follow the vainglorious than the shrewd. This last is what makes them dangerous. For there need be only one man within their ranks who displays a capacity to lead, and they will feed his ambition until there is nothing but rubble on which to stand. And worse, let there be two such men, and the state must suffer the slow death of civil war. In short, military men are no different from other men, save that they wield deadly weapons and threaten all with their pride and vanity.

A word of advice, then. Beware of soldiers. Use them only as tools, because they have neither the wit nor the endurance for the building of states. If they once believe that they have the power, little will keep them from destroying the state. The army must, therefore, be like a handmaiden to those who control the realms. Do not be afraid to destroy those within it who begin to amass too great a following or who show any signs of ambition.

XVIII. THE LAW

 Our final topic is the second part of Messer Niccolò's precept for stability: the law. I save it till the last because I do not believe it contributes to the welfare of states as much as those who have come before me claim. For the most part, they conclude that the law protects the people and enlarges freedom. But freedom is a dangerous weapon in the hands of a people. The mob cannot distinguish between license and liberty, more often than not taking freedom to be the first, and, in so doing, dragging the state into anarchy. For that reason, the law must work to limit freedom. Accepting this as the law's purpose will prove no difficulty once educational institutions begin to produce young men who share the Overseer's vision and who consider a passion for stability more inspiring than some hollow desire for liberty or the like. But in the early stages of the new state, the aim of law will not be joined so easily to the character of men. The difficulty will arise because the people, as they have been taught, will believe that stability derives from law. This is a false belief the new state must quickly correct.

Law is a reflection of men's wills. Nothing more. There is no supreme precept in this world that determines the rights or wrongs of any act. Punishment alone establishes the justice of all actions. Thus both law and penalty are arbitrary, because they are created to suit political, economic, and social expediency. Laws are no more trustworthy than the men who create them, and stability can never rest on human caprice.

But do not take the laws from the people. The laws are like a well-worn blanket in which the people wrap themselves. Grant them their childish sanctuary; speak highly of laws, enact new ones from time to time, repeal the old, and always let the people believe that they have the laws to thank for the state's well-being.

Furthermore, it is best to keep the laws simple. What to do; what not to do. What punishment; what reward. Let the people see that without the laws, they themselves would be forced to order the state, set limitations on actions, control those around them. They will gladly leave responsibility with the law so as to keep their lives as simple as possible. And in granting the laws authority, the mob yields all power to the Overseer and Prefects. Men seek to avoid complexity whenever possible. Let the law cater to that desire.

This last is a lesson that extends beyond the law. In all things, a state should look to simplify, and, in so doing, to make men more docile. As things become less complex, so, too, will men. Imagination, always a danger to a state, will cease to provoke. Let men become dull with passion (a passion conceived and promoted by the Overseer and the Prefects), and they will lose all desire to challenge authority. In education, teach men to be simple; clog their thoughts with rudiments (hatred is the most diverting) so that they will cease to develop their own ideas. Once leaders drive invention and ingenuity from men's hearts and minds, the people can pose no threat to stability.

XIX. THE IDEAL FORM OF GOVERNMENT

 Thus far, I have made every effort to avoid the fanciful advice offered by those who have written before me. Nowhere have I explained how states ought to direct themselves, nor how men ought to act. I have chosen the more honest, if bleaker, path so that my words may be of some use to men who seek supremacy in a real world, and not in some land of fantasy. Why, then, do I now claim that I can describe the ideal form of government? Such things are not for men with practical goals.

The reason is simple. For those who still question the usefulness of the three realms, who cannot see why chaos is essential in creating stable government, and who deny the need to expand through aggression and machination, my conclusions will seem unattainable. Truly, the government of which I speak is only possible if all three realms work together in perfect harmony. Then and only then will true supremacy produce a government that on the surface appears to cater to the caprices of men's desires without giving up any of its authority. Republic, tyranny, democracy—these names are meaningless save for the comfort they offer the hearts and minds of men.

I also use the word ideal for another reason. Nowhere in these pages do I describe how a particular state may put these words into practice. Nowhere do I recommend the period of tutelage under which each Prefect will develop his skills. Nowhere do I name the exact area in commerce, or the exact political failure that will send the old regime into ruin. And nowhere do I describe the course of study to be taught in the schools. The words hatred, expansion, aggression, and machination have provided the only detail. But why? Because circumstances must dictate the policies chosen, because each state requires a different target of hatred, because the most susceptible areas within commerce and trade vary among states, because expansion sets its own direction, and because power follows its own whims.

It is an ideal because no one, including myself, can foresee the demands of the future within the three realms. But take note. I do not call it an ideal because it cannot be won. What I have written can lead men and states to stability. Whether those men have the skill and courage to read the circumstances of their times and act accordingly is all that stands now between ideal and reality.

XX. AN EXHORTATION TO ACTION

 Yet I wonder now whether the time has arrived to create a new state, and whether a few men might attempt to launch so magnificent a change. It is too true that fear has infested activism, indulgence has replaced direction, and empathy has diluted everything. And still I most assuredly answer yes. Never before has so much conspired to offer so propitious a setting and so great an impetus for a change in the wielding of power. In the very presence of this Luther indicates how easily men may be led to abandon all that is dear to them in the name of some unknown and untried authority. Use this renegade German, most holy of Fathers, as a symbol of corruption; show him as the canker that will destroy all of Europe; destroy him and his followers and, in so doing, set power free so that it may explore and conquer as it wills.

The destruction of this Luther, though, must come only as the culmination of the endeavor, the final moment before chaos may come to the light. Let other, smaller instances of destruction pave the way so that his death will sound the clarion cry for all those ready to step beyond the corrupted world he has inspired. Let the chaos build, event to event, until they rise together and strike fear and uncertainty into the people's hearts. One tiny eruption matters for naught. One on top of another, on top of another—that is something of true worth; that is something that, over a period of several months, will be sure to bring chaos. Remember, too, dear Father, these tremors need not be of real moment. Their genuine effect is of little consequence so long as their perceived threat is vast.

I cannot claim with certainty that my scheme is infallible, but the short schedule I offer below is one such way to bring about the chaos that is so vital to the capture of true supremacy. I ask only that you read it, and hope that it may inspire you to your greatest exploits.

    i. Do not be afraid to destroy that which you hold most dear. The Cathedral of Santa Maria dei Fiore must be the first to fall victim. It is a symbol of your strength, of the will of our Father Christ, and thus stands as a bulwark of our faith. Let the people believe this Luther is responsible, that he is the threat. They will respond accordingly.

ii. The Spanish Ambassador must fall next. Charles will see this as an intrigue and it will raise the spectre of war. A people fearful for their own survival will embrace whatever security you may offer.

iii. The ports at Civitavecchia and Portopisano must meet with disaster; only in this way will the merchant trade be brought to its knees. At the same time, the Pazzi Bank must be taken to ruin—mismanagement is the surest course, and there are those whom I have placed at your disposal within the Pazzi family who are willing and eager to serve that end. You need only call upon them.

iv. You must threaten a second expulsion of the Jews from Rome, set them as a pariah on which all may focus their hatred. But do not expel them. Allow them to remain so that the people's aggression may fester. When the time comes, you will make examples of them in public festivals.

v. Permit several wells within Rome and Florence to be infested with contagion. This must endure only for a short period, but it is essential to make the threat of plague very real. Bad health and chaos go hand in hand.

These are but the beginning, most Holy Father. Indeed, it is best to try a first trial of conjecture by experience, some few incidences within one city of worth—Venice is perhaps the wisest choice—to ensure that the climate is rip for the chaos. Once tried, let go the reins and allow chaos her way with the continent.

I have kept the other events on the schedule with me so that we may together conceive and execute this most daring of plans. Do not chastize me for keeping them hidden. A poor man must keep something for himself. I shall remind you, though, that the final act will be the death of the Devil himself, this Luther who stands between mankind and salvation. It is the schedule I have devised that will make that possible.

There are those who stand ready to rule the three realms; those I have trained to understand the subtleties within each realm and to look to you as their guide, their Lord, their Overseer in the days to come. Let them be your servants. Let them remove the pestilence and use this Luther as an excuse to alter the very nature of supremacy. These men, once boys without vision and passion, now realize that the realms are everywhere the same—in every town, every city, every nation. Let them grant you command of them all.

God has conferred upon you an opportunity in the guise of a religious monster. He offers you this sacrifice so that you may exert your will and share in His glory. None would deny the righteousness of your actions were you to act now, swiftly, and with the vengeance such evil inspires. Power claws at the door, ready to leap forward and swallow up this demon. God Himself offers you the key to set power free. Take it, my Lord, and create for our Savior a world of perfect order and stability here on earth.

Acknowledgments

A first book carries many debts, but I must single out:

Rob Roznowski, Rob Tate, and Dan Elish for their insights on early drafts, but more so for their friendship.

Peter Spiegler and Mark Weigel, whose knowledge of the working of markets was invaluable.

Rob Cowley and Byron Hollinshead, whose wise counsel was eclipsed only by their encouragement.

Doug Hertz, who set the manuscript on the road to William Morris.

Matt Bialer of William Morris, whose enthusiasm, judgment, and expertise turned this first-time author's introduction to the world of publishing into a real pleasure.

Kristin Kiser of Crown, who made both the process of editing and my instruction in the craft of writing fiction a delight.

Professors Anthony Grafton and Theodore Rabb of Princeton University, who cast scholarly eyes on *On Supremacy*.

The likes of Machiavelli, Hobbes, Hegel, and Mill, the true inspirations.

And, of course, my family—they know why.